"The preeminent writer of historical fiction."

—*USA Today*

"There is no question she is the best at what she does."

—Associated Press

"One of the great storytellers of our time."

—*San Francisco Book Review*

"Gregory excels in plucking . . . women out of their secondary places in the historical chorus and placing them stage center in starring roles."

—*Booklist*

"Philippa Gregory is the crème de la crème."

—*The Huffington Post*

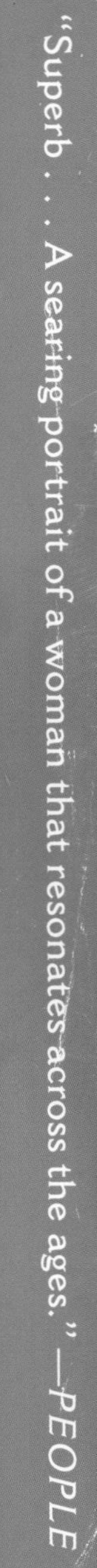

# Praise for PHILIPPA GREGORY

"The queen of royal fiction."
—*USA Today*

"There's no question that she is the best at what she does."
—Associated Press

"A mesmerizing storyteller."
—*Sunday Telegraph* (London)

"One of historical fiction's superstars."
—*Historical Novels Review*

"Gregory . . . always delivers the goods."
—*New York Post*

"Gregory defines what it means to be a writer of historical fiction."
—*RT Book Reviews*

*By the same author*

*History*

The Women of the Cousins' War: The Duchess, the Queen, and the King's Mother

*The Plantagenet and Tudor Novels*

The Lady of the Rivers
The Red Queen
The White Queen
The Kingmaker's Daughter
The White Princess
The Constant Princess
The King's Curse
Three Sisters, Three Queens
The Other Boleyn Girl
The Boleyn Inheritance
The Taming of the Queen
The Queen's Fool
The Last Tudor
The Virgin's Lover
The Other Queen

*Order of Darkness Series*

Changeling
Stormbringers
Fools' Gold
Dark Tracks

*The Wideacre Trilogy*

Wideacre
The Favored Child
Meridon

*The Tradescants*

Earthly Joys
Virgin Earth

*Modern Novels*

Alice Hartley's Happiness
Perfectly Correct
The Little House
Zelda's Cut

*Short Stories*

Bread and Chocolate

*Other Historical Novels*

The Wise Woman
Fallen Skies
A Respectable Trade

# TIDELANDS

PHILIPPA
GREGORY

WASHINGTON
SQUARE PRESS

ATRIA

New York London Toronto Sydney New Delhi

An Imprint of Simon & Schuster, Inc.
1230 Avenue of the Americas
New York, NY 10020

This book is a work of fiction. Any references to historical events, real people, or real places are used fictitiously. Other names, characters, places, and events are products of the author's imagination, and any resemblance to actual events or places or persons, living or dead, is entirely coincidental.



First Washington Square Press/Atria Paperback edition February 2020

WASHINGTON SQUARE PRESS / **ATRIA** PAPERBACK and colophon are trademarks of Simon & Schuster, Inc.

For information about special discounts for bulk purchases, please contact Simon & Schuster Special Sales at 1-866-506-1949 or business@simonandschuster.com.

The Simon & Schuster Speakers Bureau can bring authors to your live event. For more information or to book an event, contact the Simon & Schuster Speakers Bureau at 1-866-248-3049 or visit our website at www.simonspeakers.com.

Manufactured in the United States of America

5 7 9 10 8 6 4

The Library of Congress has cataloged the hardcover edition as follows:

Names: Gregory, Philippa, author.
Title: Tidelands / Philippa Gregory.
Description: First Atria Books hardcover edition. | New York : Atria Books, 2019. | "Atria fiction original hardcover"—Title page verso. | Includes bibliographical references.
Identifiers: LCCN 2019005706 (print) | LCCN 2019008103 (ebook) | ISBN 9781501187179 (ebook) | ISBN 9781501187155 (hardcover : alk. paper) | ISBN 9781501187162 (pbk. : alk. paper)
Subjects: | GSAFD: Historical fiction.
Classification: LCC PR6057.R386 (ebook) | LCC PR6057.R386 T53 2019 (print) | DDC 823/.914—dc23
LC record available at https://lccn.loc.gov/2019005706

ISBN 978-1-5011-8715-5
ISBN 978-1-5011-8716-2 (pbk)
ISBN 978-1-5011-8717-9 (ebook)

# TIDELANDS

# TIDELANDS, SUSSEX, MIDSUMMER EVE, JUNE 1648

The church was gray against a paler gray sky, the bell tower dark against the darker clouds. The young woman could hear the faint stir of the shingle as the tide came in, whispering across the mudflats, recoiling from the beach with a little hiss.

It was the height of summer, the eve of midsummer, the apex of the year, and though the night was warm, she felt chilled, for she had come to meet a ghost. This was the walking night for the dead, this night and their saints' days; but she did not think that her drunken violent husband had been under the care of any particular saint. She could not imagine angelic eyes on his erratic progress from sea to alehouse, and back again. She did not know if he was run away, or dead, or pressed as a sailor in the disloyal fleet that had turned on their king and now sailed under the rebel flag for parliament. If she were to see him, she would know he was dead for sure, and she could declare herself a widow and think herself free. She had no doubt that if he had drowned, his ghost would be coming, dripping water through the misty graveyard, on this white night of midsummer, when the sallow gleam from the west showed the sun refusing to sink. Everything was out of its place and time on this full-moon Midsummer Eve. The sun unset, the throne upset, the world overset: a king imprisoned, rebels in power, and a pale moon, white as a skull amid gray flying banners of clouds.

She thought that if she were to meet her husband's ghost drifting like a sea fret through the dark yew trees, she would be the happiest that she had been since her girlhood. If he was drowned, she was free. If he was among the walking dead, she was certain to meet him, for she had the sight, as her mother had, as her grandmother had, back through the generations, through all the women of her family, who had lived here forever, on the tidelands of the Saxon shore.

The church porch had old wooden benches made from warped ships' timbers on either side of the entrance. She tightened the shawl around her shoulders and took a seat, waiting till the moon, hidden now and then by unraveling clouds, should reach its midnight height over the church roof. She leaned back against the cold stones. She was twenty-seven years old and as weary as a woman of sixty. Her eyes closed; she started to slide into sleep.

The creak of the lych-gate and rapid footsteps on the shingle path of the graveyard woke her at once, driving her to her feet. She had not thought that the ghost of her husband would come early—in life he was always late for everything—but if he were here, then she must speak to him. Breathlessly, she stepped from the church porch, nerving herself to face whatever wraith was coming towards her from the darkness of the graveyard, on the whispering breath from the incoming sea. She could smell the brine on the air, she could sense his advance, perhaps soaked in seawater, perhaps trailing seaweed—and then a young man rounded the corner of the porch, recoiled at the sight of her white face, and cried out: "God save me! Are you of this earth or the other world? Speak!"

For a moment, she was so shocked that she said nothing. She stood very still and stared at him, as if she would see through him, her eyes narrowed, trying to see beyond her earthly vision. Perhaps he was one of the undead: undrowned, unhanged, walking in this night, which was their night, under the midsummer moon, which was their moon. He was as handsome as a faerie prince from a story, with long, dark hair tied back at the nape of his neck, and dark eyes set in a pale face. Behind her back she clenched her thumbs between her fingers in the sign of the cross, her only defense against being seduced, or carried away, and her heart broken by this young lord from the other kingdom, from the other world.

"Speak!" He was breathless. "Who are you? What are you? A vision?"

"No, no!" she contradicted him. "I'm a woman, a mortal woman, the ferryman's sister, the widow of Zachary the missing fisherman."

Long after, she would remember that the first thing she told him was that she was a mortal woman, a married woman, a widow, anchored in this world by the power of a man.

"Who? What?" he demanded. He was a stranger: these names meant nothing to him though anyone from the tidelands would have known them at once.

"Who are you?" She could tell he was gentry by his beautifully cut dark jacket, by the lace at his throat. "What're you doing here, sir?" She looked behind him for his servants, for his guard.

The empty graveyard stretched out in the eerie half darkness to the low wall of knapped flints shining darkly in the moonlight as if they had been washed over and left wet. The thickly crowned trees leaned over, casting a darker shade on the dark ground. There was nothing to see but the light of the moon throwing the shadows of the headstones onto the ragged scythed grass, and nothing to hear but the soft sigh of incoming tide under a full moon.

"I can't be seen," he muttered.

"Nobody here to see you." Her abrupt dismissal of his fear made him look again at her oval face, her dark gray eyes: a woman as beautiful as a Madonna in an icon, but drab here in the unearthly half-light, her tattered kerchief hiding her hair, shapeless in her ragged clothes.

"What are you doing here at this time of night?" he asked suspiciously.

"I came to pray." She would not tell this stranger that it was well known that a widow would meet her dead husband if she waited for him in the churchyard on Midsummer Eve.

"Pray?" he repeated. "God bless you for the thought. Let's go in then. I'll pray with you."

He turned the heavy ring handle on the door and caught the bar as it lifted on the other side so that it made no sound. He led the way into the silent church, quiet as a thief. She hesitated, but he waited for her, holding the door open without another word and she had to follow him. When he closed the door behind them there was only the dim light from the old stained-glass windows, gold and bronze on the stone-flagged floor. The sound of the rising sea was shut out.

"Leave the door open," she said nervously. "It's so dark in here."

He opened it a crack and a ribbon of pale moonlight stretched along the aisle to their feet.

"What did you come here for?" she asked. "Are you a gentleman from London?" It was the only explanation for his clean collar and his good leather boots, the little pack that he carried, and the warm intelligence in his face.

"I can't say."

She thought he must be one of the agents traveling the country seeking recruits for either parliament or king, except that nobody ever came to Sealsea Island, and he was alone without companions, or even horses, as if he had been dropped from the sky like a stormbringer, swung low from the clouds, for ill-doing to mortals, ready to blow away again on a summer gale.

"Are you smuggling, sir?"

His short laugh, nipped off when he heard his voice echo eerily in the empty church, denied it.

"Then what?"

"You cannot tell anyone you saw me."

"Nor you tell of me," she returned.

"Can you keep a secret?"

She sighed a cloudy breath in the cold musty air. "God knows I keep many."

He hesitated, as if he did not know whether or not he dared to trust her. "Are you of the new faith?" he asked.

"I don't know the rights or the wrongs of it," she said cautiously. "I pray as the minister tells me."

"I'm of the old faith, the true faith," he confessed in a whisper. "I was invited here, but the people I was going to meet are away, and their house, where I would have been safe, is closed and dark. I have to hide somewhere tonight, and if I cannot meet with them, then I must somehow get back to London."

Alinor stared at him as if he were in truth a faerie lord, and a danger to a mortal woman. "D'you say you're a priest, sir?"

He nodded as if he did not trust words.

"One sent from France to do the heretic services with the hidden papists?"

He grimaced. "Our enemies would say that. I would say I serve the true believers in England, and I am loyal to the ordained king."

She shook her head, uncomprehending. The civil war had come no nearer than Chichester, six miles north, when the little town had collapsed under a brisk siege from the parliament forces.

"They handed over all the papists when Chichester fell," she warned him. "Even the bishop ran away. They're all for parliament round here."

"But not you?"

She shrugged. "No one's done anything for me or mine. But my brother's an army man, and very true to them."

"But you won't hand me over?"

She hesitated. "D'you swear you're not a Frenchman?"

"An Englishman born and bred. And faithful to my country."

"But spying for the king?"

"I am loyal to the ordained King Charles," he told her. "As every Englishman should be."

She shook her head, as if grand words meant nothing to her. The king had been driven from his throne, his rule shrunk to his household, his palace was little Carisbrooke Castle, on the Isle of Wight. Alinor knew nobody who would declare loyalty to such a king, who had brought war into his country for six long years.

"Were you going to stay at the Priory, sir?"

"I may not tell you who would have hidden me. It is not my secret to tell."

She made a little impatient noise at his excessive secrecy. Sealsea Island was such a small community, not more than a hundred families; she knew every one of them. It was obvious that only the lord of the manor would have offered hiding to a papist priest and royalist spy. Only the Priory, the one great house on the island, had a bed and linen fit for a gentleman like this. Only the lord of the manor, sir William Peachey, would dream of supporting the defeated king. All his tenants were for parliament and for freedom from the crushing taxation that came from king and lords. And she thought it was typical of Sir William to make such a dangerous offer and then carelessly fail to honor it, leaving his secret guest in mortal danger. If this young man were caught by parliament men they would hang him for a spy.

"Does anyone know you're here?"

He shook his head. "I went to the house where I was told to go, the safe house, and it was all dark and locked up. I was told to tap a special knock on a garden door, but no one came. I saw the bell tower over the top of the trees, so I came here to wait, in the hope that if they are asleep now, they will answer later. I didn't know where else I might go. I don't know this place. I came in by ship on the high tide, and it looked like a wasteland of sea and mud for mile on mile. I've not even got a map!"

"Oh, there's no map," she told him.

He looked aghast. "No map? Why has it not been mapped?"

"It's the tidelands," she told him. "The shingle bar before the harbor, and the harbor itself changes with every storm. The Chichester people call it 'Wandering Haven.' The sea breaks into the fields and takes back the land. The ditches flood and make new lakes. It never stays the same for long enough to be measured. These are the tidelands: half tide, half land, good for nothing, all the way west to the New Forest, all the way east till the white cliffs."

"Is the minister of this church one of the new men?"

"He's been here for years and he does as he's told, now he takes his orders from the new parliament. He's not whitewashed the walls or broken the windows yet. But he took down the statues, he keeps the altar at the crossway of the church and prays in English. He said that good King Henry set us free from Rome a hundred years ago, and this King Charles wants to take us back, but he can't. He's defeated. He's ruined, and parliament has won the war against the king."

The stranger's face grew dark with anger. "They've not won," he insisted. "They'll never win. They can't win. It's not over yet."

She was silent. She thought that it was long over for the king, who was imprisoned, his wife fled to France, leaving two little children behind, and his son, the prince, gone to the Netherlands. "Yes, sir."

"Would he denounce me, this minister?"

"I think he'd have to."

"Is there anyone here of the old faith? In hiding? On this island?"

She spread her hands as if to show him her ignorance. He saw that her palms were scratched and scarred from the shells of lobsters and crabs and the rough twine of the fishing nets.

"I don't know what people hold in their hearts," she said. "There were many for the king in Chichester, some of them papists; but they're killed or run away. I know no one except one or two old ladies who remember the old faith. Most people are like my brother: godly men. My brother fought in the New

Army under the general. General Cromwell is his name. You'll have heard of him?"

"Yes, I've heard of him," he said grimly. He paused, thinking hard. "Can I get to Chichester tonight?"

She shook her head. "The tide's coming in now, and it's high tonight for midsummer. You can't cross the wadeway to the Chichester road till morning, and then you'd be seen. Won't your boat come back for you?"

"No."

"Then you'll have to hide till low tide tomorrow evening, and go across the wadeway at dusk. You can't take the ferry. My brother's the ferryman, and he'd arrest you on sight."

"How would he know me for a cavalier?"

Her smile lit up her face. "Sir, no one looks like you on Sealsea Island! Not even Sir William is as fine."

He flushed. "Well, if I have to stay on the island, where can I hide?"

She thought for a moment. "You can lie in my husband's shed till tomorrow evening," she offered. "That's the only place I can think of. It's not fit. He kept his nets there, and his pots. But he's been missing for months and nobody ever goes there now. I can bring you food and water in the morning. And when it's light, perhaps you can go to the Priory, just over there. You could go in the morning privately and ask to see the steward. His lordship's away from home, but the steward might take you in. I don't know. I can't say what they believe. I don't know."

He bowed his head in a thanksgiving. "God bless you," he said. "I think God must have sent you to be my savior."

"I'll show you the net shed first, before you bless me for letting you sleep there," she said. "It's not for the likes of you. It stinks of old fish."

"I have nowhere else," he said simply. "You are my savior. Shall we pray together?"

"No," she said bluntly. "We'd do best to get you into hiding. I don't think anyone else will come here at this time of night, but you never know. Some like to think themselves very godly. They might come to pray at dawn."

"You came here to pray," he reminded her. "Are you godly? Are you one of the godly believers?"

She flushed at her own lie. "I didn't really," she admitted.

"Then for what?"

"Doesn't matter."

He ignored her embarrassment, assuming that she had come to meet a lover in some sordid village affair. "Where is the net shed, and your home?"

"At the top of the harbor, near the ferry-house, across the rife from the mill."

"The rife?"

"Broad Rife," she said. "The river that flows into the head of the harbor. It moves with the tide, ebbs and flows, but it never runs dry. It's high now. It's been such a wet summer, the wade-way's not been dry for weeks."

"Your brother's ferry crosses the rife when the tide is full?"

"And there's a wadeway at low tide for people to walk across."

"I would not put you in danger. I can find my own way if you tell me the direction. You don't need to lead me."

"You can't. The harbor's like a maze of paths and there are deep pools and channels," she explained. "The sea comes in faster than a trotting horse, and spreads across the land quicker than a man can run. You can get stuck in the mud or cut off on a path, or trapped by water. There are quicksands that you can't see till your foot sinks beneath you and you can't draw it out. Only us who were born and bred here ever cross the mire. I'll have to take you."

He nodded. "God will bless you for this. He must have sent you to guide me."

She looked doubtful, as if God had not been generous with his blessings in her life. "Shall we go now? It'll take us a while to get across."

"We'll go," he decided. "What shall I call you? I am Father James."

She recoiled from the priestly title. "I can't call you that! I might as well go to the justices and get arrested at once! What's your real name?"

"You can call me James."

She gave a little shrug as if she was offended by his discretion. "I bear my husband's name," she replied. "They call me Goody Reekie."

"What shall I call you?"

"Call me that," she said pertly. "Since you don't tell me your true name why should I tell you mine?"

She turned from his surprised face and led the way out of the church, waiting patiently as he bowed low to the altar, kneeling on one knee and putting his hand to the ground. She heard him whisper a prayer for his safety and hers, and for all those serving the true faith in England tonight, for the king in his cruel captivity, and the prince abroad.

"My husband's missing," she remarked, as he joined her at the door. "He's been gone for more than half a year."

"God bless him, and keep you," he said, making the sign of the cross over her head. She had never seen the gesture before, and she did not know to bow her head and cross herself. Nobody had publicly crossed themselves in England for nearly a hundred years. The people had lost the habit, and those who were still Roman Catholic were careful to keep their faith hidden.

"Thank you," she said awkwardly.

"Do you have children?"

She opened the heavy door to the porch, looked out to see that the graveyard was deserted, and then beckoned him to follow her. They walked in single file between graves where the stones were so thick with old moss and lichen that only a few letters could be seen.

"Two still living," she said over her shoulder. "I thank God for them. My daughter is thirteen and my son is twelve."

"And does your boy fish in his father's place?"

"The boat's missing too," she said, as if that were the greatest loss. "So we can only fish with a line from the shore."

"Our Lord called a fisherman before he called anyone else," he said gently.

"Yes," she said. "But at least he left the boat."

A laugh broke from him at her irreverence, and she turned and laughed with him and he saw, again, the bright warmth of her smile. It was so powerful and so illuminating he wanted to catch her hand and keep her smiling at him.

"The boat matters so much, you see."

"I do see," he said, taking hold of the shoulder straps of his pack, keeping his hands away from temptation. "How do you manage without boat or husband?"

"Poorly," she said shortly.

At the low wall of rough stone flints at the edge of the graveyard she hitched up her brown skirt and hemp apron and swung her legs over the stile, as lithe as a boy. He climbed after her and found himself on the shore, on a little path no wider than a sheep track, with quickthorn hedges closing in on both sides and meeting over the top, so that the two of them were hidden in a tunnel of thick leaves and twisted spiky boughs. Walking ahead of him, she bent her head and wrapped her elbows in her shawl, striding out in her wooden pattens, following the erratic course of the narrow path. The sound of the sea grew a little louder as she scrambled down a bank, and then they were suddenly in the open, lit by the fitful moon in the pale sky, on a beach of a white shingle. Behind them the bank was topped by a big oak tree, its roots snaking through the mud, its down-swinging branches bending low to the beach. Ahead of them was the marsh: standing water, sandbanks, tidal pools, mud, reed islands, and a wide winding channel of water with branching silted streams swelling and lapping over the mud, flowing in little waves that broke at their feet.

"Foulmire," she announced.

"I thought you said it was called Wandering Haven?"

"That's what they call it in Chichester, because it wanders. They never know where the islands are, they never know where the reefs are; the rivers change their beds at every storm. But we, who live on it and know all its changes, who change our paths in obedience to its moods, who hate it as a hard taskmaster, call it Foulmire."

"For the birds? Fowl-mire? Bird-marsh?"

"For the mud: foul," she said. "If you misstep it holds you till the sea comes for you and you are foully drowned. If you get free you stink like a foul thing for the rest of your life."

"Have you always lived here?" he asked, wondering at the bitterness in her voice.

"Oh, yes," she said. "I am mired. I am bound as a tenant to a neglectful lord and I cannot leave. I am wife to a vanished man and cannot marry, and I am sister to the ferryman and he will never carry me across to the mainland and set me free."

"Is all the coast like this?" he asked, thinking of his landing, when the captain had steered them in the dark, past reefs and over shallows. "All so uncertain?"

"Tidelands," she confirmed. "Neither sea nor shore. Neither wet or dry, and no one ever leaves."

"You could leave. I will have a ship," he said lightly. "When I finish my work here, I will sail back to France. I could give you a passage."

She turned and looked at him and once again she surprised him, this time by her gravity. "I wish to God that I could," she said. "But I would not leave my children. And besides, I have a terror of deep water."

She walked on ahead of him, scrunching on the shingle beach that wound between the bank and mud where the water was seeping inwards. A roosting seagull whirled up ahead of them with an unearthly call, and he followed her shadow over shingle and mud and the driftwood, hearing the steady hiss, as the sea, somewhere out in the darkness to his right, came constantly closer, flooding mudbanks, drowning the reeds, always coming unstoppably on.

She scrambled up another bank to a path that ran higher, above the tidemark, and he followed her between gorse bushes where the nighttime flowers were drained of their color and glowed silver rather than gold, but he could still smell their honey scent on the air. An owl hooted near him and made him start as he saw it, dark in the darkness, wheeling away on wide silent wings.

They walked for a long time, until the pack on his back became heavy and he felt as if he were in a dream, following the wooden heels of her pattens, the dirty hem of her skirt, through a world that had lost meaning as well as color, on a winding track through desolation. He pulled himself up, and whispered an "*Ave Maria*," reminding himself that he was honored to carry the word of God, the precious objects for the Mass, and a ransom for a king; he was glad to have to struggle on a muddy path through an unmapped shore.

The sea seeped farther inland as if it knew no boundary. He could see the water creeping through the driftwood and straw on the shingle below them, and on the other side of the bank the ditches and ponds were swelling and flowing back inland as if it were, as she had said, a place that was neither sea nor shore but the land itself that ebbed and flowed with the tide. He realized that for some time he had heard a strange hissing noise overlaying the sound of the lapping water, like the seething of a giant stewpot, like the bubble of a kettle.

"What is that? What is that noise?" he whispered, stopping her with one hand on her shoulder. "Do you hear it? A terrible noise! Strange, like the water is boiling."

She halted, quite unafraid, and pointed out into the middle of the moving water. "Oh, that. Look, there, out there, in the mire, can you see the bubbles?"

"I can see nothing but waves. God save us! What is it? It sounds like a fountain?"

"It's the hushing well," she said.

He was absurdly frightened. "What is it? What is that?"

"Nobody knows," she said indifferently. "A place in the center of the mire where the sea boils as it comes in. Every high tide, so we pay no attention. Sometimes a stranger takes an interest in it. A man told my brother it was probably a cave, underneath the mire, and the bubbles pour from it when the sea fills it. But nobody knows. Nobody's ever seen it."

"It sounds like a seething pot!" He was horrified by the strangeness of the sound. "As if it were hell boiling over!"

"Yes, I s'pose it's fearful." She had no interest in it.

"What does it look like when the sea goes out?" he asked curiously. "Is the ground hot?"

"Nobody's seen it when the tide is out," she repeated patiently. "You can't walk to it. You'd sink and the mire would hold you till you drowned on the next tide. P'raps it's a cave—and you'd fall into it. Who knows? P'raps there really is a cave that holds all the sea, the waters that ebb and flow underneath all the world. P'raps it's the end of the world, hidden away here in Foulmire, and we've been living on the doorstep of hell for all these years."

"But the noise?"

"You can take a boat over it," she offered. "It bubbles like a cauldron and it hisses loudly. Sometimes it's so loud that you can hear it in the churchyard on a still night."

"You can sail out to see it?"

"Well, I wouldn't," she specified. "But it can be done, if you've nothing else to do."

He guessed that there was never a day in her life when she had nothing else to do.

She turned and walked on again. She had no interest in the threatening hiss that grew louder as the bank curved towards the harbor, and fainter as they moved away.

"Were you ever at school?" he asked, trying to imagine her life, living here in this desolate landscape, as ignorant as a flower. He lengthened his stride and walked beside her as the path widened.

"For a few years. I can read and I can write. My mother taught me her recipe book, and the herbs, and her skills."

"She was a cook?"

"A herbalist. A healer. I do her work now."

"Did anyone ever speak to you of the old faith? Did anyone teach you the prayers?"

She shrugged. “My grandam preferred the old ways. When I was a girl sometimes a traveling priest would come to the village and hear confessions in secret. Some of the older people say the old prayers.”

“When we get to the net shed, I should like to pray with you.”

He saw the ghost of her smile. “You’d do better to pray for your breakfast,” she said. “We don’t eat well.”

The path narrowed and they went single file again, the thorns pressing on either side of them. Somewhere in the woods away to his left he could hear the piercing song of a nightingale, singing to the pale sky.

He thought he had never traveled through so strange a landscape with so alien a companion. He had followed his vocation throughout England, going from one wealthy house to another, hearing confessions and celebrating the Mass, usually in hiding, but always in comfort. His dark good looks had served him well. He had been petted by the richest ladies of the kingdom, and respected by their fathers and brothers for risking his life for his faith. More than one beautiful girl had sunk to her knees and confessed to disturbing dreams of him. Their desire had never touched him. He was sworn to God and never distracted. He was a young man of only twenty-two years old; he reveled in the chance to test his fervent convictions, and in the sense of his own righteousness.

He had been promised to the Church since boyhood, and his teachers had trained him and inspired him, and then sent him out into the world to travel in secret, meeting with royalists and sharing their plans, going from one besieged palace to another, carrying funds from the exiled queen, plans from the imprisoned king, promises from the prince. He had been in some dangerous and frightening places—slept in priest’s holes, hidden in cellars, served the Mass in attics and stables—but he had never before spent the day with no refuge, alone on an unmapped shore, or followed the footsteps of a common woman who held his safety in her roughened hands.

He felt for the gold crucifix that he wore under his fine

lawn shirt and gripped its awkward outline. Superstitiously he glanced at the mud beneath her feet to be sure that she was making footprints like a mortal. Even though he could see the sharp tracks of the wooden pattens, he crossed himself, thinking that she was an unearthly guide to an ungodly land, and if it were not for the power of his faith he would think himself lost indeed, walking through a world of ancient elements: water, air, and earth.

They walked on, for perhaps an hour in silence, and then she turned sharply left and scrambled up the harbor bank and he saw, dark against the dark sky, a ramshackle hovel, walls of driftwood infilled with dried mud, thatched with reeds from the marsh. It looked like sea wrack thrown up by a high tide. She leaned against the ill-fitting door that creaked as it opened.

"The net shed," she announced.

It was pitch-dark inside, the only light from the moon coming in glimmers through the cracks in the walls.

"Do you have a candle?"

"Only in the house. You can't show a light here. It'd be seen from the mill on the other side of the mire. You'll have to sit in darkness, but it'll be dawn soon and I'll bring you breakfast and some ale."

"Is your house nearby?" He was apprehensive at being left here alone in the dark.

"Just along the bank. And it'll soon be light," she reassured him. "I'll come back when I can. I have to set the fire and fetch the water. I have to wake my children and give them breakfast. Then, when they're gone for the day, I'll come back. You can sit here on the nets; you can sleep."

She took his hand—he felt the roughness of her scarred palm—tugged at it so that he bent down, and she pushed his hand against the rough twine of a heap of nets. "There," she said. "The old nets. It's not good enough for you but I don't know where else you can go."

"Of course it's good enough for me," he assured her, his voice eager and unconvincing. "I don't know what I would have done if I had not met you. I would have slept in the woods and been washed away by the hissing waters." He tried to laugh; she did not.

"If you hear anyone coming, or if anyone tries the door, you can kick out the back wall. We're on the edge of the ditch; you can roll down into it. If you run along the bank to the right, it'll lead you inland to the ferry and the wadeway, left to the woods. But nobody ever comes here, nobody should come here."

He nodded, but in the dark, she could not see him.

"I know it's not fit," she said uneasily.

"I am grateful for it. I am grateful to you," he said. He realized that he was still holding her hand and he pressed it to his lips. Instantly, she jerked her hand away, and he flushed in the darkness for his stupidity in showing her a courtesy that she would never have known. The wealthy ladies of the safe houses were accustomed to being kissed. They extended their white hands to him and raised their fans to their eyes to hide their blushes. Sometimes they would go down on their knees in a flurry of silk and kiss his hand, hold it to their damp cheeks in penitence for some trivial sin.

"Excuse me," he tried to explain. "I just meant to say that I know this is a great gift. God will remember what you have done for me."

"I'll bring you some gruel," she said gruffly. He heard her backing towards the doorway and saw the crack of moonlight as the door opened. "There's not much."

"Only if you have some to spare," he said, knowing that there would not be any spare food in her house. She would go without to feed him.

She closed the door quietly and he felt for the pile of netting and tugged at it a little to spread it out. The stink of old fish and the foul harbor mud rose with a buzz of sleepy flies. He gritted his teeth against his repulsion, and sat down. He drew his booted feet up and tucked his cape around him, certain that there were rats. He found that even though he was desperately tired, he could not bear to lie down on the ill-smelling knots.

He reproached himself for being a fool, an unfit priest without wisdom or experience, a foolish boy sent out to do mighty work in great times. He was afraid of failing, especially now, when so much depended on him. He had confessions to hear and secrets to keep, and in his mind, battened down, he carried a plan to free the king. He was afraid that he had neither the courage nor the determination to carry it through and he was about to pray to be a strong emissary, a good spy, when he realized that he was mistaken: he was not afraid of failing, he was afraid like a child, afraid of everything, from rats in the net shed, the hushing well outside, and somewhere beyond it all the vengeful armies of Cromwell and the tyrant's black-eyed stare.

He sat in the darkness and waited.

Alinor hesitated outside the door of the net shed, listening for him moving inside in the dark, as if he were a strange animal that she had penned. When he was quiet, she turned and ran along the bank to where her own cottage stood, facing the mire, a one-story building thatched with reeds, set square in a little herb garden fenced with driftwood.

Inside her cottage everything was just as she had left it, the embers of the fire on the hearth under an earthenware lid, the runes drawn in the ashes to prevent a spark, the children in the bed in one corner of the room, the pot of gruel by the fireplace with the lid clamped on, to keep it from rats, and the roosting hens in their corner, who clucked sleepily as the cool air, smelling of mud and brine, blew in with her.

She took a bucket from the fireside and went out, inland, along the shoreline where the high tide was lapping at the mud and the reeds. She climbed up the bank, and down the other side using rough-cut steps, to the deep freshwater dipping pond. She held on to a worn post to fill her bucket, then lugged the slopping load back to her own cottage. She poured a bowl of water and set it on the table, took off her cloak and washed her face and hands, using the homemade gray fatty soap, rubbing her fingers with particular care, painfully aware that the priest had held them to his lips and must have smelled the lifelong scent of fish, smoke, sweat, and dirt.

She dried her hands on a scrap of linen, and sat for a little while, staring out of the open door where the sky—pale throughout this white night—was getting brighter and brighter. She wondered why—since she had failed to meet a ghost—she should feel so bewitched.

She shook her head, as if to pull herself back from the shadowlands, and rose up from her stool, to kneel before the fire, using a rag to lift the earthenware cover from the embers. With the back of her other hand she erased the runes against fire that were drawn in the cool ashes. She fed the glowing heart in the middle of the ash with little twigs, and then more driftwood, and when it caught she set the three-legged iron pot in the heat, added water from the bucket, and stirred the soaked oatmeal inside, bringing it slowly to the boil.

The children, in the one bed, slept through the sounds of preparation. She had to wake them, touching each one on the shoulder. Her daughter smiled in her sleep and rolled over to face the rough wooden wall, but her boy sat up and asked: "Is it morning?"

She bent down to hug him, burying her face in the warmth of his neck. He smelled of himself, sweet as a puppy. "Yes," she said. "Time to get up."

"Is Da home?"

"No," she said flatly. The perennial question no longer gave her a pang of grief for her son. "Not today. Get dressed."

Obediently Rob sat on the edge of the mattress and pulled his jacket on over the linen nightshirt. He pulled up his breeches and tied them with laces to the jacket. He would go bare-legged and barefoot to his work today. He was crow-scaring at Mill Farm after morning school. He sat up at the table and she poured gruel into his bowl.

"No bacon?" he asked.

"Not today."

He took up his spoon and started to eat, blowing on each mouthful and sucking it loudly. She gave him a cup of small ale; no one at Foulmire ever drank the water. She turned back to the bed, sat on the edge, and touched her daughter's shoulder.

Alys rolled over and opened her dark blue eyes to look at her mother as if she were part of a haunting dream. "Did you go out?" she asked.

Alinor was surprised. "I thought you were asleep."

"I heard you come in." The girl sighed as if she were about to sleep again. "In my dream."

"What did you dream?"

"I dreamed you met a cat in the churchyard."

The two of them were intent. "What color?"

"Black," the girl said.

"What happened?"

"Nothing. That was all. You stood before him and he saw you."

Alinor thought of this, held it in her seer's vision. "He saw me?"

"He saw you, he saw everything."

Alinor nodded. "Don't speak of this," she said.

The girl smiled. "Course not." She pushed back the covers of the bed and rose up, standing tall at her mother's shoulder, her fair hair in a plait down her back, her skin Saxon-pale. She turned to her pile of clothes at the foot of the bed and pulled on her skirt of felted wool, dried mud crusted on the hem, and a patched shirt. She sat on her stool at the table to wash her face and hands and then took the bowl to the door and threw it over the herbs outside.

Alinor took her stool beside her children and clasped her hands. "Father, we thank thee for our daily bread," she said quietly. "Keep us from sin forever and ever. Amen."

"Amen," they said in a chorus, and Alinor served her daughter and herself, leaving a portion in the pot.

"Can I have that?" Rob asked.

"No," Alinor said.

He pushed back his stool and knelt on the floor for her blessing. She put her hand on his matted curls and said: "God bless you, my son."

Without another word, he took his cap from a hook behind the door, pulled it on his head, and opened the door. The sound of seagulls crying and the salty morning air poured into the darkened room. He went out, banging the door behind him.

"He'll be early for school," Alys remarked. "He'll be playing football against the church door again."

"I know," Alinor replied.

"You look strange," the girl told her mother. "Different."

Alinor turned her face to her daughter and smiled. "In what way?" she said. "I'm the same as yesterday."

Alys saw the deceit in the way her mother's eyelashes veiled her gaze. "You look as you did in my dream. Where did you go?"

Alinor gathered up the empty bowls and stacked them on the table. "I went to the church to pray for your father."

The girl nodded. She knew very well it was Midsummer Day. "And did you see him?" she asked, very low.

Alinor shook her head. "Nothing."

"So perhaps, he's still alive? If you didn't see him, then he's not dead. He could still come home."

"Or perhaps I have no sight."

"Perhaps that. Perhaps you met a black cat and he truly saw you."

Alinor smiled. "Don't speak of it," she reminded her daughter. She thought of the priest, waiting for his gruel in the net shed. She wondered if he had truly seen her, like the black cat of her daughter's dream.

The girl ran her fingers through her thick fair hair and pushed it back from her face, then pulled her cap over the golden plait. She sat down to put on her boots. "I wish to God we knew," she said irritably. "I don't miss him, but I'd like to know I can stop looking for him. And it's not fair on Rob."

"I know," Alinor said. "Every time a ship comes to the tide mill quay I ask for news of him, but they say nothing."

The girl lifted up a boot and poked her finger through the hole in the sole. "I'm sorry, Ma, but I need new boots. These are through at the toes and the sole."

Alinor looked at the patched uppers and the mended soles. "Next time I have money, next time I go to market," she promised.

"Before winter, anyway." The girl pulled on her worn boots. "I might bring a rabbit home tonight. I set a snare yesterday."

"Not on Sir William's fields?"

"Not where the keeper ever goes," she said mischievously.

"Bring it home and I'll stew it," Alinor promised, thinking of the extra mouth to feed if the priest did not leave till the evening ebb tide.

The girl knelt before her mother and Alinor rested her hand on the tender nape of the girl's neck. "God bless you and keep you safe," she said, thinking of her daughter's young prettiness, and the miller and his men who watched her as she crossed the yard and joked of the husband she would have in a few years' time.

The girl smiled up at her mother as if she knew her fears. "I can fend for myself," she said gently, and went out, shooing the hens out of the door and out of the gate so that they could pick their way down to the shoreline.

Alinor waited till she heard the crunching sound of footsteps on shingle recede, as her daughter walked along the shore to the ferry crossing at the rife. Only when she could hear nothing outside but the calling of the seabirds did Alinor spoon the warm gruel into the spare bowl, her missing husband's bowl, and take his carved wooden spoon and his own wooden cup filled with small ale, and carry them back along the bank to the net shed.

She tapped at the door and went in, ducking her head below the crooked lintel. He was asleep, sprawled over the nets, his good woolen cape spread under him, his beautiful curling hair tumbled around his face. She observed his pallor, and the dark long sweep of his eyelashes, the sleeping strength of his body, his chest and arms and the length of his legs in the expensive riding boots. Nobody would take him for anything but a stranger, foreign to this impoverished island off the south coast of England. One glance would tell anyone that he was a nobleman. He was as out of place, sprawled on the stinking nets in the ramshackle shed, as she would have been among the silks and perfumes of the king's court, in the old days, when the king had a court in London.

She thought it was disrespectful to wake him, but then the cooling bowl in her hand reminded her that if she left the gruel beside him and he woke to found it cold and congealed he would be nauseated. So she bent down, put the cup of ale on the floor, and gently shook the toe of his boot.

His eyelashes flickered at once and he opened his eyes and sprang to his feet in one movement. "Ah! Goodwife," he said.

She held out the bowl and the mug of small ale. "Gruel," she said. "I know it's not good enough for you."

"It comes from you, and it comes from God, and I am grateful," he replied. He put the bowl and spoon and mug on the floor and he knelt down and spoke a long whispered grace in Latin. Alinor, not knowing what to do, bowed her head and whispered "Amen" as he finished, though she had been told by the minister—they had all been told—that God did not speak in Latin, that God spoke in English and should be addressed in English and that everything else was a sham and a heresy and a papist mockery of the truth of the Word.

He sat cross-legged on the nets as if they were not crawling with vermin, and he ate the gruel like a hungry man. He scraped the wooden bowl with the wooden spoon and drained the cup of small ale.

"I'm sorry, there's no more," she said awkwardly. "But I'll bring you some fish soup if you're here at dinnertime."

"It was very good. I was hungry," he said. "I am grateful to you for sharing your food. I hope that you did not go without to feed me?"

She thought with a brief pang of guilt of her boy, who would have eaten more at breakfast. "No," she said. "And my daughter might bring home some meat for dinner."

He narrowed his eyes as if he was trying to conjure a calendar and see if there was a holy day or a fast day that he should observe. He smiled. "It's St. John's Day. I shall be glad to dine well, but if there is only a little I beg that you take it for yourself and your children. You do a great service to me and for God by hiding me here. I don't want you to go hungry. I am accustomed to it."

Her face lit up as she laughed, and he was struck again by her sudden transformation. "I wager I'm more accustomed than you!"

He had to stop himself from touching her smiling cheek. "You're right," he conceded. "Fasting is my choice, part of my faith."

"I thought I'd guide you to the Priory this morning," she offered. "If you want to try the steward there, and see if he'll take you in."

"I should be glad of your help. I should be glad to meet with him. Do we go back the way we came?"

"Yes," she said.

"Then I can find my own way. I'll go alone. I won't put you in danger."

"It's the mire," she reminded him. "I have to guide you. I can walk ahead of you, so that we're not seen walking together."

He nodded. "You must keep your distance."

"Very well."

They were silent for a moment. "Will you sit?" he invited her. "Sit and talk with me?"

She hesitated. "I have to go to my work."

"Just stay a moment?" He wondered at himself, seeking her company when he should have been using the solitude for prayer.

She sank to the floor, tucking her feet under her rough woolen skirt. The room was shadowy, smelling of salt and seaweed and the foul undertone of marsh mud. The floor was tamped-down earth, the nets flung carelessly one on top of another, the lobster pots rotting with their load of old seaweed and shells.

"What should you be doing, if I were not delaying you?" he asked her.

"This morning I'd be weeding in the garden, and cleaning the house, picking the herbs, for drying or distilling, probably spinning. This afternoon I'll go up to my brother's house at the ferry, to start barley in the brewhouse for our ale. I'll make bread from the yeast. Sometimes I work at Mill Farm—in the dairy or bakery—or I weed or dig or harvest, depending on the season." She shrugged. Clearly there were too many tasks for her to list. "As it's Midsummer Day I'll pick herbs again this evening, those in my own garden and those that I grow at the ferry-house, and I'll distill in the ferry-house stillroom. Sometimes, someone sends for me, for childbirth or sickness. I go to church some evenings. It's good to sit, just for a moment."

"You must be lonely?"

"No—though I miss my mother," she conceded.

"Do you not miss your husband?"

"I'm glad to be rid of him," she said simply. "Except for the loss of the boat."

"He was unkind to you?" He gripped his hands in his lap to stop himself covering her clasped hand with his own. He thought the man must be a monster to hurt such a woman as this—and what was the minister of the church doing, what was her brother doing that he did not protect her?

But she shook her head. "No worse than many. I never complained of it. But he took a lot of feeding, and a lot of working for. It was tiring to be his wife, wearisome. But without him we've got very little money and few ways to earn it, and no way of saving. I fear for my girl—working at Mill Farm every day—as pretty as she is. She's got to marry in two or three years and where I'm going to find her dowry, I don't know. And I fear for my boy, growing up and not even his father's fishing boat to inherit. He'll get the ferry after my brother, I suppose, but not for years, and then it's a hard life. I don't know what'll become of either of them." She shook her head as if she had puzzled over this often. "Nor of me, either. God keep us all from begging."

"You can't beg," he said, shocked. "You can't be reduced to begging."

"Well, we borrow," she admitted, and he saw from the ghost of her smile that she meant that they poached game from Sir William's lands.

"God does not forbid borrowing if it's only rabbits," he told her, and was rewarded by a mischievous gleam. "But you must be careful . . ."

"We are," she said. "And Sir William only cares about his deer and the pheasants. Perhaps we'll buy a boat somehow. Perhaps times'll get better."

"Don't you have a man who would take your husband's place?" he asked, thinking of her waiting for someone at the church on Midsummer Eve.

He was shocked by her disdain, as she turned her head away. He had met duchesses with less hauteur.

"I shan't marry again."

"Not even for a boat?" He smiled.

"Nobody with a boat would have me with two children," she observed. "Three mouths to feed."

"Is your daughter like you?" he asked, thinking that she must be as pretty as a princess in a story, like a princess in disguise.

"Not really," she answered with a smile. "She has high hopes, she listens to her uncle, thinks that anyone can be anything, that the world is laid out before her, that everything has changed. She's all for parliament and the people. I don't blame her. I can't help but hope for better for her, and for Rob."

"Your son?"

Her face warmed at his name. "He's born to be a healer. He's got my mother's gift. From a baby he was out in the herb garden with me, learning the names and their potency. And I've taught him how they're used, and sometimes he comes with me, for a sickness, or a death. If I could only keep him at school so he could have book learning! A cunning man with learning can make a good living among people with money, in a town perhaps." She shrugged. "Not here. I get paid in food and pennies for the herbs, and my patients are all poor people. The only gentry are at the Priory. I nursed her ladyship before she died, and I physicked her son a few months ago. Twice a year I go to the stillroom and restock it and make it tidy, but when his lordship is ill, he sends for the Chichester physician."

"You are a cunning woman?" he asked. "What things can you do?"

"Herbs and healing only," she answered carefully. She guessed that he would know nothing of the many careful gradations between healers who used natural cures and those who drew on dark arts and could sicken a whole village. "I'm a midwife. I used to have my license, when the bishop was in his palace and could grant a license—before he was thrown out and ran away. I can draw a tooth and set a bone, cut out a sore and heal an ulcer, but I do nothing else. I am a healer and a finder of lost things."

"You found me," he said.

"Were you lost?"

"I think that it is England that is lost," he said seriously. "We cannot put our king from his throne, we cannot choose how we worship God. We cannot put parliament over everything. We cannot make war against the king appointed by God to rule us."

"I wouldn't know."

He hesitated. "You said last night that your brother is for parliament?"

"He ran away to fight and he would have stayed with the New Model Army; but when my father died he had to come home again to keep his right to the ferry. Our family had the rights to the ferry for generations, and we are tenants of Ferry-house."

"It's the only way to cross to the mainland? Your brother's wherry?"

"It's not a wherry," she corrected him. "It's more like a raft on a rope across Broad Rife," she said. "Broad Rife flows between Sealsea Island and the mainland. It's not deep—you can wade across at low tide. The wadeway is cobbled, so you can't get stuck in the mud. My brother keeps the wadeway, and ferries people who don't want to get their feet wet, and women going to market carrying their spun yarn or their goods, and at high tide the wagoners, or Sir William, who loads his horses and carriage on the ferry when the water is too high."

"He rows people across?"

She shook her head. "He pulls on a rope. It's like a big raft, a floating bridge, big enough to take a wagon. At mid-tide the current's very strong. The ferry is hooked fore and aft to an overhead rope so that he doesn't get swept away by the tide and out into the mire, and then out to sea."

He saw that she went pale at the thought of it. "Have you always been afraid of water?" he asked curiously. "Living here, on the shore?"

"The daughter of the ferryman and the wife of a fisherman." She smiled. "I know full well that it's foolish, but I have always had a terror of it."

"Then how will you fish when you get your boat?" he asked.

She smiled and gave a little shrug, rising to her feet and picking up his bowl and his cup. "I'll have to find the courage," she said. "I can row and I can throw a net, and the children can help me. I won't ever go out to sea on the deep waters. I'll stay inside the harbor bar. And then, if your side gets your way, and the king comes to his own again and the church goes papist, I can sell fish in the market and at the doors on all the fast days."

"I will send you money for a boat when I get home," he promised her.

She smiled as if it was a pleasantry. "Where's your home?"

He hesitated, but he wanted to trust her with the truth. "I live at my college in France," he said. "My family sent me to the English college at Douai when I was a boy of twelve, and I stayed on and took my vows as a priest. When the war started, they were glad that I was safely out of the way. My father fought against parliament and was defeated, wounded at Naseby. Now, he and my mother are in exile, with the queen in Paris, and I am a seminary priest, sworn to come to England to bring people back to the true faith."

"Isn't it very dangerous to come to England?"

He hesitated. There was a death sentence for spying, and a death sentence for heresy. His college were proud of their history of martyrs, and kept candles burning before a wall of their carved names. When he was young he had longed to be one of the sainted dead. "My college has sent many martyrs to England, ever since King Henry turned from the true Church. The Church was changed, despite people's wishes, more than a hundred years ago; but we never changed. I am following where many saints have trod." He smiled at her wondering gaze. "Truly, I choose this. And there are many safe houses and many friends to help me. I can cross the country and never leave Roman Catholic lands. I can pray in a hidden sacred chapel every night. Now, the parliament has gone too far against the king, the army even more so. Now is our chance. All over the country, towns and villages are declaring for the king and saying that they want him back on the throne. People want peace, and they want to be free to worship."

"Won't you go back to your college till then?" she asked doubtfully, thinking that the day would never come.

"No. There is one thing, a great thing, I have to do before I can go home." He resisted the temptation to tell her more.

She guessed at once. "You're never going to the Isle of Wight?" she whispered. "Not to the king?"

His silence told her that she was right.

"So you see why you should not be seen with me," he said. "And I will never admit that I met you, that you hid me. Whatever happens, whatever befalls me, I will never betray you."

Gravely she nodded. "If you want to go to the Priory, we should go through the mire while it's low tide. We can see the steward as he has his breakfast, and if he won't have you in the house, there'll still be time to walk back through the mire before the tide gets too high."

He got up from his seat on the nets, brushed down his jacket, and swung his cloak around his shoulders. “We go through the mire?”

She nodded again. “We shouldn’t meet anyone. Hardly anyone comes here. As we get to the Priory we’ll be in the hollow lane of bushes. If you meet anyone there you can just drop over the bank into the ditch and hide. If you have to run, follow the line of the ditch and it will take you inland. You can hide in the woods.”

“And what will you do?”

“I’ll say that I never saw you following me. That I was going out to the beach for tern eggs.” She turned and opened the door. “Wait here.”

Suddenly, like a cannonade on the still air, there was an explosion of noise, a cascade of water, and then a terrible rumbling sound.

“What’s that?” he demanded, starting up, hand to his precious pack.

“Just the mill,” she said calmly. “They’ve opened the millrace and now the millstones are grinding. It’s noisy on a calm day.”

He followed her out into the brightness of the morning. The mudbanks and the water pools gleamed like tarnished silver, stretching to the horizon, dazzling and strange. The grinding and the clanking noise went on, as if someone were rolling back the iron gates of hell on a stone pavement.

“So loud!” he said.

“You get used to it.” She led the way down the bank onto a little spit of shingle that went into the mud of the mire and then petered out at a shallow riverbed. He walked at her side, his pack on his back, the heels of his riding boots sinking into the cloying mud and coming free with a horrid little sucking sound. Suddenly the shallow ditch beside him rushed with a gout of water that made him jump.

She laughed. “That’s the millrace, the water from the tide mill.”

“Everything is so strange here,” he said, ashamed of flinching from the water, which was now pouring along beside them, in the landscape that was otherwise so still. "My home is in the North, high hills, moorland country, it's very dry. . . . This is like a foreign land to me, like the Lowlands."

"The miller opens the sluice gates on the millpond, so the water pours in to turn his wheel," Alinor explained. "And then the water rushes out to sea."

"Every low tide?" he asked, watching the torrent beside them.

"He doesn't mill every tide," she said. "There's not enough demand for flour. But he stores grain and sends it to London when the price is right."

He heard the resentment in her voice. "You mean that he profiteers? He buys the corn cheap and sends it away to sell at London prices?"

"He's no worse than anyone else," she said. "But it's hard to see the grain ship going out with her sails spread when you don't have the money for a loaf yourself, and you can't earn enough to buy flour."

"Doesn't his lordship set the price of the loaf? He should do."

She shrugged. A good landlord would set the price and make sure that the miller took no more than a scoop of wheat as his fee. "Sir William's not always here. He's in London. He probably doesn't know."

The track she was following was invisible to him as it turned away from the mill stream, to the higher ground of a little island of shingle and then another, set amid a waste of soft mud. The harbor water was gurgling and receding all around them, all the time. Sometimes they were on the firm footing of a shingle spit, with a deep pool on the seaward side, where he saw shoals of tiny fish left by the receding water; sometimes they walked over sand ridged by the departing sea and he remembered the danger of quicksands and stepped in her footprints. Often, he thought she could not possibly know the way around deep creeks that ran through the featureless marsh. But she turned one way and then another, tracing her way through, sometimes on the seabed, sometimes through the reed banks, sometimes on the wavering shore where half-submerged stanchions and mud-buried groynes showed that someone had once built a dike and claimed land, but then lost it again to the indifferent sea.

When she turned inland after more than an hour of walking, they went into an overhung lane where quickthorn trees pressed close on each side. He made sure that he was so far back that he could drop out of sight the moment that he saw someone, or heard her exclaim a greeting, and yet close enough that he could follow her as she took the twisting path that led them towards the high roofs of the Priory, just visible above the thick trees. Brambles trailed across the path, tugging at his sleeves. This path was rarely trodden: the farm workers preferred the road, and when the king was on his throne and Sir William had his favor, all the grand visitors drove their carriages from the mainland over the wadeway at low tide and entered by the ornamental gates to draw up to the double front door where a row of liveried servants bowed as the carriage doors opened. But the liveried servants had run away to fight for the New Model Army, and there had been no grand visitors since the war started and Sir William had joined the losing side.

The trees gave way to a scrubby-hedged meadow of badly mown hay, and the two of them went quickly across the open ground to the shelter of the high wall of knapped flints banded with red brick. Alinor paused, her hand on the ring handle of the wooden door.

"Is this your safe house? Were you expected? Shall I tell the steward your name?"

"I did hope to come here," James admitted. "Sir William said he would meet me here. But I don't know how much he told his steward. I don't know if you are safe going in there and speaking of me. Perhaps I should go in alone."

"Safer if you stay here. I can say that I met you by chance, and I've brought you to him. You wait here." She gestured to a stack of hay, carelessly built of poor grass in the seashore meadow. "Get behind that, and keep a lookout. If I don't come back within the hour then something's gone wrong and you'd better run away. Go back along the shoreline; stay on the bank. You can hide until the tide's low again this evening, and wade over the causeway at dusk."

"God keep you safe," he said nervously. "I don't like to send you into danger. His lordship assured me I would be safe here. I just don't know if he will have told his steward."

"If he sends me to trick you, to bring you in for arrest, I'll take my apron off as a signal," she said. "When I'm coming, if I'm carrying my apron in my hand, run away."

She was pale with fear, her lips tightly compressed. She turned without another word and went through the door in the wall into the kitchen garden. She walked past the tidy beds of herbs and vegetables to the kitchen door of the Priory, stepped out of her wooden pattens, and tapped on the door.

The cook opened the top half of the door, smiled to see that it was Alinor, and said: "I need nothing today, Goodwife. His lordship isn't home till tomorrow and I don't make eel pie for anyone else."

"I came to see Mr. Tudeley," Alinor said. "It's about my boy."

"There's no work," the cook said bluntly, lifting the lid on a giant stewpot and stirring the contents. "Not with the world as it is, and nobody knowing what will happen next, and no good coming to anyone, with the king missing, and parliament up in arms, and our own lord up and down to London every day of the week, trying to talk some sense into them, and nobody listening to anyone but the devil himself."

"I know," Alinor said, following her into the hot kitchen. "But still, I have to speak with him." She felt a pang of hunger bite in her belly at the waft of beef broth. She pursed her lips against the rush of water in her mouth. The cook raised her head from her work, mopped her sweating face with her apron, and shouted to someone inside the house to see if Mr. Tudeley would see Goodwife Reekie. Alinor waited by the door, and heard the servants ask if she was to be admitted, and then a footman put his head in the kitchen and said: "You're to come in, Goodwife."

Alinor followed the lad along the corridor past the storerooms to the paneled door of the steward's room. The footman swung it open and Alinor went in. Mr. Tudeley was sitting at the rent table, papers spread before him. "Goodwife Reekie," he said, barely glancing up. "You wanted to see me?"

Alinor bobbed a curtsey. "Good day, sir," she said. "I did. I do."

The boy went out, closing the door behind him, and the steward waited, expecting that she would ask to be excused her rent for a quarter. Everyone knew that the Reekie woman and her children were hand-to-mouth; nobody had much sympathy for the deserted wife of a drunkard.

"I was at church last night and I met a man who told me his name was James," she said in a frightened rush. "Father James. I've brought him here. He's waiting by the haystack in Seaward Meadow."

"You brought him for me to arrest, a recusant priest?" Mr. Tudeley asked her coldly, looking over his steepled fingers.

Alinor swallowed, her mouth dry, her face frozen. "As you wish, sir. I don't know the rights and wrongs of these things. He said he wanted to be brought here, and so I brought him, with no one the wiser. If he's a friend of his lordship then I have to obey him; if he's an enemy then I'm reporting him to you."

Mr. Tudeley smiled at her white-faced anxiety. "You're not acting on principle then? Not joined your brother's party, Goody Reekie? Become one of these prophesying preaching women? D'you want to see him burned for heresy? D'you want to see him hanged and drawn for treason?"

"I ill-wish no one," Alinor said rapidly. "And I believe as my lord does. Whatever Sir William thinks right. It's not for me to judge. I don't want to judge. I brought him to you, so that you'd do the right thing, Mr. Tudeley. I brought him to you, for you to judge."

Her pale earnestness reassured him. He got to his feet. "You've done very well." He reached into his pocket and brought out a handful of pennies. He counted out twelve, a shilling in copper, two days' earnings for a farm laborer like Alys. "This is for you," he said. "For serving his lordship though you didn't know, and you still don't know what he wants. For being a good servant in the deepest of ignorance." He laughed shortly. "For doing the right thing, though you don't know what you do, as ignorant as a little bird!"

Alinor could not take her eyes from the pile of coins.

He reached into the drawer and pulled out a purse, opened the drawstrings, and put a small silver coin down beside the pile of pennies. "And look," he said. "A silver shilling. To buy your silence. You're a poor woman, but you're no fool and you're not a gossip. Not one word of this, Goodwife. It could not be more important. We're still at war, and nobody knows who the victor will be.

"If anyone speaks of this it will be the worst for you. Not for me—I will deny it and nobody would listen to your word against mine. Not for his lordship, who is not even here. Not for the man who waits by the haystack—he will be far away, as fleet as a hare before the hounds. It will be you that they throw in the water for false faith, for false dealing, for false speaking. It will be you that they say is a spy, a traitor, or at least a gossip. You that they swim in the rife with your skirts dragging you down and the sea coming in. Do you understand me?"

"Yes," Alinor croaked, her throat tight with fear. "Pray God it never happens. I swear I'll say nothing. Yes, sir."

"So we will say that you came to me today to see if I had work for your boy, and I said the two of you could come and weed the herb garden, pick what needs drying this summer, and tidy the stillroom. And we will pay him and you the usual rate: sixpence a day each. You will spend these pennies carefully, one at a time, and never tell anyone where they have come from, and you will save the shilling and never say it came from me."

"Yes, sir," she said again.

He nodded. "And I will forgive you your rent for this quarter."

He turned the table on its central pivot till the drawer with the letter "R" was before him. He drew out Alinor's rent book and put a tick beside her name. "There."

"Thank you," Alinor said again, breathless with relief. "God bless you, sir."

"You can go now. Tell the man in the meadow to come in quietly by the door that the tenants use on rent day. Do you understand? Tell him to make sure that no one sees him. And you and I will never speak of this again. And you will never speak of it to anyone at all."

"Yes, sir," she said for the last time, and she snatched up the money as quick as a thief, slid the coins into her pockets, and was out of the room silently in a moment.

She went out through the side door that they used on rent days to make sure that it was unlocked for him, and back through the kitchen garden to pick up her pattens, and then, pushing her feet into the wooden shoe protectors, she walked through the gate and into the meadow. Anyone seeing her would think only that she was taking the most direct route back to her house at the far end of the harbor. Father James, watching from behind the haystack, saw her come out of the little wooden door in the flint wall, walking lightly, her head up, her apron tied around her waist, her skirt hushing on the cut grasses, releasing the scent of hay and dried meadow flowers. The moment he saw her, the easy grace of her stride, he knew that he was safe. No Judas could walk like that. She was as luminous as a saint in a stained-glass window.

"I'm here," he said as she came around the stack of hay.

"You're to go in," she said breathlessly. "You're safe. Through that door in the wall where I came out, and left through the kitchen garden. There's a small door to the house—it's black oak—at the side of the house on the left. You go in there. It's unlocked. The steward's room is just two steps down the corridor on the right. His window overlooks the kitchen garden. He's waiting for you. His name is Mr. Tudeley."

"He did not . . . he was not . . . you are not in his power now?"

She shook her head. "He paid me," she said, trembling with relief, "for bringing you in. He's on your side. And he paid for my silence. I'm richer by far for meeting you."

He took both her hands. "And I, you," he said.

For a moment they stood handclasped, and then he released her. "God bless you and help you to prosper," he said formally. "I shall pray for you, and I shall send you money when I am back in France again."

"You owe me nothing," she said. "And Mr. Tudeley already gave me two shillings. A whole two shillings!"

He thought of his seminary, the gold plate on the altar, the glitter of diamonds and rubies on the shrines, the gold crucifix on the gold chain around his neck. Tonight, he would dine off silver and sleep on the finest linen while someone laundered his shirt and polished his boots. Tomorrow or the next day he would meet Sir William and they would hire a boat and bribe men with the fortune that he carried. Meanwhile this woman celebrated earning two shillings. "I will pray for you." He hesitated. "Who shall I name in my prayers?"

She smiled. "I am Alinor. Alinor Reekie."

He nodded. He could think of nothing to keep her, but he found he did not want to let her go. "I shall pray for you. And that you get your boat."

"I might," she said.

They spoke together and both broke off. "Will you ever . . . ?"

"If I come back here . . ."

"I don't expect to come back here," he admitted. "I have to go where I am sent."

"I won't look for you," she assured him. "I know this is no place for you."

"You are . . ." he started, but still there was nothing that he could say.

"What?" she asked. There was a slight blush on her neck just above the rough homespun gown.

"I didn't know . . ." he began.

"What?" she asked softly. "What didn't you know?"

"I did not know that there could be a woman like you, in a place like this."

The smile started slowly, in her dark gray eyes and then her lips curved and the color rose in her cheeks.

"Good-bye," she said abruptly, as if she did not want to hear another word after those, and she turned and went across the meadow towards the sea, where the tide was coming in, a dark line against a cloudy sky.

Elation at his words—"a woman like you, in a place like this"—lasted her for days, while she went about her work in the heat of the summer: weeding her garden, cutting herbs and drying them in the ferry-house stillroom, walking all the way to Sealsea village to see one of the farmers' wives who was expecting her first child after the harvest. Her husband, Farmer Johnson, was well-to-do, owning his own lands as well as renting a share of the manor lands, and he gave Alinor a shilling in advance to visit his wife every Sunday, and promised her another shilling to attend the birth. She tied the two silver shillings in a rag and hid it under one of the stones of the hearth. "A woman like you, in a place like this" sang in her head through the long hours of summer daylight. She thought that when she had saved three shillings she would speak to her brother about buying a boat. "A woman like you, in a place like this."

She repeated the words so often to herself that they came to lose their meaning. What was a woman "like her"? What was this place like, that her living here struck him as incongruous? Was there any sense that he meant the place was fine and she was not fit for it? But then she remembered his brown gaze on the neck of her gown, the warmth in his eyes, and she knew exactly what he meant and she felt the joy of his words over again.

It never occurred to her that his words were wrenched from him, that it was a sin for him to voice them, even to think them. She had been baptized into a church where ministers were allowed to marry: there had been no celibate priests or monasteries in England for a hundred years. She did not understand that it was a sin for him to even look at a woman, let alone to whisper to her with desire. She heard the words forced from him as if he could not help but speak them; but she had no idea that he would have to confess them when he returned to his monastery; he would have to tell his confessor he had fallen into a mortal sin: he had felt desire.

She did not know herself, what she was feeling. She had been married young and given birth to two children, feeling nothing but pain. She did not know what it was that made her whisper his words as if they were an invocation, what kept the words in her mind as if it were a phrase of music that sang to her, over and over.

Her son, Rob, came back from crow-scaring with three pennies for the day's work, and her daughter, Alys, contributed her week's wages of two shillings and sixpence. They both handed over their earnings without complaint, knowing that the household had to pay cash for goods: fleeces for spinning, butter and cheese since they had no cow, bacon and lard since they had no pig, a fee for baking bread in the mill oven, a payment to the miller for grinding a peck of wheat, a fee to the Priory for the right to gather driftwood from the shore and terns' eggs from the beach, a fine for failing to dig the harbor ditches last spring. Rent, when it next fell due, the tithes to the church every month, new soles for Alys's boots.

"I'm going to buy a boat," she told them. "If I can."

## TIDELANDS, SUNDAY, JULY 1648

On the first Sunday in July, all the parish attended church and looked at the blank white walls while the preacher prayed in the austere words that were all that was left of the Prayer Book since parliament had pared it away. He preached for more than two hours, that they should all become saints and witnesses to the coming of the Lord. He told them that the king, at Carisbrooke Castle on the Isle of Wight, was mortified by his sins, and that God would bend his stubborn heart to submit to a parliament of saints. They could be assured that God would never permit the Scots to march south—though the wicked king had summoned them, and they were mustering, even now, to plunder and ravish innocent English towns. God would prevent them, and God would especially smite the Irish, if they too invaded in support of the king. The parishioners need not fear. Alinor, covertly looking around at her neighbors' faces, noted that this assurance made them particularly uneasy. These were simple people: when someone told them that they had nothing to fear they knew that they were in trouble.

It was true, the minister told them, "verily true" that traitors were taking arms all over the country, royalist uprisings were happening in every county and two foreign armies invading; but the godly army of parliament would defeat them, the royal cavaliers could not win against solemn men, good men, saintly men. There would be no more papists at court. The king would beg forgiveness and be restored, and his papist queen would learn to be godly, forbidden from bringing in heretic priests. Her chapel, which had been the very center of heresy and misrule, would close, and the king would turn aside from his temptations and accept the rule of honest advisors. The royal family would be reunited, like a godly family should be. The father ordering the mother and the children, the sons obeying him; the little prince and princess, who had been abandoned by their parents, restored to them. Nothing could stop this, the preacher promised, though there was bad news from Essex and from Kent, where royal traitors were taking towns for the king. Worst of all, the whole fleet had gone over to the king, and now the prince his son commanded the ships, and would invade England deploying England's own navy. But despite all this, despite these increasingly bad odds, the godly would prevail. The battle had been fought and won, the king was defeated, and he must learn he was defeated. He was honor bound to surrender.

Alinor was conscious of Sir William Peachey, newly arrived from London where he had been demonstrating his newfound devotion to parliament, seated in his big chair, very still and attentive, his household ranged behind him. He never shook his head, no shadow ever crossed his weary face, he never even blinked. She would have thought that he was a parliament man heart and soul, he sat so still and quiet while their victory was predicted as God's will.

The minister recited the closing prayer and reminded them: there was to be no play in the churchyard, there were no Sunday feasts or sports anymore. The Sabbath was to be holy now, and holy was quiet and reflective—not church ales and dancing at saints' days. Ill behavior by any parishioner was to be reported to the church wardens. Women especially must be obedient and quiet. A godly victory demanded a godly people. They were all soldiers in the New Model Army now, they were all marching in step to the promised land.

As they filed out, sluggish with boredom, Mr. Tudeley, the

steward, was standing behind Sir William at the lych-gate, naming the tenants as they went past dropping their bows and curtseys. Alinor waited her turn, her children behind her. As a deserted wife living on the very edge of the mire, on the very brink of poverty, she came behind nearly everyone. She curtseyed to the lord and to his steward in silence. His lordship looked her up and down unsmiling, nodded, and turned away, but Mr. Tudeley beckoned her with a crooked finger.

"Sir William is to appoint a chaplain to serve in his private chapel and teach his son," he told her.

Alinor kept her eyes on the ground, saying nothing.

"Your boy is the same age as Master Walter Peachey, isn't he?"

"A bit younger," she said, moving her hand to indicate her son standing stock-still behind her.

"What work does he do, besides helping you with the herbs?"

She answered him calmly, hiding her surprise at the sudden interest in Rob. "He goes to school in the mornings, and after school he works at Mill Farm: crow-scaring and weeding. He's a clever boy. He can read and write. He will come with me next week to the Priory stillroom, as you ordered, and it'll be him who writes the labels on the bottles. He knows the names of the herbs in English and Latin and he writes fair."

"Ever in trouble?"

Alinor shook her head.

"He will serve in the household," Mr. Tudeley announced. "He will take lessons with Master Walter, and be his servant of the body, and his companion here at the Priory until Master Walter goes to Cambridge. He will be paid fifteen shillings a quarter, five shillings in advance."

Alinor could hardly breathe.

"The tutor requested a companion for Master Walter," he went on urbanely. "I suggested your boy. This comes to you as a favor from his lordship, to help you since your husband is missing. This is what it is to serve a good lord. Remember it."

She dropped a deep curtsey. "I'm very grateful."

He gave her a hard look. "If anyone asks, you will tell them that his lordship is generous to poor tenants."

She dipped a curtsey again. "Yes, sir. I know, sir."

She turned and walked to the lych-gate with Alys on one side of her, Rob on the other. The two women, mother and daughter, kept their eyes on the ground, and their white-capped heads bowed, the picture of submissive obedience.

"He doesn't know about the rabbit then," Alys said with satisfaction.

## TIDELANDS, JULY 1648

Rob did not have clothes fit to wear to the Priory and stubbornly resisted the preparations, saying that he did not want to go into service with the Peachey son and heir. He said that he did not know him, that they would not be able to play together, for how could a son of the Peachey family wrestle with the son of a fisherman, or race frogs? But when his mother told him of the food he would eat in the great hall, of the five shillings that would come to them at once, and that it would pay the next quarter's rent, buy the family a boat, and pull them out of the poverty that always yawned before them like the trough of a drowning wave, he stopped complaining and went to the ferry-house after dinner to borrow a jacket that had once belonged to Alinor's father, and a pair of Ned's old boots.

Ned walked back with his nephew at low tide, his dog, a water dog with a bright rufous coat, trotting at his heels.

"Sister," he said brushing Alinor's forehead with his lips.

"Brother," she replied.

She poured him a mug of small ale and he drank it sitting on the bench at the doorway with his back against the cottage wall, overlooking the harbor, his dog, Red, sitting at his feet, looking longingly at the hens as they pecked along the scum at the low waterline.

"I brought you one of those little tokens that you like so much." He dug into the pocket of his jacket, bringing out a tiny metal disc, snipped into shapelessness and tarnished black.

"Oh, thank you, Ned," she said with pleasure. "Where did you find it?"

"In the dipping pond behind the house. It's been so wet, I think it must've washed out of the ditch. It caught my eye. How would anyone lose a coin beside a pond?"

"So long ago," she said, turning the little token over in her hand. "It makes you wonder what they were doing there, doesn't it? So many years ago. Standing there, with this coin in her hand. Perhaps she threw it in for a wish."

It was a coin from the time of the Saxon kingdom, from when the Saxons had ruled the tidelands, pushing through the reed banks and the mud in their longboats, building their farmsteads on the islands. Alinor had collected the tokens since childhood, and kept them in her treasure box. Her mother had laughed at her as a miser with a hoard of fool's gold, but had praised her sharp eyes and told her to watch carefully in case one day she found a coin of value. Only once had Alinor found a beaten coin of silver and they had taken it to be assayed and weighed in Chichester. The goldsmith had given her sixpence for it, a fortune to the little girl. All the other coins in her collection were made of bronze or enameled silver, the valuable metal rubbed off over the years. But she had never wanted them for their value. She loved them for their age, for the sense of them belonging to a forgotten time, to people who were not remembered anymore, the coins engraved with strange symbols and shapes rubbed to invisibility.

The people of Sealsea Island called the coins "faerie gold"

and told stories of treasure hoards of priceless coins and the dark horsemen who guarded them, who would strike a thief blind and seal his eyelids with molten silver, but everyone knew they were just sea wrack: washed in and out by the sea, found in waterside mud, and valueless.

"Why would his lordship take Rob into service?" Ned asked as Alinor spat on the little coin and polished it on the hem of her gown, held it up to the setting sun and tried to decipher the blurred image. "Why pay him so well?"

"This looks like a lion," she said, admiring the little token. "It really does. Do you think it's a coin from old England?"

"Aye, perhaps. But why Rob?"

"Why not?" she demanded. "Don't you remember when I cured Master Walter of his croup last May? Rob came with me then. He picked the herbs from their garden and helped me in their stillroom. We've been there a few times since the death of her ladyship. We're going back tomorrow to harvest their herbs and dry them. Mr. Tudeley said it was to help us since the disappearance of Zachary."

"They could have helped before. He's been gone more than six months."

She shrugged. "They don't count the days like us."

"They don't count anything," he said resentfully.

"I know, but if Rob can earn good money and get an education at the same time then perhaps he can do better than his father. Maybe he can get away from here, perhaps even to Chichester."

"If they don't lead him into sin. Sir William was for the king, not for parliament. He might have surrendered and begged for pardon but he doesn't serve in the new parliament, and he's not mustered for the New Model Army. By rights, he should be calling up his men and marching north against the Scots. If he ever meant his promise to parliament, this is his chance to prove it. But I doubt it's a godly household."

Alinor glanced sideways at her brother, at his shock of thick brown hair and his stocky shoulders. He was bitter at being called away from the army just as they were winning, forced to come back to pull the ferry over a muddy rife, when he had got away from the island and thought that the world was changing forever and that he was part of that change.

"You'll always guide Rob," she assured him. "He won't forget your teachings. He knows where he comes from, and what we believe."

"What d'you believe?" he challenged her. "I don't know what you believe."

Her gaze slid away from him. "Ah, I'm like our mother and grandmother, Ned. I don't always understand; but sometimes I feel . . ."

"He'll never be an army man," he said regretfully. "He'll never serve under Cromwell. He's missed his chance at that. And now you're putting him into service to a cavalier lord . . ."

"His lordship was pardoned, and he paid his fine for backing the king," she said, resolutely turning her mind from the memory of the priest walking into the Priory, confident it was a safe house for a papist, for a royalist spy. "Rob takes after you. He won't forget what's right. And Sir William will serve in a godly parliament, whatever regrets he has for the old days. It's over for the king and his lords. You told me so yourself."

"I don't trust him, nor any of them who say they're sorry and get their lands back as if there's no harm done, when hundreds of good men will never come home again. I'd have had Rob in the army; I'd have had him march to war on the side of God. If he was my boy, I'd send him out to my old troop now. There's still a chance the Scots will come down on us. Some say the Irish are coming."

"Surely the war's over?"

"Not till the king signs a peace treaty, and means it."

"Ned, I can't let my boy go," she said apologetically.

"Not even to serve the Lord?"

"He's all I have."

"And now, if he's wearing Peachey livery, he won't even take the ferry after I'm gone," he said resentfully. "So I came back to keep the ferry and the house in the family for nothing."

"You might have a son of your own," she said gently, though he was a widower at thirty.

He hunched his shoulder. "Not me. We ferrymen make poor husbands."

"Ah, God bless her," Alinor said quietly. Ned's young wife, Mary, had died in childbirth, Alinor helpless to save her. "God forgive me that I couldn't—"

"Long ago," he said, shrugging off the pain. "But I'd not take another wife and put her through that."

"Another wife might not—"

"So Rob should be my heir and take the ferry!"

"He still might! He won't serve the Peacheys forever. It's only till Master Walter goes to Cambridge. But even a few months in the schoolroom will be the making of him. He'll be able to go anywhere, to any family, anywhere in England. That's better for him than being stuck here."

"But you and I are still stuck here!"

She frowned at the bitterness in his tone, and put her hand on his. "I've never hoped for better, I don't hope to leave. But now, with Rob's wage, I'll be able to buy a fishing boat, and start putting something aside for Alys's dowry. And just because we're stuck here doesn't mean we can't dream of something better for our boy."

"I s'pose," he said grudgingly. "But dream for Alys, too. That's a girl with high hopes! She's going to make her way in the world."

"Perhaps," Alinor said uneasily. "But it's not a very good world for a hopeful girl."

They sat in silence for a moment. Red, the dog, glanced at them both as if wondering if anyone would throw something into the water for him to fetch.

"You never thought like this before you went away," she remarked. "You'd never have said 'stuck here' then."

"No. Because then I never knew there was a world north of Chichester. But when I was with the army at Naseby, I talked with the other men—men who had come from all over, all over the kingdom, all of us coming together to fight for what we believed, knowing that God was guiding us, knowing that the moment was then—it started me thinking. Why should the king own all the land, every acre of it, and you and I perch on a spit of shingle halfway into the mire? Why should the Peacheys have all the fields and the woods? Shouldn't all the lands belong to all the people? Shouldn't every Englishman have his own plot to grow his own food, so that nobody starves in a rich country?"

"Is that what they say in the army?" she asked curiously.

"It's the very thing that they are fighting for," he said. "The talk that started with the rich men of London complaining about their taxes turned into a roar from the poor men of England asking: What is right? What about us? If the king is not to own everything, then neither should the lords, nor should the bishops. If the king is not to own everything, then every Englishman should have his own garden and the right to fish his own river."

He had surprised her with his vehemence. "You've never spoken of this before."

"My nephew was never apprenticed to the service of a royalist lord before!" he exclaimed angrily. "With the king held, but plotting as if he'd never lost a battle, and cavaliers up in arms all around the country, the Scots coming down on us, the Irish raising troops! Have you heard the news from Essex?"

She shook her head. "Only what the minister said."

"They've declared for the king, the fools. The army's had to march on Colchester and set a siege against royalists."

She looked aghast. "They've never started fighting again?"

"And the ships of the parliamentary navy have gone over to the king. We've lost the admiral's own flagship and half a dozen others."

"What will they do? Will they sail into London?"

"Who knows what they'll do, the traitors? Ship in the Irish? Rescue the king from the Isle of Wight?"

"Oh, Brother, don't say it's war? Not again."

"It'll be war forever until the king agrees to make peace, and keeps to his word," Ned predicted. "He says one thing to parliament and then sends for the Scots and the Irish. Even the Welsh. The army should take him themselves, force him to swear peace, and then make him keep his word."

"I thought he was in prison at Carisbrooke Castle?"

Ned shook his head in disgust. "He's holding court as if he were at Whitehall. He drives in his carriage all around the island, visiting the lords and ladies as if he were newcome to his throne. They say that he's welcome everywhere he goes. He never stops writing his letters and planning his escape. I thank the Lord that the commander of the castle is Robert Hammond. He's a good man. I know him myself; he had his own troop in our army. At least he can be trusted to keep the king safe, and in the end, I swear we'll put him on trial for making war against his own people."

"On what charge? Wasn't it parliament that rebelled against the king?"

"He raised his standard first. He turned his guns on apprentice lads and clerks. He armed his lords and set them up on great horses to ride us down. He turned against us. You're signing your boy up to the wrong side, Sister. Nobody is going to love a cavalier at the end of this summer, when they're all defeated."

"I don't want him on any side," she said fretfully. "I just want him in a good place, and my daughter with a dowry, and a fishing boat to earn my own living."

He subsided and took a deep draft of ale. Red put his soft chin on his master's knee. "Ah, I can talk. Talk is all I do now. For all that I marched and prayed and fought, as soon as Da died I came home to the ferryboat. I was on the winning side with my heart set on it, and now I ship a cavalier lord to and fro whenever he hails the ferry. And he never pays me a penny because the ferry is his, and I am his tenant, and he probably thinks the water of the mire is his too, the mud beneath it, and the sea beyond it."

"You had to come home." She wanted to comfort him, her

only brother and only neighbor. "And we'd have lost the ferry if you hadn't, and the house and our livelihood with it. There were plenty who would have been glad to take Father's place. In Sealsea alone were dozens. They would have been queuing at the Priory gates begging for the right to it. You kept it for us, and you kept our house too. And—as it's turned out with Zachary gone—I'd be a beggar without it. We eat out of your kitchen, and we drink out of your brewhouse."

"Ah, it's your home, not just mine. I don't even want it. My troop is marching north against the Scots and I'm not there. I feel like a coward."

"You're no coward," she said fiercely. "It takes courage to do the right thing. And it was the right thing to come home and keep Ferry-house and the ferry in the family. Where would we be now, if we had lost it?"

"We'd all be relying on you," he said with a wry smile. "You and your new boat. But I did come home, and we've kept the ferry, and you don't have to take a boat out if you can't bear it. I know it's the last thing you want to do, a woman like you."

She heard the echo of the words: "a woman like you in a place like this" and he was surprised to see her face light up, as he had never seen her look before, not since their childhood.

"You say everything in the world has changed," she said, and she did not sound fearful. "Perhaps I will change too."

# TIDELANDS, JULY 1648

Alinor walked with her boy on the seashore path to the Priory through a haze of midges and mosquitoes that rose as their steps crushed driftwood and dried reeds at the high-water mark. The tide was coming in; they could hear the bubble of the hushing well as they turned inland, away from the rising waters, across the Priory meadow, the haystacks as pale as straw in the late summer sunshine.

She said: “You’ll come home on Michaelmas Day and I’ll see you every Sunday in church.”

He was pale with fear. “I know,” he said shortly. “You’ve said it a dozen times.”

“I’ll come to the kitchen and ask after you on Friday. You can tell the cook if you want to see me before then, and she’ll tell me.”

“You said.”

She nodded. “If you really don’t want to go, you don’t have to. We can manage.”

“I’ve said I’ll go.”

She turned the handle on the wooden door set in the flint wall and suddenly remembered leaving the priest, Father James, to hide behind the haystack while she spoke to Mr. Tudeley. The metal handle was warm from the sunshine, the timbers of the door dry to her touch, just as they had been on that day last month. She felt that she was wrong to think of that moment, of that man, when she was sending her own son into service.

"Come on then," she said, giving him a smile for courage, dismissing the day that a priest had looked at her with desire and said: "a woman like you."

They went through the garden, to the kitchen door. The cook looked up from the table where she was kneading an enormous ball of dough, floury to the elbows. "You're expected," she said. She looked Rob up and down. "Good lad," she said. "You mind your manners here and this will be a great chance for you."

He pulled his hat off his head. "Aye, mistress."

"You say 'Yes, Mistress Wheatley,'" the cook corrected him.

"Yes, Mistress Wheatley," he repeated.

"Stuart will take you up," she said, turning her head and shouting towards the hall. "Where is that man?"

Stuart appeared in the doorway, a thin man dressed in the Peachey livery with down-at-heel shoes.

"Look at the state of you!" she scolded, without any hope of improvement. "Take Goodwife Reekie's boy in to Mr. Tudeley. He's expecting him. In his room. And then come straight back here. You're wanted to get the platters down."

He nodded to Rob and turned towards the door that led to the steward's room.

"Wait! Say good-bye." Alinor caught her son as he was following obediently, without another word to her.

He turned back to her, his face pale and closed, and dropped to his knee before her. She put her hand on his curly head in her blessing and then she bent down and kissed him. "Be good," she said inadequately. She had no words for how much she loved him, how much she hated leaving him here. "God bless you, son. I will see you at church on Sunday."

He rose up, his cheeks red with embarrassment at the emotion in her voice, yet anxious not to reveal his own feelings, and picked up the little sack of his belongings. He had almost nothing: a change of linen, his spoon and his knife. He followed Stuart out of the door.

Mrs. Wheatley laughed at Alinor fighting her tears as she watched her son leave. "Ah, give over," she said kindly. "He's not going to sea to fight against the prince. He's not pressed for the army and marching into the wild North to fight Scotsmen."

"I thank God for it."

Mrs. Wheatley thumped the dough into a bowl and set it under a cloth beneath an open window to prove in the sunshine. "Will you take a glass of small ale before you go?" she asked. "Put a smile back on your pretty face?"

"Thank you," Alinor said, taking a seat on the bench at the table. "Can I come at the end of the week, to ask how he's doing?"

"Yes, you can bring me some samphire."

"I will. And, Mrs. Wheatley, will you keep an eye on him?"

The cook nodded. "It's a great chance for the lad."

"I know it. But will you send for me if he doesn't suit? If there's any the least sign of trouble?"

"What could there be? He'll get his schooling for free—his own tutor, not the day school—and his board, and he gets paid, and all he has to do is put up with the young master."

"Is he difficult? I saw him last year when he was ill and he was a lamb then . . ."

"He's a Peachey," was all the cook said. "He's the next lord. He was born to be difficult. But he's not vicious. Your boy has fallen on his feet, to be sure."

They heard footsteps in the stone-flagged passageway to the kitchen and Mrs. Wheatley immediately fell silent, picking up a jug of buttermilk and measuring it into a bowl. Mr. Tudeley put his head around the kitchen door.

"Ah, I thought I might find you still here, Mrs. Reekie. I have this for your boy's first quarter."

Alinor took the purse, heavy with five shillings, in her hand and tucked it in the pocket of her apron. "Thank you," she said. "And thank you very much for the opportunity for Rob . . ."

Mr. Tudeley waved away her thanks and withdrew. Mrs. Wheatley nodded at Alinor. "No more than you deserve," she said stoutly. "With two young children to bring up and no husband to be seen. And Rob's a good boy, I'm sure. I'll keep an eye on him, don't worry."

"Yes, I know," Alinor agreed, reluctant to leave even now.

She bobbed a curtsey to Mrs. Wheatley and went out through the door to the walled kitchen garden, and crossed it, looking back at the house, searching the windows of the tall building in case her son was looking out. There was no one there. The leaded panes of glass reflected the dazzle of the sun high in the noon sky. She could see nothing. She raised a hand in case he was looking out for her and turned to walk home. She felt as if she were leaving a part of herself behind.

On Friday morning Alinor left a sleepy Alys in the warm bed, and went out in the dawn light to pick samphire on the shingle seashore while it was still fresh, damp and salty with the sea fret. The tide was on the ebb. She could see the little waves breaking on the sandbar, far out to sea, and the horizon was a glorious line of gold with low-lying banks of cloud catching the light of the sunrise. The little birds ran back and forth in the shallow water, sometimes wheeling away in a flock, to settle a few yards farther down the beach. At six o'clock by the stable clock she tapped on the kitchen door of the Priory and when Stuart opened it, his hands dirty with wood ash from the fire, she walked in and put down her basket on the dresser.

"Aye, there you are," said Mrs. Wheatley, flushed from the heat of the bread oven where she was shoveling in rolls with a long-handled wooden peel. She closed the door with a thick woolen cloth over her hand and came over to look at the basket, pulling away the fresh green leaves from the top to make sure that the crop underneath was as good.

"Tuppence?" she offered.

"Certainly," Alinor said pleasantly, though it was cheap.

"You'll be hoping to see your boy," the cook guessed. "You

can come up to the chapel with me for morning prayers. You'll see him then."

Alinor shook her wet shawl out of the door and put it on a hook, then pulled her cap lower over her fair hair. "If I may," she said.

"I knew you'd be desperate to see him," the cook said shrewdly. "But he's well. He's not pining. At any rate, he eats well enough, he's not off his feed."

Stuart gave a short laugh. "He's not that!"

"Did I ask you?" the cook demanded, and Stuart ducked his head and went out to stock the wood basket, as a bell in the hall sounded three times.

"We can go now," Mrs. Wheatley said, rinsing her hands under the pump at the kitchen sink and drying them on the cloth at her waist. She laid aside her stained apron, revealing a clean one underneath, and led the way out of the kitchen.

The two women went down the stone-flagged corridor towards the entrance hall. Three dairymaids were waiting outside the carved wooden door to the Peacheys' private chapel, lined up before the wall in silence. Alinor and Mrs. Wheatley joined them. His lordship's valet, Stuart, another footman, a couple of grooms, and two gardeners took the opposite wall.

Alinor heard the Peachey family descending the great wooden stairs. First, his lordship, magnificent in dark red velvet with a rich lace ruff, tall hat on his head, cane in his hand, gloriously overdressed for a country morning, for attendance at his own private chapel. His eyes flicked incuriously over his household and stable staff; he did not even notice Alinor. Behind him came his son, dressed more plainly in a brown suit of knee breeches, and a jacket over a linen shirt with a short white collar. He was bareheaded with his light brown hair brushed smoothly, falling to his shoulders. He recognized Alinor, who had nursed him in two illnesses, and he smiled at her and turned to speak to the boy who followed him down the stairs. It was Rob. Alinor would have known him in a heartbeat for her boy, her beloved boy, but he was transformed. He was wearing an old dark green suit of Walter's with a clean white linen collar edged with a little lace, white woolen stockings to his knees, and black shoes with buckles. Everything was a little too small for his long legs and growing frame, the jacket sleeves showed his bony wrists, the breeches were pulled too high; but he looked nothing like the boy who had emerged unwashed from the cottage by the mire to play barefoot in the churchyard before school.

When he saw his mother, his beaming smile was just the same, and Alinor's face shone back at him. With a tiny lift of his shoulders he showed off the jacket and the white lace collar, and Alinor nodded her silent admiration. As Sir William arrived at the foot of the stair, Mr. Tudeley, the steward, stepped forward to greet his lordship, and Rob came to his mother, knelt for her blessing and then bounced up, and hugged her tightly.

"I knew you would come," he said with a giggle in his whisper. "I knew you would."

"I had to see you. I couldn't wait till Sunday. Is everything all right?"

"It's well," he said. "It's very well." He released her and fell into line with the Peachey procession. His lordship walked down the hall, his high heels clicking on the stone floor, his beribboned cane tapping a counterpoint to his stately progress towards the chapel doors, followed by his son, Mr. Tudeley, and then Rob. All the servants curtseyed or bowed as his lordship went by, and then followed in strict order of precedence as the double chapel doors opened wide for them, and there, bowing to his lordship in the doorway, in a suit of dark black with the austere white collar of the reformed preacher, was Father James.

He rose up from his bow and preceded the Peachey family to the ornately carved seats in the chapel. He went past them to step behind the bare communion table, which was placed firmly at the crossways of the chapel. There was nothing on the table but the Bible in English, and the Prayer Book, approved by parliament, open at the morning service. There was nothing to betray him as a priest of the Roman Catholic Church: no vestments, no candles, no incense, no monstrance displaying the sacred host. It was as clean and clear as any chapel in the land. Oliver Cromwell could have prayed in the Peachey pew without troubling his conscience.

His lordship took his place in his seat, his son beside him, Rob a little farther along, and the household assembled behind them. Alinor, standing beside the cook, a few pews behind Sir William, could not take her eyes from Father James as he bent his dark head and read the bidding prayer. He raised his head and, for the first time, he saw her.

His expression changed at once. She knew that her own face was frozen. It felt like a physical shock to see him after thinking of him with such secret delight for so long. She had thought that they would never meet again; and yet here he was, under the same roof as her son, just a few miles from her home. Dutifully, Alinor bent her head and repeated the new prayers. She watched him from under her eyelashes as he moved slowly and confidently through the phases of the service, from the bidding prayer to the declaration of faith.

When he looked up from the Prayer Book and their eyes met again, he seemed intent only on the words of the service. He did not acknowledge Alinor, and she kept her head down, trying not to watch him, wondering if he had won a place for Rob in the Peachey household as a great favor to her, or if he had put her son in grave danger: in a royalist house with a recusant priest.

The household took communion in strict order of precedence—bread only, no wine at the plain wooden table set square in the middle of the chapel like a dining place for common men. Sir William went first, his son next, the steward behind him. Alinor smiled to see her son follow the steward. As a companion of the young lord he went before all the servants. Alinor followed Mrs. Wheatley and found herself in front of Father James, her hands cupped to receive the holy bread from his steady hand.

She took it and swallowed it and said "Amen" clearly before she moved away. Her mother had always been particularly observant of the ritual of the church service. A wisewoman should always make clear that she had swallowed the bread and was not smuggling it out for use in healing magic. Alinor could almost hear her mother's voice as she went back to stand behind the Peachey family pew. "Take care. Never cause folk to question. You have to be—always—in the bright light of day."

Alinor knelt and buried her face in her hands. Having rescued a papist, brought him to a royalist safe house, put her son into service under a cavalier lord, and lied to her brother, she feared she was very far from the bright light of day.

Mrs. Wheatley nudged her. "Amen," she said loudly.

"Amen." Alinor rose to her feet and joined in.

It was the bidding prayer that released them. Sir William rose to his feet, remembered not to bow towards the old stone altar, which stood ignored, swept bare of the rich gold and silver, under the eastern window of the chapel. His lordship turned his back on the consecrated ground as if it were not his family's long-revered sacred space, and led the way out. Everyone followed him. Only the priest stayed in the chapel, his head bent in prayer in the silent whitewashed room.

"I go to breakfast now." Rob appeared at his mother's side as the household dispersed to work. At once Alinor put her arms around him and kissed the warm top of his head.

"Is everything all right?" she asked him quickly. "Are you well treated?"

"Yes, yes," he said. "I get beef for breakfast, and ham if I want it."

"You go," she agreed. "I'll see you at church on Sunday."

A quick smile and he was gone, trotting after Walter. As he came alongside, he deliberately bounced against Walter and the noble-born boy jostled him back as if they were both village children in the churchyard. Alinor, watching, realized that her son was happy, and his companionship with the son of the lord of the manor was a real friendship.

Mrs. Wheatley led the way back to the kitchen, took up the

peel, and shoveled fresh-baked rolls from the bread oven. She passed one to Alinor, who put it in her apron pocket and felt the warmth against her hip.

"Thank you," Alinor said, grateful for much more than the bread.

Mrs. Wheatley nodded. "I knew you'd pine for him. But he's doing well enough, as you see, and Master Walter is a friendly boy. There's no spite in him."

On impulse, Alinor kissed the older woman's cheek. "Thank you," she said again, and took up her basket, unpacked the samphire leaves into the cool larder, and went out of the kitchen door into the kitchen garden. Dawdling down the paths, pretending to look at the growing herbs in the late summer blowsy richness, she arrived at the gate to the sea meadow. Only then, as she put her hand on the latch and turned to see Father James coming out of the house, did she admit to herself that she had been delaying in the hope that he would come after her.

She found she was blushing and hot, and worse, she had nothing to say. She remembered that she should not speak of the first time they had met. That was a secret of grave importance. But if she did not speak of that, how could she say anything to him? She should be greeting him with deference, as a complete stranger, a guest of her lord, a minister of the church. But if they were strangers he would not be striding past the herb beds towards her, his handsome face alight with joy at seeing her. She did not even know what to call him, but he came so quickly towards her and took both her hands in his warm clasp that she could say nothing but: "Oh." "Oh," she said.

"I knew that I would see you again," he said hastily.

"I . . ." She withdrew her hands and at once he released her.

"Sir William has taken me on as his chaplain. I pass as a minister of the reformed religion. Nobody in the household but Mr. Tudeley knows any different. Your boy doesn't know. He doesn't attend Mass, nor does Walter. The Mass is completely secret, held only at night when the household is asleep. He is in no danger. He doesn't know what I am," he said in a rush.

"He mustn't know," was all she could say. "He's been raised . . . and his uncle served under Cromwell himself. He mustn't . . ."

"I know. Mr. Tudeley warned us when I said I would like Robert to share Walter's lessons."

"You got Rob hired for my sake?"

"I owe you a great debt," he said. "You took me in and hid me and brought me to safety."

She nodded at his formal tone. He spoke as if she were one of the faithful—morally bound to assist a priest—as if there had never been a moment in the meadow, as if he had never said: "a woman like you."

"It was nothing." She was cool in return. "My duty to Sir William. I know not to speak of it."

"And besides," he said.

"Besides?"

Now it was his turn to be lost for words. "I wanted . . . I want . . . I hoped I might do something that would help you. I would have sent you money, but I thought this would be better."

"That was kind of you, sir. But I need nothing."

"Because I—" He broke off.

"Because you?"

He took a breath. "I have never known a woman like you before."

"'A woman like you in a place like this,'" she quoted his words back at him.

He flushed. "Such a stupid thing to say."

"No! I was so pleased! It meant—"

"Not that I think there is anything wrong with Sealsea Island."

"It's very poor," she said simply. "It must look very poor to you, who are used to so much better. Finer."

"I've never met a woman finer than you!"

They were both shocked at his sudden honesty. It was as if they both heard the words and would have to go apart from each other in silence and think what they meant.

"I'd better go," she said, her hand on the latch but not moving.

"Yes," he said. "Can you buy the fishing boat now?"

He watched her smile and then she raised her eyes to meet his.

"I'm getting it next week," she said with simple gratitude. "I'm going with my brother to see an old skiff at Dell Quay."

"Will you sail it home?"

"Oh, no. We wouldn't go all the way by sea around the island. I wouldn't dare. We'll borrow a cart from the tide mill and fetch it down the lanes. It's only a little way by land, five miles."

"And will you be brave enough to take it out on the water?"

"I must be," she said steadily. "I have to be."

"Will you take me out? I could bring the boys. Your son must know how to fish—he could teach Walter."

Together they considered this; they imagined this next step.

"I don't see why not," she said slowly, imagining how it would look to the servants in the household, what they would say at the mill if they saw the boat on the water with the four of them on board. "Would Sir William allow Master Walter to go out in a little boat?"

"Why not? And Robert can guide us to your cottage. There would be nothing wrong in that."

"Nothing wrong," she agreed with him.

It was odd that their last words, as she bobbed a curtsey and went through the door to the sea meadow, was that there could be nothing wrong. They both knew that it was wrong: she should not be hoping that her son would bring him to her, and James knew very well that he should not meet her again.

# TIDELANDS, AUGUST 1648

Rob led the chaplain and young Walter to the cottage along the shore path, in the heat of the afternoon, leaping like a goat over the briny puddles and pattering up and down from beach to bank and from tussock of reeds to dry land. Walter, in smart buckled shoes, slipped and slid after him, complaining of the mud and the incoming tide. Father James followed behind. The tide lapped inwards, closer all the time, seeping up the beach so quickly that they had to clamber from the shore to the high path on the bank as they got to the cottage. They could hear the hiss of bubbling water in the hushing well.

Rob exclaimed at the sight of the skiff moored at the end of the rickety pier outside his mother's cottage, and at his mother coming towards them smiling, a clean white cap hiding the twisted plait of her golden hair, a clean apron around her waist. Rob bounded forward, knelt for her blessing, and then bounced up to kiss her. "You remember Master Walter," he said. "And this is our tutor, our chaplain, Mr. Summer."

Alinor bobbed a curtsey to Walter. "How are you, sir?" she asked him. "You look a deal better than in the spring."

"I'm well," he said. "Father says I'm as strong as a bullock."

Alinor made a little curtsey to Father James, but he stepped forward and took her hand and bowed over it as if she were an equal. "I am pleased to meet you," he said. "I've heard much of you from your son, and I have admired your work in the Priory stillroom."

"Oh, it's very neglected," Alinor said. "We've done very little there since Lady Peachey's death." She glanced towards Walter as she mentioned the death of his mother, but he and Rob were already heading down the little pier to where the skiff was bobbing on the deep water of the channel, nudging the rotting stanchions of wood as the tide pushed it inward.

"Have you been out in the boat? Did you find the courage?" Father James asked her quietly.

"My brother took me the first time. I'd not been on the water since Zachary went missing."

"Your husband?"

"I used to row for him when he was lobster potting."

"And do you think you will manage it alone?"

"I can," she said, swallowing her fear so that her voice was steady. "As long as the water's not too deep, or the tide running too fast."

He nearly laughed at her determined expression. "Ah, Mrs. Reekie, even I can see you're not a natural waterwoman."

"I'm not." She smiled back at him. "But I know I can take the boat out with a line and troll for mackerel, and I can use a net, and I can row to the islands where the gulls nest, and take the eggs, so already I'm set to make a better living than before. I have to be brave. This is a great chance for me, for my children. I'll never go out of the harbor, I'll never put out to sea, but this is our trade. Everyone on this island is a fisherman. I have to do it too! And if I were to be so lucky as to catch a salmon and sell it to Sir William—well, then I would have paid for the boat with one day's work."

"I thought that you bought the boat with the money from one day's work?" he teased her.

At once her eyes danced. "That *was* a very fat fish," she said mischievously, and made him laugh.

They were at the step up to the pier and, without thinking, he put his hand under her arm to help her, as if she were a lady and he were courting her. She felt the warmth of his hand on her arm and she did not draw away but they both looked studiously at their feet until she had stepped up and he released his grip.

"The lines are in the boat," she told the boys. "And the bait."

Rob stepped easily from the rickety pier into the boat, and then held it for Walter, as it rocked against the pier. James hesitated and looked at Alinor. "Will you get in next?" he asked her, offering her his hand.

She sat down on the timbers of the pier so that she could lower herself into the boat without assistance, settling herself on the central seat. James untied the rope, stepped down into the boat, and seated himself beside Alinor, taking one of the oars. "Shall we row together as the boys fish?" he suggested.

She agreed and turned her face away from him, but he could see her color rising as they were shoulder to shoulder, moving together, each placing the oar and heaving gently, moving in rhythm as the boat eased away from the land and into the channel. The water inside the harbor was calm, though they could hear the seethe of the hushing well in the center of the deep waters. The tide was flowing in, the current moving fast, but they rowed easily out into midchannel and then held the boat still, as the boys baited their hooks with earthworms and dropped them over the side.

"Disgusting!" Walter exclaimed delightedly. "Where d'you get worms from?"

"I dug them for you." Alinor smiled at him. "And if you want to catch fish again, you can dig your own. However disgusting."

The little boat bobbed as the tide pushed it inland, and Alinor and James held it steady. "Is that the ferry-house?" James asked her, nodding to the low cottage at the far end of the harbor.

"Yes, my family home, where my brother lives now as ferryman. There's the pier before it, and the ferry is moored on the other side. And see? Just across the rife, on the mainland, that's the granary store on the quay, and the tide mill and the miller's house."

"Will he be milling today?"

"No, he mills when the tide goes out. The tide comes in and fills up the millpond and when it ebbs he opens the sluice, the water pours into the millrace, and turns the wheel. He was milling on the afternoon ebb. I was in their dairy today, churning butter. Alys, my daughter, is there every day, she works in the house, and mill, and farm."

"I've got a bite!" Rob said suddenly. He pulled up his line and there was a writhing shiny-scaled mackerel. Confidently, he unhooked it and dropped it into the woven reed basket in the bottom of the boat.

"Is that what they look like?" Walter demanded, peering in. "I've only ever seen them cooked."

"There's bound to be more," Alinor assured him. "They travel together, like scoundrels. Bob your line up and down, Master Walter."

James watched her as she feathered her oar to keep the boat steady, copying her, so the push of the inflowing water did not force them into the deep channel that ran towards the ferry-house.

"Now you can see my brother's ferry," she said, nodding towards the channel before them and the big raft moored before the ferry-house. "And farther up the channel, inland, is the wadeway. It's underwater now so you can only see the cobbled bank that runs down to it."

He saw the swirl and rush as the river flowing out past the ferry-house met the incoming sea.

"Is it very deep?"

"It rises more than six feet, and it's fast. Everyone can cross at the lowest point, and people drive or ride. But everyone takes the ferry at high tide, or goes all the way round inland. You have to take the horses from the traces and take them across on the ferry and then take the coach across separately, so it's a lot of work."

"I'm surprised his lordship does not build a bridge."

She shook her head and a lock of golden hair fell from the modest cap. "There's no good ground for building," she said. "It's all sand till you get to the tide mill quay. And the mire moves in every storm. The wadeway gets washed away every spring tide, or in the winter storms. Master Walter's father spends all his time rebuilding it, doesn't he, sir? We'd never keep a bridge up. It's all sand and silt."

"So your brother is the gatekeeper to the entrance to the island?" James remarked. "Like a porter on a drawbridge to a castle."

She smiled. "Yes. And our father before him, and his father before him."

"Since when?"

"Since the Flood, I suppose," she said irreverently, and then exclaimed: "Oh! Excuse me . . ."

"You don't offend me," he laughed. "I'm honored to be rowed by a daughter of Noah."

"I think I've got one!" Walter exclaimed. "Like a pull?"

"That's it," Alinor confirmed. "Pull it out gently, gently, and swing it into the boat."

He pulled too hard and the fish came flying out of the water, swinging into Alinor's face.

"Watch out!" Father James said, catching the line and holding it away from her as the boy reached out to take the fish, and then flinched, as it writhed on the hook.

"I can't . . ."

"If you want to eat it, you take hold of it," Alinor advised him.

The tutor laughed. "She's right. Take hold of it, Walter, and unhook it."

Grimacing, the boy unhooked the fish and gasped as it wriggled from his hand and dropped into the basket, as Rob exclaimed: "Another! I have another!"

They were in the middle of a shoal of fish and as soon as they baited their hooks they were pulling them from the water. James and Alinor kept the boat in the middle of the channel as the boys fished, exclaiming at their catch and counting as the basket filled up, until Alinor said: "That's enough, that's all that you can eat today, and all that I can dry."

"Don't you sell them fresh?" James asked her.

"If my husband had a big catch on a Friday I would take it

to Chichester Saturday market, but it takes two hours to walk there, and two hours back again. You can't sell fish in Sealsea village—everyone catches their own—though I sometimes sell them at the mill. The farmers' wives buy fish when they come to get their corn ground, or if a grain ship comes in they'll buy some. Mostly, I dry them for sale, or salt them down."

"Shall we row back in?"

"Can't we go out to the hushing well?" Rob asked her. "Walter has never seen it."

Alinor shook her head, and she and James timed their strokes together and rowed back to the pier. She shipped her oar and stretched out her hand to the pier timbers to pull the boat in, while Rob stood to drop the looped mooring rope over the worn pole.

"You'll have to wait till you can row yourselves to go there," she told Walter.

"Why won't you go there, Mistress Reekie?" Walter asked her.

She steadied the boat as the boys got ashore, and Father James followed them. Then she stood up and handed them the basket of fish, balancing easily against the rocking of the boat.

"I am a foolish woman and I have a horror of deep water," she told him. Father James put out his hand to help her onto the pier and she took it.

"But you've lived all your life on the water," Walter remarked.

"All my life on the mire," she corrected him. "Tidelands: neither land nor sea, but wet and dry twice a day, never drowned for long but never drying out. I never go out to sea; I don't even go out to the deep heart of the harbor. My work has always been on the land with the plants and herbs and flowers. I'm only recently a boat owner, thanks to your father hiring Rob."

Rob tied off the boat loosely so that it could fall with the tide.

"And now, shall I cook your fish for you?" she asked the boys.

"Can we cook it? On a fire with sticks?" Rob begged.

"Oh, all right." She smiled, and James could see the love she had for her son. She turned to him. "Will you eat with the boys?"

"If I may," he said. "Shall we all dine together?"

"You may not want to. Rob hopes to eat like savages around a fire."

He had to stop himself tucking the tumbling lock of hair behind her ear. "Let's be savages." He smiled.

Rob and Walter gathered driftwood and Alinor brought the embers from the damped-down fire in the cottage. James, going to help her, looked around the single room, the bed that she shared with her daughter, the stools where they sat, the table where they ate. It was a typical cottage for a poor working family, and he was struck how the bleak poverty strangely contrasted with the sharp and sweet smell of the place. It smelled of lavender and basil, like the Priory stillroom. Usually a hut like this would stink of old food and excrement, the heavy scent of unwashed people sleeping in their working shifts, but here the salt air blew in through the open door and the room was filled with a grassy smell of drying herbs. In one corner of the room there were cords strung from beam to beam, festooned with posies of herbs. Beneath them, a corner cupboard held a collection of glass jars, and on either side were shelves holding metal trays filled with wax for extracting perfume.

"Your stillroom?" he asked her.

She shrugged. "My corner. I have more room in the ferryhouse. I use my mother's stillroom there, as I used to do with her. This is just for the things from my garden here, while they're fresh."

Under her direction James sliced bread from the big loaf under the upturned pot on the table, and carried out four slices to serve as trenchers for the fish. The little fire was burning brightly.

"Will your daughter come home in time to eat with us?" he asked.

"No, she works late in summertime," Alinor replied. "She

won't be back till sunset. I'll cook her a mackerel and save it for her."

Alinor cut and cleaned each fish, throwing the entrails into a pot for later use as bait, but leaving the heads and tails on. She gave the gutted fish to Rob, who skewered each one on a stick and handed them round. Alinor went to the house to wash the scales and blood from her hands and came out with four cups of small ale. Rob watched her give his missing father's cup to James, but he made no comment.

When the skin on the fish was burned to a blackened crisp and the flesh inside was moist and hot, Alinor told the boys: "That's done. You can eat them." Walter nibbled his from the charred stick, but Rob put his between two hunks of bread and took mighty bites. When they had all finished eating they sat in silence, looking at the fire as the sun lay on the horizon, and the tide seemed to stand still, lapping at the pier but rising no higher. The hens came running up from the shoreline and rushed towards Alinor, confident of their welcome and hoping for crumbs. She greeted each one by name and gave each a little piece of her bread, and they pecked around her feet and clucked softly.

"We have to go," said Rob. He looked to his mother and was surprised to see her gaze turn from him to his tutor.

"Oh, do you?"

James rose to his feet as if he did not know what he was doing. The hens scattered from the stranger; but he did not see them. "Yes, yes, I suppose we do. That's sunset now. We should go."

"I'll lead the way back to the Priory," she offered.

James wanted to agree, but there was no reason that she should guide them when her son was there.

"I can show the way," Rob said, puzzled.

Slowly she rose from her fireside seat, and her boy came into her arms. She hugged him, and when he knelt for her blessing she put her hand on his head, whispered a prayer, and bent and kissed him. She dipped a little curtsey to Walter. "I'm glad you came," she said to him. "You can come anytime, for your mother's sake as well as your own, you know."

He flushed. "Thank you," he said awkwardly, for she was a Peachey tenant and they were, in any case, his fish. "Rob and I will come again."

The two of them started down the path to the Priory, side by side, companionably silent. Alinor was left alone with James.

"Shall you come again?" she asked him, her tone carefully neutral.

"Yes," he said, rushing into speech. "Yes. I want . . . I really want . . . May I come again? May I come back now, as soon as I have taken them home?"

She had a dizzy sense of the world turning too fast around her. She looked up and felt a jolt of desire as his brown eyes met her dark gray gaze.

"You can't come through the mire on your own."

"I'll come the long way round. I'll follow the road," he said.

"Yes, you can come back tonight," she agreed, and as if to deny her words she turned from him and kicked the embers of the fire so they were darkened and cool, and then she went along the bank towards her cottage without looking back at him.

The waxing yellow moon had turned the water of the mire to a yellowy shine, and the land to tarnished black as James turned off the main road at the ferry-house, walked quietly past Ned's back garden, and then loped along the sea bank to Alinor's cottage. He had left the boys in the schoolroom, evening prayers done, tasked with reading and completing some mathematical exercises, and putting themselves to bed. James did not know what was ahead of him. He did not know if he would find Alinor alone, or if her daughter would be there. He did not know, if he found her alone, what he should say, or what he should do, nor what she might allow. He could not imagine how he had dared to ask to return, nor why she should have consented. He knew that he must not break his oath of celibacy. He was sworn to the

Church; he could not consider a woman as a lover, he should not even be alone with a woman outside of the confessional. But, at the same time, he knew he could not stay away.

As he walked along the path from her brother's house, ducking below the blackthorn boughs, the high tide licking the raised bank, he did not think what he was doing, only that he could do nothing else. He thought he was a fool to run through the dusk to see a woman who was little more than a cottager, a poor woman, a woman far beneath him in the eyes of the world. But he knew that he could not help himself, and he was reveling in the sense of his own helplessness. Promised to God, engaged in a conspiracy for the King of England, he should have no time to fall in love. But as he ran, he knew very well that was what he was doing: he was falling in love. He could not stop himself feeling a leap of joy as he recognized that he was falling, unstoppably, in love with a woman as if he were an imaginary knight in a poem and she the greatest of ladies in a castle.

She was waiting for him. As he saw her slim silhouette at the outermost end of the rickety wooden pier, her dress gray against the gray waters, her white cap pale against the night sky, he knew that she had gone out to the end of the pier so that she could watch the bank path and see him walking towards her. Instead, she had seen him running like a lover to his love. He skidded to a walk at the sight of her as she came down the pier, stepping carefully over the rotting planks, so that as he arrived where the steps met the bank and held out his hand to help her, they were handclasped before they had even said one word.

At the touch of her hand, her scratched rough palm, he could not help himself: he drew her closer towards him and put a hand around her waist, feeling the warmth of her body through the homespun cloth. She did not resist him but stepped into the circle of his arm and raised her face to look at him. They gazed at each other silently and then, as if the exchange of looks had been an exchange of vows, he dropped his head to hers and their mouths met.

She was willing. Years later he would remember that, as if it absolved him from guilt. She was longing to be loved, she was longing to be loved by him.

Her kiss was sweet. It was the first time in his life that he had kissed a woman and he felt desire rush through him as if his knees would go weak beneath him. He felt her relax against him as if she too were feeling a wave pass through her, as irresistible as the flow of the tide.

"I should not," she said when she took a breath. "I don't even know if my husband is alive or dead."

"I should not," he said, finding the words awkward in his mouth as if he had no speech but only the power of touch. "I am an ordained priest."

She did not move from him, she did not take her eyes from his face, his mouth, his dark gaze.

"Kiss me again," she said quietly, and he did.

They stood enwrapped in each other's arms, his body pressing against her, his mouth on hers, his arms tightening around her, and then she moved a little away from him and at once he let her go. In silence, just a halfpace apart, they waited to see if they would move together again, if he was going to take her hand and lead her into the little cottage to make love in her missing husband's bed. She shook her head, as if he had said words of desire out loud, but she did not speak.

"I will come to you again next month, in the evening at this time," he said as if a month apart would teach him what to do and what to say to her, while today each was dazed by the other's closeness.

"Next month?" she queried, as if it were a year away. "Not till next month?"

"I have to go away tomorrow," he said.

She made a little gesture as if she would take his hand and delay him. "Not back to France?"

"No, no. But I have to serve ... I have made a promise ... I will go and I will return."

She guessed at once it was the secret business of his Church, and the king imprisoned on the Isle of Wight. "Into danger? Are you going into danger?"

"Yes," he admitted. "But I hope to be back with you within the month."

She heard, as a woman in love will always hear, the promise of love more than the meaning of the sentence. "Here, with me," she repeated.

"Without fail."

"Can't you refuse to go?" she demanded. "Can't you say you've changed your mind?"

He smiled. "But I have not changed my mind," he said. "I think as I did about everything, and I cannot break my word. There are men depending on me; there is a great man depending on me. Nothing has changed . . . except . . ."

She was silent, while she waited for him to say what had changed.

"My heart," he told her.

## TIDELANDS, AUGUST 1648

Alinor worked as usual, through the next weeks of summer storms and sudden days of heat, which made a haze on the mire that looked like palaces and streets and warehouses. The visions made her wonder what James was seeing, if he was admitted into great buildings or was walking down beautiful streets, far bigger and cleaner than Chichester, far grander than anything she had ever seen, if the gates of palaces opened for him, if there were garden doors into beautiful houses.

She walked to Chichester market and at the secondhand

clothes stall she bought Alys a pair of boots, hardly worn and with a good sole that would keep her feet warm and dry through the coming autumn and winter. She bought linen shifts and caps for both of them, and a new petticoat for Alys. She bought a ribbon to trim it, since Alys had so few pretty things. It was too hot to imagine that winter would ever come, but the second-hand clothes were cheapest in August, so Alinor bought her daughter a winter shawl and a cape of waxed cloth that would keep her dry when she had to go out across the ferry to the tide mill or work outside.

Alinor attended church and saw Rob, she picked fruit in the ferry-house garden, she worked in the Mill Farm dairy. She delivered hanks of spun wool to the wool merchant and received, in return, her pay and a bale of fleeces for spinning. She went through every day, her eyes down, her behavior demure, as if she were not burning up inside, white cap on her feverish forehead, gray dress wrapped as tight as an embrace around her waist. She took the boat out on a turning tide at slack water and laid four lobster pots, holding her nerve, though the boat rocked as she leaned over the side. She drew them in again next day, heaving against the weight of the pot and the rope, with two snapping monsterlike lobsters inside. She baited the pots again with stinking fish, threw them out, then rowed to the mill quay with her catch, and sold it to a couple of farmers' wives for fourpence each.

"You look well," Mrs. Miller said, staring at Alinor's flushed smiling face as she pocketed the pennies.

"I'm just the same," Alinor said, though her heart pounded too fast.

"I don't know how you can bear the work." Mrs. Miller looked disdainfully from Alinor's soaked hem to the stinking bait jar. "Especially this work. In this heat."

"Oh," said Alinor, as if she had not noticed.

She went to her beehive and watched the bees coming and going with their determined purpose from the little doorway at the foot of the skep. "Something has happened to me," she told them. "Something very important." She listened to the warm comforting rumble of the hive as if the swarm was agreeing that it was important to them too; but she did not tell them what it was. She weeded her vegetable bed on her knees with her little hoeing stick, the sun hot on her back. She stood up, suddenly dizzy, her hands empty, as if she were walking in her sleep, and remembered the morning when she had looked through the cottage door at the unearthly whiteness of the sky and thought herself enchanted.

The wheat in the harborside fields was a rippling sea of gold, ready for harvest, the miller more and more fearful of a summer storm in this year of terrible rain. Finally, Mrs. Miller declared that they would start the harvest, and all the poor cottagers nearby were summoned to Mill Farm for the work.

Alys was one of the binding gang that followed the reapers, picking up the cut wheat, binding it into a stook, and loading it into the wagon. It was painfully hard work and when Alys came home, her arms were scratched by the stalks and her back was aching from bending and lifting and throwing stooks into the wagon. She worked from dawn—harvest days were long days—and her face was white with exhaustion. She was paid for extra hours with a small loaf of wheat bread baked in the mill's big bread oven, in the harvest bake—one for each reaper and binder on top of their daily pay. It was a luxury that the Reekies only tasted at harvesttime. The rest of the year they baked their own coarse bread of mixed grains.

Alinor bathed Alys's arms and face with elderflower water. She fed her nettle soup to ease the stiffness in her back and arms. Alys drank her soup and ate her bread in silence.

"I'm fine," she said, as soon as she had finished, pushing back her stool and heading for bed, pulling off her skirt and filthy shirt. "It's only as bad as always. I forget how vile the work is. The fields go on forever."

"Soon be finished," Alinor reminded her, picking up the bowls. "I'll wash your gown and linen overnight. You can wear your new shift tomorrow."

"I swear next year I won't do it," Alys said as she rolled into bed, almost asleep. "I swear next year I'll have work somewhere else: clean work, easy work. Indoor work. You know, I'd sell my soul for indoor work."

"I hope that you get it," Alinor said gently; but she could not imagine what work Alys would find that could pay her a wage to live on.

"And that Jane Miller—" Alys broke off, almost too sleepy to speak.

"Jane?"

"Eyeing up the miller's lads, just because her father owns the mill. Giggling with Richard Stoney. She's such a stupid whey-faced thing . . . I'd like to push her in the millpond."

Alinor smiled. "You go to sleep on a pleasant thought," she counseled. "And have kindly dreams."

"I am," Alys whispered. "That is a pleasant thought."

Alinor took the washing bowl outside the cottage, and as she was wringing out the skirt and rough linen shirt, and spreading them on the rosemary bush to dry, she saw her brother, Ned, picking his way on the bed of the mire from shingle bank to dry sand on the hidden shortcut from Ferry-house to her cottage. He brought a half round of cheese—a fee for ferrying a wagon going and returning from Chichester market. They sat together, outside the cottage on the bench facing the mire as the low tide ebbed farther and farther away until all around them was dry land, and the water was a silvery line on the horizon at the bar of the harbor. He watched her as she ate a tiny slice.

"Are you sick?" he asked. "Is it quatrain fever?"

All the people who lived on the side of the mire had marsh fever three or four times a year. They were accustomed to the onset of cold shivers and the sweats that would last perhaps a week, and then pass off. Alinor gave her patients willow and mint tisanes for their fever, and grew marigolds and lavender at the door and windows of the cottage to discourage the insects that brought the illness in their bite.

"No, I'm well," she said, though the high color in her cheek and the brightness of her eyes contradicted her.

Across the mile of mud, they heard the squeal of the sluice gate key opening the millpond, and then the roar of water in the millrace. They heard the wheel creak and turn and the sound of the grinding stones. Then the water poured out into the dry channel in the mire in a sudden deep flood.

"You've not heard from Zachary?" Ned asked, thinking that she might have had news of her missing husband. "You look feverish."

"No," she said, finding a smile and meeting his eyes. "No. Nothing. It's just me! I am filled with impatience: I have spring fever in the wrong season. Canterbury tales after Midsummer Day! I think it must be Rob leaving home, and knowing that I can start to save a dowry for Alys, and I have a boat of my own. I feel as if I am young again and free, and could go anywhere or do anything."

He nodded, putting her rapid speech and the brightness of her eyes down to the wildness that was always a danger, even in the best of women. They could not help themselves. They were like the swallows that were swooping round and round, rejoicing in skimming and dipping in the mill rife, flirting with the warm air, building tiny perfect homes in houses and barns: wild and tame at once, here for summer, gone in winter, perfectly inconstant. He thought his beautiful sister was like a swallow, and that she should never have been tied down to one place. Certainly, she should never have been given in marriage to a man who was so much of the earth that he had probably sunk himself in deep waters and was even now rotting under barnacles on a seabed.

But there had never been a choice for her: she was a woman and had to marry, as all women do, and she was a poor woman who would never go anywhere, however bright her face and breathless she might be. Their mother, knowing that her own death was coming near and nearer, had insisted that Alinor marry, hoping to leave her safe, not knowing that Zachary himself was a wandering haven, no more trustworthy than the shore, vagrant as the tidelands.

"You'll never get Alys married if she's inherited your wildness," he said sternly.

"Ah, she's a good girl," Alinor said, immediately defensive of her daughter, sleeping inside the cottage. "She works so hard, Ned. She wants a better life, but you can't blame her for that! And—see—I only dream."

"Dreams are worthless," he ruled. "And anyway, how are you finding the boat?"

The smile she turned on him was so dazzling, it could be nothing to do with the boat. "Rob came over from the Priory two weeks ago with Master Walter and his tutor, and we all went fishing."

He could see nothing in this to make a woman look as if the world was opening up before her. "Catch much?"

"Yes." She gestured to the bank. "We made a fire. We ate together. We were just there." She laughed.

Her joy was a mystery to him. He finished his cup of ale and got to his feet with a grunt at the twinge of pain from the rheumatism that twisted his joints from a childhood of hauling on the damp rope of the ferry and working in all weathers at every high tide.

"Don't be foolish," he warned her, uneasy at the thought of her dreams and the light in her eyes. "Don't forget where you are, who you are. Nothing changes here but the waters. The rest of the country can run mad, turn upside down, but here only the sea changes daily and only the mire goes where it will." The rumble of the mill, as ominous as thunder rolling over the flat drowned land, emphasized his warning.

"I know," she reassured him. "I know. There is no hope; nothing can happen." But the light in her face denied her words.

"If your lad would only work the ferry for me till the end of the summer, I'd go and volunteer for Oliver Cromwell in the North," Ned said. "They say he's marching men to meet the Scots. A hard march, from Wales, a long march. He'll need men who know how to do it. General Lambert is holding the Scots at bay, but he can't do it alone."

"Rob can't take the ferry," she said quickly. "He's bound to the Priory until Walter goes to Cambridge."

"Hasn't the tutor gone away?"

"A few more days, Rob tells me. The tutor's left them lessons."

"I'd give my eyeteeth to be on the road with my troop, to be beside my brothers for another battle, to defeat the enemies of the country and bring the king to justice," Ned said. "King Charles has to answer for this now. He's called the Welsh to rise against us, and now he's summoned the Scots down on us. God knows what he's promised to the Irish. He uses them all against us, against us English, his own people. He has to be finished, once and for all."

Alinor compressed her lips on contradictions. "I don't know," she said. "I can't speak ill of him."

"Of him?"

"Of the poor king."

"Then you understand nothing," he said with brotherly contempt. "You may be very learned in your flowers and your herbs and your healing, but you're a foolish woman if you don't know that Charles is a man of blood and has brought nothing but grief to us. He never means peace when he says he wants peace. He never thinks that he is defeated when his own sword has been taken from his hand. He has to stop! I swear to God I think we will never make him stop."

She rose to her feet as he became angry. "I know, I know," she soothed him. "It's just that I don't want Rob going to war, or Alys trapped in a country at war. I don't want you going away again, and of course I don't know where Zachary is this evening." She felt that tears were burning behind her eyes. "There are good men in danger, going into danger—" She broke off, unable to speak of James and the secret conspiracy that she knew was taking him away from her. "I don't know what to pray for," she said in a sudden rush of honesty. "I don't even know what to wish for, except for peace . . . and that it was all over . . . and I was free . . ."

"Ah," he said, his anger leaving him at the sight of her tears. "Ah, you pray for peace, you're right. And there's nothing for you to fear. Colonel Hammond will have the king safely mewed up at Carisbrooke. Parliament and the army will agree what must be done with the king, and even if parliament are such fools as to come to an agreement with him, they won't let him raise troops to shed our blood again. We've won against the king, and we've probably won against the Scots, too, and even now the news of the battle is coming south as we sit here. It might be all over already, and it's me who is a fool, pining to march north, thinking I could return to the days when I was among my comrades, led by Cromwell and commanded by God. It's probably all done already."

"Yes," she said. "I can pray that it's over."

Alys was slow to wake, her arms and back aching. The two women had the rest of the white loaf for breakfast with Ned's cheese.

"So delicious." Alys dabbed up every crumb. "I think I shall marry the miller and eat wheat loaf every day of my life."

"You'll have to get rid of Mrs. Miller," her mother pointed out. "And I think you'll find that she won't make way for you."

"How I'd love to be rid of her!" Alys remarked. "I should throw the two of them—her and her helpless husband—off the quay, and marry their son, and inherit the mill."

The miller's son was a little boy of six years old named Peter. Alinor had delivered him herself. "And Jane could be your sister-in-law," Alinor smiled. "That'd be a happy house."

"I'd marry her off somewhere," Alys asserted. "But nobody'd have her."

"Oh, the poor girl," Alinor said. "Don't be unkind, Alys. Anyway, have they nearly finished the harvest?"

"Nearly, just one field to go. I was binding and stacking all day. Will you come this afternoon for gleaning?"

"Yes, I'll bring your dinner," Alinor promised.

Alys bowed her head in a prayer of thanks and rose from the table. "It's funny Rob not being here," she remarked. "Aren't you lonely all the day?"

"I'm so busy I don't have time to be lonely."

"Because you look as if you're listening for something."

"For what?"

"I don't know. A footstep?"

Ashamed of herself, Alinor remembered watching James run along the sea-bank path, jumping the wet puddles like a boy running to his lover. "I'm not listening for anyone," she lied.

"I didn't say for anyone, I said for something."

"I know."

"I didn't think that you missed my da anymore?" the girl asked gently. "We don't—Rob and me. You needn't worry for us."

"I don't," Alinor said shortly.

"D'you just wish sometimes that everything was different? Aren't you sick of everything? Not the king and the parliament—because I just don't care for either of them—but something different for us. Something real, not preaching."

"I wish I could see your future," Alinor replied seriously. "I know you shouldn't be stuck here, on the side of the mire, and no chance of marrying anyone but a farm lad or a fisherman, and no chance of earning more than pennies. But I haven't the money to apprentice you to a trade, and I don't know where you'd go into service. I don't think you'd suit service—I'd be afraid for you, in service."

Alys laughed. "You're right there! I don't want to be a servant to anyone. Not to a husband nor a master."

"Alys, I do so wish for more for you."

"You wish more!" the girl exclaimed. "Dear God, I pray on my knees for more! Has there been all this fighting and shouting and all the arguing among the men, and the only hope for women is a husband who's a little bit better than a beast, or a wage of more than sixpence a day? What about Uncle Ned's new world? What about land for everyone?"

Alinor looked at her bright-faced daughter. "I know," she said. "There's a lot of talk, but there's no new world for people like you or me."

"You mean women," Alys said sharply. "Poor women. Nothing ever changes for us."

Alinor heard the bitterness in her daughter's voice and felt that she was to blame for having brought her into this world that favored men. "It's true," she said.

The girl knelt for her mother's blessing, and Alinor stooped and kissed her daughter's neat white cap. Alys rose up, and went out of the door. Alinor sat for a little longer on her stool at the table, facing the corner of the room where she kept her herbs and oils, and the little wooden box where she kept her treasures. It held her mother's recipe book for remedies, the agreement for the cottage between her missing husband and Mr. Tudeley, and her red leather purse of valueless old coins. It did not seem much for a lifetime of hard work. Then she whispered to herself: "A woman like you in a place like this," and rose up, and took her basket, and her little knife, and went out to cut herbs while they still were damp with dew.

It was a cool dawn, with strands of gray mist lying along the channels in the mire, melting the boundaries between land and sea and air. Alinor shivered in the morning chill, drawing a shawl over her head as she shooed the hens out of the cottage and down to the shoreline. She looked across her little garden to the harbor, where the water was shrinking away, draining from pools into swiftly ebbing channels, leaving acres of wet mud, sandbanks, and reedbeds. As the tide inched back to the sea, the little harbor birds, dunlin and knot, chased after it, running in and out of the waters on their long legs, suddenly flying up with their rippling calls, and then settling again in a flurry, to run to and fro. At the harbor mouth Alinor could see the flat gray of the sea, and the indigo line of the faraway horizon. From the far side of the mire came the thunderous rumble of the mill wheel turning. If James had already gone to France and was homeward bound, he would have a calm crossing. If he had gone to the king at Carisbrooke Castle, he could sail back to Sealsea harbor in three or four hours. If he had gone to meet the Prince of Wales at sea with his ships, then he could have gone out to sea and back within the day. Since she did not know where he had gone, there was no point in looking to the dark horizon for his sail. As a fisherman's wife she knew this well, but still she looked for him.

It was going to be another hot day, once the mist burned off. He had said that he would return within the month, but she knew him so little, she did not know if he was a young man who would remember a promise made to a woman, especially to a poor woman of no importance. Perhaps he was in danger, and could not choose when to go or stay? Or perhaps he was a man who was careless with his words, as men are, and he was not counting the days as she was counting them? Or perhaps the kiss had meant nothing, and the words had meant nothing either.

She turned her back on the harbor and bent over her herb beds, picking the herbs that were unfurling their fresh leaves, tying them in little posies and tossing them in her basket. When she had harvested one bed, she moved on to another until she had picked everything that was fresh, and then she went back into the house and tied them on the strings that looped from one beam to another. The earlier dry posies she took down and put into little wooden boxes, each labeled with Rob's careful script with the name for the herb, sometimes the Latin names, sometimes the old names that her mother had taught her: eyebright, heartsease, and scurvy grass.

She brushed the crumbs from the wooden plates out of the front door and felt the warmer air. The sun was burning off the mist. She watched the garden birds fly down to feed—the robin that lived in the garden all year round and a pair of blackbirds that nested and reared their young in the blackthorn hedge that ran behind the little cottage. She rinsed the two cups, from her breakfast with Alys, in the last of the clean water, then tipped the bowl over the plants at the side of the door. She picked up the empty bucket and walked to the dipping pond, on the inland side of the bank, holding the worn post as she lowered the bucket into the clean water. She heaved the slopping pail back up the steps, stood the bucket by the open door, and ladled water into the three-legged iron cooking pot that sat among the red embers. She took one of the fresh bunches of herbs and set it to seethe in the pot. Her mother's recipe called for some honey, and she spooned a careful measure from the jar where the comb oozed. Leaving it to simmer, she went outside with a sacking bag, an old flour bag from the mill, to gather driftwood for the fire. She walked along the line of the high tide, picking up twigs for kindling and bigger pieces of wood. When the sack was filled she hefted it onto her back and walked back to the cottage.

The water in the pot was almost boiled away, the herbs a dark green sludge in the bottom. Alinor poured it into a tray and set it to dry on the table; threw a piece of clean muslin over it to keep off the flies.

The sun was rising through the thick banks of rain clouds, and it was getting hot. Alinor put on her working hat, with the wide brim over her face and the fall of linen over the back of her neck to protect from the dangerous glare of the morning sun, and went back out to the garden at the side of the cottage where she grew vegetables: peas, beans, and cabbages. As she dug at the sturdy deep roots of a dock leaf, her hens saw her, and came rushing up from the shoreline. They scratched companionably, looking for worms and little insects in the turned earth, clucking contentedly at Alinor, and she scolded them gently. "You go down to the shore, don't you scrape up my plants." One copper-brown hen pecked up a little worm and made a funny grunting noise of appreciation. Alinor, alone under the arching sky with the empty harbor before her, laughed as if she were with friends. "Was that good, Mistress Brown?" she asked. "Tasty?"

Alinor worked all the morning, and as the sun started to slowly descend from the midday high, she went into the house, cut four slices of day-old rye bread, took two smoked fish from the rack at the chimney, a pitcher of small ale from the cool damp corner, and put them all in a little sack to eat with Alys before they started gleaning.

The tide was flowing in, there was only a quiet hiss from the hushing well as Alinor walked along the raised bank to her brother's house and found him picking plums from the fruit tree. "Want some?"

"I'll take some for Alys's dinner. I'll come tomorrow and pick the rest for bottling and drying."

"It's a good year. Look at the branches."

They admired the tree, the branches bowed down with the purple fruit. Alinor ate one. "Sweet," she said. "Very good."

"Going to the mill for gleaning?"

She nodded, glancing at the ferry bobbing as the in-rushing tide met the flowing river.

"I'll take you over," he offered. He led the way down the steps to where the ferry was moored to a post, pulling on the rope and sidling in the tide. He untied it and looped the painter around the overhead rope, which stretched from one side of the swirling deep water to the other.

"Running fast," Alinor observed.

"It's been such a wet summer," he said. "I've never known the rife so high at harvesttime. Come on."

She stepped down to the raft and held to the rail that ran on either side. He smiled at her fear. "Still agauw? The ferryman's daughter?"

She shrugged at her fears. "I know. I'll walk home on the wadeway."

"You'll get wet feet," he warned her. "It's high till dusk tonight."

"Hold tight to the rope," she begged, as the current took the raft and pushed it farther up the rife, and the rope on the overhead line went taut and the ferry rocked.

Ned went hand over hand to haul the ferry across the swiftly flowing rife. They reached the other side in moments and she was off the raft and up the steps to the safety of dry land before he had even tied up. "See you tonight," he said. "You'd best come on the ferry. No point getting soaked."

"Thank you," she replied, and started off down the track along the shoreline to where the mill and the granary stood beside the stone quay with the deep water lapping at the quayside.

For once, it was peaceful in the mill yard. The water wheel was stilled; there was no rushing torrent in the millrace. The millpond was quietly filling, the great sea gates pushed open by the incoming waters, the little waves lapping up the pond wall, the water level rising steadily. Inside the mill the great grinding stones were parted and the cherrywood cogs detached. The miller was bagging up flour, and the two lads were humping it to the quayside, ready for the high-tide ships of the flour merchants.

"Good day, Mr. Miller," Alinor called as she went past the open door.

He was white as a ghost from his flour-dusted hair to the hem of his white apron. But his smile was warm. "Good day, Mrs. Reekie! Come for gleaning?"

"Yes, and I've brought Alys's dinner."

"She's a lucky girl to have you for a mother. Will you come to the harvest supper? Shall we have a dance, you and I?"

Alinor smiled at the old joke. "You know I won't dance. But, of course I'm coming."

She waved her hand, and walked across the yard between the mill and the house, through the gate at the north of the yard and into the wheat fields. The fields looked shorn, the wheat stooks dotted around on the stubble. As Alinor went through the open gate, a flock of rooks rose up before her, one after another like a string of black rosary beads.

Alys was in the line of binders, working alongside the other women laborers, following the reaping gang of men. Most of the men were stripped to the waist, their backs blistered from the sun, but the others, godly men, some of them puritans, wore their shirts modestly tucked into their breeches and tied at their sweating throats. The men were working in a line across the field in a punishingly hard rhythm: grasping a handful of wheat stalks, bending and slashing at the stalks with the sickle, straightening up and throwing the bunch behind them. Alys and other women followed them, gathering the cut stalks into armfuls, tying them with a twisted stalk, piling them in a heap for the wagon. Every so often Mrs. Miller or her daughter, Jane, came out of the house, crossed the yard, and stood at the gate to the field, her hand shielding her eyes, glaring across the field to make sure that the reapers were doing their job, and not leaving uncut wheat for the gleaners.

Alys was pale with exhaustion, her hands and arms scratched from hugging the stooks, her apron filthy, her hair falling loose under her working cap, walking in the line with the other women, bending and gathering the cut wheat, straightening up, tying it, stacking it, bending again. She was working alongside women from Sealsea Island that she had known from childhood; but there were also day laborers come from inland, and half a dozen women were travelers, a harvesting gang that went from one farm to another through the summer. They were paid by the job, not by the day, and they set an exhausting pace that Alys had to match: she was struggling to keep up.

Alinor waited at the gate and was joined by half a dozen other women who had the gleaning rights to the mill fields. They stood together, commenting on the richness of the crop and the heat of the day until Jane rang the bell in the mill courtyard and everyone in the field turned from their work to the shade of the hedgerow and the dinner break. The gleaners went into the field, some to meet husbands or children with their dinner. Alinor walked across the spiky stubble and wordlessly held out the pitcher of small ale to her daughter. Alys drank deeply.

"Thirsty work," Alinor said, looking at her beautiful daughter with concern.

"Filthy work," the girl said wearily.

"Nearly done," her mother promised her. "Come and sit."

The men gathered into one group, passing around flasks of ale, eating the food they had brought from their homes. The women gathered at a little distance. One woman untied a swaddled baby from her back and put him to the breast. Alinor smiled at her. It was one of the babies that she had delivered in the spring.

"Is he feeding well?" she asked.

"God be praised, he is," the woman replied. "And I still name you in my prayers for coming to me in my time. D'you want to see him?"

Alinor took the baby into her arms and gently pressed her lips to his warm head, marveling at the warmth of his skull, and the tiny plump hands.

No one else spoke as they drank and ate their first food since breakfast. When Alys had finished the thick slices of bread and the last of the smoked fish, Alinor returned the baby to the young mother, and she and Alys shared the plums from Ned's plum tree.

"I'm surprised at you eating fruit in the sunshine, Mistress Reekie," one of the women remarked. "Aren't you afraid of the gripe?"

"These are from my brother's garden. We've eaten them every summer and never taken ill," Alinor explained.

"I'd never eat fruit with the sap in it," one of the older women declared.

"I stew most of them," Alinor agreed. "And I pickle some, and make jam, and I dry a lot of them."

"I'll buy two jars of your stewed plums," one of the women offered. "And a jar of dried plums. We had your dried gooseberries at Christmas and everyone wanted more. How much'll they be this year?"

Alinor smiled. "Tuppence a jar, for them both. I'll bring them to you with pleasure," she said. "It's been a good year for gooseberries too."

"I'll take a pound of them," another woman offered.

The women stretched out their weary legs. Some of them lay back on the prickly stubble.

"Tired?" Alinor asked her daughter quietly.

"Sick of it," the girl said irritably.

The bell, warning them that rest time was over, clanged in the mill courtyard. Mrs. Miller was a strict timekeeper. The men got to their feet, cleaned their sickles, and started to walk to the mill yard. They would bring the wagon, fork up the stooks, and take them to the barn for threshing.

Alinor handed a bag with a shoulder strap to Alys. The women who held gleaning rights on the mill fields formed themselves into a line at the foot of the field. They were careful to spread out fairly so that no one woman was given a broader sweep than another and they looked jealously down the line to see that no one was taking an advantage. Mothers and daughters, like Alinor and Alys, took care to stand wide apart to give themselves the maximum area. The line moved forward.

Wearily, the women who had worked all day for cash, now labored for themselves, bending to the ground to pick up every fallen ear of wheat, even individual grains. In some strips an inexperienced reaper had missed a stand of wheat, or crushed it down as he stood, and there the gleaners could snatch handfuls of grains. Slowly, they moved like an advancing line of infantry across a battlefield, never getting ahead of each other, holding their advance, holding the spacing between them. Alinor, her eyes fixed on the ground, bending and picking, bending and picking, was almost surprised to come to the blackthorn hedge at the end of the field, and realize that they had finished. Her bag was filled with ripe pale heads of wheat.

"Both ways," one of the older women declared.

Alys muttered resentfully, but Alinor nodded. Nothing should be wasted, nothing should be missed. "Both ways," she agreed.

The women changed the line, as well as turning the direction, so those who had been on the hedge at the left and those who had been on the extreme right were now at the center, so that no one would walk the same part of the field twice. Once again, they edged forward, their eyes on the ground, their hands snatching at heads of wheat, even scraping individual grains, pressing everything into their gleaners' bags, some of them filling their upheld aprons. Only when they came to the hedge at the end of the field again did they straighten their backs and look around them.

The sun was low in the sky, sinking into drifts of gold and rose clouds. Alinor looked at Alys's heavy bag and her own. "Good," was all she said.

They walked together to the mill yard. Mrs. Miller had the scales out in the yard and was weighing the gleaners' wheat, and marking the weight on a tally stick, as a record. Alinor and Alys tipped the contents of their bags into her scale and snapped off the few stalks. Mrs. Miller added weights on the scale until she said begrudgingly: "Three pounds two ounces." Her daughter, Jane, marked the hazel stick with three thick gouges around one end and two small cuts at the foot and then sliced it in half with a little hatchet. Alinor took their half with a word of thanks, and put it in her bag. Jane Miller tossed the other into the tally stick box as a record of what the Reekie women were owed in flour, when the wheat was milled.

"Bring some of your cordial when you come tomorrow for harvest home," Mrs. Miller told Alinor, as she turned to weigh another gleaner's load. "My back feels like it's on fire, bending over this all day."

Alinor nodded. "I'm coming to glean in the afternoon. I'll bring it then," she said.

The water in the harbor was low, the millpond brimming, gates gently bumping together, pushed shut by the dark weight of the water in the deep pond. As the weary women walked to the white-painted gate of the yard, one of the miller's young men walked around the millpond wall, balanced like an acrobat on the top of the gates, the dark waters lapping below him. He shouted boldly: "Good night! See you tomorrow!" to Alys.

All signs of her fatigue fell away in a moment. She could have been a princess hearing a tribute. She did not answer him, but she inclined her head, smiled very slightly, and walked on. Alinor, watching her, saw her weary daughter transformed.

"Who was that?" Alinor asked, hurrying her steps to catch up.

"Who?"

"That young man?"

"Oh, I think that's Farmer Stoney's son, Richard," she said.

"Farmer Stoney from Birdham?"

"Yes."

"Handsome young man," Alinor observed.

"I've never noticed," Alys said with immense dignity.

"Quite right," her mother replied with a hidden smile. "But I noticed, and I can tell you: he's a very handsome young man. He's the only son, isn't he?"

"Oh, for heaven's sake!" Alys exclaimed, and strode ahead of her mother along the track to the ferry, so that when Alinor came up, Alys was standing beside her uncle Ned in the ferry, one hand on the rope, waiting for her mother.

Alinor paused on the bank, as some of the other women and a few of the reapers hurried past her to take their place on the ferry to go to their homes on Sealsea Island. Alys went among them, collecting the copper coins and calling out the promises to pay to Ned. Only when the ferry was full and ready to go did Alinor go down the bank and take tight hold of the side of the craft, and she was first off at the other side. The women laughed at her. "She'd be no good as a barker for you!" they teased Ned. "Nobody would ever take your ferry if they saw your sister's face!"

Alinor raised a hand at the old joke. "I'll come to pick plums tomorrow before gleaning," she said to Ned.

He nodded. "I'm always here," he said. "The good lord knows that I am always here."

Alys and Alinor went about their chores in the shadowy cottage in weary silence. Alys opened the door for the gently clucking hens and they hurried into their corner of the cottage to roost. Both women drank a cup of small ale, and then Alinor washed her face and hands in a bowl of water and Alys followed her, using the same water and throwing it out of the door on the lavender and marigold plants. She knelt before her mother as Alinor combed out her fair hair and then plaited it for the night, resting her hand on her daughter's head for a blessing. Alys, still on her knees, turned towards the bed and said her prayers, burrowed in like a mole.

"Sweet dreams," Alinor said gently, and saw her daughter's hidden smile.

Alinor twisted her own thick locks in a knot and tucked them under her nightcap, laid her shirt and gown over her stool, and got into bed in her linen shift. They lay side by side in bed together.

"I'm as tired as a dog," Alys remarked, and fell asleep at once, like a child.

Alinor lay silent, her eyes wide open in the darkness. Perhaps tomorrow he would come back. Or perhaps the day after. Then she too fell asleep.

Just after midnight she started up at the loud knocking on the door. Her first frightened thought was that her husband, Zachary, had come home and was pounding on the door in a drunken rage, as he used to do. Then, as she jumped from the bed and went to the door and shot the bolt, she thought, confused by sleep, that the war had started again and the soldiers for the army, or the cavalry of the king, were knocking down her door. Her last thought, as she threw the door open, was that it was James, come for her; but there, on the doorstep, was Farmer Johnson of Sealsea.

"Thank God you're here. It's Peg," he said shortly. "You must come, Mrs. Reekie. Her time's come early, I think. We need you at once. I came as fast as I could. Come now! Can you come now?"

At once her dreams and fears vanished. "Farmer Johnson."

"I've got a pillion saddle on my horse waiting for us at Ferry-house. Come! Please come!"

"One moment." She closed the door on him and in the darkness pulled on her skirt and jacket that were laid on the stool. She found her cap, and pulled it on.

"What is it?" Alys asked sleepily from the bed.

"Mrs. Johnson's baby, come early," Alinor said pushing her feet into her boots.

"D'you want me to come with you?"

"No, you go to work in the morning. If it all goes well—God willing—I'll meet you at gleaning and harvest home. If I'm kept overnight, you stay at Ferry-house."

Alys nodded in the darkness, turned over, and went back to sleep immediately. Alinor picked up her sack, a box of dried herbs and some bottles from the cupboard, and stepped out into the cool nighttime air. The tide was coming in, seeping over the mud and climbing the bank towards the cottage and the sleeping girl.

"Quickly," said Farmer Johnson. "What's the safest way?"

"Follow me," Alinor told him, and led the way, sure-footed along the top of the bank, the waves lapping in the darkness below them till she could see the ferry-house, her family home, as a dark bulk on the skyline. Her brother, woken by Farmer Johnson's gallop up the road, held a lantern for the two of them to walk round the front of the house by the dark rife, to the road, and then led the farmer's horse to the stone mounting block beside the track to Sealsea village.

Farmer Johnson heaved himself into the saddle and Alinor stepped onto the mounting block and then seated herself behind him, her feet on the pillion step, her back supported by the saddle.

"Hold tight," her brother said, and she nodded and took a grip of the farmer's wide belt.

"Look for Alys in the morning," she replied. "She's working at the mill tomorrow. Make sure she has some breakfast."

"Aye. God bless you, and the godly work you do."

The farmer clicked to his big horse and the animal started to walk, and then went into a shambling canter. Alinor held tight, one hand wrapped inside his belt, the other gripping her sack of precious bottles and herbs clinking in her lap. The mud track to Sealsea village was deeply rutted and puddled, but they stayed on the grassy verge, and as the sky lightened they could see the way ahead of them. After two miles, the horse recognized his home, dropped down into a walk, and turned into the gateway of the farm. Ahead of them the riders could see the moving lights in the downstairs windows as the servants went to and fro. Alinor felt the familiar sense of excitement at what was before her: anxiety that she would be faced with some complication of birth, confidence in the vocation that she had learned from her mother, that she had taught herself, that she was born to do. She had an illuminating sense of standing at the gateway to life and death and feeling no fear.

The farmer pulled up the horse and turned in the saddle, holding Alinor's sack of physic as she stepped down to the mounting block, and then he handed her the precious sack and dismounted himself. "This way, this way," he said, leaving the horse to stand at the door as he hurried Alinor inside.

"Here's Goodwife Reekie," he said to an older woman, whom Alinor recognized as his mother.

"At last!" she replied rudely. "You took your time!"

"Good morning, Mistress Johnson," Alinor said politely. "How does Margaret do?"

"Poorly," the woman said. "She can't sit down and she won't lie down either. She's tiring herself out walking up and down."

"For God's sake!" Farmer Johnson cried out. "Why didn't you make her rest? Goodwife Reekie, make her rest!"

"Let me see her," Alinor said calmly. "Farmer Johnson, would you ask them to boil up some water and bring it in a bowl? With soap and linen? And some hot mulled ale for her to drink? And d'you have any wine you can heat up for her?"

"I'll get it, I'll get it all!" he assured her. "Boiled water in a bowl and mulled ale and mulled wine. I'll get it all."

He rushed towards the farmhouse kitchen, roaring for servants, as his mother led Alinor up the wooden stairs to the master bedroom.

The room was stifling hot, a fire of heaped logs in the fireplace and the windows shuttered and covered with tapestries. In the center of the room, one hand gripping the post of the bed, was Margaret Johnson, very pale in a stained nightgown. Her own mother was pulling ineffectually at her hands and urging her to lie down on the bed and rest, for assuredly this could go on for days, and she would die of exhaustion before the baby came, or die of hunger during labor.

"Alinor," she said in a little gasp as Alinor came through the door.

"Now, Margaret, how are you going on?" Alinor spoke gently.

"My waters have broken; but now nothing is happening," she said. "And I am so hot, and so grieved. I think I have a fever—could I have a fever? And I am breathless."

"You might have a fever,". Alinor said, taking in the disordered room and the ill-concealed panic of both the older women, the housemaid piling another log on the fire. "But it is very hot in here, and you are bound to be breathless if you are walking around and talking."

"I told her so," her mother confirmed, "but she'll listen to no one, and we wanted them to send for you hours ago, but Mother Johnson said no, and now she's tired herself . . ."

"Do you have any lavender in the garden?" Alinor turned to Farmer Johnson's mother. "Could you gather me some fresh heads for the floor?" She turned to Margaret's mother. "Could you go and see that they are bringing the water I asked for?"

"The house is at sixes and sevens," the woman replied. "I

daresay they've let the kitchen fire go out, and there is nothing for anyone."

"If they can't manage the birth of a baby, I'm sure I don't know why," Mrs. Johnson said rudely. "I had ten in that very bed. One was born dead and one came before its time . . ."

Alinor herded the two women from the room before Mrs. Johnson could tell more terrifying tales, and suddenly there was a silence broken only by the crackle of new wood burning in the fireplace. "It is very hot," Alinor remarked. "Don't put another log on."

The maid shrank back, as Alinor drew back the tapestry and opened the window.

"Night air?" Margaret said fearfully.

Alinor dropped the tapestry so no one would see that the window was opened but a cool breeze came into the room and Margaret sighed with relief.

"Spirits'll come in," the maid whispered. "Don't let spirits in!"

"No, they won't," Alinor ruled. "Shall we get you into a clean nightgown?"

Margaret's mother came through the door with a bowl of water. "Thank you," Alinor said, taking it at the threshold and heading her off. "And the mulled ale?"

"We could all do with a glass," the woman agreed, and went back to the kitchen as Alinor closed the door.

"Why don't you sit down and let me wash your face and hands?" Alinor suggested.

Margaret protested faintly that washing must be dangerous in her condition, but she watched Alinor add some lavender oil to the warm water. The sharp clean scent filled the room and Alinor gently patted Margaret's temples and the back of her neck with the warm water and the oil, washed her hands, taking them gently and rubbing them with oil, and then washed her own.

Margaret sighed and then held her big belly and groaned. "I feel as if my guts are turning over."

"So you should," Alinor said with satisfaction.

"I don't want to lie on the birthing bed," Margaret protested.

"Not if you don't want," Alinor said pleasantly. "You can stand or sit or kneel as you like. But let's be still and calm."

"I have to walk about. I feel so restless!"

"Walk in a moment," Alinor suggested. "But sit still now while they bring you some ale to drink."

"Is it going to take a long, long time?" Margaret demanded nervously. "Is it going to be torture?"

"Oh, no," Alinor said. "Think of a hen laying an egg. It might be quite easy."

Margaret—who had been filled with terrors by the older women—looked incredulously at her young midwife and saw her confident smile. "Easy?" she demanded.

"It might be," Alinor said smiling. "Perhaps."

It was not as easy as a hen laying an egg, but it was not torture, and Margaret did not see the gates of heaven opening up before her, as her mother-in-law had confidently predicted. She gave birth to a boy, as her husband secretly wanted, and Alinor, receiving the miracle of the bloodstained, warm, squirming baby into her steady hands, wrapped him in a clean linen cloth and laid him on his mother's breast.

"Is he all right?" Margaret whispered, as the other women in the room—the two mothers and three friends who had arrived to bear them company—drained a glass of birth ale to the mother and baby.

"He's perfect," Alinor said, snipping and tying off the cord. "You did very well."

"Shall you baptize him?"

"No, he's in no danger, and the new churchmen don't like it done by a midwife."

Quietly and carefully she washed Margaret's parts and bound them up with moss. "I will come later today and every day for a week with fresh moss," Alinor promised.

"And you will stay," the girl insisted. "And help me with him?"

"I will." Alinor smiled. "As long as you want me. But you will see, soon you won't want anyone in your way. He will like you best."

The young wife looked torn between fear and love. "Will he? Won't he prefer . . ." her eyes slid to her overbearing mother-in-law, ". . . someone who knows what to do? Better than me?"

"You will find he is all yours," Alinor confidently predicted. "For him there will be no one better than you. And both of you will learn what you like best together."

"Can I see my son? Can I see him?" was the shouted demand from the other side of the bedroom door. Farmer Johnson would not be allowed into the bedroom nor see his wife for another four weeks, but his mother carried his son out to him. They could hear the loud exclamations and blessings, and his words of love for his young wife, and then Mrs. Johnson brought the baby back in again.

"He won't have the baby baptized at church," she said in a shocked undertone to Alinor. "Says it's papist ritual and a God-fearing father names his own child at home. What d'you think of that, Mrs. Reekie?"

Alinor shook her head, refusing to be drawn into the new argument. "I don't know the rights and wrongs of it."

"And he says she's not to be churched." Margaret's mother nodded at her dozing daughter. "How can that be right?"

Alinor maintained her silence: all the new church sects were determined to be rid of all ritual, to cut any traditions that were not named in the Bible. "He's a godly man," she said diplomatically. "He must know what's right."

"Says he's prayed on it," Margaret's mother sniffed. "And so my girl gets up and goes about her work without a blessing. What about giving thanks for escaping death and danger?"

"We can all give thanks that she had a safe birth," Alinor said. "In church or out of it."

"Thanks are due to you too," the older woman said. "You

have all your mother's gifts. You have a way with a woman at her time that is like magic."

It was a dangerous word to use, even in praise. The older women turned and looked at Alinor to see what she might admit.

"There's no magic," Alinor insisted. "It's not magic. Don't say such a thing! It's just trusting to the Lord and having attended so many births."

"And yet you don't have a license from the bishop?"

"I had my license, of course; but His Grace hasn't been seen in his palace at Chichester for months, not since the siege. I've asked, and asked, but nobody knows how a midwife gets her license now."

Both older women shook their heads. "Well, someone has to give you a license," Mrs. Johnson ruled. "For there isn't a woman in all of Sealsea Island who would have anyone else attend them."

"Though it was a pity about your sister-in-law," Mrs. Johnson added.

An old pang of grief shook Alinor. "Yes," she agreed. "Some things are mysteries. It's God's will, not ours. I'm so glad that Margaret came through safe."

"And a man midwife is just ungodly. What shameless woman would want a man at a time like this?"

"I'm glad it went so well," Alinor said, gathering up her things: the sharp knife for cutting the cord, the clean string for tying it off, the oils in the bottles, the tincture of arnica and the St. John's Wort for the bruising and the pain. "I'll come back this afternoon."

"Come in the morning?" Margaret's sleepy voice came from the bed.

"It's morning already," Alinor said, lifting the corner of the tapestry and seeing the pearly light of the summer day. "Your first morning as a mother. Your baby's first dawn."

"You'll see a lot more dawns," her mother-in-law predicted grimly. "All the babies in our family wake early."

The young wife was drowsy on her pillow in the best bed. "Don't be late." She opened her eyes and smiled at Alinor. "I shall look for you this afternoon."

"I won't be late," Alinor promised. "You can count on me."

Farmer Johnson sent her home in the clear dawn light, riding pillion on his horse behind the groom, to her brother's ferry-house. Alinor was seated high on the plow horse, a tiny crescent moon like a clipped silver coin in the light sky above her, water rising in the rife, when she saw a figure on the other side. He was riding down the road towards the ferry. She recognized him at once: James Summer, the man she loved, come home to her as he promised, within the month.

Alinor dismounted from the farmer's horse, said a word of thanks to the stable lad, and stood and watched her brother pull the ferry over the water, hand over hand on the overhead rope. She saw James lead his horse down the bank, and its nervous steps onto the rocking ferry. The two men crossed in silence, and then they went either side of the horse to lead it off the ferry and up the cobbled bank on the island side.

"He should know it by now, he's done it a dozen times," Ned remarked to James, patting the horse. "I've seen horses get used to cannon and musket fire within a day. He's an island horse, he knows the ferry, he's just playing with you."

"Did you see cavalry in the war?" James asked. He turned and gave Alinor a smile just for her, shielded beneath his hat. "Good day to you, Goodwife Reekie. You're up very early?"

"Yes. At Marston Moor," Ned said, naming Oliver Cromwell's first great victory. "That was all in the hands of the cavalry. And many of us had never seen fighting but had only practiced standing and facing a charge, marching to the right, falling back and reforming, in the fields. But the horses bore it as if they knew it was the right thing to do."

"So I heard," James said blandly. He paid over his penny for the one-way passage and Ned tucked the coin into his pocket.

"I think your lord was on the other side," Ned goaded the stranger. "Sir William? On the losing side. God commanded the victory to the godly and Sir William was in the wrong. He wasn't lord of everything, that day."

James sidestepped the challenge. "I didn't know him in those days. I was appointed only last month to tutor Walter and prepare him for Cambridge."

"From what?" Ned asked suspiciously.

"I beg your pardon?"

"What were you doing before?"

"Teaching another family," James lied easily.

"And you teach my nephew too, don't you? I'm Rob's uncle, Mrs. Reekie's brother."

"I do," James said cheerfully. "And I know of you, of course, Mr. Ferryman. Robert is a very keen clever young man. When Master Walter goes to university I should think Robert could get an apprenticeship, perhaps as a clerk to a physician. He knows more about medicines and herbs and oils than I do. He's a very unusual young man." He slid a smile at Alinor, who still sat on the farmer's horse, looking at the two men.

"The apple doesn't fall far from the tree," Ned said proudly. "And she learned from our mother, and she from hers and so it goes backwards."

James smiled at Alinor again, his eyes searching her face, wondering at her silence. Still, she said nothing. He did not know, but she was thanking God for the sight of him, marveling that he had come, as he had said he would, conscious of her own simple joy at his handsome face, of the rich tumble of his dark curly hair, of the beautiful line of his mouth. He had come as he said he would—that was what surprised her most. He had kept his promise, and the warm rising of her desire felt like gratitude that he should be the man that she hoped, that he should be fit for her love, as natural and as unstoppable as the incoming summer tide.

"She's been out all night attending a birth," Ned spoke for her, and then turned to her: "Is all well? God bless them in their travail?"

"Yes, she has a boy," Alinor answered, recalled to herself. "Strong and well made. She's well herself. I'll go back to see them later."

"And will you rest now?" James asked her.

She smiled at his ignorance. "No, no, of course not. I have all my work to do in the cottage and garden," she said. "And this afternoon I'll come here to pick the plums, go to visit the mother and baby, and then go to the mill for gleaning and for the harvest home. Is Sir William coming to see the harvest in?"

At once he realized this was a chance for them to meet. "I don't know. I'm on my way there now. But if Sir William attends I will come with him and bring Walter and Robert."

"I should like to see Rob," she replied. "Sir William usually attends the harvest home at the mill. The mill is the biggest farm in his estate."

"I hope to come then. Shall we see you there?"

"At sunset," Alinor said.

"Is there dancing?" he asked, as if they were a girl and a boy, and he might bow before her, take her hand and lead her out.

"After dinner," she said. "Just a fiddle and the harvest dances."

He did not dare to ask if he might dance with her. "I should so like . . ."

"What?" she asked, instantly alert. She thought of his hand on her waist; she thought of their steps going together.

"To see you at harvest home," he said lamely. He nodded to her brother, bowed to her, climbed on the mounting block, and rode his horse down the track to the Priory without looking back.

"Pleasant enough, though fine as a lord," Ned said carefully, watching her.

The face that she turned to him was blandly serene. "I'm so glad he's teaching Rob," was all she said. "It's a great chance for him."

"Started work but went away the very next week," he pointed out.

"He left them studies to do. Rob told me they read in the library every morning and do the exercises he set them: translating and mathematics and map reading—all sorts."

"Is he a godly man?" he pressed her.

"Oh, I should think so. He preached a fine sermon in Sir William's chapel and stood before a table. He didn't use the altar at all, and all the gold and silver and all the fine embroidered cloth must have been taken down and packed away. There were no tapestries or statues or anything fine. He's one of the new men."

"Well enough," he said, denying the uneasiness he felt at the brightness of her face and the way that the gentleman had looked at her, as if he were surprised to find a woman like her in a place like this. "Well enough, I suppose."

She nodded. She was completely calm. Ned could not reach her; he could not understand her.

"Seems very friendly," he said, as if it were a failing.

"I don't find him so. He's just his lordship's tutor. He just takes Master Walter out and about to see the things he should know, and Rob with him."

"Handsome man," he remarked.

"Do you think so?" she asked, just as Alys had said to her of Farmer Stoney's son at the mill. "I hadn't noticed."

As soon as James Summer arrived at Mill Farm with Sir William, Master Walter, Rob, and the groom, he knew it was a mistake to come. It was obvious that they were the family from the great house, the landlords: riding out, ready to be amused by peasant celebrations. Sir William was on his charger and Walter rode his father's hunter, James was on a high-bred black riding horse, and even Rob had the handsome cob once used to pull the ladies' carriage. The four of them, overhorsed, overdressed, followed by the groom, rode through the white-barred gate into the mill yard as if they were royalty: condescending to observe village customs, patronizing the people's sports.

Mr. Miller came out into the yard and bowed low to his landlord, his little son Peter beside him. Mrs. Miller burst out of the kitchen door, flinging off her stained work apron, trying to look as if she were a lady of leisure and had not been basting the roasting ham. Jane raced after her, pulling her best cap over her dark hair. James flinched at the bleached whiteness of the Miller women's best aprons, the stiffness of the frilled lace, and the falseness of their smiles.

Workingmen who declared themselves godly, who knew well enough that Sir William had sided with the king, reluctantly doffed their caps and nodded their heads to their landlord, then turned away. They disapproved of him, of the old order, and the old ways. There would be no corn dollies and dancing and bringing the harvest home for them. But those who liked the old ways, and who liked a drink and were looking forward to a feast, set up a cheer for Sir William, hoping that he would pay for the harvest ale. The women smiled and waved at Walter and curtseyed low to Sir William. They could not take their eyes from James Summer, high on his black horse, his profile like one of the carved stone angels in the old churches. Alinor took a sharp breath and looked away from him. She tried to smile at her son, but she found her cheeks were hot and she was painfully aware of the knee-high dust of the field on the hem of her homespun skirt and the damp stains at the armpits of her shirt.

"Mrs. Miller," Sir William said pleasantly to the miller's wife, who dropped like a sack of corn into a deep curtsey, "I'll take a glass of your home-brewed ale."

She bustled back to the house to fetch the best pewter tankard, while Mr. Miller stood at his landlord's horse's head, waiting for Sir William to condescend to dismount.

"Good harvest?" his lordship inquired, glancing at the granary and the piles of stooks waiting to be threshed, the clean-swept threshing floor.

"Medium," the miller said carefully. He would have to pay a

tithe from the harvest to his landlord and another to the church. There was no point in boasting.

"You will stay for dinner, my lord?" Mrs. Miller asked breathlessly, nodding to her daughter to pour the first of the harvest ale, handing her the precious tankard. "Your lordship, and of course Master Walter and . . ." The invitation tailed off as she took in the glamorous looks of the stranger and longed for an introduction.

"This is Mr. Summer," his lordship announced generally. "A Cambridge man, my son's tutor."

There was a little ripple of interest. That he was a Cambridge man suggested that he was a godly man. Everyone knew that the heart of reform was Cambridge, while Oxford had been the wartime headquarters of the king. James Summer tipped his hat to acknowledge the attention and made sure that he was not looking towards Alinor. She was looking carefully down at her dusty boots tied up with string.

"All welcome," the miller said grandly, overcoming his unease at what dinner for the gentry would cost him in the long run.

Sir William dismounted heavily and his groom took his horse. The miller's lad, Richard Stoney, came forward and took the others and led them into the stables. Rob went to his mother and his sister among the gleaning women, kneeling for Alinor's blessing and then bobbing up to hug her.

Alinor kissed him, conscious of her sweating face and dirty hands, and then curtseyed to Master Walter, his lordship, and the tutor. James glanced at her, but could not cross the yard to approach her with everyone staring at him.

"We're just bringing in the last wagon," Mrs. Miller said, pleased. "You can see it come in, your lordship. Mr. Summer, you must know that we grow the best wheat in Sussex here."

"A middling good harvest," her husband supplemented quickly. "A lot of blight this year from the rain . . . terrible rain. And that's before the rats get at it."

"So I see," James said pleasantly, glancing through the granary doors.

"And Alys Reekie is Harvest Queen," Mrs. Miller said begrudgingly. "The young people chose her. They wouldn't have any other, though there were girls with better claims, God knows."

James, looking at the beautiful girl with interest, could see that there was no contest for the title of queen of the harvest. With her regular clear features and her dark blue eyes, she was far and away the prettiest girl among the gleaners. They had taken off her modest white cap, and her golden hair was tumbled down over her shoulders. They had thrown an embroidered white smock over her working clothes, and placed a crown of wheat on her fair hair, gold against the gold.

"And Richard Stoney is Harvest King."

"Are we ready?" Mr. Miller demanded as the last cart rumbled in. As the men hurried to unload it, Richard Stoney came from the stables and received a crown of plaited wheat on his brown curly head.

Mr. Miller ceremonially closed the barn doors, the young women gleaners, Jane Miller among them, and the young men reapers lined up before it, as if to block entry, and Alys and Richard went to their places on the far side of the yard with the lads catcalling and the girls singing out Alys's name. His lordship, knowing the harvest games, waited for the young couple to stand side by side, and called to them: "Ready?"

"Aye!" Richard answered for them both.

Sir William shouted: "Go!" and the young couple dashed across the cobbled yard towards the barn doors, dodging and twisting as their friends sprang towards them, pelting them with jugs of water and handfuls of chaff, trying to prevent them entering the barn. They fought their way through, pushing and ducking, swerving and gasping. Richard grabbed Alys's hand to pull her from a mob of boys as the adults cheered them on, until finally each of them got a hand on the great iron ring of the barn door, pulled it open, and declared that the harvest was safely home.

Everyone cheered. Alinor saw the bright looks that the young couple exchanged, and the way they immediately turned away from each other to return to their friends, Richard exuberantly bouncing towards the harvest lads, who jostled him and pulled at his straw crown, as Alys ran to the girls, flushed and giggling. Mrs. Miller served the harvest ale, first cup to Sir William, and the thirsty harvesters gathered around for their cups as Alinor turned to find James at her side.

"Your daughter is a very beautiful girl," he observed.

"She is," she said quietly.

They were painfully tongue-tied in company. They wanted to speak nothing but secrets; and they could not be seen to whisper. "You got home safely from your travels?" was all she could say.

"Yes," he said awkwardly. "Yes, I did. Did you go back to the young mother? Is she well?"

"I went this afternoon, and I will go again tomorrow," she confirmed. "I like to visit a young mother with her newborn baby, even if she has her own mother at her side."

He was about to ask if he might come to see her at the cottage tonight, after harvest home; but he broke off. Her brother was coming down the track from the ferry to the mill yard, his old dog, Red, winding around his feet.

"I have to see you," James said urgently. "Not here. Not in front of all these people. Alone."

"I know, I know," she breathed.

"Can I come tonight?" he whispered; but before she could answer Ned walked up to his sister, and acknowledged James with a brief nod.

"Good day, sir," Ned said abruptly. "I see you came to visit the poor people of the parish. I suppose you like the old ways: Harvest Queen and Harvest King."

"As long as the harvest games are modest." James tried to steady himself.

Ned turned to Alinor and demanded: "I take it you won't be dancing?"

"No. But Alys can, can't she?"

Ned frowned and was about to refuse.

"There can be no objection to dancing at harvest home," James interrupted. "Oliver Cromwell himself does not object to a glass of wine and godly merriment."

"Not pagan dances," Ned said stiffly. "And harvest home with the Harvest King and Queen is both pagan and monarchical."

James tried to choke back a laugh but Ned was red to his ears and looked angry. "My sister's situation is awkward." Ned turned on him. "You wouldn't know, Mr. Summers, but this is a small island, and nobody has anything to do but gossip."

"No one says anything against me," Alinor argued. "And everyone knows that Alys is your niece and a godly child. She can dance with her friends, Brother. Surely she can!"

"As you wish," he said sulkily. "But you should both leave before the harvesters get drunk."

"Of course. You know I always do."

They had set up trestle tables laden with dishes in the mill yard. Sir William stood at the head of the table and the miller and his wife stood at the foot. "Will you say grace, Mr. Summer?" he invited.

James had to leave Alinor without another word, take his place, put his hands together, and say a prayer.

Ned listened suspiciously for any old-fashioned doctrine, but James Summer recited the grace in simple comprehensible English, as plain and unvarnished as any army preacher.

"Amen!" said everyone, and seated themselves all in a jumble, on the benches and the stools, except for Sir William, who took the great Carver chair, brought from the house, at the head of the table. The miller sat on one side of him and James Summer on the other. Rob was seated farther down the table opposite Walter, Mrs. Miller at the foot with her daughter at her right hand. Sir William drank a glass of the Millers' ale, but did not dine. He sat for a little while and then nodded to his groom for his horse. "So, you have my good wishes, and I will leave you," he announced. He glanced at James Summer. "The boys can stay to dance if they like," he said.

"I'll bring them home in good time," James promised him.

Sir William closed one eye in a knowing wink. "Let them have a cup of ale or two and a dance with a pretty girl," he said. "Maybe a kiss and a romp behind a haystack if the fathers are looking the other way!" Some of the nearby men guffawed at the bawdy suggestion, but most were coldly silent.

James did not dare look towards Ned, who was bristling with indignation. "No, no, they will behave themselves," he said repressively.

His lordship laughed, as if to say that he did not care about good behavior at harvest home, and stepped up on the mounting block to wait for his horse. His groom brought his charger to the block and held it while his lordship heaved himself into the saddle, gathered up the reins, and nodded to the Millers and the diners in the yard. "Good Harvest!" he said, and smiled when they raised the cups and mugs and repeated the toast. Then he turned and rode away, his groom following him.

Alinor felt her brother's eyes on her. "What's the matter?" she demanded.

"It makes my blood boil, how he speaks," Ned exclaimed. "He lost the war, his king is in our keeping, and yet still he rides around as if he owns the place—because he does still own the place! How can everything change and nothing change? How can he say that Master Walter can take a girl behind the haystacks, as if the girls are at his bidding! As if they are as light as that old goat's mistress in London town?"

"Hush," Alinor said swiftly. "Don't spoil it."

"It's spoiled for me already," he said furiously.

"Why the long face, Ned?" the blacksmith from Birdham called to him. "I'd have thought you'd have been pleased with the news from the North?"

Ned's head went up like a hound hearing the hunting horn. "I've heard no news from the North," he said. "What've you heard?"

A number of men turned to the blacksmith. "And how d'you know anyway?" someone demanded suspiciously.

"Because I shod the horse of a man carrying the newspapers,

and he gave me one. He was carrying the *Moderate Intelligencer* for sale. Showed it to me and read it to me. Gave it me in payment." He brandished an ill-printed twice-folded paper.

"Read it!" someone exclaimed.

"I don't read so very well," he confessed. "But he told me it was good news for parliament."

"I'll read it," Ned said impatiently. "Give it here."

The men gathered round him as he spread it flat on the table and, ignoring the dishes as they were brought from the mill kitchen, spelled out the words.

"*From Warrington, 20th August*," he said slowly. "*A godly victory.*"

"Victory to the army?" someone asked.

"God be praised. Wait, wait, I'm reading it. Yes. It looks like a true report. Someone reporting from the battle. It says that Oliver Cromwell joined with John Lambert's Horse—they mean his cavalry—in time to catch the Scots at Preston and split them in two. It's a victory. God has saved us: the Scots are broken."

"God bless us: we're safe?"

"Does it say how?"

"Many dead?"

"Bad weather, hmm hmm, listen . . . I'll read it . . ."

*After a tedious and weary march, enduring many difficulties and pressures, through the unseasonableness of weather and extreme badness of ways: Lieutenant General Cromwell joining with the Northern Brigade, came on Thursday, very early in the morning, our army marched towards Preston, where the enemy lay all about, both Scottish and English. The enemy was sufficiently alarmed by the resolute going on of our men who thereupon drew up on a Moor two miles Eastward from Preston. Our forlorn—*

"What?" demanded one of the women reaping gang.

"Our 'forlorn hope,' our men in the front, with the hardest job to do," Ned explained, and went on reading:

*. . . with gallant courage, notwithstanding the deepness of the ways and the enclosures which were much to our disadvantage, still pressed on, charged several of the enemies' bodies, routs them and gains their ground.*

"They were fighting alone?"

"Desperately," Ned said, his brow knotted.

*Our forlorn had several encounters and behaved themselves gallantly, and about 4 of the clock in the afternoon, as soon as the narrowness of the lanes and passages would permit, our Infantry comes up to the relief of our forlorn and to the heat of the battle with an extraordinary cheerfulness.*

"At Preston?"

"So it says."

"Isn't that a long way south for the Scots to come?" someone asked nervously. "Isn't that far south? Nearly to Manchester?"

"Yes," Ned answered dourly. "It's dangerously far south. We can all thank God that He sent General Cromwell to stop them there. Before they got even closer."

"He did stop them? It says, for sure, that he did stop them?"

"I'll read you the rest . . ."

*The contention was sore and desperate, some of our men being wounded and the horses slain, for we gained hedge after hedge, which they had strongly manned and one part of the lane after the other with abundance of hazard as well as gallantry—*

Ned broke off again. "It sounds as if it was deep lanes and thick hedges, difficult for an army to advance, and the enemy had manned the hedgerows against us. But listen . . ."

*The enemy still gave ground, our horses forced them through the Town of Preston and cleared it.*

"Preston?" someone asked again.

"Preston," Ned confirmed.

"God save us!" said one of the women.

Ned read on. "It's a victory," he said. "Against great numbers. We pursued them to Warrington and put them to the sword." His face was shining. "It says here . . ."

*Our word at first was Truth, in the middle of the fight, an addition was made Truth and Faith. It was Truth we acted in and it was Faith we acted by.*

He raised his head. "I wish to God that I had been there. But just hearing about it makes me closer to the Lord . . . Truth and Faith the watchwords of the battle, General Cromwell in command!"

"Mr. Ferryman, I'll thank you to take that dirty paper off my table," Mrs. Miller interrupted him sharply. "And not to make a fool of yourself and spoil the harvest home with war news. And send that dog of yours out of my yard."

Nothing could wipe the joy from Ned's face but he took up the paper as he was ordered and told Red: "Go bye. It's great news for the parliament and the army," he muttered.

"It's more news of war, and some of us have had plenty of that," she overruled him. "Besides, we have guests. And they might not care for your great news."

Walter flushed and looked awkward, but James Summer was completely bland. "At least, there will be no fighting here," he said smoothly. "All good men must want peace. Perhaps, Mr. Ferryman, you would read the newspaper in full to those who want to hear after dinner? I should be glad of news myself."

"You don't know already, sir?" Ned demanded sharply. "When you've been away for weeks, and just came down the Chichester road yourself? Nobody mentioned it to you, on your way here, from wherever you have been? They didn't know there? Whoever they were? Wherever it was?"

"No, I hadn't heard anything," James lied. He had been told

the disastrous news of the Scots' defeat at a safe house in Southampton. His host had been white with shock: "The Scots have turned back. They won't save him. God save the king, God save the king, for now I think he is lost."

James had cursed the bad luck of a king mustering such unreliable allies as the Scots, but failing to launch his own son's fleet. Led by a competent general, this invasion could have turned the course of the war. But the best royalist generals were dead or dismissed, and the king was not on the field under his standard, but in prison, sending streams of contradictory orders.

"Actually, I came along the coast, not from London," James said smoothly, hiding his chagrin. "I knew that the army had marched north to meet the Scots; but this victory is news to me."

"And no reason that a gentleman should explain himself to the ferryman," Mrs. Miller interrupted. "Mr. Summer, Your Honor, would you be so good as to carve the meat, sir?"

An enormous ham was placed in front of James, as the principal guest, and he took up the knife and carved it while the miller broke into a great game pie, Mrs. Miller spooned out chicken broth into the wooden bowls and passed them around, and Jane, her daughter, went to the dairy to fetch more butter.

"Not too thick," Mrs. Miller instructed, keeping a jealous eye on the portions.

"It's a good-sized ham," he praised the meat.

"My own," she said. "And I'll have another four of them in the chimney this winter. I take great pride in my hams."

James fought to keep his face straight. He did not dare to glance down the table to see if Alinor had heard this boast. "You have a very handsome farm," he recovered, passing the platter with the slices cut thin.

"There are some that will taste meat this evening at my table that won't have it again till Christmas," she said complacently. "I believe in the old ways. Low wages but a well-spread board: that's how you run a good farm."

"I'm sure you're right," he agreed, knowing that the wages would be cut to the bone.

"Some of our neighbors—well, I don't know how they get by," she confided. "Scraping a living from the hedgerows, feasting like birds on berries and raw herbs." Her envious gaze drifted down the table to Alinor and her daughter.

Around them everyone was helping themselves to food, passing bread, meat, the broth, cooked vegetables, and pouring the specially sweetened harvest ale.

"Hard times," James said generally.

"Take Mrs. Reekie for one . . ."

Despite his sense that he should silence the gossiping woman, James could not help but lean forward.

"On the edge of starving last winter, I swear it. Knocking on the yard door and asking for work, anything. It was charity to buy her herbs. But now, from nowhere she has a boat, her son is in service at the Priory, and her daughter is making eyes at Richard Stoney and him a farmer's son, the only son, and certain to inherit the farm! How's that come about? For I know for a fact that her brother has nothing but the ferry and whatever was left of his army pay, and her husband has been gone for months."

"Robert is my pupil," he said cautiously. "He's a good companion to Master Walter and paid for his service. Mrs. Reekie is well liked at the Priory."

"By who?" she exclaimed as if scoring a point. "Who likes a common cottager so much that her son is suddenly Master Walter's companion? Two months ago, the lad was bird-scaring for me after school, and glad of the work. Barefoot half the time. So where did she get the money to buy the boat? When she couldn't afford shoes?"

James, knowing very well that it was a bribe for her silence about him, muttered that perhaps she had savings.

"Savings?" She snorted. "She has none! I say to my husband, please God that she does not fall on the parish, for we're a poor church, and can't support everyone, especially women who are neither widows nor wives, with a son and a daughter to keep. We can't support a woman who may have beauty but not enough wit to keep her husband at home."

"She has her craft and her boat and her herbs," he protested. "I am sure she can keep herself."

"She has no business keeping herself!" Mrs. Miller protested. "She's neither a widow nor a wife, and when she walks across the yard, the work stops dead as if the Queen of Sheba was dancing on my cobbles. If her husband is gone, she should declare herself a widow and remarry—if anyone will have her, given what they say about her. If he's alive, she should get him home. Then we'd all know where we are. She's nothing but a worry as she is. Nothing but a worry to good wives. Who would give her money for a boat? And why? It'd better not be Mr. Miller, that's all I can say!"

James finally understood the objection to Alinor. "She can't be a worry to an established housewife like yourself," he said soothingly. "There can be no comparison. Look at the dinner you put on today! Look at where you are in the world! The respect you are shown! You are blessed indeed. Mr. Miller must know that in you he has a helpmeet appointed by heaven."

She flushed a little under his attention. "It's not easy for me," she reminded him. "Everything that I have, whether it is respect, or hams in the chimney, I have worked for. Every penny of my little savings I've worked for. Years of money I have saved up. Jane's dowry is ready, for the first good husband to offer for her. You don't find me without a penny to my name! But where does Goodwife Reekie get her money from? Her own husband swore she had faerie luck; perhaps he spoke true for once. How can she buy a boat if not by some double dealing? I tell you one thing: whenever she has something to sell, my husband buys a dozen of them—as if he needs lavender bags!"

James managed a false laugh, as if he thought the Millers' grudging generosity to Alinor was funny; and unwillingly, Mrs. Miller smiled too. "Ah, well," she said, recovering her temper. "No one is more charitable than me to our poor neighbors. I pride myself on my Christian spirit."

James nodded his head approvingly. "It does you credit," he praised her. "A woman so great as you in the neighborhood must show compassion to those who have less."

"Was it Mr. Tudeley who chose her boy to be server to Master Walter?" she lowered her voice. "I thought it must be him."

"I really don't know."

"But why would a man like him, his lordship's steward, give a boy like Rob such a chance?" She slid a sideways glance at him. "I trust and pray that she has not played tricks on Mr. Tudeley. They say she can . . ."

James maintained a discouraging silence.

". . . summon," she said: an odd ambiguous word.

"Rob was chosen for his skills in the stillroom," James repeated. "And because he's a very clever boy."

She hesitated. "I know she's a good woman. I had her myself to the birth of my boy. But times are changing and if she can't get a license for midwifery what is she to do? She might be an honest woman now, but what of the future?"

James glanced up and found Alinor's dark gaze was steadily fixed on the two of them, watching them as if she could hear every spiteful word. He could not smile reassuringly while Mrs. Miller was pouring poison into his ear.

"Surely the only reason she cannot get a license from the bishop is because there are no bishops in the new parliament?"

"Aye, that's what she says," Mrs. Miller said grudgingly. "But everyone knows she's lost more than one poor woman, dead in childbed. Her own sister-in-law . . ."

"She would get her license if they were being issued?"

"But they're not! And so she has no license! And anyone can say anything against her."

"*Does* anyone actually speak against her?" James asked. He longed to have the courage to add: "other than jealous wives and women with half her looks?"

"It's only natural that they should. With men being such fools, and her in and out of the house when a wife is laid up. And her looking—" she broke off. She could not bring herself to acknowledge Alinor's luminous beauty. "Like she does," she said lamely.

"I hadn't noticed," James said firmly.

"You had not? I thought you went fishing with her?"

James was horrified that he was part of the gossip whirling around Alinor. "No, I took Master Walter in the boat with Robert," he corrected. "She rowed."

"And the rest of it," she said coarsely.

He looked at her, his eyes cold, thinking that he must silence this woman at once. She must be stopped from gossiping, or sooner or later the parliament spies would hear of his stay at the Priory, and they would suspect him, Sir William, and the whole ring of conspirators. "There is no rest of it."

"I know full well that she cooked your catch on the beach."

So he had been spied on; but he could not know how much this woman knew about him and his cause. "She did," he said levelly. "Just as Mrs. Wheatley would cook our dinner at the Priory. I don't think Master Walter and I could undertake to be our own cooks."

She recoiled from the familiar scorn of a gentleman silencing a vulgar woman. "Yes, of course, excuse me, of course, I understand."

"Sir William would not like any sort of gossip about Master Walter's companion," he said.

She nodded, but she could not resist going on: "But you understand that she's a poor woman; she's not fit company for the lord's son, nor for you. How did you even meet her?"

"We hired her when Master Walter wanted to go fishing," he said, denying her to protect his own secrets.

"Because her own husband said she had faerie luck, and that her children were born beautiful and without pain."

"He said that?"

"Born, like faeries, in silence and laughed with their first breaths. I wish the best for her, poor thing," she said. "I don't begrudge the lavender bags. It's a pity that she has fallen so very low. But you have to remember that she is a cottager, little better than a pauper, and from a long line of wisewomen."

"Midwives and herbalists," James corrected her.

"Who knows what they do? And I can't stand the daughter."

James took a slice of ham as the platter was returned to him, keeping his eyes down so that he did not look at Alinor. He felt nothing but nausea at the feast, and revulsion for the Millers.

"No, I imagine you can't."

As soon as dinner was done, all the women helped carry the dishes to the farm kitchen and scrub them clean, while the men lifted the heavy table from the trestles and cleared the yard for dancing. A couple of barrels and a door made a raised dais for the fiddler and the tabor player, and they played for the old circle dances, men on the outside, girls inside, dancing slowly one way and then another, a little pulling this way and that, as boys and girls positioned themselves so that they were opposite their desired partner. Alys took hands with Richard Stoney and they processed through the archway of upraised arms as if they were dancing on their wedding day. He was a lanky brown-haired boy with a merry smile, and he never took his eyes from the tall blond girl at his side.

Alinor watched him and glanced over to see the proud beam of his mother, and thought that next week, or the week after, she should walk over to the Stoneys' farm and see what dowry they were wanting from a daughter-in-law. Richard was their only son—they had no other children—the farm would be inherited by him. They could look for a far wealthier bride than Alys, but they would not find a prettier girl in all of Sussex. They were indulgent parents, and if she was Richard's choice, then they might agree to a down payment now on betrothal, and more over the next few years as Alinor earned it.

James was trapped with the Millers, watching Master Walter and Rob as they joined in the circle. The dancers laughed and twisted and turned as the fiddle ripped out an irresistible tune. Alinor knew that it was impossible for James to break free from his hosts and dance like his pupils. All the godly men and their wives had gone home as soon as dinner was over—a minister of the reformed Church should do nothing more than watch the first dance and then leave—but she could not stop herself thinking that perhaps he would come to her. For a moment, she fell into a dizzy imagining of him taking her hand and leading her into the circle. She thought of the swell of envy that would follow them, of the familiar flush of jealous rage on Mrs. Miller's cheek, of how the young women of the parish would whisper behind their hands that of all the girls he could have chosen, of all the young wives he could have honored, of all the plump matrons who would have swooned as they took his hand for a country dance—of everyone—he led out Alinor Reekie, the tall, willowy, excessively beautiful Alinor Reekie, who cast down her eyes like a modest woman and then looked up and smiled at him like a woman in love.

Alinor was so absorbed by this reverie of social triumph that she had a little jolt of surprise when she saw James standing before her. The coincidence of daydream and reality overwhelmed her. She was certain that he had come to ask her to dance, that despite everything he would take her hands and, deaf to her whispered refusal, his hand would come around her waist and their steps would match. She gave a little gasp of delight and stepped towards him, her hand out, her eyes bright, her lips smiling a welcome.

But he was cold. "I will take Master Walter and Robert home now," was all he said.

"You . . . don't dance?" she stammered.

"Of course not." He sounded stern. "And neither may you."

"But I never do!" she protested. "I was never going to! I just thought . . ." She stepped a little closer. "You won't stay?" she whispered. "Stay a little longer?"

He frowned at her and stepped back. "No. I certainly won't."

She was astounded. "What have you been hearing?" she demanded. "I know you were talking about me with Mrs. Miller. What has she been saying to you?"

He was wrong-footed, caught gossiping like one of the spiteful neighbors. "Nothing! She said nothing but what I knew already: that your husband has left you, that you find it hard to manage."

"If she told you that I am unchaste it is a lie!" she said fiercely. "If she told you that her husband, Mr. Miller, favors me, then it is another. I never speak to him but in the yard before everyone! He never says a word but what everyone could hear. Is that what she said that makes you so . . . so . . ."

He was mortified that she had seen him listening, and had guessed what was being said. "She could have no influence on me. I wasn't listening. I have no interest in village gossip."

"She fears I will fall on the parish, but she is afraid of everyone falling on the parish," Alinor said rapidly. "Her husband is church warden: he has to raise the funds for poor relief. It is her terror that they will have to provide for the poor wretches, the poor women—"

"Calm yourself. It doesn't matter what she says—"

"It does matter! It does! It matters to me! She doesn't care for anyone's reputation but her own but if she told you she fears a pauper bastard from me then she is slandering me!" The tears started in her eyes, and she gave a little choked sob. "I have known her since I was a girl and she's never had a kind word for me—"

"Hush!" he begged her. "Everyone is looking!"

He wanted to catch her in his arms and say there was no shame that could touch her. But far more he wanted to get away from her before she openly cried out. He wanted to be far away from this woman, engaged in some pointless fishwives' squabble with her neighbor, weeping in public at a harvest home. A poor woman, with dirty fingernails, in a mud-stained gown, his friend's meanest tenant, perhaps the chosen bawd of the manor's steward, surrounded by her equally poor neighbors, who were all staring at him. Only the young people ignored them, whirling in a circle dance, Walter Peachey hopping about with somebody's unsuitable daughter, as if there were no degree and order in the world anymore, as if the defeat at Preston had killed the proper distance between masters and men, between gentlemen and wretches, as well as the last hope of the royalists.

It was unbearable: “For Christ’s sake, be quiet!”

She froze at his oath, and shot him a horrified glance from under her drenched eyelashes.

“I cannot be watched,” he whispered urgently. “You know I must not be observed. I have to serve my cause. I cannot have people noticing me. I am going now. I cannot be seen with you while you are in this state. Everyone is looking at us. I cannot have you draw attention to me.”

She changed in a moment, her beauty suddenly pale and contemptuous, her tears frozen. “You go,” she advised him. “I don’t care. Go at once. I don’t care for your cause. I cared for you and I was a fool. But I won’t be a fool again.”

Without another word, with the disdain of an offended queen, she turned on her heel and walked away from him, walked to her brother, and left James all on his own, hopelessly exposed to the inquisitive stares of the mill yard, all of them wondering how Alinor Reekie—the poorest woman at the harvest home—dared to snub him: the greatest guest.

He could not sleep. He turned around and around on the smooth linen sheets of his luxurious bed in the Priory, getting more and more restless until he welcomed the fever in his pulse and the heat under his skin, and he went down to the private chapel barefoot, and laid himself down on the cold stone before the bare altar in the position of penitence: feet together stretched out, facedown, arms spread, like a prone crucifixion. He felt his desire for her like a pain in his belly. He pressed his hands to the cold stone floor and imagined the curve of her cheek against his palm. He pressed his cock, which was hard as iron, into the icy limestone and felt the relief as it shriveled against the cold. He was forbidden to think of her as a lover by his oath to his God, to his king, to his conspiracy, to his class, and to his own honor. But as the cold seeped into his hot skin he knew that he was faithless to his God, to his king, to his conspiracy, to his class, and to his honor. All he could think of was the brilliance of her eyes and the flush of her cheek when she swore that she had cared for him once, but she would not care for him again.

Even in his heat and his distress he felt a little gleam of triumph that she had told him that she cared for him. He knew it—he had known it when she came so willingly into his arms off the rickety pier—but he was a scholar and he loved words; he loved that she had said: "I cared for you."

That was where he must leave it, he thought. He ought to feel relieved that she had confessed her love and said it was gone. He should be glad that she had dismissed him, even though her pride was impossibly misplaced—she had forgotten the social order that placed her far below him. A woman like Alinor Reekie could not complain of the behavior of a gentleman like him. But better for him, in these dangerous times, that she turned from him, than if she betrayed them both with a foolishly adoring gaze. Better that he never saw her. She might come to prayers at the Priory and present herself at the communion table, but he need do nothing but serve the communion as the minister in the private chapel. If he did not seek her out, they would never meet again.

Of course, he must see her at St. Wilfrid's Church the very next morning, as it was Sunday, but he would be far at the front, first in the church behind Sir William, and she would be where she belonged—far behind, in the gallery with the other poor women, the faint scent of sweat and fish rising from their damp shawls. She would never dare to approach him; he would not look for her. He would never again speak to her privately and, in time, this ache of longing would pass. Men on both sides in this war had lost their limbs, were crippled for life having fought for their beliefs. He thought that he—whose war had been so privileged, so hidden—had finally taken a wound as grave as theirs.

He would recover. His war was elsewhere: his duty was across the Solent with the king in Carisbrooke Castle. He should never have thought of her. He had been mad to look at her just because she was beautiful, to feel tender towards her because she risked her own safety to rescue him. He would confess the sin of desiring her, and be forgiven for having gone so close to temptation. He must take Mrs. Miller's spiteful slander as a timely warning and pray that the madness was over, and this greensickness of love would pass quickly too.

"You're so white—are you sick?" Alys asked her mother.

"Something I ate at the Millers'," Alinor replied.

"Envy? She serves a lot of that," Alys suggested. "Is that why you left early?"

Alinor nodded. "I'm fine now."

"But wasn't it the most wonderful harvest home ever? Not even she could spoil it. Richard said . . ."

"Richard said?"

Alys flushed. "He said I am as beautiful as a real queen."

"Nothing but truth! You looked beautiful, and you danced beautifully."

Alys beamed. "And it's nice to see Rob."

"Yes."

"They were all mad for his tutor, Mr. Summer, weren't they? Mary couldn't eat her dinner for making eyes at him. Jane Miller couldn't speak a word."

Alinor forced a smile. "He's a handsome gentleman. And a novelty. Did you dance with Richard Stoney again, after I left?"

Alys ducked her head down. "I didn't dance with anyone else. I just couldn't. And he wouldn't ask anyone else. I love him, Ma, I really do."

Alinor took a little breath. "My little girl in love?"

"I'll always be your girl, but I do love him. And he loves me."

"He's said so?"

The girl flushed a dark rose. "Oh, Ma, he's spoken to his parents. Weeks ago, he spoke to them. He wants to marry me! He asked me last night, Ma. He's given me his promise."

"He should've spoken to me before he said anything to you. You're not yet fourteen. I was thinking of meeting his parents and asking for a long betrothal and—"

"He's been courting me for weeks," the girl said proudly. "That's long enough for me to be sure. And I liked him from the first. But anyway, they want a girl who'd bring them some land, who has furniture, her own pewter plates, who's got an inheritance. Things I'll never have."

"We can save up," Alinor said bravely.

They both looked around the little cottage, the sparse worn goods, the wooden trenchers on the plain cupboard, the table and stools that Alinor had inherited from her mother, the hanging bunches of drying herbs, the treasure box containing the tenancy paper, and the red leather purse, filled with nothing but old tokens.

"We have no savings but dried leaves and faerie gold," Alys pointed out.

"I could talk to them," Alinor said.

"My father should go," Alys said resentfully. "It shouldn't be you, on your own."

"I know," Alinor said. "We're unlucky in that."

The two women put on their capes and their wooden pattens and started the walk to church. Behind them on the bank path came Alinor's brother, Ned, his dog at his heels, and behind him a few farmers with their families from farther inland. The women waited for Ned to catch up, and walked three abreast with him, dropping into single file when the thorns of the path closed in.

"You'll be happy with the news from Preston, Ned," Alinor remarked. "It sounds like a great victory."

"Praise God," he said. "For if the Scots had got past Cromwell I don't know where they would've stopped. We could have lost all of England to them, and they would have put the king on the throne again. But, God be praised, we won, and they are driven back and the king will know that he has no friends left in the world."

"A friendless king," Alinor said wonderingly, as if she were sorry for him.

"He's never had any friends," he said harshly. "Only courtiers and paid favorites. Some of the most wicked and vicious men in England in his service."

Together they paused and looked towards the sea, where the waves were breaking white at the mouth of the harbor.

"Just over there," Ned said wonderingly. "Think of him, so close, just a few hours of sailing time, on the Isle of Wight. And he must know by now that no one's coming for him. His son's fleet can't land, the Scots are running back to Edinburgh, his wife can't raise the French for him, the Irish haven't landed. He's going to have to beg our pardon and rule with our permission."

"What if he were to be rescued?" Alinor asked.

"There's nobody who can rescue him and get him to his son's ships," her brother ruled. "There's not one of them with the courage or the wit to break him out."

"It's hopeless for him?" Alinor said, thinking of James Summer, the friend of a friendless king.

"Forlorn," Ned replied, condemning the king, ignorant of his sister's thoughts. "He's a real forlorn hope."

They climbed over the stile in the church wall and walked in silence along the path past the graves of their parents, their grandparents, and generations of Ferryman. The porch, where Alinor had waited for the ghost of her husband, was filled with bright sheaves of corn, though some of the godly men of the church complained that this was paganism. The old black door of the church stood wide open. Red, Ned's dog, lay down where he always lay, outside the porch, and lolled out his pink tongue. The villagers went without speaking to their usual places: Ned to stand at the back on the left with the men, behind the prosperous families, Alinor and Alys up the stairs to the gallery with the other poor women. Nobody bowed to the altar, nobody ever crossed themselves anymore.

Sir William and his household entered the church, and all the men doffed their hats and all the women curtseyed, except the very godly one or two who would not bow to a temporal lord. Alinor looked for her son, saw his quick smile, ignored his tutor, whose brown gaze was steadfastly directed downwards on his well-shined boots. The Peacheys entered their pew and Mr. Miller, the church warden, closed the door on them with exaggerated respect. The St. Wilfrid's minister stepped behind the plain communion table and started the new authorized service with a long extempore prayer, thanking God for giving His forces the victory against the misguided Scots in Lancashire.

The service was long, the sermon unending. Alinor and Alys, on the hard benches of the gallery at the back of the church, kept their heads down and hid all signs of impatience. From the shelter of the wings of her cap, Alinor glanced down only once from her seat in the gallery to the Peachey pew and saw James's head bowed low, his hands clasped before him. He was either in deep prayer, or in the posture of a man enacting godly piety while his head was filled with heretical and dangerous thoughts. She did not even wonder which was the case. She felt that he had gone far from her, as if he had already set sail to an unknown destination, to take part in a secret plot. He had told her—and she had believed him—that his cause was more important than their newly discovered desire. Alinor, abandoned by her husband, was familiar with rejection, accustomed to coming in second place, third place, last place. She bowed her head and prayed for the pain to pass.

At the end of the sermon, while the more devout of the congregation exclaimed "Praise Be!" and "Thanks be to God!," the minister stepped forward towards the Peachey pew, waited for Sir William to rise to his feet, and from that moral high ground, the two of them turned to scold the congregation, one of them representing the temporal powers, the other, spiritual authority.

"And on this Sabbath day, which the Lord has demanded that we keep holy, we have to call a sister to the altar and remonstrate with her," the minister said. "It is our duty, and the order of the church court."

Alys turned one swift sideways glance on her mother. Alinor showed her ignorance with widened eyes. Both of them stiffened and waited for what was coming next, wondering who would be named as guilty.

"A woman who has been the complaint of her neighbors, whose own husband has said that he cannot rule her," the minister intoned. "Her trade has been uproar and some allege that she has been unchaste. Who gave evidence against her at the church court?"

"I did." Mrs. Miller stood up from the middle of the church, where the prosperous tenants had their seats, her daughter and little boy either side of her.

"Course she did," Alys breathed to her mother. "She's got a bad word for everybody."

"Mrs. Miller, of the tide mill," she announced unnecessarily to the neighbors who had known her from childhood.

"And what did you allege before this court?" the minister asked her. "Briefly," he reminded her. Everyone knew that Mrs. Miller, once started, was hard to halt.

"I said that I had seen her at gleaning go behind a hedge with a man of this parish and come out with her dress disordered and her hair down."

There was a mutter of speculation around the church as to who might be the "man of this parish," but clearly his identity was going to be kept secret. The sinful woman would be denounced, her partner would maintain his reputation. Besides, it was hardly a sin for a man; it was his nature.

"And before that," Mrs. Miller continued, "she traduced her

husband, calling him an old fool, and on market day at Sealsea market she took his purse from him and gave him a buffet and told him that she would learn him."

"Did anyone else speak against her in court?" Sir William asked.

"I did." One of the Sealsea Island farmers' wives stood up. "She came to my house on my night for spinning with my friends, and she called me a doting fool for letting my husband keep my money from my spinning. She slapped my face and she pulled off my cap when I said that her child was not of her husband's begetting, which everybody knows."

"I spoke against her, sir." The Peachey cook, Mrs. Wheatley, rose to her feet from behind the Peachey seats. "She came to the Priory door and she was four eggs short of her tithe, and she said if there was no king, and no bishop, then there was no lord either, and she need pay no tithes and you could do without your eggs."

"And then there was the ride," a voice called out from the back of the church, from where the poor tenants stood. "Don't forget that!"

"There was a skimmington ride," Mrs. Miller explained to Sir William. "The boys rode a donkey backwards, past her house, with a lad wearing a petticoat over his head, to show that she was unchaste and a disgrace to our village."

Sir William looked so grave that anyone could have believed that he did not keep an expensive mistress in rooms near the Haymarket in London. "Very bad," he said.

"And so the church court sentenced her to stand before this congregation in her shift holding a lighted taper to show her repentance for the rest of this day till sunset," the minister said rapidly, bringing the summary of the trial to an end and moving to sentence.

The church wardens, Mr. Miller among them, opened the door of the church and Mrs. Whiting came in from the porch, in her best linen shift, holding a lit candle in her hand, barefoot and with her hair down to show her penitence. She was a woman in the middle of her life, broad at the hips and the belly and her long hair was streaked with gray. She was ashen-faced with misery.

"Ah, God keep her," Alinor whispered, high above her in the gallery. "To shame her so!"

"Isabel Whiting, you are brought before your neighbors and this congregation to expunge your disgrace. Do you repent?"

"I do," she said, her voice very low.

"Do you swear to be neither lustful nor violent in future?"

"I do."

"And obey God, and your husband, who was set by God Himself above you to be your master and guide?"

Almost, they heard her sigh at the weary drudgery that he would exact. "I do."

"Then you must stand here, inside the church till sunset, when the church wardens will come to release you. Stand barefoot and shamed, as your candle burns down, while anyone may come to reproach you, but you may not reply or speak any word. Look into your heart, sister, and do not offend God or your neighbors again."

The minister turned to the congregation, spread his arms, and gabbled the bidding prayer. The woman stood before him, facing the neighbors who had denounced her, her face set and bitter, the light trembling in her hand, while somewhere in the church her husband, who had beaten her, and the man who had taken her behind the hedge shuffled their feet and waited for when they might leave.

After church Sir William paused in the churchyard as his tenants came up and bowed or curtseyed. Alinor and Alys followed Ned to pay their respects and Sir William waved Rob to step aside to kneel for his mother's blessing and rise up for her kiss on his forehead. Alinor was pale and distracted, thinking of the woman, named as an adulteress left to do penance barefoot in the church behind them, wearing only her shift, holding her candle in a shaking hand. Alinor was well aware of the power of the Millers and the community when they moved as one, and she knew that they moved as the mood took them, against whoever they despised, and a woman could not speak for herself.

"We're going to go sailing!" Rob announced to his mother. "Across the sea."

She could not stop herself looking towards James, but she turned her eyes quickly on the steward, Mr. Tudeley.

"Sailing?"

"Mr. Summer is taking the boys for a visit to the island next week," he announced. "Sailing to the Isle of Wight."

"Oh." Alinor turned back to her son, who was bobbing with excitement.

"We're going first to Newport," Rob exulted. "We'll stay the night. Maybe two nights."

"But why?" Alinor asked. "What for?"

"Geography," Rob said grandly. "And mapmaking. Mr. Summer says we might even see the king! Wouldn't that be a sight to see? Sir William knows him, but Walter has never been presented. We can't speak to him, of course. But we might see him in the streets. Mr. Summer says that he walks out."

"I thought he was at the castle at Carisbrooke," Alinor remarked, fixing her gaze on her son's bright face and looking neither at her brother nor at James Summer, knowing that both of them were listening intently. "I thought he was imprisoned."

"His Majesty is being released to a private house at Newport, to meet the gentlemen from parliament and reach agreement with them," Mr. Tudeley told her.

"And we'll probably see him!" Rob added.

"I'd rather you didn't go," Alinor said urgently, putting her arm around Rob's shoulders and turning him away from the circle around Sir William. "You know, your uncle Ned won't like it at all!"

"I have to go with Walter," Rob pointed out. "I'm his companion. I have to accompany him!"

"Yes, but—"

"And it's not as if the king's still at war. He's in Newport to meet with the men from parliament. It's all at peace now. They're meeting him at Newport to make peace and he'll be released. I'd like to see him, now it's all over. Think of me, seeing the King of England!"

"I'd still rather you didn't," Alinor repeated.

Rob was suddenly attentive. He looked up at her pale face. "Why? What's the matter? Is it the sight, Mam?" he asked quietly.

She shook her head. "No, nothing like that. It's just that . . ."

"What?"

"Oh, poor Mrs. Whiting, and having to stand before the church . . ."

"That's got nothing to do with us," he rightly said.

"I know her, and yet I said nothing in her defense," she said.

"There was nothing to say." Alys came up quietly to the two of them. "Everyone would have turned on you, and on the three of us, if you'd spoken up for her. And besides, she did go behind the hedge. I saw her."

"Yes, but—"

"How's this got anything to do with me going to the Isle of Wight?" Rob demanded.

"It hasn't!" Alinor owned. "You know how I feel, Rob . . . it's just—"

"Is it the sea?" he guessed. "The deep water?"

"The sea," she said, grasping at the word as if her fear of the ocean could explain the sense of dread that she felt at her son going to Newport to see the defeated king. Going to Newport in the company of his tutor—the king's spy.

## TIDELANDS, SEPTEMBER 1648

James Summer, Rob, and Walter took ship from the mill quay in a coastal trader bound for the Isle of Wight, Southampton, and westerly. Richard Stoney, Alys, and a couple of the mill girls watched them go. Rob waved as extravagantly as if he were leaving for the Americas and might never return as the two-masted ketch went slowly down the deep channel, with the crew on either side watching for sandbars and shouting the depth.

James went to starboard to look for the little cottage perched on the harbor bank, as ramshackle as if it had been washed there by a high tide. The door was standing open and he wondered if Alinor was watching the ship from the dark interior. He guessed that she was unhappy at Rob sailing to the island, but she had not asked him not to take the boy. She had not spoken to him at all. Not even after church when she made her curtsey to Sir William and rose up to find James's brown eyes on her face. She had behaved—just as he had prayed that she would—with icy discretion. She had withdrawn from him as if she had never known him, as if she had never held him, as if she had never opened her lips to his demanding mouth. He had prayed to be released, and she had let him go at once, as if she had never whispered that she wanted to be with him, that she wanted to be with him alone. Even as she curtseyed to him, she looked beyond and away from him. He would have thought that he was nothing to her, that he had never been anything to her. He would have thought that he was unseen.

And of course, as soon as she withdrew from him, he wanted to catch her hand, to say her name, to make that gray gaze turn back to him. As the poorest tenant on the estate, a woman that he had stooped to notice, she should have been alert for the least sign of his forgiveness. But it was as if he were invisible to her. He had to stand at Sir William's shoulder and let this woman, this nobody, walk away from him as if he were nothing.

Now, as the sails of the ship caught the wind and the craft moved a little forward, he looked for the poor cottage that was her home, which she had opened to him as a refuge when he had nowhere else to go. He could see a trail of smoke from the chimney, he saw that the door stood open, he could even see a movement in the dark interior: the glimpse of her white cap. Then, as he watched, she came out of the doorway and stood on the cracked stone of her front step so that he could see her. She raised her hand, her scarred worn hand, to shade her eyes. He could hardly believe it: but she was looking for him. She saw him; she saw the ship that was taking her beloved son into danger, using him as a shield against inquiry, as an alibi in the incredible treason that he was about to commit. He thought she must be ill-wishing him, as he did the one thing that she must dread—taking Rob into deep waters. But then he saw her raise her hand to his ship, in a blessing, as any sailor's wife would wave to a sail and whisper, "Godspeed! Come safe home!" He saw her stand, watching him. It was unmistakable. She loved him, she had a love deeper and wider than his, for she forgave him for his stupidity and his unkindness, and she was wishing him Godspeed on a journey, even though he was serving the king and taking her boy across the deeps.

He leapt up to balance on the rail of the boat, he gripped the rigging, he leaned outwards over the dark water rushing under the prow. He could hear the ominous hushing of the receding tide as it sucked them towards the harbor mouth, but he wanted her to see him. He stretched out his arm to wave to her. He wanted her to know that as he left Foulmire, the one thought in his mind was not his cause, which he had put before her, nor his king, who should come before everything, but her: Alinor.

## NEWPORT, ISLE OF WIGHT, SEPTEMBER 1648

The town of Newport was as busy as a fair day; nothing like this had ever happened on the island before. The arrival of the king to the house of the wealthy townsman Mr. Hopkins gave the provincial street the status of Whitehall Palace. When the parliamentary negotiators arrived, Newport would be at the plumb center of the affairs of the kingdom—"of the world"—according to the dizzied Newport royalists. All the gentry flocked in from the outlying towns and villages to stay with friends and cousins, to dawdle through the narrow streets in the hope of seeing the king. They attended St. Thomas's Church; they scrambled for the front pews to kneel behind His Majesty at prayer; they sent their servants round to the Hopkinses' kitchen door to learn what was cooking for the royal dinner. Noblemen, with their ladies, sailed from the mainland on their own ships, or chartered passages to pay their respects to the king who, though defeated, could never be vanquished. All the royalists who had attended the king at London, at Oxford, in victory and facing defeat, now reappeared, learning that he was set free again. Whatever anyone might say, whatever he himself might do, the king was the king, and it was apparent to everyone that sooner or later he would return to London and to his throne.

And would he not be certain to remember the gentlemen and ladies who had called upon him in his time of troubles? Would he not reward those who had invited him to visit, stretching his parole in lengthy jaunts around the island, sent him game from their estates, fruit from their forcing houses? Would he not repay those favored few who had ridden with him in the enormous lumbering royal coach which had been shipped with such trouble, to block the narrow lanes of the island? When he was Charles the king again, would he not be obliged to remember those who had treated him with the most obsequious respect when he had been Charles the prisoner?

Mr. Hopkins's house was as easy to enter as the royal court had been in the grand old days in London, when any wealthy man might walk in to gaze on his monarch and the royal family. The king believed that his dinner table should be on view in his dining hall, as an altar should be on view in church. There was divinity in both. Here in Newport, although there was a brace of guards on each door, they did not challenge anyone: if a man was richly dressed, he could enter. The king was free to come and go as he wished, bound only by his given word not to leave the island. The street outside was crowded all the day with gorgeously dressed well-wishers, parading up and down the freshly swept cobbles, remarking loudly on the simplicity of the town and the poverty of the buildings, besieged by common people wanting a glimpse of a man who claimed to be semidivine, constantly circled by beggars and the sick. King Charles was famous for the healing powers of his long white fingers. A sick man or woman could kneel before him and be restored with one light touch of the hand and a whispered blessing. No one was refused access to the king's powers. Already a young woman was claiming that he had cured her blindness with his divine grace. Everyone knew that the king was not a mortal man. He had the holy oil on his sacred breast, he was the descendant of ordained kings, he was only one step down from the angels.

James took care to keep the boys away from the sickly paupers, and paid a guard a small coin to allow them to stand below the window where, they were assured, the king was studying papers sent from parliament. Everyone said that the parliamentary commissioners would arrive within the week and they would work through the many clauses of an agreement with the king so that he might return to his throne and rule with the consent of the houses of parliament. Now the Scots were defeated, the king and parliament would have to agree: he had lost his last gamble. He would always be king, but no longer could he impose his will on the people. Finally, he would have to come to an accord. Peace—after two civil wars—would come to the country and the court.

The boys waited, craning their necks to look up at the overhanging window; the church bells of Newport started to chime all around the town for six o'clock. There was an excited murmur among the crowd, one side of the leaded window swung open, and the graying head of the King of England poked out. Charles looked down at the people waiting below, he smiled wearily, and raised one heavily ringed hand.

"Is that him?" Rob asked, the nephew of an army man, born and bred a roundhead, unable to keep the disappointment from his voice.

"It is," James confirmed, pulling his hat from his head and looking upwards, hoping to feel a flush of loyalty, of passionate devotion, but experiencing nothing but anxiety.

"No crown?"

"Only when he's on the throne, I think."

"Then how can you be sure it's him?" Rob persisted. "Without a crown? Could be anybody."

James did not say that at his seminary the novices had been shown portrait after portrait of the dark tragic face of the king to assist in their prayers for his safety. He did not say that he had dreamed of the day when the complicated conspiracy would finally fall into place with loyalists on the island, the Prince of Wales's fleet waiting offshore, and a loyal ship's captain engaged to sail at midnight with a mystery passenger. "I suppose

I just know," was all he said. "Nobody else would wave from his window."

"Hurrah!" Walter suddenly jumped up and down and waved. "Hurrah!"

The heavy-lidded eyes turned towards the sudden cheer and the king raised his hand again to acknowledge the boy's fervent loyalty. Then he withdrew, the window was slammed shut, and the shutters closed.

"That's it?" Rob asked.

"Same every day," a woman beside them answered him. "God bless him. And I come every day to see his sainted face."

"We'll go to dinner," James said, before the three of them attracted any attention. "Come on."

They went back to the Old Bull on the Street, where James had reserved private rooms, and James ordered a hearty dinner for the two boys, allowing them each a glass of wine. "I'm going out while you eat," he said. "I want to take a look around and find a ship to take us home tomorrow or the day after."

"Can't we come?" Walter asked. "I want to look around too."

"I'll come back for you," James promised. "We can walk through the market and along the riverside before we go to bed." He pulled his hat low over his face and went out.

The streets were still busy as he went down the narrow lanes to the harbor and looked at the boats bobbing at the quayside. The dull clatter of the cleats against the wooden masts reminded him of all the other quaysides, of the many ships in his young life of constant traveling. Every port had the same rattle of rigging, just as every town had an hourly carillon of church bells. He thought that one day he might have lived so long at peace that he would be able to hear it without knowing that it called him to secret dangerous work. He hoped that one day he might hear it without dread.

"Is there a ship, the *Marie*, in port?" he asked a man, who was pushing past him with a coil of rope under his arm.

"Come and gone," the man said shortly. "Were you meeting her?"

"No," James said, lying instantly. "I thought she was always here."

"Because if you had been meeting her, I would have told you that the master told everyone that he would not meet his good friend after all, and he set sail this morning."

"Oh," James said. A small coin found its way from his pocket to the waiting hand. The man hefted his rope and started to go on.

"Any idea how I can hire another ship?"

"Ask 'em," he said unhelpfully, and pushed past.

James paused for a moment, almost winded by the disastrous news. Everything had depended on the ship sailing at midnight, as they had agreed, but now the ship had failed him. His only comfort was that the openness of the failure probably showed that they were not detected. The master had cold feet at the thought of rescuing the King of England, and had set sail, but he had not been arrested. The plot could still go on with a new ship. James would have to find a master so loyal to the king that he would take the risk, or so easily bought that he would do it for money. James looked up and down the quayside and thought that there was no way of judging, no way even to ask the question without running into terrible danger.

He did not dare to draw attention to himself, going up and down the quayside before dinner. He thought he had better come back later, stroll around the quayside taverns, find a way to have a more discreet conversation. He closed his eyes for a moment so that he would not see the forest of masts. His life had been on a knife-edge for so long that another venture did not excite him. He just felt bone-weary. More than anything he wanted this rescue to be successfully done, and all over. He did not even anticipate a sense of triumph tomorrow. He had set his heart on freeing the king, he had set his name to contracts and letters, and he had set himself to the task. He was faithful; and he thought that God would guide him, so he turned from the harbor to make his way back to Mr. Hopkins's house. The door, set into the rear garden wall, was unlocked and unguarded, and James slipped into the darkened garden and went quietly towards the kitchen door, which stood open for the cool evening air.

It was chaos inside. The king was a picky eater, but his importance had to be advertised by serving twenty different dishes at every meal. It was a strain on the provincial cooks, who were running out of recipes and ingredients. There were a few guards that James could see through the open door to the dining hall, but their task was to follow the king when he walked abroad, not to prevent anyone from coming into the house. The king's own servants were responsible for keeping his rooms free of unwanted strangers and admitting noble guests, but they were newly appointed and did not know their way around the rambling house, nor friend from stranger. The king had added half a dozen courtiers to his entourage since being released from the castle, and they too had their servants and hangers-on who came and went without challenge. There were too many strangers for anyone to notice another.

James waited for a few moments in the garden, watching the disorderly service, and how the servers ran to and fro from the kitchen, through the dining hall, and up the stairs to the king's rooms. Then he took off his hat, straightened his jacket, and boldly went through the back door as if he belonged there. It was stifling: there was a roast turning on the spit over the fire, saucepans bubbling on little braziers of red-hot charcoal, vegetables stewing by the fireside, and bread being shoveled from the ovens. The servers were rushing in and out, demanding dishes for their own tables, sometimes snatching a dish intended for Mr. Hopkins's table. Mr. Hopkins's cook was among it all, trying to keep order, her apron stained, her face sweaty with anxiety and heat.

"The king's carver," James said to her, respectfully. "Can I assist you, Cook?"

She turned in relief. "Lord, I don't even know what he's had yet. Have you not taken the joint up to him?"

"I am here for it now," James said smoothly.

"Take it! Take it!" she exclaimed, gesturing to a leg of lamb that stood on the table being dressed clumsily by a kitchen server with bunches of watercress.

"This is for the lords!" the server exclaimed.

"Take it!" She thrust it at James. "And tell me if anything is missing from his table."

James bowed and went through the door, past the guard at the foot of the stairs, and up to the door of the king's rooms. The porters at the royal door hesitated, but James held the dish high and said, "Quick! Before it gets cold!" and walked unhesitatingly towards the closed door, so the porters threw it open for him.

They closed it behind him, and James, never hesitating for a moment, walked into the king's dining room and put the dish on the table before him.

The servant behind his chair, the page holding his gloves, the server with the wine, his fellow with the water did not look twice at James as he took up the long sharp knife and carved paper-thin slices of lamb and fanned them out on the Hopkinses' best silver plate. He bowed and put the plate before the king, leaning over his shoulder. With his face so close to his ear that he could feel the tickle of gray ringlets and smell the French pomade, he whispered: "Midnight, tonight. Open your door."

The king did not turn his head and gave no sign of hearing.

"Clarion." James said the password that he had been given from France, the password that said that the plot came from the queen, Henrietta Maria herself.

The king lowered his head as if he was saying grace, and his hand, hidden beneath the table, made a small gesture of assent. James walked backwards to the door, bowed his head to his knees, and withdrew.

Back at the Old Bull inn, the boys were eating sugared plums and cracking nuts, and jumped up as he came in.

"Is there a fair?" Rob asked. "It's so noisy."

"There's a market and some strolling players," James said. "We can go and see what's going on." He found that he was grinning broadly, almost laughing in his relief that the first stage, getting access to the king, had been so easy. He had been planning this and working with great men to consider every step, yet in the end he had simply walked towards a door and the porter had opened it for him. He almost did not care that he had no ship. If the luck was running his way, it would run all the way to the high seas and the rendezvous with the prince's fleet.

"Does the king come out again tonight?" Walter asked.

"No, he only waves from his window before his dinner and then they close the shutters for the night. But we might see him tomorrow. I think he walks out in the morning," James said, knowing that the king would be on the prince's ship at dawn. "He goes to church."

"Is he free to go anywhere?" Walter asked.

"When parliament decided to make an agreement with him, they had to release him so that he could sign the documents as a free man. Now he can go anywhere that he likes on the island; but he has given his word not to leave."

"Is there a dancing bear?" Rob demanded. "I've never seen a bear."

"I shouldn't think so," James replied. "This is a godly town, or at least it used to be. But we can stroll round the market, and you can buy a fairing for your mother. Perhaps some ribbons for her hair." He found that his throat was suddenly dry at the thought of her fair hair.

"No, she always wears a cap," Rob replied. "But if there are some little tokens for sale, I'd get them. She likes old coins, little tokens. Come on."

The two boys walked through the market, looking at the stalls and laughing at the tricks of a small dog who was trained to jump through a hoop and would stand on his hind legs at the command of "Ironsides!" The stalls went down the narrow streets towards the harbor where the River Medina wound through the town, and the boats bobbed at the quayside. James was looking out for ships that had newly arrived, or might be ready to set sail, when Rob suddenly exclaimed: "Da! My da!"

James wheeled round and saw a brown-faced, dark-haired man jerk up his head at a familiar voice. He caught a glimpse of the strange face, looking astounded. Then the man turned and plunged away into the crowd.

"That was my da! That was my da!" Rob shouted. "Da! It's me! Rob! Wait for me!" He took to his heels, darting forward, worming his way through the crowds, and though the man's dark head bobbed ahead of him, Rob was quicker. When James and Walter caught up with him, he had laid hold of the man and pitched himself into his arms. "It's me!" he announced, joyously certain of his welcome. "It's me! It's me, Da! Rob."

The man's guilty eyes met James's gaze over his son's head. "Rob," he said, patting the boy's back. "Oh, Rob."

Rob was fawning like a puppy. "Where've you been?" he said. "We didn't know! We've been waiting and waiting! We thought you were drowned!"

James saw that the stranger was looking at him with a sort of desperation, as one man to another, in this terrible failure of fatherhood.

"They thought you had been pressed into the navy," James prompted.

"Ah! I was. That I was!" the man said, suddenly glib. He hugged his son and then stepped back to see his face. "I didn't recognize you, you've grown so tall. And dressed so fine! I can see you've done well enough without me!"

"We haven't! Where've you been?" Rob insisted.

"It's a long story," the man said. "And I'll tell you all of it some day."

"Why didn't you come home?"

"Why didn't I come home? Why, I couldn't come home, that's why!"

"But why not?"

"Because I was pressed, Son. Snatched up by the navy press gang off my boat and taken to serve in the navy for the parliament. Served as a common seaman and then rose through the ranks since I knew the seas around Sealsea Island and all the way to the Downs."

"But why didn't you send a message to Ma?"

"Bless you, they don't let you go ashore! They don't give you high days and holy days off! I was on my ship and spoke to no one but the other poor curs who were pressed alongside me."

James watched Alinor's son, raised to love and trust, struggle to believe his father. "You couldn't even get a message to us? Because we waited and waited for you to come, and Ma still doesn't know if you're alive or dead. I'll have to tell her when I get home. She'll hardly believe me! She's been waiting. We've all been waiting for you to come home!"

"Oh, she knows." He nodded rapidly. "It's better for her to act as if she doesn't. But you know your ma, Son. A woman like that—she knows in her bones. She knows in her waters. She doesn't need a message to tell her what's what. The wind and the waves tell her. The moon whispers to her. The birds in her hedge are her familiars. God knows what she knows and what she doesn't know, but you needn't worry about her, ever."

An icy sweat of sheer hatred washed over James as he saw the boy struggling to comprehend this, the puzzled frown on his young face, as the faithless father told the boy that his mother was faithless too.

"I don't think she does know," Rob said tentatively. "She would've told us when we asked where you were."

"Well, you're doing well enough for yourself anyway," his father said cheerfully. "Fine clothes and fine friends." He turned to James. "I'm Zachary Reekie," he said. "Captain of the coastal trader *Jessie*."

"I'm James Summer," James said, not offering his hand. "Tutor to Master Walter Peachey here, and to your son, who is his lordship's server of the body and companion."

"In the Peachey household?" Zachary demanded of his son. "Didn't I say there was no need to worry about your mother? What did she have to do to get you in there? Imagine I know! Is Mr. Tudeley still the steward there?"

Rob flushed scarlet. "My mother keeps the stillroom for the Priory," he stumbled.

"It was I who asked for Rob to be Master Walter's companion," James said, making sure that his cold rage did not creep into his smooth tone. "Mrs. Reekie was wise to accept the place for him. He is in service and paid by the quarter, and when Master Walter goes to university I hope to get Rob apprenticed to a physician. He is skilled with herbs and medicines and he's studying Latin with me."

"Oh, aye, that's what we say, is it?" Zachary said unpleasantly. "I'm glad it has turned out so well for us all." He turned as if he thought they might let him go, but at once Rob laid hold of his arm.

"But you will come home now, Da? Now that you're not in the navy anymore?"

"I can't immediate," he said, looking again to James for help. "I got out of the navy when they went over to the prince. When the ships went to Prince Charles, I got away. I couldn't have looked your uncle Ned in the eye if I had served the king! Now could I? But I had to indenture myself to the ship *Jessie* and so I'm bound to serve in her for another year. She's a coastal trader, all around England and all around France. I'm never here. Never stop sailing. But as soon as I've served my time I'll come back to you, for sure."

"But what shall I tell Ma?" Rob pressed him.

"Tell her that! Ask this tutor of yours to explain. He understands, don't you, sir?"

"Very well," James said levelly.

Rob looked at him with hope. "You do?"

"I understand that your father was bound to the navy and is now bound to a trading vessel. That's quite usual. He'll be able to come home when his term is over, but we can tell your mother that he is alive and well, and will return."

"If it suits her," Zachary said. He turned to James and, unseen by his son, closed his eye on a wink.

James swallowed distaste. "But you must have a drink with us and talk with your son now we have so luckily found you," he said heartily. "It's such a chance! We only came to Newport to see the sights of the island and catch a glimpse of the king, and we have found you."

Walter did not look as if it were much of a treat for him, but Zachary brightened at the invitation to take a drink. "We can go in here," he said, indicating one of the quayside alehouses. "I have a slate here and I wouldn't mind bringing them some trade." He winked again at James. "Gentry trade," he said. "Carriage trade. That'll surprise them."

"Certainly," James said pleasantly, and led the way into the room, looking around quickly to ensure that although it was a poorhouse, serving fishermen and the harbor traders, it was not bawdy or unsafe for the boys.

Walter and Rob took their seats at a small table in the corner while the men stood at the doorway to the kitchen to order their drinks. Zachary entered into a brief whispered discussion with the landlord that James cut short by saying, "Tell him I will clear your slate."

"Kindly of you," Zachary said, instantly suspicious.

"I may have work for you," James said.

"Happy to help a friend of the Peacheys. Or perhaps you're a friend of my wife?"

James was stony-faced at the slur on Alinor. "This is for the Peacheys," he said. "I think I may be able to put some business your way."

"Oh, aye," Zachary said, agreeably. "Boys, would you take a slice of beef and bread? I know boys are always hungry."

Walter, uncomfortable, shook his head.

"We just dined," James explained. "They'll take a glass of small ale and then they'll go back to our inn."

"Fair enough," Zachary said. "I'll take a measure, since you're buying." He nodded to the landlord, who poured a spirit from a blackened bottle under the table. Zachary raised his earthenware cup in a toast to his son. "It's good to see you, my boy," he said fondly. "And looking so fine!"

The boys were awkward at the table. Rob did not take his eyes from his father's face but asked no more questions. After a while, James told them that they could make their way back to the inn and go to bed. "I will make arrangements with your father," he promised Rob.

"Will you, sir?" Rob's brown eyes were trustingly on his face. "Shall we see him tomorrow?"

"I'll ask him to breakfast with us."

"Thank you, sir, because . . . I have to ask him . . . I have to be able to explain to my mother how it was."

James thought of Alinor's poverty and the terrible risk to her reputation since this man had abandoned her and their two children. "I'll speak to him," he promised, and was ashamed at his own duplicity when the boy's face cleared.

The men waited until the boys had left and the door had closed behind them.

"What d'you want with me?" Zachary said bluntly. "You needn't cony-catch me."

"I need your ship," James said. "I agreed with a coastal trader to meet me here, but he has failed. I need to commission a voyage out to sea."

"Which way?" Zachary asked sarcastically. "For this is an island. It is out to sea in every direction."

"South, towards France."

"That's what I do, once a week."

"You're the ship's master?" James confirmed. "You can sail when and where you want?"

"Provided I have a load and can turn a profit," Zachary said. "My owner trusts me to manage the business."

"I want you to meet a ship offshore and transfer some goods," James said. "You don't need to know more."

"Smuggling?" Zachary asked quietly. "It can be done, but it is expensive."

"I will pay you," James promised him. "I will pay you well."

"Would this be a barrel sort of goods? Or a chest sort of goods? Or more like a person?" he asked.

"You don't need to know that," James said. "All you need to know is that you will be well paid, and set sail a few minutes after midnight. I will come with you. Not the boys."

"And how much am I paid for this nighttime jaunt? With Your Honor as shipmate? With these goods?"

"Twenty crowns as we leave, twenty crowns on the quayside when we come back; and no one the wiser," James said.

Zachary tipped back his chair and put his sea boots on the barrel that served as a table. "No, I don't think I'll take it," he said, smiling at James over the top of his cup. "It's too much for ordinary smuggling and I'm no smuggler, I must tell you. And it's too little for shipping the king off the island. If that's your game, you'll be hanged for it."

"It's what my other ship would have been paid," James said coolly. "It's the right price."

"No, it isn't. For—see? He wouldn't do it for the price. Your fine friend didn't appear. You don't know why?" His sharp glance at James's face told him that the handsome young man did not know why his ship had failed. "So, if he wouldn't do it for the money, I don't think that I will either."

"I think you will," James said. "For I can call the watch to arrest you, and I can tell the magistrate that you have abandoned a wife and thrown her children onto the parish at Sealsea. I can tell them that you deserted from the parliament navy and serve as a smuggler. I can tell them that you are an adulterer and possibly a bigamist. I can tell them that you are wanted on Sealsea Island, perhaps elsewhere. Your own son would give witness that his mother is waiting for you to come home and that the Sealsea church wardens want you for your tithes."

"She is not!" Zachary slammed the table with the palm of his hand. "She's not waiting! Damn you for all the rest of it, but don't tell me that. She don't miss me, she don't want me. The boy might look for me, but she won't."

"I know that she does," James said steadily, thinking of the white-faced woman waiting for this man's ghost to speak to her on Midsummer Eve.

Zachary leaned forward confidingly. "Not her, because she's a whore," he said frankly. "One honest man to another: she's a whore and a witch. They married me to her, though I had my doubts, but her mother—another witch—wanted my boat and my nets and my catch, and thought that I would keep her girl safe, in difficult times. Thought I would make a fortune. Maybe I swore that I would. Maybe I made all sorts of promises. I was so mad for her—and who do I blame for that, eh? I built our house right next door to her mother in the ferry-house so that they could carry on their trade as wisewomen together, and I looked aside when they did what they did. I brought home fish, I sent her to market for me, and I took the money she brought back. I had plans for another boat, but I was unlucky a few times. I was as good a husband as any on the island. I didn't know what tricks that they would play on me. My wife and her mother, God curse them.

"One child we had: a daughter as beautiful as a faerie-born child. What did I know? Only that they had foisted a changeling on me from the moment that I saw her. Then came Rob—look at him! He could read as soon as he could walk, though I can't spell my name. He knew the herbs as soon as he toddled into her garden. Used to name them by smell. Who smells leaves but a faerie child? They're not my children. Nobody could ever have thought that they were my children! Look at them!"

"Then whose?" James demanded tightly.

"Ask her! She knows who she meets when she goes out into the full moon, when she goes out at Midsummer Eve, when she goes out to dance in the darkest of the nights of winter. She knows where she got these children. But I swear to you, it was not from me."

James braced his shoulders against a superstitious shudder. He forced himself to speak steadily: "This is nonsense. Are you saying that you left her for no better reason than this?"

"Damn her to the deep! She left me!" Zachary exclaimed. "I

may have been the one that was pulled out of the alehouse and thrown into the navy, but it was her who left me, years before that. She unmanned me; she can do it with a look. I could do nothing in her presence. I grabbed her once and was going to force her, but my hand went weak and my blood went like ice. I was going to make her do her duty by me—you know what I mean, a man has rights over his wife, whether she was willing or not—but I couldn't. She looked at me with eyes like a curse, and I went as soft as a dead fish. I swear to you, she was killing me. I could do nothing with her: not beat her nor swive her. She was killing me from the cock up."

"She was?"

"She drained me of life, I tell you. I could be no husband to her, and when I went with some drab I couldn't do the act there either, for thinking of her. What is that but a curse on me? And after her mother died, it got worse. I thought that when her mother died her power would go, but it was as if she added the old witch's power to her own. I was a baby in my own house. More of a baby than Rob, less of a voice than Alys. The press gang took me away, but by God I was glad to go!"

"Would you ever come back?" James asked.

"Never! Never! I'd rather die than go back to her. I'd rather drown. She's a whore, I tell you. A whore to faerie folk. She's a witch, I tell you. She can make a child without a man; she can prevent a child despite a man. She can kill a child in the womb and blast a man's cock with one icy breath."

"Dear God, what are you saying?" James could no longer hide his fear at the man's words—the worst things a man could hear: a woman that could shrink his potency, kill his children. "I know her! This isn't possible for a woman like her. It isn't possible for any mortal woman!"

"You can say that, Priest," the man said, his voice low. "You can say that who has never seen her naked, who has never touched her warm skin, who has never longed for her. But the taste of her mouth is like drinking henbane—she makes you thirsty for more and more, and then she drives you mad."

"I'm no priest," James said, quickly, ignoring what Alinor's husband said about the woman he loved.

Zachary's lip curled. "As you wish," he said coldly. "But something stinks of incense here and it's not me."

There was a silence between the two men.

"Anyway," James said, trying to recover his authority, trying to banish the image of Alinor whoring to a faerie lord, "I have no time for this nonsense. I am offering you a voyage or arrest. Which will it be?"

"Twenty crowns to take the trade out, to a meeting of your saying. Twenty crowns to bring you back?"

"Yes," James said.

"And we never speak of this again, and you take that boy back to her and tell her that you never saw me?"

"I can't make him lie, but I can make up some excuse."

"So that she does not look for me?"

"She would not come looking for you."

"She has the sight, fool. She can see me if she pleases, unless there is the deep sea between us. She cannot see me through deep water, I know that. She's afraid of deep water because she has no power over it. But if I ever sail into Tidelands again the mire will boil beneath my keel and throw me up like sea wrack before her door, and she will destroy me with one look."

"You speak like a madman."

"What d'you think killed her sister-in-law?" the man suddenly demanded.

"What?" James was thrown off course again. "What sister-in-law?"

"See how little you know her?" He turned and shouted over his shoulder for another drink. The landlord brought it in silence, and silently James waited for him to pour, and for Zachary to take a thoughtful swig.

"Go on," James said through his teeth.

"So you don't know that either! Her sister-in-law. Ned's wife. Her that she didn't like. What killed her, d'you know?"

"I didn't even know . . ."

"Exactly. You know nothing. She struck her dead from jealousy. So the poor mortal woman would not bear the child in her womb."

"She would never do such a thing."

"She did. I know it. For it was my child."

"You put Edward Ferryman's wife with child?"

"Yes, and my wife killed it, for spite."

There was a long silence. Zachary drained his mug and pushed it towards James, hoping for more.

James took a shuddering breath against these horrors, casually asserted. "Stop this slander. It means nothing to me. I don't know these people, and I don't care about them. We are here to make an agreement: that you will sail for me."

"You're here for an agreement. I'm here for drink."

James nodded over his shoulder to the landlord to pour another draft. "Will you sail for me or not?" he demanded, his voice very low.

"I will."

"And if I agree to tell her that you will never return, do you swear that you will not?"

"Willingly. Didn't you hear me? I'll never go back to her."

Zachary stuck out a dirty hand. Reluctantly, James shook it. When the warm palm with the old scars pressed against his own, he was reminded with a shock of Alinor's skin.

"Ah, you've touched her," Zachary guessed with spiteful satisfaction as James blanched. "You've touched her and she's got your soul in thrall too."

James walked back to the Old Bull inn and up the rickety stairs to the boys' low-ceilinged room. They were in their nightshifts in the big bed together.

"I prayed for my father," Rob confided.

"That was good," James said. "We'll see him again tomorrow. He'll come here for breakfast. You go to sleep now."

He watched them: Walter sprawled out to sleep, arms across the bed, feet to each corner, and Rob hunched into a ball. Then James quietly went from the room, downstairs to the private dining room.

Two men were seated on either side of the fire. As James came in, they rose up and clasped his hand, but no names were mentioned.

"You've seen him?"

"I have. I told him it's to be midnight. And I've met the boatman, and agreed a price," James confirmed. "You've bribed the guard?"

"Easily done," the other said. "He's not guarded as he was at Carisbrooke. That was the agreement with parliament, and they are true to it. They offered that he should be free to come and go here, limited only by his parole. They think an agreement is his only hope: fools."

"If I am caught at the Hopkins house don't wait for me. Get him away at all speed. The ship is the *Jessie*, by the quay and ready to sail."

"I thought it was the *Marie*?" the second man demurred.

"He failed me. It is the *Jessie*."

"Have you paid him?"

"Twenty crowns to go, twenty when we are safely home."

"I'm going with him to France," the first man said, "if he will allow me. I'm not coming back."

"I have to return with the boatman to finish my mission here," James said. He felt in his pocket and gave the second man a heavy purse. "But you can hold this for me. Be on the quay to pay the *Jessie* when it returns."

"You won't carry it?"

James shook his head.

"You don't trust him not to steal it and throw you overboard?" The man was appalled. "What kind of comrade is this? On a venture like this?"

James was silent for a moment. "I don't trust anyone," he answered, hearing the ring of truth in his own words. "I don't trust anyone, in this land which is sea, in these harbors that are not havens, in these ebbing tidelands."

"What?"

"Anyway, if I don't get down to the quay, get the person we have come for safely aboard, and pay the boatman."

"What d'you mean, if you don't get down to the quay?"

"If I'm caught," James said flatly. "If I'm dead."

At five minutes before midnight the three men pulled on their tall hats and wrapped their thick cloaks around their shoulders. James assumed that it was the damp air that made him shiver and long to stay by the fire for one minute, just one minute more.

"I'll go ahead," he said. "You come behind me and wait below his window, and you wait on the quay."

"As agreed," the first man said, irritable with fear. "For God's sake, can we get on?"

All the windows were dark at the Hopkins house. There were no guards to be seen, but James had a suspicion that the commander of Carisbrooke Castle, an experienced army man, would have posted men to watch the doors, whatever promises the parliament might have made about the king's freedom. The Hopkinses' porter on their front door had been bribed to look away at midnight, but there was no way of knowing if there were spies hidden in the dark doorways or leaning against the dark walls. James peeled off from the main road and entered with assumed confidence through the garden door, walked around the vegetable and herb beds to the kitchen door. It was unlocked for early deliveries. James turned the handle and stepped into the quiet kitchen.

The spit boy rose up from his truckle bed by the fireside. "Who's there?"

"Sssh, it's me," James said familiarly. "I didn't know if anyone had remembered his sops in wine?"

"What?"

"The king. He takes bread and wine at midnight. Has anyone taken it up?"

"No!" the boy exclaimed. "Lord! This is always happening. And his servers have gone to the inn, and the cook gone to bed."

"I'll do it," grumbled James. "I do everything."

"D'you have the key to the cellar? Shall I wake the groom of the servery: Mr. Wilson?"

"No. The king doesn't drink from your cellar. He has his own wine, in his own room. I have the key. You go back to sleep. I'll serve him."

He took a glass and a decanter from the cupboard in the hall and walked up the stairs. The door to the king's room was locked on the inside, but as he approached it across the creaking floorboards of the landing he heard the clock on St. Thomas's Church strike midnight, and at the same time the sound of an oiled bolt sliding back. He felt a sense of complete elation. He was on the threshold of the king's bedchamber, the king was opening the door, the boat was waiting. "This is triumph," James thought. "This is what it feels like to win."

The king opened the door and peered out.

"Clarion." James said the password, and dropped to his knee.

"Rise," the king replied indifferently. "I'm not coming."

James turned an incredulous face up to the king. "Your Majesty?"

The king stepped back into his room and beckoned James in, nodding that he should close the door. His lined face was bright: a cornered man getting the last laugh. "Not tonight."

"The porter is gone from the door. Your son, His Royal Highness, is waiting for you with his fleet. I've got a man under your window and another on the quay, a ship to take you to the prince. We're safe to go now . . ."

His Majesty waved it all aside. "Yes, yes. Very good, very

good. But we'll do it another day, if needs be. I have them on the run, you see. They're bringing me an agreement."

James felt his head swim with dismay, and then he remembered the frightened man waiting under the king's window. "I have to send some men away," he said. "Men in danger, waiting for you. I can't stay myself, if you're not going to come. But I beg you to come, sire. This is your chance—"

"I am making my own chances." The king had already turned away. "You can go."

"I beg you," James repeated. He heard his voice quaver and he flushed, shamed before his king. "Please, Sire . . . Her Majesty the Queen sent the money herself, for me to hire the ship. She commissioned me to rescue you. I am under her orders."

The king turned back, his smile vanished. "I don't need rescuing," he said irritably. "I am the best judge of my actions. I know what is happening. Her Majesty has nothing but a woman's wit: she cannot know. They are coming to me on their knees with handsome proposals. The Scots' invasion taught them that they have to make terms with me or next I will bring the Irish down on them. They have seen that the country rises up for me. They begin to understand my power; it is never-ending, it is eternal. They can win a thousand battles—but I still have the right. The parliament knows they cannot rule without a king. Without me."

James felt the rise of a treasonous rage. He wanted to lay hold of the man and drag him to safety. "Before God, Your Majesty, I swear that you should come now, and then you can negotiate from a place of safety, with your wife and son at your side. Their future depends on you, as does all of ours. However good the offer, whatever parliament promises you, you would be safest talking to them from France."

The king drew himself up. "I will never leave my kingdom," he said firmly. "My kingdom can never leave me. God ordained I should be king. That cannot be set aside. We will come to an agreement, my subjects and I. I shall return to London and Her

Majesty the Queen will join me there, at my palace at Whitehall. I shall not steal away like a thief in the night. Tell her that." He nodded James to the door as if to dismiss him.

"I cannot go without you! I swore!"

"It is my command."

"Your Majesty, please!"

Charles made a little gesture with his hand, a little cutting-off gesture. There was nothing James could do but leave: stepping carefully backwards as royal protocol demanded, never turning his back, going steadily until he felt the brass ring latch of the door press into his back, and he checked.

"Your Majesty, I have risked my life to come for you," he said quietly. "And a loyal man is waiting on the quayside to go with you to France. He has said good-bye to his own family and his country. He will go into exile with you and not leave your side till you are in safety. We have a boat, we will take you to your own son. He is waiting for you with his fleet on the high seas. Your safety and freedom are waiting. Your future—all of our futures—depends on you coming away now."

"I thank you for your service." But the king had already seated himself and turned to his letters. "I am grateful. And when I come to my own again I will reward you. You can be sure of that."

James, thinking wildly that he would never be sure of anything, ever again, bowed low and went out of the room. As he stood on the shadowy landing he heard the door close quietly behind him and the bolt slide shut. He thought it was the most final noise he had ever heard, like the dull thud of an executioner's axe through a neck and onto the block.

Downstairs, in the street, the nameless man flinched like a frightened dog when he saw the figure come from the darkened doorway. "Your Majesty," he breathed, and dropped to his knee.

"Get up, it's me." James pushed up the brim of his hat to show his face. "He won't come."

"Mother of God!"

"Come on," James whispered. "Back to the inn."

They went swiftly, by a circuitous route, down the dark alleyways and then along the quayside to fetch their comrade from his hidden doorway. The three of them slipped in the unlocked front door, and into the dining room. As soon as the door was shut, James pulled off his hat and threw down his cloak. He flung himself into a chair and buried his face in his hands.

"Why didn't you make him come?" one of the men demanded.

"How?"

"Christ! You should have told him!"

"I did."

"Doesn't he know the danger he's in? That we're in? How could he let us go through all this for him, and then not come? We've been planning this for weeks!"

"Months. He thinks they will make an agreement."

"Why didn't you insist?"

"He's the king. What could I say?"

"When parliament comes, what if they can't agree?"

"He's sure they will," James said through his clenched teeth. "I begged him to come. I warned him. I did everything that I could. He was determined. I pray to God that he's right."

"But why not come? Why run away from imprisonment at Hampton Court, breaking his word of honor, his parole, but not run from here? When we've got a ship waiting and his son at sea?"

"In the name of God, I don't know!" James swore, driven to despair. "I wouldn't be here if I didn't think it was the right thing, the safest thing, the only thing for him to do. But how could I make him come! How could I?"

The second man had not taken off his hat, nor even unfastened his cloak. "I'm off," he said savagely. "I won't do this again. Don't try to find me or invite me. Don't call on me for help. This has been a night I won't repeat. This is my last time. I am finished in his cause. He has lost me. I cannot serve him. They warned me he was changeable and talkative as a woman. But I would never have thought he would let his friends, men sworn to his cause, stand in the street in mortal danger while he chose not to bother."

James nodded in silence as the man let himself out of the door and they heard his footsteps go quietly across the hall and the front door open and close.

"Shall you come back?" the first man asked unhappily. "Try again?"

"If I'm ordered, I must obey. But not like this again. Never like this again. Forcing men to serve him, swearing them to his cause. I even brought two boys into this danger to hide the plot. I put my life at risk, yours, even the villain on the *Jessie*. I have been a mortal fool for a man who does not want my service, who didn't even ask my name, who didn't even give me a message for his wife, who sold her jewels to pay for this. I shall have to go back to her and tell her he would not come. I have failed. I have failed him, and I have failed her because of him."

"Good night," the man said abruptly. "I pray to God that we never meet again. I will swear that we never met, and I will never speak of it. If I am captured I will deny all this, and you will do the same."

"Amen," James said, slumped in his chair.

The man paused at the door. "Even if they burn you, I trust you not to say my name, and I will not speak yours. I don't want to die for nothing."

"Agreed," James said bitterly, as if it was all nothing, as if loyalty was nothing, as if death by burning was nothing. The man let himself out into the night.

James sat in silence by the dying fire, sick with the draining away of his courage. He found his hands were shaking and that all he could see, as he watched the embers, was the triumphantly gloomy face of the king with his dark sorrowful eyes. James thought himself to be a fool to have given his life to such a man and such a fanciful web of plots. The king he had sworn to serve wanted none of his loyalty, and the woman he desired was a whore to the faeries and had murdered the wife and baby of a mortal man. He thought he was very far from God, and very far from grace, and a long, long way from his home.

At dawn in the morning when a man might reasonably be up and about, James went down to the quayside. The air was cool and smelled of salt in the light breeze. The sky was peach pink. It was going to be a beautiful day. If they had sailed overnight as they had planned, they would have had a good wind homeward and the sun on their backs. They would have moored on a peaceful quayside, paid off Zachary, and gone their own ways to their homes. No one would have known that the king was gone until they served his breakfast, late in the morning. The king would have been breakfasting in France, the Stuart monarchy safe in exile, certain to invade; Cromwell's rebellion doomed. James looked to pink clouds at the east and thought that never in his life had he seen a sun rise and felt such darkness.

Zachary was asleep, curled up under a sail in the stern of the little trading ship. He opened his eyes and sat up as he heard the sound of James's riding boots on the stone quay.

"Miscarried," he observed. "Like the babies she says she will deliver that come out blue. Unsatisfied—as she always is."

"Yes," James said shortly. "But I know nothing about any babies."

Zachary hawked and spat over the side. "Her hands are stained with them," he said conversationally. "She smells of them: dead babies. Had you not noticed? But—anyway—what happened to you? Nothing good. Were you caught? Doing whatever you were doing?"

"No."

"Probably half the island knows anyway," Zachary said pessimistically. "He's not famously discreet, your master. Everyone I know has taken a letter from him and learned his ever-so-secret code."

"I don't think so."

"Well, you'll pay me the forty crowns for my silence," he observed.

"Twenty," James said flatly. He took the purse from his pocket and tossed it over. Zachary caught it neatly, and it disappeared into the folds of his tattered jacket. "So you failed," he said spitefully. "Your mission was a failure and so are you."

"I failed," James said. "But no one the wiser, and no harm done."

"But I am wiser. I know of you and where you came from. Who you came from. Where you live. I think you'll find that is harm done."

"You know," James agreed. "But I know of you, so we are equal in that. Will you come to have breakfast at the inn and see your boy this morning?"

Zachary shook his head. "Not I."

"What am I to tell him?"

"Tell him I went out last night and drowned."

"I can't do that."

"Then tell him whatever lie you can stoop to. For clearly you are not wedded to truth. You have broken your vows and you lie to those who trust you. You lie to your hosts and to their servants. If you have a lover, and I think we both know her name . . ." he paused and leered at the thought of Alinor, ". . . then, for sure, you lie to her, for she's no royalist. She can't be faithful to any cause or mortal man. You're no better than me. In fact, you're worse than me, for I ran for my life from a witch, but you are running back to her. And she will eat your lying soul and steal your child."

"I am not running back to her!"

"Then you're lying to yourself as well."

"And there is no child."

"There will be if she wants one."

James paused and gritted his teeth on hatred. “I will not help her to find you in any way, and I will tell your son that you took a message for me and have not yet come back.”

Zachary nodded indifferently. “I sail on the morning tide anyway,” he said. “I’ll be gone for days, weeks. If the boy comes looking for me, he won’t find me.”

“Good-bye,” James said shortly.

“Godspeed, Priest,” Zachary said, getting a threat into the last word as James turned and walked away.

James went through the day in a daze. The boys wanted to watch the king go to church, but James could not bear to see that mournful face again, so he sent them on their own and they came back full of excitement that the king had saluted the crowd of well-wishers, that someone had raised their voice against him, that some cavaliers had started a brawl, that the king had laughed and gone back to his house, then waved to the crowd from his window, and that everyone said that the parliament men were coming in the next week to give him his crown back.

“D’you want to ride over to Cowes?” James asked. He found that every minute in Newport was unbearable. “We could take a ship to Portsmouth from Cowes, and then hire horses to ride home.”

“Can we?” Walter was exuberant. He cuffed Rob around the head. “Say yes!”

“Yes! Yes!” Rob exclaimed. “But did you say my father was coming to breakfast? Can I see him before we go?”

“He took a message for me to Southampton and he’s not returned,” James lied smoothly. “He said that he might be delayed. We might see him at Cowes. We might not. But I am afraid that he’s not coming home to your mother, Robert. He said he wouldn’t come home. I am sorry.”

“But what is she to do?” Rob demanded. “What if he never

comes home? She can't live off the herbs and the midwifery. Did he say he would send money? And there is Alys to be provided for. She needs a dowry. Her father should give her a dowry, sir."

James swallowed his own sense of despair. "I will talk to your mother," he said. He knew that he longed to talk to her. "If we can get you an apprenticeship, then you will earn good wages. You could do well, Robert. You could be her support. If your sister marries well, then your mother can live more cheaply at home. She's got the boat now; she can earn her own keep. She does not depend on your father. She is skilled, and when she can get work she is paid well."

"The women won't use a midwife who is neither a wife nor a widow," Rob said, flushed to his ears. "They think it's unlucky."

"I didn't know," James said quietly, realizing how much he did not know about Alinor and her life. "Perhaps she could go and live inland, where people don't know her, where she could pass as a widow?"

"Why can't he come home, and make everything right?" The cry came from the boy as if it were wrested from him.

James could not meet his eyes. "These are troubles between a man and a wife," he said lamely. "I am sorry for you and for your mother. But if your father will not do his duty, I cannot make him. Neither can you, Robert. It's not your fault."

"The church wardens would make him!"

"They would, but he won't come back to face them."

"She will be shamed," the boy said bleakly. "And they will call me a bastard."

They rode to Cowes, Walter in buoyant spirits but Rob was very quiet. Then they spent the night at an inn on the quayside, and took a ship across the Solent. It was a calm crossing and when they landed in Portsmouth they hired horses and took the coast road, riding east, through fields and little villages with pretty waterside churches. They stayed overnight at Langstone in an old fishing inn. James woke to the smell of the sea and the cry of seagulls, and thought that for the rest of his life he would hear that mournful calling as the sound of defeat. Then they rode on, east through the marshy tidelands of Hampshire and across the county border to Sussex. When they came down the road that led south to her brother's ferry and the wadeway, James narrowed his eyes against the low sun, looking for Alinor, where he had seen her before.

The tide was on the ebb, the water was dazzling in the rife. He almost thought that she would be waiting for him, her pale face bright with joy at seeing him. The light on the water was so bright, and he was so certain that she would come to meet him, that he saw her, her hood pushed back from her white cap, looking over the mire towards him. But it was a mirage, a false seeing in the haze of the waters, a chimera. It was her brother who came from the ferry-house, his dog at his heels, and he pulled the ferry over to them, and helped to load the hired horses.

"You can go along the bank and see your mother if you like," James said quietly to Rob as Ned hauled the ferry, hand over hand on the rope. "Walter and I will go on to the Priory. I can lead your horse."

Rob nodded.

"Why, what's the matter with you?" Ned demanded, hearing the dullness in James's voice and seeing Rob's drooping head. "Are you sick, Rob? Is there something wrong, Mr. Summer?"

"Just weary," James said. He had not known that the despair he felt in his belly was showing in his face. "I think we're all weary."

"So the sight of the king did not cheer you?" the ferry-man remarked. "His touch did not cure you of all ills?"

James reminded himself that nobody here knew that he had failed in his mission and the purpose of his life was wasted. "No. The boys liked to see him."

"You a royalist now, Rob?" his uncle demanded, as the ferry grounded on the bank.

"No, Uncle," Rob replied quietly. "But I was glad to see the king in person."

"And his coat!" Walter interpolated. "You should have seen his hat!"

The boys led their horses off the ferry onto dry land.

"Looks like he's going to haggle on and on with the parliament men," Ned said to James. "But I reckon the army will have something to say about any deal. He won't wrap the army round his little finger, whatever tricks he plays on parliament. The soldiers won't forgive him for starting the wars again, after we all thought we were at peace. The country's turned against him like never before, for that. No one will forgive him that."

"I don't know," James said wearily, stepping ashore and pulling at his horse's bridle. "God knows what they will come to, and what it will cost us all."

"You don't take in vain the name of our Lord on my ferry," Ned reproved him.

"I apologize," James said, through cold lips, leading his horse up to the mounting block, climbing into the saddle, and taking Rob's reins. "My good wishes to your mother, Rob."

Alinor was striding along the bank path to Ferry-house garden to pick blackberries when she saw the silhouette of her beloved son against the afternoon sky, as he walked from the rife. He did not bound like a colt in the field, but walked as if his feet were heavy, his head down as if he were hurt.

"Holloah!" she shouted, and ran towards him. As soon as she took him in her arms, she knew that there was something wrong. She sniffed at him like an animal scenting ill health: the different houses where he had lodged, smoke from different kitchens in his hair, a different starch in his collar, the smell of the sea and the salt of the harbor on his coat. Then she stepped back and looked into his face and saw how his shoulders were hunched, and his face turned down. "What is it, son?" she asked him gently. "What ails you?"

"Oh, nothing, nothing," he said dully.

"Come home, come inside." She led the way back to the cottage without another word, dimly understanding that he would not speak under the arching sky with the gulls crying and the sea lapping at the bank as if it were flowing inshore and would make all the world into tidelands.

"Were you going somewhere?" he asked her.

"Just to pick blackberries. I can go later."

She did not close the front door on the little room, but kept it open so that she could see his face in the bright afternoon light. He dropped onto his stool. He had sat there when he was a boy and cried for some small hurt. She wanted to hold him now, as she had done then.

"Where's Alys?" he asked.

"She's having her dinner at Stoney Farm with the Stoney family, and staying the night there. She's fine. But what is it with you?"

"I . . . It is . . . We met . . ."

Inwardly, she cursed the priest who had taken her boy from his home, over the seas, and brought him back speechless with distress. "Are you hungry?" she asked him, to give them both time.

"No!" he exclaimed, thinking that she could not waste her bread on him, that it would be hard for her to earn it when everyone knew that she was an abandoned wife.

"Have a cup of ale, then," she said gently, and went to the jug and poured them each a cup. Then she sat beside him, and clasped her hands in her lap to keep herself still. "Tell me, Rob. It's probably not that bad. It's never as bad—"

"It is bad," he insisted. "You don't know."

"Tell me then," she said steadily. "So that I do know."

"I saw my da," he said quietly, his face downcast. "At Newport, on the island. He had a ship, he's master of a coastal trader. It's called the *Jessie.*" He snatched a quick look at her face. "Did you know?"

"No, of course not, I'd have told you."

"He could've come home to us months ago," he said. "But he didn't."

She gave a little sigh. "This doesn't shock me," she promised him. "Nor hurt me, neither."

"I saw him, and I called his name, and he saw me and he ran," Rob said, his voice quavering a little. "I didn't think it at the time, but now I think that he knew me at once, and ran from me. But I went after him like a fool, and Walter and Mr. Summer after me."

Now she flushed, a deep humiliated blush that rose from her neck to her forehead. "Master Walter and Mr. Summer were there, too?"

"Course they were! They met him."

"Oh, no!"

"Yes." He nodded. "Awful. We all went with him into an inn, a small dirty place where he had a slate. I think Mr. Summer paid for everything. And he said he'd been pressed by the navy, the parliament navy, and escaped from them when they went over to the prince, and then he got a passage on a coastal trader. He said he'd come to breakfast with us the next morning, but he didn't. He went on an errand for Mr. Summer and never came back. We thought we might see him in Cowes, but though I went down to the quayside he wasn't there, and they hadn't seen his boat. Mr. Summer says that he won't come back here."

With one hand shading his eyes so he did not see her face, he stretched out his other hand and she gripped it tightly.

"I don't even know there was an errand," he said, his palm clamped over his eyes. "It may be that they lied to me, thinking I was a child, thinking I am a fool. Maybe he just ran away, and Mr. Summer lied for him."

"This isn't your fault." She felt that she could wail with pain that anyone should turn from Rob, that his own father should run from him. "This is the fault of the man that Zachary is, not the boy that you are. He can't live with me: p'raps that's my fault. But it's nothing that can be blamed on you. You've been a son that anyone would be proud of, and Alys a daughter that anyone would love. Zachary cannot live with me, nor I with him. But that's our fault. It doesn't fall on the two of you."

"Did you ever think he'd come back?"

"I didn't know," she confessed. "As the months went on, I thought it less and less likely, but I didn't know. Just this Midsummer Eve I went to the graveyard in case his ghost was walking, so that I'd know for sure that he was dead. God forgive me, Rob, I was hoping he was dead so that we wouldn't have to think of him anymore. When I didn't see his ghost, I knew he must be alive, and was choosing not to come home to us. But it's still not your fault, Rob."

She felt a pulse of shame that she had met the priest in the graveyard when she should have been undertaking a vigil for the ghost of her husband, and now he had met Zachary, and they had spoken together of her. She could not imagine what Zachary might have said. If he had repeated the wild accusations he used to make—of her taking faerie gold for whoring in the other world, of her witchcraft and unmanning him—she would be shamed before James Summer forever. If he had convinced James that Ned's wife had died because Alinor was negligent or worse: murderous; then she might face questioning. She closed her eyes at the shame and the danger that Zachary could still bring her. They sat side by side, both blinded with distress for a moment.

"It's not your fault, Rob," she repeated steadily. "And much of it's not my fault either."

"What'll we do?" Rob asked anxiously. "If he doesn't come back? You've got the boat now, but you can't sell fish to fishermen, and when Walter goes to university I'll have to find other work, and nothing'll pay as well. And Alys can't marry without a dowry."

"I don't rightly know what we'll do," she said, trying to sound cheerful. "But I have the herbs and the babies. I've been paid by Farmer Johnson. Everyone will go on having babies, God bless them. And if peace comes, and the bishop comes back to his palace, then I'll get my license from him, and I'll be able to charge more and I'll be called out to more homes."

"Not when they know that Da's left us," Rob contradicted her. "Not when they know you're not a widow nor a wife. You'll never get your license then. Even if the bishop comes back. You won't be a woman of good repute. They won't even let you into church; you'll have to stand in the porch. They won't let you in for communion."

"Perhaps people won't mind too much. Nobody liked Zachary."

"They'll call me a bastard!" he choked.

"They'll be wrong," she said steadfastly. "And you need not answer to it."

He was silent for a moment. "Should we move away?" he asked. "Somewhere that you could call yourself a widow, and Alys and I could find work, and people wouldn't know?"

"No parish would have us!" She tried to smile but he could see the pain in her face. "No parish would admit a widow woman with two children! They'd be too afraid that we'd fall on the parish and cost money. Mrs. Miller is afraid already, and we were born and bred here and have paid our tithes for generations. And besides, you know, gossip'd follow us, and it'd sound worse to strangers, people who didn't know Zachary, and don't know what he's like."

"I can't face it here."

"Yes, I understand. I do understand, Rob. But, at least here we have the garden and the boat and your uncle. I have my stillroom and my dairy and the brewhouse in Ferry-house. I work the garden with your uncle. There's always work at the mill. They think well of you at the Priory, and Mrs. Wheatley, the cook, is a good friend to me. We'll just have to make up our minds to tell everyone that Zachary has left me, so there's no more talk of whether or not he's dead. It'll be bad for a month or two; but then something'll happen and everyone'll become accustomed." She tried to smile at him reassuringly. "You'll see. Some poor woman will hop over the stile and be shamed in church before us all. They'll find something else to gossip about; they'll talk about someone else."

"They will blame you and they will look down on you, and you've done nothing wrong!" he said fiercely.

She nodded grimly. "Yes, maybe. But I have a good reputation as a hardworking woman with some skills, and that won't change. Zachary was not well loved and nobody'll miss him. I didn't even miss him, but for the boat and his earnings."

He nodded. "You'll have to live without a husband for the rest of your life. And you're—I don't know—thirty?"

She smiled. "I'm twenty-seven years old. Yes, I'll be a single woman for the rest of my life; but that's no hardship for me. I have you and Alys, and I want for nothing more."

"You might find someone you love," he said shyly. "Someone might find you."

"Nobody will ever find me here." She gestured to the open door and the stretches of mud and slowly receding brackish water outside, as the low rumble of the tide mill started up like thunder, and there was a sudden gout of green water in the rife. "Nobody will ever find a woman like me in a place like this."

James met with Sir William in the library after Walter had gone to bed. The candles were burned down in their sconces and the deerhound slept before the fire. Sir William was in his great chair by the fireside, James on the other side in a smaller chair. Both men had glasses of French brandy, smuggled by the hidden traders who came to the tide mill quay on the high tide dark nights, and left without showing a light. James was wearily explaining the king's plan to trick the parliament and his refusal to leave.

"He wouldn't come? Not even for the password?" Sir William repeated incredulously.

James shook his head. "No, sir, he would not."

"You warned him of what might be?"

"I warned him, and I told him that it was his wife's own plan and his son was waiting in his ship offshore. I begged him. He wouldn't come."

"God save him, this is a damnable mistake." Sir William held up his glass in a toast. James clinked glasses and sat back in his chair.

"Are you sick?" Sir William cocked an eye at the younger man's pale face.

"Perhaps a little fever. Nothing important."

"So d'you think there's any chance he might be right? That parliament will come to an agreement with him?"

"Newport is filled with royalists who boast that it doesn't matter what he signs. They say he will sign anything, and once he's back in his palace he'll avenge his advisors that parliament executed, restore the queen, and bring the royal family back to London. He'll take back his power and destroy his enemies. Everyone says that it doesn't matter what he signs now—he will restore himself."

"I doubt it. I really doubt it. The parliament men aren't fools. It has cost them dear to get here. They've lost sons and brothers, too. They won't throw it away on an empty agreement when he has given them every reason never to trust him. My own ferryman doesn't trust him! Anything they offer would have to be binding. They'll tie him down with oaths. They won't just hand him the treasury and the army for a handful of promises."

"I was told that he will consent to nothing less," James said wearily.

"Impossible!" Sir William said scathingly. "Besides, it's not his army anymore. This is the New Model Army, they're all Cromwell's men. They'll never serve under a king; they have their own ideas! They're a power to themselves, they think for themselves. Not even the parliament can control them—how ever would he?"

James clenched his hands on the carved arms of his chair, trying to master a wave of dizziness. "Yes, sir. But that's the very reason that parliament will have to agree with him: to avoid the demands of the army. Some parliament men hate the army worse than they doubt the king. Some would rather have a tyrannical king than a tyrannical army—who wouldn't? They're divided among themselves, whereas he is determined . . ."

The older man nodded. "It's a gamble," he said. "A royal gamble. You have to admire him for taking it."

James, very far from admiration, took a sip of brandy. "I don't know where it leaves us," he said. "I don't know where it leaves me."

"I'll wait until I'm summoned again to serve him," Sir William spoke for himself. "But I'll never put my son in danger again. It's hard to accept that he would let us come to his door before refusing. Did he not think of the danger to us? And what about you? Will you have to go back to your seminary for your orders?"

"I suppose so." James put a hand to his forehead and found it was wet with sweat. "They'll never understand how I failed. I was told to set loose a lion; I never thought it would stay in its cage. Of all the things that I feared might go wrong, I never thought of this. I'm at a loss. I was to see him safe on his son's ship, and then go to London. I am ordered to report to London as soon as he was safely away. I suppose now I shall go back to them and say he has stayed, and I have failed. I will have to go to the queen and tell her that I have spent her fortune for nothing."

"You're very welcome to stay here. The chapel needs a chaplain. Walter needs a tutor. Nobody doubts you. You're safe here."

"I'd be glad to stay overnight, but I am under oath. Tomorrow I must ride to London."

"You don't look fit for it."

James felt his very bones ache. "I have to report. There'll be another plot. There'll be more journeys along hidden ways. There will be another task for me: and I am sworn to obedience."

"Well, please God they don't ask more of you than to lie low and wait for better times. You've been living on the brink of danger for months, and you look as sick as a dog."

"It's been weary work," James conceded.

"What if they send you back to him, to do it all over again?"

"I am sworn to serve," James repeated, feeling the words sour in his mouth and his heart hammering. "I pray for peace."

"So do we all," his lordship said. "But always on our own terms. Shall we pray now?"

"Matins?" James offered, looking at the French clock that ticked on the stone chimney breast. It was past midnight.

"Yes," Sir William said, getting to his feet. "And will you leave tomorrow?"

"At dawn," James said, thinking of the two boys in his care, of his plans for them, which would not now happen, and of the woman that he had sworn he would never see again, and now he never would.

James, in his white shirt and riding breeches, but with his holy stole around his neck, went quietly around the private chapel lighting candles. Sir William knelt before his great chair, his eyes closed, his face buried in his hands. Turning his back on his congregation of one, James prepared the bread and the wine for the Mass at the old stone altar at the east end of the church and spoke the prayers in Latin, his voice never rising above a quiet monotone. Sir William did not need to hear clearly. He joined in the confession and the preparation of the host in Latin, knowing every word from his childhood in a family that had never surrendered their faith, not during the years of Elizabeth, not during the years of Edward, not during the years of Henry.

The sense of despair that James had felt when he realized that he had spent months preparing an escape for a king who would not leave drained from him as his hands moved deftly among the goblets and the pyx, turned the page, poured the wine, broke the bread. He turned to find Sir William kneeling on the chancel steps and gave him the holy bread and a sip of the sacred wine. He knew, without any doubt, that at that moment Jesus Christ, the risen Lord, was in the bread and in the wine, that it was His body and His blood, that James and Sir William had dined at the table of the last supper, and that they had defeated death itself. He knew himself to be a sinner and he knew himself to be mired in doubt; but still he knew that he was redeemed and saved.

He muttered the final prayer in Latin: "Abide with us, O Lord," and heard Sir William whisper the response: "For it is toward evening and the day is far spent."

"As the watchmen look for the morning . . ."

"So do we look for Thee, O Christ."

"Come with the dawning of the day . . ."

"And make Thyself known in the breaking of bread."

James had a sensation under his ribs, which he thought must be his heart breaking, just as Christ's heart broke on the cross. He had given up the woman he loved for the king that he must save, and he had failed to save him and learned to doubt her. He would never see his king again; he would never see her. He would leave her in poverty and the king in imprisonment. He was only twenty-two and he had failed in everything his duty and his heart had prompted him to do. "God forgive me," he said, and without another word, sank to the floor as his knees buckled beneath him, and he lost consciousness.

They sent Stuart the footman to fetch Alinor, three miles round by road, as he did not know the tracks across the harbor and was fearful of the tide coming in and drowning him, and of the ghosts of drowned men swimming after him. But when he hammered on the door of the cottage he found Alinor and Rob in the half-light of the smoldering fire, hours after good Christians should have been in bed. He recoiled in fear at the sight of the wisewoman, waking in the dark hours, with her son beside her.

"Not abed?" he asked fearfully. "Up all night?"

Alinor rose. "Is someone sick?"

"It's the tutor," he replied. "Sir William said to come at once."

Rob handed Alinor her physic basket, already stocked with oils and herbs, pulled on his cap and jacket, and led the way across the mire to the Priory, by shore and bank and hidden path, lit by the half-moon gleaming on the rising water. They were at the Priory sea meadow as the moon came from behind a bank of cloud to make the eastern waters of the harbor shine, and they crossed the kitchen garden in the eerie light.

The chapel was closed and quiet, all the gold and candles hidden away by Mr. Tudeley and his lordship. They had dragged James back into the library, stripped him of his stole, and left him on the rug before the fire, fearful of lifting him up the stairs.

"Did he say anything before he fainted?" Alinor could not look at him, so deathly pale; sprawled on the hearthrug, just as he had sprawled in her net shed, when he had slept beneath her roof and she had thought him as beautiful as a fallen angel.

"He said, 'God forgive me,'" Sir William said. "But he could not be possessed by devils. He is a godly man and he was in . . . in a state of grace."

One swift glance from her gray eyes told him that she understood what he and the exhausted priest were doing at midnight. "Did he complain of fever or chills?" she asked, putting her warm rough hand on his cold sweating face.

"Yes, and he was weary," Sir William said. "And melancholy."

She had a very good idea why he was tired and sad. "May I use the goods from your stillroom?"

"Of course. Take whatever you need. You know what's there. But, Mrs. Reekie: you don't think it is the plague?"

It was the one question that Alinor dreaded, worse than whether a baby might be breech or malformed. If it was the plague it was almost certain to be fatal for everyone in the room, for half the household, for most of the village. Their death sentence had already been written and could not be recalled. There was nothing she could do against plague. She was likely to be the first to die. That was how it was. Everyone knew it.

"I can't tell," she said. "Not till I search his body for the marks."

"But could it be?" Sir William demanded. He had retreated behind his chair. "He was at Newport. Dear God, he took my son, Walter, to Newport and to Cowes."

"And mine," Alinor reminded him.

"They could have met with anyone. He could have taken the plague from a ship. They could all three have taken it. They came home by ship to Portsmouth."

"I'll need to examine him," she repeated, hiding her own dread. "I can't say yet."

Sir William would not take the risk of the man staying in his house another moment. "Get him carried over to the stables." He turned to Mr. Tudeley. "Carry him on the rug so he's not hurt. Leave the rug there. We'll lock him in to be on the safe side until we know." He turned to Alinor. "Mrs. Reekie, I have to ask you, will you go in with him and nurse him till he is well?"

"I can't," Alinor said flatly. "I have a son and daughter of my own. I will examine him, but if he has the signs I can't be shut in with him. I've never been a plague nurse."

"I beg you," he said. "I will pay you well, very well. Go in with him now and examine him. If he has it—God forbid that he has it—I will get a plague nurse from Chichester to come and be locked up with him and you shall come out, before she arrives, before we declare it, and go to your own cottage and not stir until it is over. If he does not have it I will still pay you three shillings a day to nurse him until he is better."

She hesitated.

"You don't want him to be put into his bed in the boys' room," he reminded her. "Not with your son and mine. Better for us all, if you nurse him in the stable loft."

She looked at James's white face, at the fall of his dark curling hair, his black eyelashes lying on his pale cheek, the darkening of his chin and upper lip that marked him as no angel but a mortal man. She saw the rapid rise and fall of his chest and how the cold sweat darkened the curls on his forehead. She knew she could not bear to leave him. She could not bear to hand him over to the rough care of a strange woman.

"Ten shillings." His lordship raised his bid for the safety of his household. "Ten shillings a day, till the plague nurse comes. Every day."

"I'll do it," she decided. "Rob can fetch what I need from your stillroom, but then he must stay away."

The rooms above the stable, hastily vacated by the grooms, were light and airy with dappled windows not of glass but of thin cut horn set at each end into the eaves. Down below, the hunters stirred and snorted in their stalls and the room smelled comfortingly, of clean straw and hay and the warm oaty smell of horses. Stuart and two of the grooms lugged James, still wrapped in the hearthrug, up the ladder and laid him on the bed.

"I'll send over food," Mr. Tudeley said, keeping his distance, halfway down the ladder. "You can pull it up on the rope."

"And a bucket of hot water for washing and a pitcher of cold water. A big jug of small ale and some little dishes for mixing. I'll need fresh bread, cheeses, and meat for when he wakes, and at noon someone must bring breakfast," Alinor instructed. "I'll need a pail for a chamber pot, and strewing herbs."

"Of course, he'll be served as an honored guest, and you too, Mrs. Reekie," Mr. Tudeley said. "Shall your boy come and sleep here with you?"

"No," she said firmly. "He'll stay in the house with Master Walter. I'll sit up tonight with Mr. Summer and if he is well tomorrow, God willing, he can come back to the house and I will go to my own home. This is just for a night."

"You will tell us at once," the steward said nervously. He would not mention the word "plague."

"I'll tell you the moment that any marks show, and you'll call another nurse and I'll hand over to her," Alinor assured him.

"I'll send over everything," Mr. Tudeley promised, then descended the ladder and closed the hatch behind him. Alinor waited a moment and then went over and bolted it from her side, so that no one could come up the stairs unexpectedly. She and James were quite alone.

She went to where they had left him, limp as a corpse in the rug, and she unfolded him, as if she were unwrapping a precious parcel. As the carpet fell away, he sighed and seemed to gasp for air. Alinor lifted his head and shoulders a little and slid a bolster behind his head. He seemed to breathe easier and a little color came into his cheek. She found she was looking at his pale mouth and remembering how he had kissed her.

She unbuttoned his fine lawn shirt. The buttons were made from mother-of-pearl. She touched each one, seeing the sheen on it, and then opened his shirt so that she could see his chest and his belly.

His shoulders were broad, his chest and belly flat. He was well muscled as a man who rides and runs every day. A dark trace of hair ran from his belly down towards his breeches and Alinor, who had undressed her drunken husband more than once, unlaced his breeches without hesitation and peeled back the flap. For the first time she saw him naked. She saw the darkness of his thick hair, the strength of his sleeping cock, the muscled line of his haunches. She looked at him for no more than a moment and felt her desire like a fever of her own. Carefully, she eased the breeches from under him, bending over him and smelling the clean warm male scent of him; she had to stop herself dropping her head to kiss his belly and laying her cheek against his hot skin.

She peeled the riding breeches off him, down to his boots, and then she unlaced the boots and slipped them from his feet, then the fine hose. He lay before her naked, except for his open shirt and jacket.

There were no red spots of smallpox. She lifted one arm and

then another and felt in his armpits. There were no swellings of the buboes that were a certain sign of plague. There was no sign, on any part of his smooth creamy skin, that anything was wrong with him except the heat of him: he was burning up with fever.

Gently she raised him higher on the bolster, and felt him nestle towards her and groan a little as if he were in pain. She buttoned up his shirt again to protect him from cold, and she felt a passionate tenderness as she did so, as if she were tending to Rob or Alys when they were babies. She left the rich carpet underneath him, and she covered him with one of the blankets from the other bed. Most physicians would heap blankets on a feverish patient and add a warming pan to burn out the fever. Alinor treated her patients as she had treated her children, keeping them cool and still. Again, she put her hand against his forehead. She could almost feel the heat pulsing through the blue veins at his temples. She put two fingers inside his shirt collar on his neck and felt the drumming of his heartbeat.

There was a call from the yard outside, and she went to the window and opened it to find Stuart, the serving man, with linen and small ale, a bucket of hot water and some washing bowls, some linen towels and a box of herbs and oils chosen by Rob from the stillroom. There was a pulley and a rope above the window for raising sacks of grain. Alinor lowered the hook and Stuart sent up the basket loaded with a tureen of soup, and bread and cheeses on platters, then all the other things he had brought, until he said: "Will that be all, Mrs. Reekie?" as if Alinor were a guest and not a servant like him.

"That's all," she said. "Tell Rob to come here after breakfast. I'll speak to him from here. But nobody is to come in until I know what ails the tutor."

"Beg pardon, Mrs. Reekie, but d'you think it might be plague?" Stuart whispered fearfully.

"There are no signs now," she said cautiously. "I will watch him today in case of the signs. There are no marks on him yet. Wait there." She went to her basket of herbs and brought out a bunch of dried sage, and tossed it down to him. "Light this at the kitchen fire," she said, "and then blow it out and bring it to me still smoking."

He was gone only a few moments and brought it back, smoldering in an earthenware bowl. Alinor lowered the rope and he put it in the basket and she pulled it up.

"Does it summon spirits?" he whispered. "Are you calling them up?"

Alinor shook her head. "It cleanses the air," she said firmly. "I do no work with spirits or anything like that. Just herbs and oils, like anyone else."

He nodded, but he did not believe her.

"That's all," Alinor said, thinking that however often she denied the rumors of magic they clung to her, and to all the women of her family, like the mist from the mire.

"God bless us all," Stuart gasped, and scuttled to the kitchen door.

Alinor took the stems of the smoldering sage and walked around the room, shaking the burning leaves so that the cleansing scent went into every corner. Then she set it back on the bowl and left it to smoke. She opened the sack of physic to see what Rob had sent her. There was a stick of cinnamon, a jar with a lemon bottled in oil, and a bottle of distilled holy basil from the Peachey stillroom. Alinor thought that James might have taken tertian fever, a sickness that lingered in the mire, striking visitors, and staying with them for life, coming back three times a year and so earning its name. The first bout of illness was always the worst, often fatal; the others wore the patient down, as he became feverish and delirious. Most of the Foulmire families took it as children: Rob had it as a child, and Zachary had quatrain fever every season. Alinor's mother believed it came from the bites of the flies that whined noisily in your ear as you slept, and advised her daughter to plant marigolds and lavender at windows and doorways to keep them out. It was no surprise to Alinor that the man she loved had been poisoned by the flies that lived on the waters of her home. This proved he should never have come; and, once he had left, he should never have come back. It was a sign to them both.

His fever did not break all night. She sponged him down with water and her own lavender oil. She added the oil of lemon to the soup, and she grated cinnamon over it as she spooned it down his throat, but he remained half conscious, in a fevered sleep, turning his head from side to side, and speaking words, Latin words, that she could not understand but that she feared were heresy or magic, or both.

He was only still when she held him, one arm around his shoulders, as she helped him to drink small ale, which she dosed with more lemon oil. Only then was he quiet, as if her touch cooled him, and so, as the night wore on till dawn, she held him, leaning back against the rough wooden wall, his hot head on her shoulder, her arms around him. He nuzzled his head into her neck as if he wanted the cool of her skin against his face, and he slept.

When the thick horn windows showed a cloudy light, he groaned with pain, staggered to his feet, and crammed his fists against his belly. She knew what was coming and tucked the pail beneath his buttocks as he voided himself, doubled over in agony.

"There," she said, "there," as if he were one of her sick children, and washed him with Beard-Papa water that she had brought from her home. She lowered the stinking pail on the pulley, and called to the stable boy to tip it in the midden and wash out the pail and return it. Then she washed her hands in the Beard-Papa water and made herself as comfortable as she could against the planking of the wooden wall, and once again took him in her arms and laid his head on her shoulder.

Alinor dozed, dreaming incoherent dreams of love, of a man who spoke of "a woman like you in a place like this," of a world where women were not condemned in church before the men who were sinners like them, who had sinned with them. She dreamed of Alys and her sweetheart, Richard Stoney, of Rob and the life he might live if they were not poor and born to be poor, of Zachary sailing far away and saying into the wind of the dream, as he had once said so bitterly to her: "Your trouble is that nothing real is ever enough for you."

She woke in daylight, cramped, with a sense of defeat. All her pride in her passion of the night was gone. She thought Zachary was right and that she had misled herself and misled her children, and he had spoken the truth—not when he said that she danced with faeries, but that she longed to be with them. All her life she had wanted more than the life she was born to; but this morning she knew she had sunk very low: a poor woman, about to be disgraced before her neighbors, working as that lowest of beings: a plague nurse, almost a layer-out, only one step above a porter of a plague cart heaped with dead bodies, calling for people to bring out their dead. She knew no work lower than a plague nurse, and her folly and her love had brought her down to this: locked up with a dying man, who was foresworn, and who had never said that he loved her.

Still, she held him; knowing herself to be a fool, and ashamed of her folly. But then she realized James was warm in her arms, not cold and stiffening, not sweating and dying. He was warm and sweet-smelling, like a man who would live, and his eyes were opening and his color was good.

"Alinor," he croaked, as if he was saying her name for the very first time.

"Are you better?" she asked incredulously.

"I can hardly speak. I don't know. Yes."

"Don't speak. You were very ill."

"I thought I was going to die."

"You're not going to die. It's not the plague."

"Thank God. I thank God."

"Amen," she said.

Blearily, he looked around. "Are we in the net shed again?"

"No! The hayloft at the Priory. You fell sick. D'you remember?"

"No. Nothing." He frowned. "I brought the boys home from Cowes."

"You did. They're safe. Then you had a great fever."

He struggled with the memory of the lies that he had to uphold, but he could not remember them. He could not be sure anymore what was true and what was false. "I'm so thirsty."

She offered him small ale and he drank it gratefully, but she allowed him only one cup. "Slowly, slowly, you can have more later."

"I'm not sure what I said, what I may have spoken in my sleep . . ."

"Nothing that made sense," she reassured him. "Sir William sent for me after midnight. He told me nothing. You were lying on a rug before the fire. He said only that you had fainted. When I got here, you were dazed with fever."

He nodded. "I can remember nothing."

She thought that he must spend his life forgetting half of it, and speaking of less, and now oblivion had come to him, like a curse in answer to a wish.

"His lordship sent for me and asked me to come up here with you to make sure that it was not the plague."

"You came to me . . . although you said . . ."

"Yes," she said steadily. "The lord of the manor sent for me. I had to."

"But you agreed to nurse me."

"His lordship asked me. I had to."

"You came to me," he insisted. "You chose to come."

She showed him the sweetest, most generous smile. "I came to you," she confirmed.

"And undressed me."

"I had to see if you had the marks of the pox or the plague."

"And stayed with me all night."

"To watch over your fever."

"You held me in your arms."

"It was the only way you would lie still, and not toss and turn and throw off the covers."

"I was naked in your arms."

She pursed her lips. "For your own good."

He was silent for a moment. "My God, I wish I could be naked in your arms again."

"Hush," she said, wondering how much they could hear in the stable below. "Hush."

"I will not hush," he whispered. "I have to speak. Alinor, I thought I would go away without seeing you again, I thought we would never meet. I have lost my faith—my God—I am forsworn so many ways. I have lost my king and my God and myself. But I thought there would be some meaning to my life if only I could see you again—and now you are here."

"I am not faith, nor God, nor king," she told him solemnly. "I am not even a woman of good repute. I know you met Zachary at Newport. He will have told you—unless the fever has made you forget—he must have told you that I'm a bad woman: neither widow nor wife."

"He swore to all sorts of terrors. I don't regard them," he promised. "I didn't listen to him, and I didn't believe him. I can't remember anything he said." He did not even know that he was lying to her. "I thought I would never see you again—I am ordered to leave you, and leave Foulmire—and now here we are, locked up together, almost as if it is God's will that we should never part. I swear in His name that I don't want to be anywhere else. I've lost everything but you. I thought I was dying, and when I was at the very darkest moment, the only thing I wanted was you. I could not speak, I could not think, I could not pray: all I wanted was you. I thought I was dreaming that you were holding me. I thought it was a fever dream of desire. I would not have come back to life if it had not been for your touch."

They were silent for a moment at the enormity of what he had said.

"When I tell them you're well, you'll be free to go," she warned him. "And I'll have to leave. You'll go to your bedroom at the Priory to rest and grow strong, and I'll go home and come back tomorrow to see that you continue well. Sir William may call the Chichester physician."

"Then tell them you won't know till tomorrow," he instantly replied, and when she hesitated, he said again: "Alinor, I am begging you. We have no chance, we two. We have no chance to be together in the world, but we can have today and tonight, if you will just tell this one, this little lie, we can hold each other. Tell them that you are waiting to see the fever break, or the spots come out, or whatever it is that you might wait for. And give us today and tonight and tomorrow, here alone. Nothing more. I ask you for nothing more. But I beg this of you."

She hesitated.

"You need not lie with me unless you choose to," he offered. "I ask nothing of you but to be here with you. You can see I can't force you." As he spoke he realized that he was unmanned, as Zachary had said he would be. He shook his head to clear it of the malign thought. "I don't want to force you. You shall not be constrained. I won't even touch you if you don't allow it. But, Alinor, give me a day and a night with you before I go out into that world where I have lost everything but you."

Without replying she rose up from the bed and she untied the laces down the front of her linen shift, so that he saw, for the first time, the curve of her breasts. She untied the waistband of her skirt and dropped it to the floor so that she was naked but for her open shift, and beneath it, he saw the outline of the long line of her haunches and thighs.

"If you want, we will have today and tonight," she agreed, like a woman preparing to drown in deep water. "Today and tonight," and she came to his arms, half naked.

At noon Rob came to the yard under the window. Alinor leaned out, smiled down at her son, and told him that she was sure it was not the plague but she would stay and nurse Mr. Summer until his fever had broken. She praised him for the herbs he had chosen and said that she needed no more, just another jar of oil of lemon to bring down the fever. She told him to ask Mrs. Wheatley for more small ale and for Stuart to send up their dinner in a basket. She said that Mr. Summer was sleeping and he was feverish but no worse.

"But how are you, Rob? You don't have it?"

"I'm well," Rob said, looking up at her. "And Walter is well, too. I checked him for heat and I looked at his throat. No inflammation, no spots on his back or his chest. Whatever ails Mr. Summer, I don't think Walter and me have it."

"God be praised," Alinor said. "And, Rob," she lowered her voice as he stepped closer to the wall and looked trustingly up at her. "Don't be troubled about your father. Mr. Summer won't speak of meeting him and we need say nothing. Don't speak of Zachary till I come out and we can agree what we want to say. Especially, Rob . . . don't be unhappy about him. He has made his choice and will live his life. We'll make ours. You should be happy. You have so much to look forward to."

He nodded, his eyes on her face.

"And go and tell Alys to stay the night at Ferry-house," she instructed him. "I'll be home tomorrow. And say nothing to her yet."

She blew him a kiss and he ducked his head in embarrassment, waved his hand to her, and went from the yard.

James, in his makeshift bed, watched her close the window and step back so that she could not be seen from the yard below.

"All well with him?" he asked her.

"God be praised," she said.

He found he could not say: "Amen." He thought that he could no longer speak to his God.

"I think I should make a new bed for you with clean sheets," she said. "And shall I ask Stuart to bring water for you to wash?"

"Yes," he said. "And we shall have all day and all night," he said. "This is like a dream, as if I still had fever."

At once she put the back of her hand against his forehead. "No," she said. "No fever and it's no dream."

"And tomorrow . . ."

"Let's not think of tomorrow till we have to," she whispered, and he drew her down to him, as he lay on the bed and pressed her against him.

The hours went by unnoticed. Two or three times Stuart called from the yard below, and Alinor threw on her gown and let down the rope from the window. He passed up food, water for washing, ale for drinking, but they hardly noticed how often he came, nor what he brought. Alinor made up the bed with clean linen and they both lay down together naked, made love, fell asleep, and woke to make love again. They watched the sun set over the marshes from the west window, and they saw the moon set. All night they stirred and woke and made love and slept, as if there was neither night nor day, and they needed no light but the flickering candle that made their moving bodies glow.

"I never knew that it was like this," James confessed. "When the brothers spoke of the love of a woman in the seminary I thought it was somehow harder and cruel."

"Was this your first time? Your very first?" Alinor asked, feeling a pang of guilt as if she had sinned against James and taken his innocence.

"I've been tempted," he said. "When I was in hiding and traveling from one house to another. There was a lady in London, and another at a house in Essex, I knew that I felt desire; but it always felt like sin, and I could resist it; but this feels right."

Alinor imagined that the handsome young priest had been desired by more than one woman, receiving him into her house and hiding him from everyone, delighting in the secret. She laughed at the thought of it and at once his face lightened. "You must think me a fool," he said. "To be a virgin at my age!"

"No," she assured him. "I've learned to despise a man who has been with many women and loved none. Zachary was the only man I was ever with, and he was a hard husband. They were right to teach you that at the seminary. Hard and bitter and . . . thankless." She found the truest word. "It was a thankless task being wife to Zachary."

He took a bright lock of her hair and twisted it around his third finger as if it were a ring. "And have you had no man since him?"

She looked at him. "Did he tell you otherwise?"

He shook his head. "He told me all sorts of fears and terrors," he said. "I was not asking because of his lies, but because I cannot believe that no one courted you."

"I had no desire," she told him. "If anyone had asked me—but nobody speaks of such things on Foulmire—I would have said that I was one of those women who feel no desire. For me, it was always pain and harsh treatment. Zachary said that I was cold as stone to him, and I thought there was no other way to be. I never knew that it could be like this."

He smiled at her and touched her warm cheek with his finger.

"When I delivered a baby sometimes, and the woman asked me when she could lie with her husband again, I never understood why she would want to. I would tell her she must wait for two months, until she was churched, and I used to wonder why she complained that it was so long."

"Would it seem long to you now?"

"A day would seem too long a time to wait, now."

"So now you understand love?"

"For the first time." She smiled at him. "So it is the first time for me too, in a way."

He kissed her hand. "The woman of stone has melted?"

"I've become a woman of desire."

Later in the night they woke, ravenously hungry, and ate the rest of the bread and cheese, good white bread from the Priory bread oven, smooth hard cheese with a salty crust from the Priory dairy.

"Zachary spoke of something," James said tentatively, afraid of the darkening of her eyes, of her turning away.

"Oh, he's one that never stopped speaking," she said, with a smile. "He thundered like the tide mill at every low tide."

"He said that Ned had a wife . . ." he began.

His words were like a blow. He had knocked the smile off her. At once she went as white as guilt.

"I'm sorry. I didn't mean . . . Don't say anything," he begged her. "You need say nothing. It was just . . ."

"Did you believe him? Will you repeat to Sir William . . . what he said? Whatever it was he said? Are you bound by your vows to tell the minister at St. Wilfrid's?"

"No, I'll never say. I wouldn't have said anything now but . . ."

"But he made you wonder," she said slowly. "For all your learning, and your languages, and your knowledge—for all your faith!—he made you wonder. He made you . . . afraid."

"I'm not afraid!" he started up, but she put a gentle hand on his shoulder.

"If the world was as Zachary sees it, we would all be afraid," she said gently. "For like a poor fool he has peopled it with monsters to frighten himself. He speaks of me as a woman who lies with faerie folk. He denies his own children. He says I cast a spell that unmanned him. He says that I killed my poor sister-in-law, Mary. You know, if people around here believed just one of these things, they would test me as a witch?"

He shook his head in denial of the terrible accusations against her. "They must know you're innocent!"

"You didn't know."

"I did! I do!"

"You know what they would do to me?"

"I don't know." He did not want to know.

"They have a ducking stool on Sealsea quay and they strap a woman into the seat, truss her like a kitten for drowning. The seat is on a great beam that the blacksmith—usually it's the blacksmith—pushes down on the other end. The woman goes up into the air, where everyone can see her, then he lowers her down into the water, underneath the water. They take their time and when they judge that the trial has been long enough, they bring her up and raise her in the air again, to have a look at her. If she's retching seawater, they say that the devil has protected her, and they send her to Chichester, for trial in the court before the judges, who will hear the evidence and may sentence her to death by hanging. But if she comes up white as sea-foam, and blue as ink at the lips and fingernails, her mouth open from screaming in the water, her hands like claws from tearing at the ropes, then they know she was innocent, and they bury her in the holy ground in the churchyard."

"I've heard of such things but—"

"It's the law that every parish should have a ducking stool. You must know that."

"I thought it was just a ducking?"

She showed him a thin smile. "Yes, that's what it's called. Makes it sound light work, doesn't it? And some women are only ducked. But of course, some drown."

"Sir William should make sure it is only a ducking."

She shrugged. "He should. When he's here. But it's better for Sir William that they duck a witch from time to time, and blame some poor woman for their misfortunes, than ask him whose side he took at Marston Moor, what he did at Newbury—and why they should pay their tithes to him."

"That's got nothing to do with it! He's paid his fine for serving the king. And he's been forgiven by parliament."

"We'll never forgive him," she said, speaking for her brother, for all the men who hoped for a better life without a lord. "He took a dozen lads from Sealsea with the king's cockade in their hats, and he brought only seven home."

"But that has nothing to do with it," he explained patiently. "And he's a civilized man—he would stop a witch trial. He's a justice of the peace—he would uphold the law. He's an educated man, a lawyer. He wouldn't hurt an innocent woman."

She smiled at him as if he were a child. "No woman is innocent," she remarked and her words made him shudder as if it were

Zachary speaking. "No woman is innocent. The Bible names the woman as the one to blame for bringing sin into the world. Everything is our fault: sin and death are at our door, from now till Judgment Day. Sir William isn't going to risk his own authority by stepping in to save some poor slut from drowning."

He was chilled by her cynicism, and he did not want to hear her. He wanted her back in his bed, warm and responsive. She had been hardened by the cruelties of her life and he wanted her to be soft and melting.

"But it doesn't matter to us," he suggested. "And I daresay there was nothing in what Zachary said anyway, about your sister-in-law?"

"Mary died under my care," she told him frankly. "And the world knew well enough that we quarreled like a cat and a dog in the same barn, every day since Ned brought her into Ferry-house and set her up in my mother's place. I disliked her and she loathed me. But, all the same, I cared for her the best that I knew how. I didn't know what should be done for her; I don't think anybody would have known. Her baby came too soon, and it was a bitter stillbirth for us all. Then I couldn't stop her bleeding. She died in my arms and I couldn't save her. I don't even know what caused either death: hers or the child's. I'm not a physician, I'm just a midwife."

"Zachary said it was his child, and you were jealous," he said, and instantly regretted it.

She looked at him very coolly and levelly. She drew the sheet around her shoulders as if it was a silken stole. "He told you that, did he?" Suddenly she was cold. "Well, you must be the judge of what you hear. I've never defended myself against Zachary's lies, and I'll not reply to his foul words in your sweet mouth. But if it was his child—as he boasted to me, after she was dead and couldn't answer back—then I doubt she was willing."

He shivered with distaste. He felt that he could not bear the ugliness of these people's lives on the very edge of the shore, with their loves and hates ebbing and flowing like a muddy tide, with their anger roaring like the water in the millrace, with their hatreds and fears as treacherous as the hushing well. That Zachary might have raped his sister-in-law, or seduced her, that he bedded his own wife without her consent, that her brother tolerated this, and instead of putting it right, went away to fight against the king, that Alinor's own husband denied fathering her children! James's shudder told him that he wanted nothing to do with any of them. He wished himself back with his own people, where cruelty was secret, violence was hidden, and good manners more important than crime.

Tentatively, he reached out to her; he wanted her to be the lover of his feverish dream, not the woman who struggled in this sordid world. "I believe in you. I believe in you, Alinor."

The face she turned to him was warm and trusting, her eyes brimming with tears. "You can," she said simply, and he felt that he was falling into the deepest sin as he kissed her soft mouth and her wet eyelashes as they rested on her cheeks.

After that, they kept to their promise not to think of the world outside the stable loft; not to think of tomorrow; but at dawn, making love even before they were fully awake, when her eyelids fluttered open in pleasure, she saw the dim light at the window and she said quietly, sorrowfully, "Ah, my love, it's morning."

"Not yet," he said, moving slowly above her. "That's moonlight."

"No. It's dawn. And I have to go back to my home today, and we have to tell Sir William that you are well."

He rested his head on her shoulder as he moved within her. "I can't bear it."

"Can't bear the pleasure or can't bear the parting?"

"Both. Can't we say that I am still ill? Can't we take another day? Alinor, my love, can't we steal another day together?"

"No. You know we can't. Neither of us can come under suspicion."

"I won't let you go."

She raised herself up to his kiss and her rich hair tumbled back from her face. "Let me kiss you once," she said, "and then I'll get up and get dressed."

He wanted to hold her, but she shook her head and he rolled away and lay back, gripping his hands behind his head so that he should not snatch at her, as she leaned over him and kissed him passionately on the mouth and then rested her forehead on his chest, inhaling the scent of him as if he were a rose beneath her lips. Then she peeled herself off him, as if she were shedding her own skin, and turned away, to pull her linen shift over her head so that the stiff fabric fell, concealing her.

"I can't do this," he said quietly. "I really can't be parted from you."

She said nothing, but stepped into her skirt and tied the laces at her waist with meticulous care, and then sat on a bench at the side of the room to pull on her woolen hose.

"Alinor," he breathed.

"Let me dress!" Her voice was choked. "I can't dress and speak. I can't hear your voice and think. Let me dress."

He sat up in the bed in silence while she twisted her hair into a knot at the back of her head and pulled on her white cap, crumpled as it was. When she turned to him she was, once again, the respectable midwife of Sealsea Island; and the tranced lover of the night was hidden under the shapeless bulky clothes.

"Now you," she said.

He started towards her and she put out her hand to fend him off. "Don't touch me," she begged him. "Just get dressed."

He pulled on his linen shirt. For the first time in his life he noticed what fine linen he wore, and he thought that the first thing he would do, as soon as he was well, would be to go to Chichester and buy her some beautiful shifts, as smooth as her flawless skin. He pulled on his hose, heaved up his breeches, stamped his feet into his riding boots, and turned to her.

"I'm dressed," he said. "Are you satisfied?"

Her dark eyes in her pale face were huge. "No," she said

quietly. "I am longing for you again, already. But we have to be ready to face the world and the day."

He heard the echo of Zachary in the back of his mind: that she was a woman that no man could ever satisfy. He shook his head. "Where will you go?" he asked, as if she had anywhere to go but the poor fisherman's cottage.

"Home."

"I shall stay here for a few days and then I will have to go to London and then to my seminary," he told her, trusting her with his secrets as he had trusted her with his sin. "But, Alinor, my love, it is all changed for me. I have lost my faith and failed in my mission. I have to go and tell them that, and I will have to confess, and then, I suppose, I shall have to leave. I will have to beg them to release me."

She looked alarmed. "You have to confess? You have to speak of this?"

He grimaced. "These are mortal sins. I have broken so many of my vows. I have to confess. My loss of faith is worse than this, but I have to confess this too and face my punishment."

"Will they punish me too?" she asked.

He could have laughed at her ignorance. "I won't say your name," he assured her. "They won't even know where you live. They cannot report you."

"D'you have to speak of us?"

"I have to make a full confession, great sins and lesser."

She wondered which was the greater sin and which the lesser. But she did not ask. She would not have claimed her own importance. "If you confess to them, mightn't they keep you there?"

"I don't think they will want me," he said desolately. "I have failed in everything they sent me to do. And I have lost my faith as well."

"But even so, mightn't they keep you? Can they keep you? Can they make you stay there? Can they lock you up?"

"They would not keep me against my will, I know that. But they will make it very difficult to leave. They will have to be convinced that I am sure. I can never go back, you see. If I leave, I can never return. They will see this as a betrayal of my duty and of my faith. And they have been father and mother and schoolmaster to me as well as my way to God. They will be sorry, as I am sorry."

She looked very grave. "You are sorry?"

"But I will come back to you."

The flush on her face told him what that meant to her, but she shook her head. "Don't come back for me," she said quietly. "This has been everything to me, but you can't come back here for me. I'm not fit for you. I couldn't live in your world, and you'd never live in mine."

"But we have been lovers as if the world was ending!"

"But it's not ending," she said reasonably. She found a little smile. "Outside, everything goes on. I've got to go back to my life, you've got to return to yours, whatever it turns out to be. Faith or no faith. King or no king. And even if everything's changed for you, nothing changes for me. Nothing ever changes for me."

"Have I not made a change for you?" he demanded. "Are you not a woman of desire, as you said? Will you go back to stone?"

She turned her head from him. "I won't be dead to myself again," she promised. "I won't turn back to stone. But I wouldn't survive long in my world as a woman of desire. I have to harden, or someone will destroy me."

"My family are in exile," he told her, his voice very low. "My mother and father are in exile, our lands and houses sequestered—do you know what that means?"

She shook her head.

"My father was appointed by the king to advise the Prince of Wales," he said. "When the prince went into exile, my father and mother went with him. Our lands were sequestered—that means taken by parliament, to punish us. My father and mother are now at the queen's court in Paris. But if we left the royal courts, made an agreement with parliament, surrendered to them and paid a fine, just as Sir William has done, we could get our lands back, just as he has done. I could live in my family house. It's in Yorkshire, a long way from here—a beautiful house and good farmlands. I could get it back; my mother and father could return to England."

"Would they want to?" she asked. "Would they want to live with a new minister in their church, and new men in power? Under a parliament, not a king?"

He waved away her objection. "What I'm saying is that I could get our house back, I could return home. I'd be in England again, not an exile, not a spy, not in hiding."

She tried to find a smile. "I'd like to think of you living in your house with your lands around you. I'd look at the moon and know it was shining on you, as it was shining on me. I'd like to think of you at the water's edge as the tide ebbed, while I stood on the tidemark in Foulmire."

"It's a different tide, and anyway we're inland," he said, distracted by her ignorance. "But that's not what I mean. I mean to say: I won't leave you here. I would not return to my house without you. I will take you there, to my home."

She looked at him as if he were speaking Latin, as if he were quite incomprehensible. "What?"

"Would you come with me to Yorkshire? Will you marry me?"

"Marry?" she asked wonderingly. "Marry?"

"Yes," he said steadily. "Why not? If there is no king on the throne and no bishops in their palaces, if there is no royalty nor church, if all degree is leveled and there is neither master nor man as the radicals say, then why should I not marry you?"

She held out her hands to show him the roughness of a workingwoman's palms. She spread her tatty brown skirt caked with foul mud at the hem. "Look at me," she said bleakly. "You will see that the radicals are mistaken. There is still master and man. You can't take me to your mother and ask her to accept me as a daughter-in-law. I can't go with you and be a lady in your house. The woman who is to be your wife is far above me. You can't put me in her place."

He was about to argue but she went on: "And you've forgotten? I can't marry anyway—I'm married to Zachary, and we both know he's still alive. We couldn't stand before an altar and take vows. I've two young children and they know their father. I couldn't go to your home as an honest woman, a widow. I'm not an honest woman. I've been your slut here, I've been your whore. I've lain with you without a promise. I don't demand one now. I couldn't even be your mistress. I'm not even fit for that."

He flushed as if he was scalded with her shame. "Don't say such things! You're no slut! You're no whore! I've never loved anyone as I love you! This has been sacred! Sacred! This is a first and last for me."

"I know! I know!" The first words of love calmed her. For a moment, he saw a glimpse of her smile. "For me too. Oh, James—me too. And that'll be a joy to me when you're gone and I'm left here."

"I can't leave you here," he said. "I have to be with you."

She shrugged as if the world were full of incomprehensible disappointments, and this was another. "I wish it was different," was all she said. He came closer and she stretched out her hand to him, but she was not reaching for him, she was gently fending him off. She touched his cheek with the back of her fingers. He caught her hand and pressed it to his mouth.

"Don't hold me," she said very low. "I can't leave you if you take hold of me. I can't pull away from you. I think I'll die if I have to push you away. Please let me go. I've got to leave you now."

"I'll come to your cottage tonight," he whispered. "We can't say good-bye like this."

"I'm not for you. Our worlds are very far apart."

"I'll come to you. I'll come tonight."

"Then we'll only have to say good-bye again."

"I want to say good-bye again. This cannot be the last time that I see you."

"Tonight, when it is dark," she agreed reluctantly. "But I'll come to you. It's high tide, the path isn't safe for you. I'll meet you in the sea meadow outside the Priory. Where we said good-bye before."

"Tonight," he said again as she turned, unbolted the hatch, and made her way down the ladder to the stable yard, where the grooms were sleepily watering the horses, and brushing them down.

He watched her go, the basket on her arm, the neat white cap on her head. He saw her speak a pleasant "good morning" to the grooms, and saw them turn and watch her as she walked across the yard to the house. Behind her back one lad made an obscene gesture pumping his buttocks to mimic lust, but the other did worse: he gathered spittle in his mouth and he spat on her tracks, and clenched his thumb inside his fist, in the old, old gesture of guarding against a witch.

"His lordship wants to see you," Mrs. Wheatley said to Alinor as she came into the kitchen. "Good Lord! Mrs. Reekie! I've never seen you in such good looks. You're glowing!"

"Your good cooking," Alinor said lightly. "I've eaten better these last two days than I have for weeks. I shall come to nurse at the Priory again if I can."

"Pray God we're spared illness," Mrs. Wheatley said.

"Amen," Alinor answered correctly. "His lordship is well?"

"Yes, but he asked you to go to his gun room before you leave this morning. You can go now. Stuart will show you in."

"Why does he want to see me?" Alinor hesitated.

"It can only be to thank you," the cook replied. "You saved us all from great worry, and perhaps you saved the island from sickness. Go, you've got nothing to fear."

"Thank you," Alinor said, going to the door into the house.

"Come back this way and I'll give you a loaf of bread to keep that bloom in your cheeks," Mrs. Wheatley said.

Alinor smiled and followed Stuart down the corridor towards the garden door and his lordship's gun room.

Sir William was seated at the table, cleaning his flintlock rifle.

He glanced up and nodded when Alinor knocked, came in, and stood before him.

"Goodwife Reekie, I'm grateful to you," he said, looking down the barrel. "Thank God it was no worse than a fever."

She nodded. He took care to pay attention to his gun and not to look at the curve of her breasts under the bulky jacket.

"Your son, Robert, found his way round the stillroom. He's a bright lad. He fetched all the things you needed?"

"Yes, he knew what was wanted for a fever," she said. She thought her voice sounded thin, as if the light was too bright and Sir William was too loud.

"Nobody told him what to get. He picked out the things himself?" He took up a piece of wadding and polished the beautiful enameled stock.

"He's watched me since he was a baby. He's got a gift with herbs and their use."

"James Summer said some time ago that he was fit to be a servant to a physician, or apprenticed to an apothecary."

Alinor bowed her head. "I think so, but we couldn't afford his entry fee."

His lordship put the cleaning cloth and the oil to one side, racked the gun, and sat back in his chair. He looked her up and down, and felt again the regret that she was a respectable woman and the sister of a pious man. "I tell you what, Goodwife, I'll do it for you. He's a good lad, a credit to you. He's been a merry companion for Master Walter and you've been a great help to me and my house. Just now with the tutor falling sick . . . and I know about earlier."

For a moment, she could not speak. "Your lordship!"

He nodded. "I'll get Mr. Tudeley to arrange for him to go as an apprentice, an apprentice to an apothecary, so he can get a training and a trade. Chichester or perhaps Portsmouth, I suppose."

She was breathless with shock.

"Aye," he nodded, thinking again that she was a beautiful woman. If only Sealsea Island had not been such a center of gossip, and so damnably godly, he might have brought her into his household, called her a housekeeper, and used her as his whore.

"I'm sorry, but I can't accept. I can't afford even the clothes he would need," she said. "I don't have the savings—"

"Tudeley will take care of that," he said, waving away her objection. "How's that? We'll give him a suit of clothes, and buy him his apprenticeship as payment for your . . . help. How's that?"

Her face lit up. "You would do that?"

His lordship thought that he would do much, much more, if she were willing. But he merely nodded.

"He'll be so glad. I know he'll work hard." She stumbled over her thanks. "We'll owe you a debt of gratitude . . . forever . . . I can't thank you—"

"I'll get it done," Sir William concluded. "These are difficult times for all of us, you know."

She nodded earnestly, wondering what he meant now.

"Dangerous times for some."

"Yes, sir."

"I suppose in his fever, the tutor didn't speak out at all?"

Alinor checked her breathless thanks and stole a quick look at her landlord from under the brim of her white cap, knowing that this question was the most important moment in the whole of this interview.

"Speak out? Sir?"

"In his fever. Men say odd things when their minds are affected by illness, don't they? He didn't say anything, did he? Anything that I'd not want widely known? Or known at all? Anything that I wouldn't want repeated? Not even here?"

"He didn't say anything that I heard." She picked her words with care, knowing that this was important, feeling perilously ill prepared to deal with a powerful man like her landlord. "Sir, people in fever often say fanciful things, things they wouldn't say in waking life. I never take notice, never repeat them. I wouldn't speak of things that I see and hear in the sickroom. Being deaf is part of the craft. Being dumb is part of being a woman. I don't want any trouble. The day I spent nursing him, I won't speak of, not to anyone."

He nodded, measuring her reliability. "Not to your brother, eh?"

She met his gaze with complete comprehension. "Especially not him," she confirmed.

"Then we understand each other. You can consider your son apprenticed to a Chichester apothecary."

She bowed her head and clasped her hands. "I thank you, sir," she said simply.

He put his hand into his pocket and pulled out a handful of shillings. He made them into a little tower and slid them across the table to her.

"Your wages for nursing him. Ten shillings a day. There's a pound. And my thanks."

She picked them up with a little nod and put them into her apron pocket. "Thank you."

He got up and came around the table. She stood before him and he put a hand on her arm. "You could come back tonight?" he said, unable to resist, looking down the front of her linen shift at the curve of her breast. "To visit me."

He tightened his grip and drew her towards him, but to his surprise she did not move. She did not yield to him; but nor did she shrink back. She was as steady as if she were rooted to the spot.

"You know I can't do that, sir," she said simply. "If I did that, I couldn't take my pay: it'd be whore's gold. I couldn't hold up my head, I couldn't let you be a patron to Rob. I wouldn't think of myself a good tenant to a good lord. I don't want that."

His grip felt weak, as if his fingers were powerless with cold. Still, she stood her ground, as if she were growing there, like a hawthorn tree, and he could not draw her closer. She stood like a stone, and looked at him coolly with a dark confident gaze until he felt awkward and stupid, and remembered the rumor that she could freeze a man's cock with a look.

"Yes," he said. "I suppose so."

There was a little silence. She did not seem shocked; she was neither flattered nor fearful. She stood, waiting for him to take his hand off her arm, and let her go. He supposed that men desired her all the time and that she regarded a touch at her breast, a grab at her waist, as a regular inconvenience, like rain.

"Oh, well," he said, letting her go, and returning to his seat behind his table, as if to restore himself to authority. "So: your lad. He can go to his apprenticeship when Walter goes to university."

She nodded. "And when'll that be, sir?" she asked as calmly as if he had not propositioned her, as if it was merely another thing that she had not heard and would not repeat.

Despite his own discomfiture, he smiled at her cool grace. "He'll go in the Lent term," he said. "After Christmas."

Alinor walked quickly on the hidden paths across the mire from the Priory to her home. The tide was ebbing and, as she went deeper into the harbor on the hidden ways, she could hear the suck and hiss of the waves reluctantly leaving the land, like her fears dogging her quick footsteps. As she walked past the net shed she heard the roar of the tide mill starting up, and saw the spout of water burst out of the millrace, coming directly towards her.

She turned inland and climbed the path to her cottage, opened the door, and looked around. Suddenly the place seemed very small and poor compared to the groom's loft at the Priory. Even the lowliest servants lived better than she did. She put the loaf of Priory bread under the bread cover, and saw that the fire was dark and cold in the hearth. She levered up the hearthstone and found her little purse of savings, safely buried. She took the twenty shillings for nursing James out of her apron pocket and added them to the purse with a satisfying clink of coins. Then she pressed the hearthstone back into place, and dusted the ashes over it.

She rose up, brushing down her gown, and went to the front door. For a moment, she looked around at the cramped room, the low ceiling, the beaten floor of mud. Then she turned away from her shame at her poverty, and went outside, closing the door behind her, and along the bank to the ferry.

The ferry-house door was closed, the ferry pulling at its mooring rope as the tide ebbed. The raised wadeway was nearly dry and Alinor lifted her skirt and paddled across in the cold water, and then walked down the lane to the mill.

Alys was crossing the mill yard, carrying a bucket filled with eggs. Now that harvest was over, she was working as a maid-of-all-work for Mrs. Miller, gardening in the vegetable and herb patch, feeding and keeping the hens, feeding the ducks, picking and storing the fruit, smoking hams and curing meat. She worked in the dairy too, and in the brewhouse. If they were shorthanded in the mill she would help to weigh and bag the flour. Mrs. Miller might order her to help with baking in the mill oven, and always there was the endless task of scouring and rinsing, scalding and drying the tools for the dairy, for the brewery and the kitchen utensils.

Alinor watched as Richard Stoney, Alys's sweetheart, came out of the mill at a run and tried to take the bucket of eggs to carry them for her. She fended him off, but he caught her hand and kissed it. Alys looked up and saw her mother as Richard made a little nod of a bow and darted back to the mill. The girl came to the five-barred yard gate, dipped her head for her mother's blessing, and rose up and kissed her.

"Not plague then," she said, knowing that her mother would never have kept the clothes that she had worn while nursing a plague patient. When Alinor came home from a death she always washed her hands and trimmed her hair, so that the bad luck would not follow her.

"No, God be praised. They were pleased at the Priory. It was the tutor, James Summer, and they must have been afraid for Master Walter." She smiled at Alys. "I see young Richard Stoney is eager to work."

She had thought that Alys would laugh, but the girl blushed and looked down. "He doesn't like to see me do heavy work here. He wants a better life for me. For us both."

"He does?" Alinor asked. "Did you have a merry evening at his farm?"

"Yes, they were kind to me, and we were . . ." she tailed off, her face illuminated. "You know what I mean."

"I understand," Alinor said quietly.

"So, what was wrong with Mr. Summer?"

"Some sort of fever. It broke overnight. But, Alys . . ."

"Shall I come home tonight, then?"

There was no reason to keep her daughter from her home. Guiltily, she realized that never before had she wished to be alone in the cottage. "Yes, of course," she said. "I've a loaf of bread from the Priory for your dinner."

"I'll bring some curd cheese," Alys promised. "Jane Miller and I are making it, this afternoon. Mrs. Miller will give me a slice."

"Is she here?" Alinor asked.

"In the kitchen, sour as crab apples," Alys said under her breath.

"Is her back paining her?"

"Her bottom," Alys said vulgarly, and Alinor gave her a little cuff around her cap.

"You'd better talk like a goodwife if you want me to go and see Richard Stoney's parents."

At once the girl's face lit up. "Will you go to see them?"

"If he's promised you, and you wish it, I'd better talk to his parents."

"Oh, Ma!" The girl plunged into her mother's embrace. "But why now? Why d'you think we can ask them? Did his lordship give you a great fee for nursing?"

"Yes, he did, a fortune. And something even better than a fee. He said that he will apprentice Rob to an apothecary at Chichester. It's as good as giving me ten pounds. Now I know Rob is provided for, I can put all my savings into your dowry."

Alys did not think for a moment that this would leave her mother without anything against accident. She thought only that she could be married to the young man that she loved.

"How much've you got?" she demanded.

"One pound and fifteen shillings," Alinor said proudly. "Farmer Johnson paid me well for the birth of his son, and the boat only cost us three shillings. A whole pound and fifteen shillings altogether. Sir William gave me a pound for nursing the tutor. That's more than I've ever had in my life."

"How ever have you saved it all?"

"Rob's wages." Alinor was silent about the pay for leading James to the Priory at midsummer. "And Farmer Johnson, nursing Mr. Summer just now, and the herbs and fishing, especially the lobsters."

"But it still won't be nearly enough."

"Thirty-five shillings down, and more to come?" Alinor demanded. "They'll be surprised we have so much. We can tell them that Rob is going for an apothecary. He'll earn well in the future. He'll promise some of his wages."

"It won't be enough. They thought they'd get a girl who would inherit land. They want some neighbor's girl whose father owns the fields nearby. Richard has sworn he won't have her. He's told them he wants to marry me. We've just got to force them to agree."

"We'll do the best we can," Alinor said quietly. "Tell Richard we'll call on them on the way to market tomorrow."

"Ma!" Alys gasped, her face alight, and she turned and bounded across the yard to the mill while Alinor tapped on the kitchen door and let herself in.

Mrs. Miller was leaning on the kitchen table, rolling and turning pastry, battering it with an icy roller. Alinor thought that the pastry would be as hard as the woman's heart.

"Goodwife Reekie," she said grudgingly as Alinor entered. "Alys told me you were nursing at the Priory."

"It was the young lord's tutor that was taken ill," Alinor said. "Him that was at harvest home, Mr. Summer."

Neither women referred to the jealous glance that Mrs. Miller had shot down the table at the beautiful younger woman, nor how the young lord's tutor had gone to speak to Alinor as soon as the table was cleared, and she had stormed away from the harvest home, leaving Alys unsupervised, to dance all night with Richard Stoney.

"Is he sick?" Mrs. Miller asked. "Did he take sick in Newport? I wouldn't be surprised. The island's always feverish in summer."

"Yes, he took a fever," Alinor said. "Very sudden, very hot, but he's better now."

"You nursed him?"

"Sir William insisted. He sent for me at once, to make sure that it was not plague."

"God save us!"

"Amen."

"And it was not?"

"No. I wouldn't be here if there was any danger. I wouldn't bring sickness to your door, Mrs. Miller."

"Don't speak of it," she said quickly, and knocked on the wooden table, as if Alinor could bring disease by naming it.

Alinor knocked too, a counterpoint to the rhythm of superstition. "No, of course not. I only came in to see if you wanted any of your garden herbs picked and distilled. I'm going to do a batch for myself, and some at Ferry-house. And to ask if Alys might have a day off tomorrow."

"I could do with some basil oil and oil of comfrey," Mrs. Miller said. "Of course Alys can have the day off. I don't have enough work to keep her busy as it is. She's always dawdling in the yard and talking with the men. I have to tell you, Mrs. Reekie, she's running after that Richard Stoney every hour of the day."

"I'm sorry for that." Alinor resisted the temptation to defend her daughter. "I'll speak with her. But I know she's learning so much from you. In the dairy and bakery."

"Well, of course, I can do more in a big kitchen than you can in your little cottage." Mrs. Miller warmed to the flattery. "I daresay my kitchen is twice the size of even Ferry-house. Are you two going to Chichester market?"

"Yes. Can I buy anything for you?"

"Nothing, nothing. I can't afford to waste my money on fripperies. But if you see a piece of lace, just enough to trim a collar and an apron, not too rich, not too fancy—you know the sort of thing I like—you can buy it for me, if it's not too dear. And a piece for Jane, too. I can put it in her dowry drawer."

"I will," Alinor promised. "If I see anything pretty."

"I'll give you the money," Mrs. Miller said. "You can bring it back, if there's nothing nice."

"Oh, I'll take my own money, and you can just repay me, if I find anything."

"No, it'd be too dear for you," the older woman said smugly. "I'll want something worth at least three shillings, and I know you won't have that. Turn your back and I'll get out my purse."

Obediently, Alinor turned her face to the sideboard where the Millers' well-polished pewter and one trencher of silver was proudly displayed. Behind her she could hear the noise of Mrs. Miller going to the drawer in the big wooden kitchen table, pulling it out and taking out her purse, and her "tut" of irritation as she found that she did not have enough money to hand.

"Wait a minute," she said. "Just wait a minute."

"No hurry," Alinor said pleasantly, her thoughts far away from Mrs. Miller's purse, conscious only of the heat of her lips and the ache in her body and her longing for James.

"Just a moment," Mrs. Miller said again, but now she was immediately behind Alinor, her voice strange and echoing. Startled, Alinor's head jerked up and she clearly saw, in the silver trencher, the miller's wife standing on the hearthstone, behind the glowing embers, pulling a red leather purse from a hole in the brickwork chimney. The woman turned with sooty fingers, and met Alinor's eyes, flinching at her reflected gaze. Obviously, Alinor had seen her hiding place. Alinor looked down and heard the scrape of the brick sliding back into place.

"You can turn round now," she said, flustered. "Jane's dowry. I'm short in my own purse. I'll just borrow from Jane's dowry."

"Of course," said Alinor coolly, turning and looking at the floor, not the fireplace.

"It's my own money," the woman said awkwardly. "It's me that put it by for her. Surely I can borrow from my own daughter's dowry, since I put it by for her since she was a baby?"

"I understand," said Alinor. "And I didn't see."

"It's the same purse that your mother got from the pedlar. We bought them together, years ago. Red leather."

"I didn't know," Alinor said. "I didn't see."

"I know you didn't," Mrs. Miller lied. "And I wouldn't mind if you did. I can't bring myself to keep it at the goldsmith's. I like it where I can see it. Now and then I top it up. Always have done. Of course, I don't mind you knowing where it's kept. Haven't I known you since you were a little girl? Didn't your own mother attend my birth?"

"She did," Alinor agreed.

Mrs. Miller pressed three silver shillings into Alinor's hand. "There. If you see some fine lace, not too fussy, for a collar and a pinny, you can pay up to three shillings for it."

The coins were hot from being stored behind the fire. Alinor thought that anyone who touched them would have guessed their hiding place at once. But she said lightly: "I'll look for lace for you, and bring it tomorrow afternoon."

"Very good," Mrs. Miller said. "Alys can help you pick the herbs now and then go home with you if you want. I don't need her for anything else today."

"Thank you," Alinor said, and went to fetch her daughter to come to the herb garden and pick comfrey and basil for Mrs. Miller.

In his bedroom at the Priory, James was packing a clean shirt and clean hose in a saddlebag with his Bible and a purse of gold coins, all that was left from the queen's money to buy her husband's freedom. Sir William was standing by the window and looking down into the orchard below.

"You can leave your sacred things here," he said. "I'll keep them safe for you, until you return to claim them."

"Thank you," James said. "If I don't come back, you can be sure that another priest will." He tried to smile. "My replacement. I pray that he does better than I."

"Don't take it so hard," Sir William said. "You did what you were asked to do. You reached him with a good plan and a waiting ship. You didn't miscarry. You didn't steal the gold, you didn't betray him. Half the people he employs would have sold him to our enemies. If he had wished it, he would be free now, and you would be the savior of the kingdom."

"Yes," James said. "But he did not wish it, and I am very far from the savior of the kingdom. I am a Nobody. Worse than that, I am a Nobody with no home and no family and no faith. No king either."

"Ah! You take things hard when you're a young man. But listen to me: you'll recover. You're not even well yet, just up from your sickbed. When you get back to France, tell the Fathers that you need some time. Rest for a while, eat well, and only then tell them about your doubts. It all looks better when you're well. Trust me. It all looks different when you've had a good sleep and a good meal. These are hard times for us all. We have to get through them one step at a time. Sometimes we fall back, sometimes we press forward. But we keep going. You'll keep going."

James straightened up from tightening the straps on his bag and looked at Sir William. Even the lord of the manor, a cheerful thoughtless man, was struck by the bleakness of his pale young face.

"I wish I could believe it, but I feel as if everything that I know, and everything that I am, has been knocked out of me. And all I can pray is to be allowed to do something else and live another life entirely."

"Ah, well, perhaps your road lies that way, who knows? These are times of great change. Who knows what will happen? But there will always be a welcome for you here. If they send you back to England you can return here as Walter's tutor until he goes to Cambridge, and as a welcome guest anytime after that."

"What will become of young Robert?"

"I've taken care of that. We owed Goodwife Reekie a debt, don't you think? She came as soon as I sent for her, and she went in with you when we didn't know what was wrong. She could've been locked up with a dying man, for all we knew. She risked taking the plague and God knows what would have been the end of that. She nursed you well, didn't she?"

James turned away and opened a cupboard door to hide his face. "Perfectly adequate," he said to the empty shelves.

"And she made it clear that she'll keep her mouth shut. She never said a word about finding you when you first came here. She can be trusted. I've promised her that her boy will have an apprenticeship. Mr. Tudeley will arrange it. Apothecary in Chichester. It's not cheap, but it's worth it for her silence, and it will keep her indebted and silent forever."

"I'm glad!" James said, turning back to Sir William. "That's generous and good of you, sir. She's a woman who deserves some good luck. I didn't tell you, but I ran into her husband at Newport. He told me he was never coming home to her."

"Zachary Reekie." His lordship named his missing tenant with aristocratic distaste. "No loss, if you ask me. Better for her if he'd drowned."

"Maybe, but it leaves her in an awkward position."

"No, it doesn't. Not if she doesn't see him, and no one sees him. If no one ever reports seeing him, then in seven years' time she can declare him dead, and herself a widow."

"Seven years?"

"That's the law."

"Would she know that?"

"No! How would she? Doubt if she can read."

"She can read. But I doubt if she knows the law. I didn't. If no one sees him in seven years she's free?"

"Exactly." His lordship tapped his nose, indicating a secret. "Seven years from when he first went missing. So, he disappeared—when?—last winter, I think, when the navy was still commanded by parliament, before we got the ships back. He ran away to serve them, as a rogue like him would, and never came back. So, he's been gone nearly a year, at least. In six years' time she'll be free and can take another husband. She's a young woman. If she can get through six years with her name untarnished, then she'll have a life ahead of her. There's more than one man who'd be glad to have her. I should think more than one would even marry her."

"She could remarry?"

Sir William closed one eye in a slow wink. "As long as no one has seen Zachary alive. You might remember that. If you want to do her a favor, you might remember that."

"No one has seen him," James confirmed. He felt his spirits leap up at the thought that she might be free, that he might be released from his vows, that despite what she had said, they could have a future together. "No one has seen him at all. He's dead, and she could declare herself a widow in six years."

"That's the way," Sir William said. "Pretty woman. Shame to have her wasted on the edge of the mire like that."

"I hadn't really noticed," James said cautiously.

"You must have done!" his lordship exclaimed. "She's known from here to Chichester as the most beautiful woman in Sussex. Some fool wrote a song about her a few years ago: 'The Belle of Sealsea.' I'd have tupped her myself if it weren't for having Walter in the house, and his mother not long dead, and everyone in this damn island knowing everyone else's business and turned so godly."

James felt his familiar sense of distaste at the trouble that seemed to follow Alinor even here, among her betters. "Better to leave her alone," he advised rapidly, "and then she might make a good marriage and change her luck."

"Oh, aye," Sir William conceded. "And her brother is an army man and as free with his opinions as a dog with his piss, and times so changeable. It's not like the old days when you knew where you were. My father would take a tenant's wife behind the haystack and no one would say a word but 'Thank you, your lordship!'"

"Yes," James said repressively. "It's not like the old days at all."

"Anyway, they say you can't force her," Sir William confided. "They say some fool tried to take her against her will, when she was coming home from market, and she whispered something to him that completely unmanned him. He said his cock went limp and his blood froze. He said she ruined him, before he ruined her."

"Really?"

"Gossip. Sort of gossip that collects around a beautiful woman. Especially a cunning woman. They say she can do all sorts. They called her a cock whisperer after that; said that she could blast a man with ice or harden him like a rock. Must say, I'd like to know."

James was sickened by the repetition of Alinor's uncanny skills. "It was probably nothing but that she spoke godly to him and he lost the will," he said.

"Who knows what she can do?"

"Surely, she just knows the healing herbs," James insisted.

"Maybe. They believe all sorts of nonsense on this island. Her mother was half witch for sure. But she's dead and buried in holy ground and nobody actually tried her. Her sister-in-law died in childbed; but of course the brother hushed it all up. Anyway . . . makes no difference to us. The woman, whatever she may be, has obliged us and we've paid her. And you know you're welcome back anytime. You can stay on now, if you wish."

"I'll go tomorrow," James said, glad to change the subject. "I have to go to London, and then I'll take a ship to France. I will go to my seminary and confess. If they release me, perhaps

I will be able to come back to England. Perhaps next time we meet I shall have my old name and my old house back again."

"I hope you do, by God, I hope that you do. You deserve it," Sir William said gruffly. "Remember that it wasn't your fault. His Majesty chose his own path. Pray God that he chose rightly and it gets him to his throne. Pray God that both you and he get safe home."

Alinor and Alys soaked their best caps and their linen in a bowl of water and urine as soon as they got home from the ferry-house herb garden. They left them to bleach all evening, rinsed them in cold water from the dipping pond, and then pinned them on a string beside the herbs to dry.

"I'm never going to be able to sleep," Alys said.

"You should," Alinor warned her. "I don't want to be taking a pasty-faced girl to her new in-laws."

"Pasty!" Alys objected.

"With dark shadows under her eyes like old drunk Joan."

"All right, I'll sleep, I swear it."

"I'm stepping up to Ferry-house to see your uncle. I won't be long."

"All right," Alys said. She took off her work skirt and jacket and laid them on top of the blankets. Wearing only her linen shift, and with her hair in a plait, she slid under the covers and drew them up to her shoulders. She looked like a little girl again, and Alinor stepped back to the bed to kiss her on her forehead. "Are you sure about this? You seem very young to be talking about your wedding?"

Alys's smile was radiant. "I'm sure, Ma. I'm absolutely sure. And I'm the same age as you when you married my da."

"It wasn't a very good choice," Alinor said quietly.

"But I'm as old as you were then."

"Yes."

"D'you think he'll come home?" she asked. "My da. If he hears from someone that I'm to be married, will he come home for my wedding day?"

Alinor hesitated. "Alys, I don't think he'll ever come home."

At once, Alys clapped her hands over her ears. "Don't tell me anything!" she begged her mother. "The Stoneys can only just about bear me if they think my da is missing and might come home wealthy. If I tell them he's run off they'll never consider me for Richard, I'll be next to a pauper for them."

Alinor took Alys's hands from her ears and held them in her own work-worn palms. "All right, I'll say nothing. And you can say you know nothing for sure."

"And that's true." Alys nodded. "This is the tidelands, there's nothing sure."

Alinor pulled on her cape, for the evening mist was blowing off the harbor, damp and cold, and she went out of the cottage garden and turned to the left, as if she were going to the ferry-house, as she had told Alys, but then, when she reached the top of the bank she turned again, and entered along the hidden footpath that ran behind the cottage towards the Priory and the sea. It was high tide and the smell of sea salt blew in with the ribbons of mist. When she looked to her right, inland over the low-lying fields behind the bank, she could see the white silhouette of an owl hunting along the hedgerow, silent as a ghost, its great eyes seeing through the darkness.

Alinor stayed on the high-tide path, dropping down to cross the narrow strip of dry beach above the lapping waters, back up the muddy steps to the top of the bank, tracing her way across the gray stepping-stones where a marshy field oozed into the mire: gray stones set in gray mud under a gray sky. She skirted the headland where the bell tower stood like a warning fingerpost against the darkening sky, and then she turned inland at a sunken mooring post, its base in deep water, green with seaweed. She crossed the foreshore, her boots crunching on a drift of tiny shells, and mounted the bank to the Priory sea meadow. She lifted her gaze from the uneven steps and saw him at once. He was waiting in the shade of a hayrick, hidden from the Priory windows, facing the sea path, looking for her.

Without a word, she went into his arms and they clung to each other.

"Alinor," was all he said, and then he kissed her.

Alinor leaned back against the hayrick, her knees weakening beneath her as if she might fall to the ground. She made a little movement and he released her. "Not here," was all she said.

"Not here. Will you come to the Priory?"

"I don't dare."

"Can we go to your cottage?"

"Alys is at home."

He was silent. "Is there nowhere we can go? You know the woods, the mire, the little pathways?"

"I couldn't lie with you on the mire." She gave a little shudder and at once he put his arms around her and drew his cape around her. "Not with the tide high," she said. "It'd be like drowning. Could we go to the chapel? We could sit in the porch?"

He shook his head. "I have lost my faith, but that would be too much. I couldn't—forgive me, my love—I can't."

"Of course," she said, and thought what a loose slut he must think her to even suggest it. "I didn't mean . . ."

"I want you so much I think my heart will stop," he said. "Anywhere, anywhere!"

"I don't think there is anywhere for us," she said quietly, and then she was struck by the words. "Oh, it's true. D'you see? There's nowhere for us, not on Sealsea Island, not in all the tidelands, not in the world."

"There must be!"

"And besides, aren't we here to say good-bye?"

"I can't bear to say good-bye to you in this meadow again!"

"Last time you came back, as you had promised," she reminded him shyly.

"Last time I was ordered to come back. Next time, I will come back a free man. I will come back for you."

"I don't think that can ever be."

"It will. I will be freed of my vows. I will go and see my parents, I will buy back our house in Yorkshire, and I will come for you."

Her hands twisted in his and she tried to pull away. "You know—"

"No, listen to me. I can confess my sins and be released from the priesthood." He tightened his grip as she shook her head. "That is my choice. It is what I want."

"But you were risking your life for your faith! You told me that it came before everything."

"I did. But that was before Newport. My love, I failed in my mission and I lost my faith. I lost my faith in everything: king and God. I will leave the priesthood whatever happens, and I will never again come to England as a spy. I will not serve the king again—God bless him and may he have better servants than I. I have failed him and I cannot bear to fail again. That part of my life is over."

"Even so . . ."

"Alinor, I won't change my mind. I have lost my faith, I have lost everything. I can't tell you, but there is a darkness where once there was a burning light. The only thing I care about now is you."

"Oh, my love," she whispered. "That's not how to choose a wife."

"But the thing that you don't know and that I have just learned—it is good news—you will be free of your husband. I will never say that I saw him. Robert must be silent, too. I've told Walter. In six years, if nobody sees him, and nobody tells the parish that they saw him, then your marriage is dissolved as if it never was. He passes for dead and you are a single woman."

She had not known this. She raised her eyes, clouded with doubt. "Is this true? Really? Can it be true? Six years and I am free?"

"It's seven years by law, and the first year has nearly passed."

"This is the law?"

"It is. Sir William told me himself. You will be free, Alinor, I swear it. You will be free to marry me. And I will be free to marry you."

"We only have to wait six years?"

"Will you wait?" he demanded.

"I'd wait sixty!" She pressed herself against him. "I'd wait six hundred years. But you should not . . ."

He wrapped himself around her, he pressed her back against the rick and, with his mouth on hers for silence, he made her moan with pleasure until his head dropped into the crook of her neck and she heard him gasp: "I swear. I swear it."

Alys and Alinor rose early, at first light. Alys was determined to look as smart and as clean as a town girl, and the two women took a jug of soapwort tincture, and some lavender oil, and walked up to Ferry-house before sunrise. Red, the dog, bounced to the door to greet them and sniffed the jug.

"You're up early," Ned remarked, seated at his kitchen table, a loaf of bread beside him and a mug of ale to hand.

"We've come to wash. We're visiting the Stoneys," Alinor explained. "Before we go to Chichester market."

"And why do they deserve a wash?" Ned glanced, smiling, at Alys and saw her deep blush. "Oh, I see. I'll get the copper out."

He rose to his feet and went to the scullery for the big iron pot for the Ferry-house monthly laundry. He slid the worn pole through the two carry loops at the top of the pot and he and Alys lifted it onto the kitchen hearth, while Alinor took two buckets and went to the well at the back door. When they'd set it on the little fire she poured bucket after bucket of water into it, going back for more.

"Will you have some breakfast while it heats up?" Ned offered, cutting two slices of bread.

"I couldn't eat a thing!" Alys said, though she took a slice and ate it while watching the water.

Ned raised an eyebrow at his sister. "Greensickness," she whispered. "Please God we can agree on a dowry. She's set her heart on him."

He nodded. "He's walked her to the ferry every evening since harvest home. They sit on the pier, talking and talking like there was any news here. He doesn't go till I tell her it's the last crossing of the day."

"It's hot enough," Alys interrupted. "Surely that's hot enough!"

Alinor and Ned threaded the carry pole through the loops again, took the heavy pot out to the scullery, and set it down on the brick floor.

"I'll see you later," Ned remarked. "You can leave the water in the copper for me. I can't recall when I last had a proper wash, and your water is always so sweet."

He closed the door on the two of them and they both stripped naked, washed each other's hair, and then took it in turns to pour jug after jug of water over each other. The tincture of soapwort made the water as cloudy and as slick as soap, and the oil of lavender scented the whole room. They were both shivering when they dried themselves, standing on the cold brick floor, and then they toweled their heads, dressed themselves in their clean linen and brushed gowns, and went out through the kitchen with their damp hair tumbled down over their shoulders.

Ned was on the bench outside the door, smoking his pipe and watching the bright water lapping at the pier. The tide was coming in fast, washing over the cobblestones of the wadeway, foaming in the rife against the outflowing river water. "Going to be a nice day," he remarked. "You two look as fresh as daisies."

Alys and Alinor, holding their skirts bunched up so that not a speck of mud should mark the hems, walked gingerly back along the bank and down the steps to the cottage. Their linen caps were dry and pressed smooth on top of the earthenware fire cover. They plaited each other's damp hair and then pinned the caps on top.

"How do I look?" Alys asked, turning towards her mother.

Alinor looked at her daughter, the perfect skin of a girl tinged with a rising blush, her golden hair hidden by the white cap, her wide blue eyes and her mischievous smile. "You look beautiful," she said. "I don't think anyone could resist you."

"It's his mother I'm worried about. His father's very kind to me; but she's hard-hearted. Ma, we're going to have to talk her round. Can't you take a potion, or something?"

"A love potion?" Alinor laughed at her daughter. "You know I don't do such things."

"She has to agree we can marry," Alys said again. "She has to."

"He's an only son: they're bound to want the best for him. But everyone says he can wrap them round his little finger. Will he have told them that we're visiting today?"

"Yes, and he'll have told them why. He said they'll give us breakfast. We can't be late."

"We don't want to arrive at dawn. We don't want to look too eager."

"I am eager!" Alys insisted.

Alinor had a sudden flash of memory of James's touch, and the taste of his mouth, the thudding of his heart as he pressed her against the hayrick. "I understand eagerness," she said, turning away. "I do. But first we've got to put out the herbs and the oil, and feed the hens and cover the fire."

"I know!" Alys said impatiently. "I know. I'll do the hens."

As Alys shooed the hens out of the door, took two eggs from their nests, and put them in the crock, Alinor poured flaxseed oil from the jug into a big glass pitcher packed with the last of the fresh basil leaves, and corked it tight. She made another pitcher filled with comfrey and put the two of them on a shelf outside the cottage where the rising sun would strike them, and warm them all day long till the spirit was drawn from the herbs and into the oil. Alinor went to the corner cupboard where she distilled her oils and dried her herbs, and she took a dozen little bottles and put them in her basket.

"Are you ready?" Alys demanded. "D'you have everything? Can we go now?"

"Is the fire covered?"

"Yes, yes!"

"And the marks against fire?"

Alys bent to the hearth, took up a twig of kindling, and drew the runes against house fire. "There!"

"We want it nice . . ." Alinor began.

Alys completed the phrase, laughing: "to come back to."

"I know! I know!" Alinor admitted her predictable instruction. "But it's what my mother always said, and it's always true."

"It's perfect to come back to. Mrs. Miller herself would admire it. Let's go."

The two women walked in single file back along the bank to Ferry-house. The tide was high, and a farmer was leading his big cob horse off the ferry and climbing into his saddle off the mounting block.

"Going to Chichester market, Goodwife Reekie?" he greeted Alinor.

"Yes. Are you keeping well, Farmer Chudleigh?" she called up to him.

"I am," he said. "But I'll thank you for that goose grease of yours when the cold gets into my old knees."

"I'll bring you a jar," she promised him.

"You two look like you've been new-minted," Ned complimented them. "So clean you're shiny."

Alys giggled and raised her skirt away from the muddy hoofprints on the quayside.

"Not taking any wool to market?" Ned asked his niece, holding the ferry steady for them against the pier.

"Not today," she said. "Ma is buying some lace for Mrs. Miller if she sees anything nice, and selling some of her oils."

"Ribbons for you?" he asked.

"Vanity is a sin, Uncle," she said with a toss of her pretty head that made him laugh.

The tide was flowing slowly and smoothly inward, but even so, Alinor gripped the side of the boat with both hands, and when Red, the dog, jumped into the boat beside her she gave a little gasp of fear.

"That tutor, James Summer, went north in the middle of the night," Ned observed. "Over the wadeway on Sir William's second horse by the light of the moon. Didn't call me, but I saw him. Going to London, I suppose. Didn't call for a light. Didn't stop for a chat. Doesn't talk much. Doesn't do much teaching either, does he?"

"I don't know," Alinor said.

"Does Rob know when he's coming back?"

"He didn't say."

"He looked better than when he arrived. He was sick as a dog, wasn't he?"

"Fever," Alinor said shortly, keeping her eyes fixed on the horizon.

"Will you buy a sheep's cheese for me at the market?"

"Yes," Alinor said. "We'll be back before dinnertime."

He handed her out of the boat on the far side. "You might get a lift in a wagon. You could wait here for anyone crossing."

"We'll start walking," Alinor said, and she and her daughter made their way up the road as Ned pulled the ferry back to the island side to wait for customers going to Chichester market.

After a little way, the two women turned left off the road to Chichester and took the footpath towards Birdham. The ground was marshy, but the unmarked path ran on the top of raised banks at the edges of the fields, and on stepping-stones over the streams. Climbing over stiles that crossed the hedges from one low-lying marshy field to another, they made their way to the little village, a handful of houses clustered on the road.

They both paused on the grass verge of the one-track road. "Do I look all right?" Alys asked nervously.

Alinor straightened her daughter's cap, set her cloak a little more evenly on her shoulders. "Fine," she said. "Let's wipe our boots."

Despite all their caution, the hems of their skirts were dirty from the walk, and their boots caked with mud. Carefully, they lifted their skirts and wiped the sides and toes of their boots on the grass of the verge.

"I'm sweaty," Alys said nervously. "And muddy. Damn this place, I'm always muddy. He's never seen me in a clean petticoat!"

"You're beautiful," Alinor reassured her. "And he's seen you a lot worse."

Stoney Farm stood back from the road, a low wall of knapped flints between the house and the lane, to keep the stock from straying. A grassy track led to the front door through a small orchard of fruit trees, the apple trees bowed low with ripe fruit, a picker's triangular ladder leaning against one of them.

It was a good-sized house, one of the best in the little parish, two bedrooms and a lumber room for storage under the reed-thatched roof, and below them a kitchen and two rooms: one used as a parlor and one used as a store. The kitchen ran the length of the back of the house, the brewhouse and the dairy were across the stone-flagged yard from the kitchen door, the barn and the stables made the fourth side of the square. As the two women walked towards the front door, Richard Stoney, in a suit of dark brown, and good riding boots, muddy from the stable yard, came bounding round the corner of the house and ran towards them.

"You've come! Oh, you've come!" He skidded to a halt and stopped himself embracing Alys. He made a little bow to Alinor.

"Mrs. Reekie, thank you for coming. Alys . . ." He shot her a warm conspiratorial glance. "Good day, Alys."

As soon as she saw the warm intimate look that passed between him and her daughter Alinor knew their secret as clearly as if they had told her. She was certain that they were lovers, that Alys had defied all her warnings, all the teaching from school and church, had evaded Mrs. Miller's suspicious glare, had followed her heart and not her head, and had lain with this young man.

Now Alinor understood why Alys was so determined that the betrothal should go ahead. If Richard could not persuade his parents to agree to the marriage then he and Alys would have to part, and his parents would probably take him away from the tide mill to make sure that the couple never met again. Alys would be known as a girl who had lost the man of her choice, and her eventual marriage would be widely known as second-best. If it was ever known that she had lost her virginity it would be hard to find a reputable young man for her to marry at all, and Mrs. Miller would be within her rights to turn her away from work. Most village betrothals started with a promise and a bedding, but times had changed, and godly people and families on the rise condemned young love as both unchaste and bad for business.

"Oh, no," Alinor whispered under her breath.

"What's the matter?" Alys tucked her hand in Richard Stoney's arm and turned to her mother. Defiantly, she met her mother's reproachful gaze and, in the face of her happiness, Alinor could not be angry. The young couple were beautiful together, so well matched in height and looks; she could not blame them for being unable to wait for the reluctant consent of his parents. He was dark eyed and brown as a hazelnut, with a tumble of dark curls to his plain white collar. Alys beside him looked fair and delicate, her hair, a paler gold than her mother's, modestly tucked beneath her white cap, her features as regular and pretty as a painted china doll.

"Nothing," Alinor said. "Nothing's wrong."

Alys met her eyes and flushed as if she realized that her mother had guessed her secret. "Ma?" she said uncertainly.

"We'll talk later," Alinor ruled.

Alys blushed deeply, and drew closer to Richard, as if she were claiming him. "Ma, this is the man I'm going to marry," she announced.

Richard flushed like a boy but stood with pride. "If you permit," he said politely. "I have promised. I have given my word. We are betrothed."

"Let's see what your father says," Alinor replied cautiously.

Holding Alys's hand, Richard led the way up the path to the house. Alinor followed, thinking guiltily that Ned must be right, and the wildness that he saw in her had come out in her daughter. She had failed to control the lust that lived in every fallible woman since Eve, and she had failed to teach Alys any better.

The front door opened with a creak from disuse, and Mrs. Stoney stood in the doorway, her maidservant behind her.

"Good day, Mrs. Reekie," she said formally.

"Good day to you, Mrs. Stoney," Alinor replied, struggling for calmness.

The woman turned to her son. "Go and fetch your father," she said. "He's in the barn."

Richard looked as if he did not want to leave Alys, but he went obediently as Mrs. Stoney led the mother and daughter into the best room at the front of the house. It was furnished sparsely with solid dark furniture; a large cupboard laden with expensive pewter took up all of one wall. There was one great chair with a woven back and arms, which was clearly for the master of the house, and a second chair beside it. Alinor put her basket of oils down by the door and moved tactfully to a smaller chair beside the dark wooden table, laid with a small piece of tapestry, anchored by a bowl of heavy pewter. Mrs. Stoney seated herself in the second-best chair; Alys stood beside her mother and was not invited to sit at all.

They heard the men coming in the back door and the noise of

Mr. Stoney knocking mud off his boots. Then he came into the room. He was a short, bluff, red-faced man with a ready smile and a handshake for Alinor, who rose to greet him.

"How do?" he said to her. "How do?" Then he turned to Alys. "And how's the prettiest maid in Sussex today?"

Alys curtseyed and went to him for a smacking kiss on both cheeks.

"Will you take a glass of ale, Mrs. Reekie?" he invited.

"Bess is fetching it," his wife said.

"And the young people can walk round the orchard, I suppose," he said.

Bess entered with a tray of pewter mugs, and Richard and Alys escaped.

"He loves to walk her round the farm," Mr. Stoney confided. "He's that proud of it. Our only child, y'know."

"I know." Alinor took a cup and sipped. It was home-brewed small ale and Mrs. Stoney had sweetened it with apples from her orchard. Alinor could taste the fruit. "This is very good, Mrs. Stoney."

The woman smiled at the polite compliment. Alinor observed her smugness and wondered if she would be a kind mother-in-law to Alys, who would live with them at this farm and share a house with this woman for life.

"So, our young people want to make a match of it," Farmer Stoney said to Alinor. "Richard came to me after harvest home and said he had plighted his troth without a word to me." He chuckled, shaking his head. "Boys, eh? And he's brought her back here a few times, and we like her very well. But I should really be talking with her father."

"As you know, my husband's at sea," Alinor said cautiously. "He's been gone nearly a year now. All the arrangements fall to me."

"Your brother doesn't act for you?" Mrs. Stoney inquired.

"I decide about my own children," Alinor said with quiet dignity. "My brother advises me when I need it."

"Does he know you're here today?" Mrs. Stoney demanded.

"He does."

"Well, you're no fool, I know that," the man said encouragingly. "But you must realize that we could look very high for Richard. He's our only son and he'll inherit all of this, when we're gone. There's nothing owed on the farm. I had it entire from my father, and I improved it, and I will pass it on entire. It's a tidy inheritance."

"I know," Alinor said. "It's a beautiful farm. But Alys was taken with your son even before she knew who he was, when she first saw him at the mill. She had no thought of all of this."

Mrs. Stoney sniffed, as if to say that she doubted it.

"It would be a love match," Alinor pursued. "But of course, she will bring a dowry."

"Does she have her own linen laid away?" Mrs. Stoney asked.

"No," Alinor said, thinking of the corner of the room of the little cottage, the box of treasures that held nothing but a paper contract and a red leather purse of dross. "Not yet. But by the time of the wedding, I will be able to send her with some sheets . . ." She saw the disapproving look on the woman's face. "And some wool," she added.

"This is what comes of sending him to the Millers' farm," Mrs. Stoney complained aside, to her husband. "You sent him to learn milling, but all he has learned is disobedience."

"He can make his own choice," her husband rejoined. "She's a pretty girl and she knows all that she needs to know to be a working farmer's wife. Isn't that right, Mrs. Reekie?"

"She does everything at the tide mill," Alinor confirmed. "Mrs. Miller keeps a very good place and Alys has learned housewifery there. She works in their dairy, she can milk cows, she can brew, she bakes bread, she cooks, she spins of course, and she sews. And I've taught her the herbs and the uses of them. She can read and write. You'll find her very able in the dairy and the brewery, in the bakery and even outside."

"Would she bring your recipe book?" Mrs. Stoney demanded.

Alinor flinched. She had a recipe book inherited from her mother with cures for all known ailments and injuries, the proper uses of herbs and how to grow them, use them, and distill them. It was her greatest treasure and the bedrock of her practice as a healer. "I will copy them," she promised. "I will copy them for her. And, of course, if there were any illness or trouble I would come to you for free, as family."

Mrs. Stoney looked as if it was not enough. "And these savings?" she inquired. "What dowry will she bring?"

"I have thirty-five shillings saved just now," Alinor said with quiet pride. But obviously, this was not enough; the woman merely raised her eyebrows. "I will have another ten by their wedding day if they marry at Easter," Alinor added. "And my son, Rob, will have his quarterly wages from the Priory at Candlemas. That's another fifteen shillings." Alinor tried to speak calmly about these tremendous sums of money, far more than she had ever earned before, but she saw Mr. Stoney's glance at his wife and her firm shake of her head, her down-turned mouth.

"We can't let him throw himself away," he explained.

"I can add from my fees as I earn them," Alinor said. "I attend almost all the births in Sealsea Island. I could promise a monthly payment in their first year of marriage—say—from my fees."

Mrs. Stoney pursed her lips.

"My son is to be apprenticed to a Chichester apothecary," Alinor said, her voice level, but her heart pounding. "He's to go in the Lent term when Master Walter leaves for his university. I know he would want to see his sister happily settled . . ."

"An apothecary?" Mrs. Stoney asked, and when Alinor started to explain, she interrupted: "But what use is that to us?"

"She and Rob will inherit the right to the ferry, and Ferryhouse—"

"I'm sorry," Mr. Stoney said finally, "but we're looking for a bigger dowry, to be paid in full on the wedding day. Maybe with land adjoining, maybe one of our neighbors. Not pennies as and when. Not as and when, Mrs. Reekie. It's a pity that you don't have a husband to earn a living for you. A great pity. But we can't let Richard throw himself away. For all that she's a lovely girl, and we like her very much. She would have been our choice, if the money had been right. We thought you'd have had more, to be honest. I'm sorry. We thought you were in a better way."

Alinor gritted her teeth to stop herself exclaiming that once she did have more: her inheritance from her mother, her dowry in her mother's red leather purse; but Zachary had taken it, as a husband's right, and wasted it as a husband can do, and now Zachary was not here to answer for it, and the red leather purse held only shavings of old coins.

"But she has her own wages," Alinor urged him, growing more anxious. "If you want her to keep working at the Millers', she could bring home her wages. And she can spin."

"Then he might as well marry our servant Bess!" Mrs. Stoney objected. "Maidservant wages as dowry! No, no, she's a lovely girl but if she's got nothing but thirty-five shillings and farm work wages. I look higher for my son than that."

Mr. Stoney looked as if he regretted her sharp tone. "No disrespect," he said.

"What did you have in mind?" Alinor asked. "For my brother would perhaps—"

"Nothing less than eighty pounds," Mrs. Stoney said smartly. "I'd take nothing less."

"Eighty pounds!" Alinor gasped at the unimaginable sum.

"We're going to have to refuse," Mr. Stoney said gently. "Regretfully but—"

"I have sixty pounds!" Alys interrupted suddenly from the door. She stepped into the room, white-faced, Richard behind her, gripping her hand. "I have it," she claimed. "I have savings of my own that my mother doesn't know about." One fierce glance at Alinor warned her to say nothing.

"Were you listening at the door?" Mr. Stoney asked his son, frowning.

"We came past the window and we overheard," his son replied. "We weren't eavesdropping, sir, but my mother was speaking very clearly. We must marry. We love each other."

"How much d'you have?" Mrs. Stoney asked the girl.

"I have sixty pounds," Alys said boldly. From the pocket of her gown she pulled a fat red leather purse and put it down on the dark wood table before her mother. "Sixty pounds," she said defiantly. "Sixty pounds down, and the rest to come. Is that enough?"

With a pang of terror Alinor recognized at once the heavy red leather purse that Mrs. Miller had pulled from its hiding place behind the brick in the millhouse chimney: it was Jane Miller's dowry. She opened her mouth and found she could say nothing.

"Is that enough?" Alys asked, her voice shaking. "Is it enough?"

"It's a surprise," Mr. Stoney remarked gravely. "How has a maid like you got more savings than her mother?" He turned to Alinor. "How have you got a fortune like this? Did you know she had put this by?"

"My father gave it to me," Alys spoke rapidly before her mother could reply. "His prize money from the navy. He won it serving in the navy, and when he came home last time, he gave it to me for my dowry. I was always his favorite. He gave it to me for my dowry if I wanted to marry before he came back."

"I should think your mother could have used the money often, over the past year," Mrs. Stoney said mistrustfully. "Everyone knows how hard she works. Shouldn't you have told her? And given it to her?"

"My father and my mother didn't always agree," Alys said boldly, ignoring Alinor, her eyes only on Mrs. Stoney's grim expression. "My father told me to keep his savings safe for his return, and use it only for my dowry. I have to be obedient to my father, don't I?"

She turned to Mr. Stoney, certain he would support male authority. Solemnly, he nodded: "An order from your father? Yes, you had to obey it."

"He hasn't left you, has he?" Mrs. Stoney turned to Alinor. "Deserted you? If he gave his daughter her dowry before he went? Was he planning on never coming back?"

At once Alys saw that she had overplayed her hand. Before Alinor could reply, the girl interrupted: "Oh, no! My da would never leave us! He promised to come home. He just left his savings with me, in case I wanted to marry before he returned. He's a sailor at war, he knew that he might be a long time away. There was no way of knowing how long his voyage might last. He was just trying to do the best for me."

"But you said that they did not always agree?"

Alinor, knowing that Mrs. Stoney would have seen her at Chichester market with a blackened eye, with a bruised cheek, shook her head. "I've no complaint against him and I know that he is coming home," she said steadily. "We disagreed sometimes, like many a husband and wife—nothing out of the ordinary. Zachary signed up for a voyage with a coastal trader, and then we heard that he had been pressed into the navy. Then the navy went over to the prince. But I don't doubt that when the peace comes, the sailors and the soldiers will be released, with their back pay and prize money. I don't doubt that he will come home then."

She kept her face very still, expressionless, and thought that she had promised James that she would tell everyone that Zachary was not coming home, and that she was a widow, and now here, the very next day she was declaring the contrary. But there was nothing she could do about it now, while Alys was holding the floor of the room and lying like a mountebank.

"And his pay," Alys added. "Who knows what pay he'll bring home? If he's captured a ship he'll be rich!"

"So he's serving with the prince now?" Mr. Stoney seized on another problem. "We're a parliament household, here."

Alys shook her head. "We don't know what ship he's on. He might be on the ships that stayed loyal to parliament. My father's a parliament man, like my uncle Ned. You know my uncle Ned!"

"We're a parliament household too." Alinor struggled to join the conversation, tried to drag her eyes away from the old red leather purse.

"Then shouldn't they delay marrying till he returns?" Mr. Stoney turned to Alinor. "If he'll come home when there's peace, and the parliament are talking to the king right now?"

"Perhaps—"

"No!" Alys said quickly. "That wouldn't be right at all. My da gave me his savings to use for my dowry so that we didn't have to wait for him! He told me not to delay my wedding. And there's no way of knowing when the king will agree to peace."

Alinor nodded, but found she could not speak.

"So is it enough?" Richard pressed his father. "If we both work without pay on the farm, and give you our wages from everything else? It is enough with the dowry? Zachary Reekie's dowry?"

The farmer looked at his son, and decided in his favor. "It's enough," he ruled. He picked up the purse, hefted it in his hand, judging the value from long experience. He pulled open the drawstring and peered inside at the coins of gold and silver. "Sixty pounds—I didn't expect it; but yes, it's enough."

"We could have got more," Mrs. Stoney reminded him stiffly.

"We could." He smiled at his son. "But I'd rather see you happy." He handed the purse to Alys with a warm smile. "I'll give you this back now," he said, "as I should. And you give it to Mrs. Stoney at the church door on your wedding day, with your mother's savings, and with your wages between then and now, and Richard will give you a ring and his word. It's agreed. You'll have your share of the farm on his death, and your seat at this fireside for all your life. And your son will have the farm after Richard, and his son after him."

Alys burst into tears as Richard pulled her into his arms and kissed her. Mr. Stoney rose to his feet and kissed first Alinor and then the weeping girl. Mrs. Stoney put her hand on her son's head in blessing and then kissed Alys.

"So that's that," she said to Alinor begrudgingly. "He'd set his heart on her, and she pulled a dowry out of her pocket that no one would ever have dreamed. You'd think he was enchanted."

"Yes, yes . . ." Alinor was lost for words, still stunned at the sight of Jane Miller's dowry purse in Alys's hands. Alys palmed it back into her pocket without looking at her mother.

"And your son doing so well!" Mrs. Stoney said, allowing herself some warmth. "Apprentice to an apothecary in Chichester! What a start for a young man!"

"Yes," Alinor said. She realized she was nodding, still speechless. "Yes."

"How ever did he get a place like that?" Mrs. Stoney invited her to explain.

"They like him at the Priory." Alinor found her lips were so stiff that she could hardly form the words. "He's been companion to Master Walter and they paid for his apprenticeship. He'll start when Walter begins at the university. They call it the Lent term."

"Shall we have a glass of wine? And will you take your breakfast with us?" Mr. Stoney urged hospitably. "Now we're to be family? And I'll show you round the barns and the orchards, Mrs. Reekie, and I daresay you'll want to see the herb garden."

"Yes, please," Alinor said faintly. "I would like that. I would like that. Thank you."

The two women waved good-bye to the Stoney family, and walked together in silence up the road to Chichester. Alinor felt a gripping pain in her belly, which she thought was fear, and had the taste of sickness in her mouth, which she knew was dread.

The farm was half a mile behind them and out of sight before Alys spoke. "Say something. Please say something."

"Are you mad, Alys?"

"I know! I know! I must be!"

They walked a few more steps in silence, then Alinor felt Alys's cold hand creep into her own.

"Help me, Ma."

"How can I? This is a hanging offense. This is theft."

"I know. I know."

"It's Jane Miller's dowry, isn't it? In her mother's red leather purse?"

"Yes. Of course."

"What're you going to do?"

"Put the purse back. I just had to show it. I'm not going to steal it. I'll earn what I need for my wedding day. I'd never steal for it."

"It's only six months away! We'll never earn enough. We wouldn't earn enough in six years. And if Mrs. Miller goes to her hiding place and finds Jane's dowry missing, she'll turn the mill upside down and accuse everyone. You and me first. Alys, how could you!"

"I'll get it back in hiding before she misses it. But I have to marry him."

"Because you're lovers already?"

The girl gave a little gasp, which was a confession in itself. "Because I love him so much. I'd rather be hanged as a thief at Easter than lose him now."

"I would not!" Alinor cried out. "I've spent my life trying to keep you safe and now you've lain with a man before marriage, and stolen—" She cut off her cry and dropped into a whisper though they were alone under the wide sky, and the empty track stretched north ahead of them.

"I haven't stolen. I've borrowed. He loves me. And she won't catch me. It is worth the risk."

"You think that now . . . you'll think differently later."

"I do think this now. So I acted now."

"You'll change. You'll look back and this'll seem like madness to you. And you'll think I was mad not to stop you. I was wrong not to stop you. I should've taken the purse off you, the moment you brought it out." Alinor choked on the rising bile in her mouth. "I thought it was my purse! My red leather purse filled with nothing but my little coins! I thought I was going mad."

"Then I would have lost him. You heard them."

"Even so. Better to lose him than—"

"I knew you wouldn't go against me, Ma. I knew you'd never let me down."

"I shouldn't have gone along with you. This is a hanging matter, Alys. If you're caught with that purse on you, they'll hang you for a thief."

"They won't catch me. I'll put it back. But I swear to you, that if I can't marry him, I will die. If you forbid me, I'll run away. If he were to leave me, I'd drown myself in the millpond."

Alinor thought that she was the last woman in Sussex to argue against a desire that was more than life itself. How could she blame her daughter for doing nothing worse than she had done? Alinor had risked her life, going into the locked room above the stables with James, and since then she had lied to everyone.

"We'd better go back now to the tide mill, and put it back at once. If I call her into the yard, and you hurry into the house—"

"No. I know how to do it, really I do. I know when. She always goes out at dusk, every evening, to shut up the hens. She likes to shut them up herself. She's afraid that I'll steal the daytime eggs. She's so mean. She goes out at dusk, and there's never anyone in the kitchen then. I can put it back then."

"How d'you know her hiding place?"

"I was in the yard when the corn merchants came, and she sold them corn that should have gone to the poor of the parish. They paid twice the price and the poor went hungry. It's dirty money, Ma. Every time she does a deal that she knows Mr. Miller wouldn't like, she keeps the money from him, and puts it into Jane's dowry purse. Now and then, she sneaks it out to buy herself something special, or something for Jane's bottom drawer. Once, she asked me to buy some gilt chains from the pedlar at the gate and the coins were hot and she had sooty fingers. I didn't know where she kept the purse, but I knew it must be in the chimney. I just jiggled the bricks till I found the loose one."

"This is a terrible risk."

"I know. But I had to take it, Ma. I had to stop the Stoneys from saying no today. They won't go back on their word, even if I can't get the money. Richard will help me, and Mr. Stoney loves me—he'll let me off. I'll put the purse back, Mrs. Miller will be none the wiser, and when we get to market I'll get some more wool for spinning. I'll earn as much as I can before my wedding day, and I'll give them all that I have at the church door. It won't be sixty pounds, but it'll be too late by then. They'll never cancel the wedding. I'll tell them then that I'll owe the rest."

Alinor shook her head at this solution. "It's false dealing. Alys, it's bad for us to be seen as cheats. If you cheat them on your wedding day, they'll throw it in your face every quarrel you have. They'll never trust you again."

"Richard'll never throw it against me."

"His mother will."

Alys shrugged. "Who cares? Once we're married, she can say what she likes. I don't care. It's him I'm marrying, not her. And he's worth stealing for, and cheating for. He's worth anything."

Alinor put a hand over her eyes as if the morning sun was too dazzling to bear. Vividly, in her mind's eye, she saw Alys at the church door offering an underweight purse, the Stoneys' white-lipped resentment, and her own shame.

"It's no way to start a marriage," she said miserably. "It's not how you should be on your wedding day."

Alys hugged her arm. "Ma, I know this is terrible for you, and I'm sorry. I'm sorry, but I can't be stuck here, getting nowhere. I have to marry Richard. I have to be with him. I'm young, I want my life! I can't be patient under misfortune like you. I can't wait and wait for our da to come home, as if that would ever make anything better, when we know it'd be worse! I can't creep about all humble, and hope that the neighbors are kind to my face while calling me a pauper and a faerie bastard behind my back."

"They don't say that!"

"It's exactly what they say. Look how you have to fawn on

Mrs. Miller. Look how you bow to Mrs. Wheatley. Look how you cringe to Mr. Tudeley, and that horrible tutor! We're on the edge of charity all the time. We're always leaching off someone's goodwill. I can't stand it. I'd rather be a thief than a beggar. I've got to take my chance now. I've got to live my life now!"

"Oh, don't say that of him!"

"Mr. Tudeley is a monster!"

Alinor silenced her response, shamed by her own daughter, looked at Alys but could not find the words to reprimand her. "I'm not craven," she said, her voice very low. "I don't cringe. I don't leach."

"Yes, you do," Alys said mercilessly. "Anyone can say anything to you, if they'll only buy a bottle of plums."

"I didn't know you felt like this."

"I've always hated being poor."

"Rob, too?"

"Rob doesn't matter!" Alys exploded. "This is not about your precious son, for once."

Alys's jealousy and her resentment stretched before Alinor for the first time, as if she was seeing the waste of Foulmire for the first time, in its vast emptiness, and smelling its mud.

"I can't afford to offend anyone," Alinor said quietly, the words forced from her. "If I want to earn enough to put food on the table for the two of you, I can't afford pride."

"I know," Alys said.

"And Rob is not more precious than you." She choked on her words. "Nothing in my world is more precious than you."

"I know," Alys repeated. She put her arm round her mother's shoulder and held her closely. "I know what you've done for us. I don't know half of what you've suffered—for us. You've been mother and father to us, I know. And it was too much for any woman to do on her own. I'm grateful, I am—really. But I'm only saying that I can't be like you. I can't do what you do. I can't bend under the wheel. I can't stand it. I'd rather risk everything than settle for a poor life, like you have."

"You think I've settled for poverty?"

"Yes," said Alys with the blunt cruelty of the young.

"I understand," her mother said quietly. "I do understand wanting to be proud, being in love, being reckless."

"Do you?"

She nodded, pressing her lips closed on her secret. Only last night she had been proud of her desire, entranced by lovemaking, and reckless. "I do know," she repeated.

They stood for a moment, holding each other close, then they turned and walked side by side up the road to Chichester.

"I'm sorry," Alys said quietly. "You know I love you. I didn't mean to say all that."

"I know."

They walked a few minutes in silence then Alinor spoke: "This life isn't what I intended for myself. It isn't what my mother wanted for me. She thought Zachary was a man with his own boat, who'd do well. She thought we'd be neighbors, and she and I would work together, and he'd make a better life for me. She thought Ned would inherit the ferry, and have a good wife and a child of his own, and I'd have money coming in from Zachary and we'd live next door to my brother in our home. She couldn't foresee that Mary would die, and that your father'd turn out bad."

They walked in silence for a while until they heard a shout from behind and turned to see a farmer with a wagon piled high with fleeces, his wife sitting up beside him with baskets of cheeses.

"Going to market?" he asked as they paused on the side of the road and turned to him. "Ah, Mrs. Reekie, I didn't recognize you, out of your way, on the Birdham road. Are you going to Chichester market?"

"Yes," Alinor said, smiling brightly. "And this is my girl, Alys."

"Grown like a weed," he said. "I remember you when you were a little tot. Would you like a lift?"

"Come up and sit on the bench beside me," his wife said to

Alinor. "Alys can go in the back on the fleeces if she doesn't object."

"Thank you," Alinor said gratefully, as the goodwife leaned down and offered a hand to help Alinor up to the driver's bench and Alys put one foot on the hub band, the other on the spokes, and clambered up.

"Are you selling some of your oils?" the woman asked, looking at Alinor's basket.

"Yes," Alinor said. "And buying some lace for Mrs. Miller, if there's anything good to be had."

"Terrible dear," the farmer's wife said. "I wonder she doesn't make her own."

Alinor, knowing that anything she said would be repeated, smiled and made no comment.

"But I suppose they're doing so well, she can afford to buy," the woman said.

"I don't know," Alinor said levelly.

"Oh, weren't you there at harvest home? Didn't we all see the best wheat harvest they've ever had? And don't they sell half of it for profit and send it out of the county? And her yaddering away all dinnertime with Master Walter's tutor from Cambridge, as if she were as good as him? As if she would have anything to say to him that he would want to hear!"

Alinor blandly smiled again.

"Still, she'll make no ground there. I hear he's going back to Cambridge when Master Walter goes. Taking the young lord back there, to teach him all about law or whatever it is that they do."

"I don't know," Alinor repeated.

"Such a handsome man!"

"I didn't really see," Alinor said, thinking that the thudding of her heart was so loud in her own ears that it must be audible to the woman sitting beside her.

"You must have done! He went right up to you after dinner. We were all wondering what he had to say to you."

"He was telling me about Rob. My boy is taking lessons with Master Walter. He is his server."

"Did you hope that they would send Rob as a companion to Cambridge?" the woman speculated. "Was that why you walked away from him at the dinner without a curtsey? Did you ask for Rob to go, and did the tutor refuse you?"

"No, no," Alinor said. "Nothing like that! I was unwell. I was so afraid of being sick before the company. I had to get myself home. I begged his pardon and dashed for home."

"She doesn't cure her hams properly, for all she's so proud of them," the goodwife said. "I felt queasy myself."

"What brings you on this road, Mrs. Reekie?" the farmer interrupted his wife. "Will you be wanting a lift back this way after the market?"

"No, we'll take the usual road home," Alinor replied. "We're only out of our way because we were visiting."

"Visiting who?" the wife asked curiously.

"Stoney Farm," Alinor replied.

"Aha!" The goodwife was thrilled at finally extracting a nugget of gossip. "I saw the two of them dancing at harvest home. They made a lovely pair. Am I to listen for the banns?"

"Yes," Alinor conceded. "Yes. Alys and Richard are to be married."

"In our church at Birdham?"

"Ours. St. Wilfrid's."

"Well, what a catch for you!" she said with unintentional rudeness. "The Stoney boy! And that beautiful farm. Just as well she inherits your looks, as you've got nothing else to offer."

"I think they'll be very happy," Alinor said repressively. "It's a love match."

"Best sort," the man said.

"I daresay Mrs. Stoney's not too pleased. She's had a rich match in mind for her boy from the day he was born."

"She was very welcoming," Alinor said, praying that Alys, in the back among the sheep fleeces, could hear none of this. "We're all very happy."

They got to Chichester within the hour and jumped down from the wagon with thanks.

"Ridiculous old woman!" Alys said, smiling and waving as the wagon rumbled away from them on the cobbles. "And now I stink of sheep."

"Hush," Alinor said.

Alys laughed. "Who cares what she thinks? Shall we buy lace first?"

"No, first I'll sell my oils."

Alinor led the way to a stall specializing in dried herbs, crystal stones, oils, ointments, and charms. She knew the stallholder well and he greeted her with a leering smile. "Ah, Mrs. Reekie, I was hoping to see you today. Have you brought me something good?"

"A dozen bottles of mixed oils," Alinor said.

She put her basket on the stall and looked at his stock while he lifted out each bottle and read the handwritten label. "Very good, very good. I didn't know that you had wolfsbane? You've never brought me any before."

"I found some growing wild," Alinor said. "And I thought I'd make some oil. It's a useful physic, but I doubt that there's much call for preventing wolves on Tidelands!"

"It's a very potent poison," he remarked. "Strange to see a wisewoman selling poison in the broad light of day!"

"It's a cure for fever too. One drop in a big beaker of ale is a mild treatment against fever. And you can use it on a scorpion bite."

"We don't suffer from many scorpions in Chichester," the man said sarcastically.

Alinor shrugged. "I'll take it back home if you don't want it. I can use it for treating fevers."

"No, no, I'll buy it. It's good to have it in stock, even if there is little call for it. What shall I give you for the water of aconite and the other oils?"

"Six shillings," Alinor said boldly.

"Now, now, I have to pay rent on my shop, and a servant to keep the shop. I can't spare that. But I will give you four shillings for them all."

"Six shillings," Alinor insisted. "For the twelve bottles. And the bottles and corks returned to me."

"You drive a hard bargain," he conceded. "As a beautiful woman may do."

Alinor unpacked the bottles onto his stall and he produced empty bottles from a basket at the back.

"Here, I'll give you a couple of extra bottles and corks," he said. "For the wolfsbane."

"Thank you."

"Bring me some more next monthly market," he said. "And I'll buy dried herbs by the ounce, also."

"I have some drying now."

He leaned towards her. "Can you make me something to restore manhood?" he whispered. "I have a customer who would be glad of it."

"I don't have a recipe for that," she said, discouragingly.

"You will have, I know you will have. It'll be horny goatweed and bull pizzle, ginger and something like that, boiled up together."

She shook her head. "I don't have a recipe. I can't get hold of such ingredients and if I could, I would not," she said. "I don't do anything of that sort."

He snorted disbelievingly. "Don't tell me that you turn away good business?"

"I do," she said steadily. "I make the herb remedies because I know what they do. The goodness, the God-given goodness, is in the plant, a gift from God Himself. But anything with charming and special words is halfway towards magic. My mother'd never have anything to do with it, and neither will I. She taught me to use the herbs that we all know, and not dabble in things that are mysteries—if they work at all."

"And you a midwife!" he said nastily. "I don't see why you would put yourself above the act. You pull the baby out, why don't you help the father to put it in?"

"Because I need my license," Alinor said. "And if the bishop ever comes back, he isn't going to look kindly on some woman from Sealsea Island selling love philters and casting spells. I am a midwife and a herbalist, and I do nothing else. I have to guard my reputation: it's my fortune."

"Hardly a fortune, my dear. Your reputation is hardly a fortune! Look, I'll get you the ingredients myself and pay you to come to my stillroom and make it up for me. You needn't tell a soul. It can be just between you and me. Our little secret. I don't believe that you'll turn down five shillings."

Alinor had a pang of guilt thinking of the five shillings towards Alys's dowry, but she could not rid herself of a fear of anything that looked like magic. "I'm sorry," she said again. "But I only work as a herbalist, with the herbs that I know. I don't dabble in mysteries."

He laughed to conceal his irritation and she realized at once that the remedy was for himself. He had the edgy laugh of a man without confidence; his bullying tone came from his weakness. All the talk about a customer was a blind for his own need. "Oh! If you want to turn down good business from an established customer. . . ."

"I am sorry," she said kindly. "But I can't help you."

"It's not for me," he said quickly. "But I could sell it a dozen times."

"Then you will surely find someone to make it for you," she said.

He grimaced. "Your herbs are so good—they're the best. I wanted yours. People always ask for the oils from the pretty witch of Foulmire."

"I hope they don't call me that," Alinor said coldly.

"Only in jest."

"It's no jest to me."

"So you say, so you say. I'll give you good day, and if you have the sense to change your mind you can come back to me."

Alinor accepted her dismissal, pocketed her money, and lifted her basket from his stall. He waved her away, and Alinor gritted her teeth, smiled, and said good-bye. He did not bother to reply but turned to a customer and let her go without another word. Mother and daughter made their way through the crowd to the north side of the Market Cross, to the wool merchant.

There was a little crowd around his table, women bringing back wool that they had spun and collecting their payments, women buying sacks of raw wool for spinning. Alinor bought a shilling's worth of fleece in a small sack. He took the money with a word of thanks. "Good day, Mrs. Reekie. I can fetch the yarn from you myself, if you work quickly. I am coming to Sealsea Island next month."

"I'll leave it with my brother at the ferry-house," Alinor promised him. "And if you'll take the price of another sack off my wages and leave it for me, I'll spin more."

"Working hard?" he asked with a wink at her. "Saving up for something?"

"Nothing in particular," Alinor said discreetly, though Alys smiled and blushed and looked down.

They turned from the stall, trying not to bump people in the crowded street with the bulky sack.

"What now?" Alys asked.

"I have to buy some salt, for salting down the fish," Alinor said, looking around.

"What's wrong with the salt that we make?"

"I can't make enough for a barrel of fish," Alinor said. "And it's such hard work, stirring the boiling pans and keeping the fire in all day, for such a little result."

She led the way to the stall where two rough men were shoveling from sacks of salt into smaller bags. "I'll take two," Alinor said, and handed over the pennies.

As she took the bags and turned away, Alys said: "There's the lace maker."

She was an old lady sitting on her own, on a stool with a piece of cloth spread on the ground before her to show her little pieces of lace. She had a cushion on her knee, and her swollen fingers were busy with the bobbins as the lace grew from the center of the cushion. She pulled out a pin and pressed in another, pricking out the pattern as the bobbins whirled and clicked against each other, as if they were a little army in battle on a snowy field.

"Good day, mistress," Alinor said politely.

"Good day to you," she replied, not glancing up from her work.

"I'm looking for some lace for a collar for Mrs. Miller at the tide mill," Alinor said.

"Everything you see is for sale," the old woman said. "And I should be glad of your custom, my dear. I keep myself off the parish with my work, you see."

Alys suppressed a giggle at the old lady's piping voice, and Alinor frowned at her. The two of them knelt down and turned over the pieces of handmade lace until Alys said: "This is the prettiest, Ma. Look at this." She held up a wide ribbon of lace that could be used to trim a collar. It was worked with a design of butterfly wings, a repeating motif. "Pretty," Alys said and then added under her breath: "Far too pretty for her."

"How much is this?" Alinor asked the old lady.

"That is two shillings for the yard," she said.

"Could you let me have it cheaper?" Alinor asked. "I am not commissioned to spend if it is too dear."

"My dear, all that stands between me and the parish is a yard of lace," the woman confided. "You're too beautiful to know what it is to be a poor woman and a burden on your neighbors. But within a week of me selling nothing they won't open their doors to me for fear that I'll beg a loaf of bread, or a quart of milk, though they have a whole herd of cows. Within a month they're wondering if they can move me on to another parish. They ask after my children, and why I don't go and visit them. They hope to force me to be a burden on them. It's a bitter thing to grow old and poor. Pray that God spares you."

"Amen," whispered Alinor.

The lace maker turned to Alys's shocked face. "Believe me! They can take against you in a moment. One cross word, and then they call for the witchfinder, and name you as a witch so as to be rid of you once and for all! It's a crime to be poor in this county; it's a sin to be old. It's never good to be a woman."

Alinor felt a cold shiver down her back at the words. "I have only three shillings for lace," she said hastily. "I am sorry for your troubles."

"I'll sell you two yards for three shillings," the old woman said. "And you will oblige me if you buy from me again."

She took the ribbon of lace and folded it gently, over and over, and tied it with a thread of pink silk. "Fine work," she said. "Two weeks' work and I get three shillings for it. Pray God that you are never left on your own and have to earn your own living. It's a hard world for a woman alone."

"Amen," Alinor said again. "I know it."

They walked away from the stall. "Miserable old thing!" Alys said carelessly. She looked more closely at her mother. "Don't listen to her! You earn well enough. You're nothing like her. With your herbs and the midwife business, and now your boat, and the fishing. And you have the work you do at the mill, and your own work in the garden and at Ferry-house. If they have you back to the Priory to work in their stillroom they'll pay well. And soon I shall be a rich young farmer's wife and Rob'll be an apothecary. We'll both send money home to you!"

"And she earns well enough with her lace for now," Alinor said. "But what about the week when she's too old to work any-more? You saw her hands—what happens when she can't bend her fingers? What happens the week that she falls sick? What does she eat then? Where does she get her firewood then? From her neighbors, as she said, and they'll turn against her just for asking."

She had to raise her voice against the gathering swell of noise and the two of them looked around to see what was causing people to shout and heckle. It was a young royalist supporter, standing defiantly on the steps of the Market Cross, with a rowdy crowd gathered around him.

"We will have peace and the king back on his throne by Christmas!" he shouted.

"Then we'll have war again by Easter!" someone rejoined. "Because your king is a liar!"

There was a cheer and a laugh, but most of the crowd wanted to hear what the young royalist would say.

"Let's go," Alinor said nervously, as Alys dawdled to listen.

"The parliament men know that they have to agree with the king, and they are going to the Isle of Wight to meet with him," the young man declared. "He will not be coerced, he will be returned to his throne."

"Free ale for all!"

"They will demand that he give up the royal militia and accept the rights of the New Model Army." The young man paused impressively. "He will never agree to this. They will demand a church without bishops. You know what comes of that!" Again, he glared at the crowd. "Where is the Bishop of Chichester today?"

"Slough," someone said helpfully. "Did you want him? Because he ran away as fast as his feet could carry him."

Grandly, the young man ignored the heckler. "This is the church of Henry VIII," he declaimed over the laughter. "The church of Queen Elizabeth. Their true heir, King Charles, will never abandon it. He will restore the House of Lords, the bishops . . ."

"Don't forget the Bishop of Rome!" someone shouted from the back. "Because the queen obeys him rather than her husband!"

"Come on," Alinor said to her daughter. "There'll be fighting soon."

"Our king will never agree to these demands!" The young man raised his voice, as the two women hurried away. "They cannot force him and we should defend his right to be king. We should say to our member of parliament . . ."

"Can they really force the king to give everything up?" Alys asked her mother as they went down South Street towards the road to Sealsea Island.

"I don't know," Alinor replied. "I suppose so. Since he's in their keeping. But perhaps you can't keep a king in prison."

"My uncle says the king should be tried for treason. For starting the war again and calling in the Scots. That was treason against the people of England."

"Easy to say," Alinor observed, "but other people say that a king cannot be wrong, since he is the king."

"Who thinks that?"

Alinor thought of the man she loved. "Some people say it."

"Well, it's rubbish!" Alys declared stoutly.

The two walked home, taking it in turns to carry the sack of wool and the bags of salt. A carter on his way to the tide mill overtook them on the road, and let them sit in the back of his wagon on the sacks of grains. The sky was golden with the afternoon light as the wagon turned down the lane to the mill. The waters were lapping at the quay, a breeze picking up the waves in the haven, making the waters look like shirred gray silk.

Alys jumped down to open the yard gate for the cart, and then walked ahead of him into the yard. The sluice gates of the millpond were open, the tide pouring in to fill up the pond, the little birds darting around the pond edge, feeding from the incoming waters. Mr. Miller came out from the barn at the sound of wheels on the cobbled yard and Mrs. Miller came from the kitchen door to see Alinor climbing down from the wagon.

"Here you are," she said to Alinor. "And home without the trouble of a walk, thanks to one of our customers."

"Yes," said Alinor. "We were lucky."

"Oh, there's always some man ready to help you out," Mrs. Miller said.

"Well, we were lucky today," Alinor agreed. "And look what I bought for you."

The miller and the wagoner unloaded the sacks of corn, piling them at the foot of the granary doors, ready to be hoisted upwards when the pond was full and the water released to turn the wheel and work the hoist. Alinor handed over the package of lace and watched Mrs. Miller unroll it.

"Now this is very fine," she said with rare satisfaction. "Very good. Never tell me that you got all this for three shillings?"

"I did!" Alinor said with pleasure. "I hoped you would think it a good bargain. I believe that it really is. Look at the delicacy of the pattern!"

"Chichester market!" Mrs. Miller said. "Who knew there was anything as good as this to be found at Chichester market! I would have thought to go to London for such work."

"She was an old lady. She was lace making, sitting on a little stool in the middle of the market. She didn't even have a table," Alinor said. "But all her things were beautiful."

"Well, I'm grateful to you," Mrs. Miller said with unusual warmth. "And did you sell your oils?"

"I did," Alinor said, showing her the basket with the empty bottles. "And I bought a sack of wool for spinning, and some salt for salting down the fish, so I've had a very good day."

Alys suddenly appeared at her mother's elbow, and dipped a curtsey to Mrs. Miller. "And you've had a fine day!" the woman scolded at once. "Jauntering off all the day and strolling round the market on a workday."

"We went to Stoney Farm first," Alinor said, knowing that Mrs. Miller would have to know, and would resent it bitterly if they delayed the news and she heard it from someone else. "Alys and Richard are betrothed. They will marry at Easter."

"Never!" the woman exclaimed, her mood darkening at once.

"I was sure that you would be pleased," Alinor prompted. "Since they met while working for you, and were king and queen of the harvest at your harvest home. I knew you would be pleased for them."

Mrs. Miller was struggling with her envy of anyone else's happiness. "No reason not to be pleased," she said irritably. "It's not as if I put any obstacles in their way. It's not as if I had him in mind for Jane."

"No, exactly," Alinor confirmed. "There is no reason for you not to be happy for her."

"And yet . . . well, it's a very good match for your girl. Stoney Farm! Richard Stoney! You'll be lucky if people don't say that she trapped him into it."

"Nobody would be so unkind," Alinor ruled. "It's obvious that Richard loves her so much, and she him."

"Just that it's such a good match for her," Mrs. Miller grumbled. "Strolling out of a fisherman's cottage and getting to Stoney Farm in one jump."

"There's no denying that it's a good match for her," Alinor conceded. "But she'll make a good wife to him. She has learned so much good housekeeping from you."

"She's learned nothing today, but walking around the market and spending other people's money."

"She'll make it up to you," Alinor promised, taking Alys's cold hand. "And now we must be going."

"I wish you well," Mrs. Miller said begrudgingly. "I wish you very happy."

"I know you do," Alinor replied, and picked up her sacks of salt as Alys hefted the sack of wool and walked beside her mother out of the yard. She left the yard gate open for the carter to leave, and they went towards the ferry together.

"I put the purse back," Alys said nonchalantly.

Alinor's heart skipped a beat. "I thought you said you would do it in the evening. I thought you would come back, when she closes up her hens?"

"Yes, but when I saw her come out to you to look at the lace, I knew I had a moment. I ran into the kitchen, pulled out the brick, popped in the purse, and put the brick back in a second. She'll never know it was gone."

Alinor almost staggered with the relief. "So, it's done, and you got away with it."

Alys beamed at her. "It's done, and I got away with it."

"And you'll never do it again," Alinor commanded. "Promise me, Alys. It's too great a risk. Never take anything from her again. Not even borrowing. You shouldn't have done it this time. Promise me, you'll never do it again. Think of the danger!"

The girl laughed as though no danger could threaten her. "I'll promise you that I'll never be caught," she said gleefully. "I'll promise not to end up on the gallows. A fool like Mrs. Miller will never catch me, and soon I'll have far more money than Jane Miller's dowry. You wait till I'm Mrs. Stoney, of Stoney Farm, Birdham! I won't keep my money in a chimney. I shall have my own box at the Chichester goldsmith's! I shall be a woman of means!"

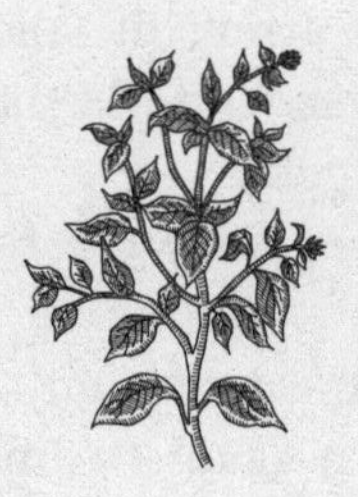

## TIDELANDS, SEPTEMBER 1648

Alinor heard nothing from James all through the month of September, but she did not expect to hear from him, and she went through the dusty days at the end of summer with a languid sense of peace. She found that she trusted him, she believed that he would go to that place—that unimaginable and mysterious place—that he called his home, and the men he called his brothers would release him from his vows. Alinor, raised in a country where Roman Catholics had been banned for nearly a century, could not imagine what rituals and oaths James might endure to be free of his blasphemous past. She thought they might frighten him with threats of endless purgatory and drench him in wine like blood and force him to eat raw flesh. Tears came to her eyes when she thought of him facing the terrible mastery of Rome. But she trusted him to be brave and confident in that world that was such a mystery to her. He had said that he would do it, and she knew that he loved her and she believed that he would convince them that he must be freed.

She was more afraid of the influence of his family, especially his mother, as she could imagine only too easily what a noble lady might say to her adored only son when he told her that he was leaving the priesthood with no greater ambition than to marry a deserted wife, a herbalist, a fisherman's widow who made a living clinging to a muddy harbor in the tidelands of England. If the Stoneys—yeoman farmers—looked down on Alys, what would the aristocratic Summers say to her drab of a mother?

James's parents were sure to forbid him to return to her. They would disinherit him rather than let him throw himself away on a woman that they would accuse of being little more than a hedge witch: little better than a pauper. But then she remembered that they too were landless, they too were clinging to all they had left after six years of civil war, far from their beautiful home, in exile with a defeated queen. They were papists and cavaliers and utterly damned. They could not return to England: both their religious faith and their political loyalty were criminal. They had been far above her when their king was on the throne and their faith accepted, but now they were not. The unimaginable gulf between her and their son had been destroyed forever with the smashing of the altars, with the breaking of the contract between king and people, with the end of deference. While the king could be captured by a mere cornet of the army and end up in an ordinary house in Newport on the Isle of Wight, then Alinor and James were no longer at opposite ends of society with a gulf between them unbridgeable as the mire. His parents must know, as everyone now knew, that the world was changed, that the humble people of England had risen up and that the rulers were no longer in their palaces. If a working farmer like Oliver Cromwell could rule England, why should a fisherman's widow not rise in the world and hope for better?

"The prince has been defeated at sea and driven back to Holland. Have you heard?" Ned asked her one evening, as he sat before the cottage door and smoked his pipe to keep the biting flies from his face. His dog lay down in the shade of the bench and panted in the heat.

Alinor brought him a cup of small ale and sat beside him to sip her own. She had the pole of her distaff pushed into her belt so that the hank of wool was as high as her head and, as she sat beside him, she plucked and twisted the thread with her free hand, keeping the spindle on the end of the thread in constant motion with little taps from her foot. The hank of wool was hot in her hand and greasy with lanolin.

"I hadn't heard. But I've seen no one since Chichester market. I've not been out of the brewhouse, or the stillroom or the kitchen. What's happened?"

"You and Alys are working all hours. Did you get a good price for that barrel of salted fish?"

"Twenty shillings! From the grain trader ship. But what about the prince?"

"I only just heard it myself. We never hear anything here. It's as if we were under the waters of the harbor, not just beside it. But Farmer Gaston's wife has a cousin come to visit from London, and he told me as I ferried him across the rife. You knew that the Prince of Wales had command of a fleet?"

"Yes, I'd heard that," Alinor confirmed, thinking of the man who had told her of the waiting fleet, of the chance for the prince.

"Our navy, the parliament fleet, has chased him out of the Thames and all the way back to Holland. He won't wait off our shores again." Ned chuckled. "Must've been hoping his father would escape from Newport and that he'd pick him up at sea, take him to France. They must've thought that the king would break his parole and escape again. So that's overset, too. The king's ships've gone, and he's trapped in Newport, the parliament men telling him how it's to be, and nothing for him to do but agree."

"The king's ships have failed him?" she asked.

"Driven back to Holland. He's got nowhere to go now," Ned said with satisfaction. "He'll have to agree with parliament and return with them to London. And I tell you, he'll find a dusty welcome there."

"But what'll become of him? And what about all the people who followed him? Those in France and Holland, those who went into exile with the queen?"

"Who cares for them?"

"It's just . . . what will happen to them, I wonder."

"You know, I think they'll reprimand the king," Ned said thoughtfully. "I think they'll take him to London and make him into a king like no one has ever seen before, a king who has to work with the parliament and the church, not one who's set over it. I think they'll give him back his house but not his throne. Maybe they'll make him Mr. King!" He laughed at his own joke. "I would bet you a shilling that they don't give him back his throne, and for sure, he'll never command an army again. He can't be trusted. Everyone can see that now: he can't be trusted."

"So will the queen come home to be with him? Will she be Mrs. Queen? And the prince? And what about the lords and ladies and those who followed her to Paris? What'll they do?"

"They'll all have to beg pardon of the people of England," Ned ruled solemnly. "That's what I'd have them do. Beg pardon. Pay a fine, swear never to bear arms against Englishmen again, and then live privately, quietly. We should treat them all as bad as papists: fined and banned from public office. They can live in England without rights, silent: like wives and children, like the madmen that they are. They can work but not command."

"But they'll be able to come home?" she pressed.

"If they want a half-life," Ned predicted. "But it'll never be the same again for them. And us. Nothing'll ever be the same again."

Alys came out of the doorway, a hank of raw wool on her distaff. She sat beside them and twirled the spindle with her foot and started to spin.

"You've got a spindle in your hand night and day," her uncle remarked.

"Dowry," she said shortly.

He nodded. "I'll give you a couple of shillings on the day," he promised. "Ten."

"I'd be grateful," she said smoothly. "Thank you, Uncle."

She did not look at her mother, nor did Alinor raise her eyes from her work. "We'll both be grateful," Alinor added. "To tell truth: we've had to promise more than we can find."

"It's a handsome farm," he conceded. "They're bound to want a good payment. When's the wedding to be?"

"After Easter," Alinor said.

"Perhaps earlier," Alys added. "If we can get the money earlier. Perhaps Twelfth Night. I should love a Twelfth Night wedding."

Her uncle shook his head. "There's no Twelfth Night in the Bible," he said. "And no call for one in a godly church."

"And that's too soon!" Alinor protested. "We'll never get anything like the money in that time."

Alys shrugged. "A later day in January then. Or February. A day without a name."

"Then you'll have to spin faster," Ned told her. "Or spin gold, like the lass in the story."

"What's the hurry?" Alinor asked her. "In bad weather and dark afternoons? Why not wait for spring?"

The pretty girl showed her most mischievous smile. "Because I want a warm bed in bad weather and dark afternoons."

Alinor gave a little frown and a nod towards the girl's uncle to remind her to mind her tongue.

"Marriage is a serious contract, to be taken in hand for the glory of God," Ned said solemnly. "Not at the whim of the lusts of the young. You'd do better to be the Lord's handmaiden, ask in your prayers, till He says the time is right."

"Yes," Alys agreed, her pretty face grave. "But how long would you have me wait, Uncle Ned? For there you are on your own, and there is Ma all alone here. I know we're a family as cool-blooded as fish, but even so . . ."

Despite himself her uncle laughed and bent to pat his dog on the head.

"We'll never get the dowry in time, if you bring the wedding forward," Alinor warned her.

"We will," Alys said confidently. "Because Richard's going to make it up for me."

"What?" Ned demanded. "The bridegroom pay the dowry to himself?"

Alys glowed with pride. "He loves me so much," she said. "He doesn't want me to worry."

"Has he got his own savings?" Alinor asked. "Has he got that sort of fortune?"

"From his grandfather Stoney. Willed to him. It's all his. And he'll give it to me. He's promised to make up, if we're short."

Alinor moved her shoulders as if a weight of anxiety had slid away. "Thank God," she said. "I've been so—"

"I told you it would come out all right."

"You're very sure of yourself," Ned remarked.

Alys peeped up at him. "I'm sure about this," she said.

## DOUAI, FRANCE, SEPTEMBER 1648

James woke just before Prime to the chiming of the great bell, *La Joyeuse*, and knew himself to be safely home, where he had been raised and educated, where he was known and loved. Here he could use his God-given name, he could speak of his parents; here he could pray for his king. Here he was part of a community, passionately religious, fiercely patriotic, a community of spies ready to return at any moment to their English homes, to bring their country back to God. His waking thought was one of glorious relief: that he had survived his mission to England, where so many young men, educated, known, and loved just like him, had not. Even before he opened his eyes, he thanked God that he had been spared, neither denounced by false friends nor inadvertently betraying himself. He had not faced a court, or death by burning. He could admit to himself now how very afraid he had been. That made him think of Alinor and her unthinking protection. She decided to hide him at the very moment that they met; she had risked her life to nurse him. He thought that she was guided by God to do the right thing, and though she was a heretic, she had served God in saving him.

As soon as her grave dark gaze came into his mind, every other thought was gone and he was lost for long moments in the recollection of her profile, and how she turned her head, and the fall of her hair. At once he was back in the stable loft, feeling her lips against his skin, but then the pale walls of his cell suddenly reflected the passing candle of the brother who tapped on his door and called "*Pax Vobiscum*," and all down the corridor came the reply: "Amen," "Amen," "Amen," as the brothers and the scholars sat up in their little beds and welcomed the gift of another day.

Only James felt that the blessing was not for him, was not given to him knowingly. His brothers and his superiors at the university and the abbey did not know how he had failed, and if they had known, they would not have blessed him. He feared they would blame him and he knew that they would be right to do so. His waking joy faded, and his confident thanks to God. He rose from his bed barefoot onto the cold stone floor, and washed his face and hands, his armpits and crotch in a bowl of cold water with a cake of best Castille soap. He pulled on his linen shift, his robe, he tied the rope belt at his waist. He pushed his damp feet into his new leather sandals, opened his cell door, and joined the line of young men, hoods over their heads, eyes down to the floor, going to the service of Prime in the abbey. Absorbed in their own prayers, none of them looked at him, or greeted him, and James felt a gulf of separation from these who had been his childhood companions.

"God forgive me," he whispered as he walked, surrounded by young men praising God, confident in the world that they would enter, certain that they would restore it to the true faith. "God forgive me, God forgive me, God forgive me my sins."

He seemed to pray with true penitence throughout the service, murmuring the familiar responses, singing the psalms. But he knew that he was not penitent, he knew that he was at war with himself. He had failed in his mission, he had failed his king and he had failed his vows. He would not list Alinor among his sins. With her, he had been truly himself, as he had never been since childhood. With her, he had a glimpse of a godly life in the world, not one in the cloister. He thought he might be a better husband than a priest; he knew at any rate that he despaired of his vocation. His passion for her gave his life meaning, where otherwise he was lost. It was a revolutionary thought for a young man who had been dedicated to the Church from childhood, but he could not help himself. He had a conviction that he had never felt before: that he did not want to be here, hiding behind high walls in northern France; that he did not want to keep faith with a king who was unable to rule; that he did not even want to restore the true religion to England. The only thing he truly wanted was to go to his family home in Yorkshire, take the woman that he loved to his house, and live there as an Englishman, at peace on his own fields.

As soon as the liturgy was over, the brothers went to the dining hall to break their fast in a silence emphasized by the quiet reading in Latin of the gospel for the day. Then one of the senior brothers rose to his feet and announced the duties of the day, the work expected of the novices, the names of those who would study, garden, farm, clean and cook, or serve in the church workshops. James was ordered to attend the senior professor in his chambers. A few of the young seminarians glanced enviously at James, wishing that they too might be sent to England, to go into hiding to spy and serve the hidden Roman Catholic faithful. He did not acknowledge them. He thought they were fools to long for martyrdom. They would not wish for it if they knew what it was like to stand on a darkened quayside and watch for a light and not know if it were a friend or an enemy. They would not wish for it if they had ever got within a second of the most triumphant victory of the war, only to see it thrown away for a whim. But he avoided their glances, bowed his head in obedience, and went on his own to the professor's rooms.

He was admitted by a clerk and found Dr. Sean seated behind his table, his stole of office scarlet against the black of his gown, a black cap of office on his head, his thin face pale and drawn. He rose from his chair and skirted the table to greet James, and hugged him, kissing him on both cheeks in the French way, and then made the sign of the cross and blessed him. "Sit down," he said warmly. "Sit down, my son, and tell me everything."

James, very sure that he could not tell everything, sat on the edge of his chair as the professor seated himself and took up a quill pen to make notes.

"You came back last night? And you have spoken to no one of your trip?"

"No one," James confirmed.

"You left the king in captivity?"

"God forgive me, I did."

"Tell me how that was? Were you not ordered to get him to a boat? And see him to his son's ship and safety?"

"I was, Father Professor."

"Then why did you fail?"

Haltingly, ashamed of himself, James explained the trip to the Isle of Wight, the associates who met him, the boys who concealed his mission, the boatman who failed him, and the replacement: Zachary. He said that Mr. Hopkins's house was completely unguarded and that the king could have left with him but would not do so.

The professor sat, his fingers steepled together as if he were praying. "Why would he not leave with you?"

"He did not explain himself to me."

"But he would not leave?"

"He laughed," James said bitterly. "And then he was angry that anyone should doubt that he could save himself. He was confident that he would be able to make an agreement with them. He told me to come again in future, if he needed me. I warned him that it was dangerous for me, and for others—that we might not be able to come again—but he didn't take me seriously. I couldn't make him take us seriously."

"You told him you were obeying his wife and son? That it was their plan?"

"I said the password, and I told him they had paid me, and given me money to bribe the boatman. He said he would not go at their bidding." James could not easily convey the king's petulance and maintain the respect that he must show for God's ordained leader on earth.

"But you got back to Sir William without detection?"

"I'm certain that I did."

"And then you were ill?"

James flushed. The professor could see the deep color at the neck of his robe.

"I was. Some sort of fever that they have on the marshes there. It didn't last long."

"Was it a sickness of the body only? Or was it of your faith, my son?"

James dropped his head. The older man could barely make out the muttered words that his faith was shaken and indeed lost.

"This is not surprising," Dr. Sean said gently. "You were very alone, a young man, and in danger of your life for weeks and weeks before you even got to the island. We gave you the greatest task that anyone from this college has ever been set, and it failed."

"I'm so sorry," James whispered. "I am shamed."

"It sounds as if no one could have persuaded the king. If he did not want to come you could not make him. I believe that you did your best and I imagine that no one could have done more."

There was a silence.

"Could you have done more, my son?"

"I have questioned myself," James admitted. "I cannot see what more I could have done. I wish I could have got him away. I think if he had come with me I would have got him safely away. I even dream of it. I go over and over in my mind. But there's no certainty. There's no knowing what would have happened out at sea, or even at the quayside. I don't think I could have done more—not without his consent. But I fear . . . I fear that I should have insisted. But how could I insist to him?"

"One setback may shake your faith but not break it," the senior man remarked. "Your vows remain intact?"

There was a long silence in the sunlit peaceful room.

"They do not," James confessed, his voice a whisper. "Father, I have sinned. I met a woman and I love her. I am so sorry, Professor. I am deep in sin."

The older man nodded. "We are all of us in sin. We were born in sin and we sin every day. But the Lord is merciful. He forgives us if we confess and return to God. You will confess and return to God."

James's head came up. "I ask to be released from my vows," he said quietly. "I will confess, and serve any penance that is asked of me, of course. But I pray that I may be released. Father Professor, I love her. I want to be with her."

The abbey bell struck the hour and in the town, beyond the window, the other church bells rang too. James listened to the competing chimes, all of them announcing the hour of prayer in this devout town. When the last had fallen silent, Dr. Sean looked kindly at the young man. "Go to the church and confess your sins and we will talk again next week."

"Next week!" James exclaimed.

The older man smiled patiently. "Yes," he said. "Of course. Did you think you would leave tomorrow? You and I will talk again next week. And in the meantime, you will speak of this only in the confessional, to the confessor that I appoint to talk with you. Nowhere else, to no one else, and you will not write to anyone either. You are still under your vow of obedience, my son, and this is how you will spend your week."

James rose to his feet, bowed, and went to the door. Dr. Sean bent his head over his paper, knowing that James would hesitate at the door.

"Father Professor, I have given my word to her that I will return to her. She is waiting for me."

Slowly the older man raised his head, his quill poised in his hand. "My son, she will have to learn patience, as will you. We serve an eternal God, not one who counts the minutes. God took a week to make the world, now He demands that you consider this important choice for a similar time. I don't think you can refuse Him."

James, baffled, bowed his head. "I can't," he agreed.

"If she is a good woman, then she will be praying too. She will need time to consider her situation."

"She is a good woman," he said, thinking of her pale face in the church porch as she waited for ghosts. "She is not of our faith, not of our beliefs, but she is a good woman."

"It is your faith that concerns us now," Dr. Sean said firmly. "Meditate on that. Take it to our Father."

"But she—"

"She does not concern us now. God bless you, my son."

"Amen."

# TIDELANDS, OCTOBER 1648

Even with both of the women spinning, and both of them picking the last of the herbs that were still growing in the late October sunshine, even with Alinor selling her oils from the summer, attending every birth, and drying the herbs that were still growing green, even with Alys working all the hours they would pay her at the Millers' farm, the money was slow to come in and hard to keep. The little household had always lived off its own—growing their own food, brewing their own ale, fishing, making and mending and never buying new. But as winter came closer the price of everything went up: tallow for soap and candles, meat of any sort, cheese and milk, wheat or rye. Even the things that they foraged—the teazels for felting, the willow twigs for sweeping—took longer to find. Alinor spent more and more time picking up driftwood for her fire, walking on the shore, which started to crackle with freezing dew, as the wintry days grew shorter, and the nights dark.

As if winter did not bring trouble enough, Alinor was ill, exhausted before she started her day, sick before she got out of their shared bed. She could not eat before midday, she could not bear the smell of cheese or bacon, and when Ned brought a boiled lobster over one evening, a payment for ferry fees from one of the Sealsea fishermen, she could not even sit at the table while he and Rob and Alys feasted.

"What's wrong with you?" Alys asked irritably, her mouth full of lobster meat. Ned sat opposite Rob, who had come from the Priory to visit and had brought a loaf of white bread with compliments from Mrs. Wheatley. Alinor, opposite Alys, had a slice of the bread and a cup of small ale. Red, the dog, under the table, fixed his brown gaze on her, as if he thought she might slip him the crust.

"I don't know," Alinor said. "I thought it was the quatrain fever but I have no signs; I expect it will pass. Perhaps it was something that I ate."

"It's been weeks," Alys pointed out. "Surely it'd be over by now if it was rancid cream or spoiled meat."

"Don't," Alinor said, the back of her hand to her mouth. "Don't even speak of them."

Ned laughed shortly. "She was always sickish," he said unsympathetically. "You should've seen her when she was breeding you." He bent his head and cracked one of the claws. "Here, Rob," he said. "Try this."

The young man and his uncle picked at the meat. "It's good," Rob said. "The claw's always the best."

"D'you get lobster at the Priory?"

"No," said Rob.

"Folk look down their noses at it, as poor man's meat, but I like it better than beef," Ned said, his speech muffled by a mouthful.

Alinor heard them as if they were far away. Her brother's careless words echoed again and again in her head. She heard a noise in her head like the rush of the waters in the millrace as she looked up and saw Alys's dark blue eyes on her, and heard a distant voice say: "Ma?" as she went down into the darkness.

She woke on the bed in the cottage, Alys at her side. She raised herself on her elbow and Alys held a glass of small ale to her lips. "Where's Rob?"

"Uncle Ned's walking back to the Priory with him. I said that you'd be fine. I said that you'd send to tell him tomorrow. I said it was women's troubles." Alys scrutinized her mother's face. "It is, isn't it?"

Dumbly, Alinor nodded.

"The worst kind? You're with child?"

Alinor swallowed. "I think so."

"You think so?" Alys was pale and furious in a moment. "You must know if you laid with a man or no. Or are you going to tell me you were forced by a faerie lord? God save us, have you been dancing with the faerie lords again?"

A deep shamed flush rose from Alinor's belly to her hot cheeks. "Of course I know. What I don't know is if I'm with child. I hadn't thought of it till Ned said . . . what he said."

"And you tell me to beware of the gallows!"

"I've done very wrong," Alinor confessed to this new, authoritative daughter. "Very wrong."

Alys rose from the bedside and stepped towards the door, flinging it open as if she would summon the icy sea breeze to blow the words from the little cottage. "You must be mad," she said bitterly. "After all you've said to me!"

Alinor bowed her head in shame.

"How could you?"

"I know, Alys. Don't scold me."

"And you dare to let my uncle tell me that I must wait for months to be married? When you've not even waited a year since our da left?"

"It's a year. It's nearly a year."

"Who is it? Mr. Miller?"

"No!" Alinor exclaimed.

"That horrible man who has the physic stall at Chichester market?"

"No, of course not."

"Mr. Tudeley, who's getting Rob his apprenticeship? Is that why Rob gets his chance?"

"No! No! Alys, I won't be questioned like this!"

"You will be!" The girl rounded on her mother. "This is nothing! Don't you think the parish will question you like this as soon as your belly starts to show? Don't you think you'll have to name the father and then stand before the congregation in your shift, in your shame? Don't you think Mr. Miller will ask you, all the churchmen will ask you, they'll demand that you say, and they'll bring in a midwife from Chichester to put her dirty hands all over your belly, and peer at your privates like you were a whore suspected of the pox?"

Alinor shook her head, her golden hair falling around her white face. "No, no."

"They'll go on and on and on at you until you give them his name and then they'll find him and make him pay his fine to the parish. And you'll go to the workhouse, and when the bastard is born they'll take him off you and send you back here as a named whore."

"No," Alinor said. "No, Alys, don't say such things."

"Back here!" Alys gestured wildly at the interior of the little cottage and the vast desolate mire outside. "Back here, as a named whore. Who's going to give Rob an apprenticeship then? Who's going to marry me? Who's going to buy anything from you but magic and love potions?"

"I'm going to be sick," Alinor announced. She stumbled to her feet and got to the open front door. She vomited on her own doorstep, sobbing at the pain of her empty belly heaving on nothing.

Like a blessing, she felt a cold cloth scented with lavender oil laid gently on the back of her neck. "Thank you," she said, and wiped her face and hands. She stepped back and sat on the bed, looking up at Alys as if her daughter were her judge.

"Were you forced, Ma?" the young woman asked more gently. "Is that what happened?"

Alinor turned from the temptation of a lie. "No."

"They won't stop asking. You'll have to tell. Did you not think of this?"

"I didn't think . . . till this very moment . . . that I was with child. I hadn't thought—" She broke off. There was no way to explain to this new challenging Alys that she had thought her sickness was heartache, that her inability to eat was pining for the man she loved, that she had embraced it, like a penance, as he too might be fasting as punishment for his love for her. She had thought the two of them were working their way to be together, he fasting in Douai, and she here, on the edge of the mire, aching for him too, eating only bread and small ale, sick for love.

"Well, think it now!" Alys flung at her. "Think now that you're ruined. And I'm ruined too. You've ruined me. For Richard can't marry me if my mother is a named whore. They won't want our money, if they think you earned it on your back behind a haystack. They won't stand for a missing father and a mother of shame. A deserted wife was a long stretch for them; a pregnant whore will be too much. You are ruined and I am ruined, too."

"Alys, I would never do anything to hurt you," Alinor said.

"You have destroyed me! You could have done nothing worse."

"I won't let this happen."

"It's happened already."

"Alys, all my life I have lived for you." Alinor stumbled over her words. "I tried to keep Zachary from you and Rob. I took blows so that he wouldn't raise his hand to you. I wanted nothing but a good life for the two of you. I've done everything I could do to raise you up from this life. I'd never bring you down."

"Well, you've brought me down." The girl slumped on the foot of the bed, facing her mother, panting and desperate. "It's even worse than you know. For I am with child, too. Unlike you, I can name my lover, and we are betrothed to marry. We did not lie together until we were handclasped. But that's why I'm determined that we marry in January before the baby comes in May."

"In May?" Alinor asked, shocked.

"Yes. There's no shame in being with child at the altar. We were betrothed. We were going to tell his parents and the minister next month. But if you're proved as a whore then Richard won't be allowed to marry me, and his family will never accept me! Then I'll be ruined, too."

"Alys!" Alinor reached out to her beloved daughter, but Alys slapped her hand away and threw herself down on the bed, turned towards the wooden wall, and would not speak.

Alys cried herself to sleep as Alinor lay sleepless, the cottage door wide open to the clear night sky, the stars sparkling like ice. The tide was coming in with an east wind behind it, the coldest wind of all. The sound of the lapping water filled the cottage as if the tide would climb the bank, wash them both away, and make the whole world into tidelands.

At midnight Alinor got up, wrapped her shawl around her shoulders, ignored the protesting cluck of the drowsy hens, and went outside to sit on the rough bench against the cottage wall, closing the door on her sleeping daughter. She watched the moon high in the sky, shining a silver path on the water of the harbor, until she thought it was an invitation to her, a message from the old gods of the Saxon shore, who did not fear death but embraced it as their last voyage. She thought that perhaps the best thing she could do for her daughter, for her son, for herself, and for the man she loved was to walk down to the shore and fill her pockets with stones and follow that gleaming path, colder and colder, wetter and wetter, until the icy waters closed over her head and the sound of rushing water in her ears muffled the cry of the sleepless seagulls.

Quietly, she got to her feet and went through the garden gate, her hand lingering on the worn gatepost. She looked back at the shabby little cottage and then climbed the bank to the high path. Through the tunnel of thornbushes, she walked in moonlight and shadow, along the bank until she came to the white shell beach under the down-swinging branches of the oak tree. The bank had been built as a sea wall years ago, centuries ago, and the sea had worn it away at the foot and tumbled the foundation stones—river stones, rounded by water—on the white shell shore. Alinor lifted one and slid it in the pocket of her gown, and another, for the other side. She felt their weight drag her down. She picked up another—the biggest, the heaviest—to hold it tightly and walk into the icy water that lapped closer and closer. She thought that all her life she had been afraid of deep water and now, in her last moments, she would face that fear and not fear it anymore. She thought that it would drag at her poor skirt, chill her warm body, lap against her belly, her ribs, that she would shudder when it reached her warm armpits, her neck, but that finally she would dip her head and taste the brackish salt of it and know that she would go down into the muddy depths of it, without protest and without fear.

She did not move. She stood at the edge of the sea, the stone heavy in her grip, and watched the moon's dappled reflection, silver on the dark water as the waves crept up the shore, closer and closer. She heard the water lap at her feet and she stood still as the tide turned, and listened to it recede. But she did not move. She did not step along the silvery path of the moon, she did not walk into the water. She stood silent among the quiet sounds of the night, and certainty came to her.

She did not weep for herself, not for Alys, not even for Rob. She did not yearn for James to rescue her, she did not think of him with anything but love. She had loved him and lain with him, she had trusted him and she believed in him still; but she did not expect him to help her in this dark night. She did not think that anything would be illuminated by the dawn, she did not pray to a forgiving God, for she did not expect Him to listen to a woman like her, in a place like this.

She had no faith in her purpose or in her courage. She had no faith in herself as the cold murky waters lapped at her feet. But slowly she found that she had one belief—only one belief: that she would last through this night, that she would last through any night to come. She knew that she would not drown herself. She knew that she would not be broken by this terrible misfortune any more than she had been broken by the cruelty of Zachary or by the loss of her mother. She thought that the one thing that she had learned in this life, which had so many troubles and so few joys: she had at least learned to survive. She knew she could endure. She thought that all her life—raised by a courageous woman in hard circumstances, abused by a violent husband, loving two children and bringing them up in poverty—had taught her this lesson: to survive. She thought it was the only thing that she truly knew to do. She thought that she had found, embedded in her heart, like a drowned field post in a mudbank, a great determination to live.

Alys woke in the morning, as fresh-faced as a child, her eyes clear and her beauty undimmed by the night of crying. She found her mother making gruel and setting out the bowls on the table as if it were an ordinary day.

"Ma?"

"Yes, Alys?"

"What are you going to do?"

"I am going to eat my breakfast and so are you."

"But—"

"Eat first and then we'll talk. You have to eat. Especially now."

Alys pulled out her stool and sat at the table and ate as she was bidden. When she had finished and pushed back her bowl she said: "And now, tell me what you're going to do. You can't let anyone know your sin."

"But you can?"

"It's not the same. Richard and me were handfasted in the sight of God. He's going to marry me. His parents will have no objection to me coming into their house with a new son and heir on the way. They'll welcome me. In the old days half the girls in the parish used to be married with a big belly, you know that yourself. And only the strictest people mind, even now. Everyone's glad to see that a bride is fertile. There's no comparison to you and your adultery."

Alinor bowed her head. "You know for sure that his parents won't object?"

"They're not puritans, and they know that I'm not loose. We were both virgins when we lay together and we were betrothed. They know we've been courting for months. My baby will have a good name and a beautiful farm for his home." She broke off. "At least he would have done. Until now. Until this. Now, God knows what'll happen. Nobody'll let you work for them, nobody'll dream of having you as a midwife. You'll never get your license and no respectable place would have Rob as an apprentice." She dropped her face into her hands and rubbed her eyes. "Ma! Think! Not even Uncle Ned will stand your friend or be your brother when he knows. He'll deny you. And how will you manage here without his kinship? How will you even eat if you can't use the ferry-house kitchen garden?"

Alinor was silent.

"You won't be able to stay here! They'll torture you. Mrs. Miller and all her friends, the parish council, the church court . . ."

"I know," Alinor said quietly.

"Nobody will buy your herbs. They'll come to you for nothing but love potions and poisons."

"I know."

As if Alinor's stillness made Alys more determined, she rose to her feet and looked down at her seated mother. "It's not possible for you to bear this child," the girl said quietly. "You know the herbs to use, you know how it's done. You'll have to get rid of it. You know how. You'll have to get rid of it."

Alinor looked up into her daughter's stern face.

"It's not been long, has it?" asked the girl. "You've only been sick for a few weeks?"

Alinor nodded. She found she could not speak.

"Then it can be done and no one the wiser. I'll go to work at the mill now. I'll come home this afternoon early, saying I'm ill. You can take whatever you need to take at noon, and I'll care for you. I'll do whatever you need. I'll look after you, Ma, I promise. You shall tell me what you need to eat and drink, and I'll not leave you till it's over. I'll change your linen and care for you as it happens."

Alinor said nothing.

"You have to be rid of this," Alys pressed. "Richard can't marry me if you are shamed, and that would break my heart and his, and our child would be born out of wedlock. You'll have a bastard child, and a bastard grandchild. We can't survive that. Your child is the ruin of us all: you, me, and Rob. You have to end it. I've never asked you for anything, Ma, but I am asking you for this."

Her mother sat silent, her face white.

"Your shame is my shame," the girl repeated. "When the Stoneys hear you're with child they'll throw me off. I'll never see Richard again. Then we'll both be stuck here, both of us, with our bastards, without husbands. Don't you think they'll turn us out, with our big bellies on us? Don't you think Mrs. Miller, and all the goodwives like her, will have us out of the parish before we can make a charge on it? And every husband shouting that we should go, to show that it wasn't him?"

"Two babies," was all that Alinor could say.

"Two bastards," her daughter corrected her. "Pauper bastards. They'll die in the poorhouse together. No one will let us raise them."

"I'll think about it." Alinor drew a breath. "I will think about it today and tell you tonight."

"You should have thought before," her daughter said crudely.

Alinor flinched as if she had been struck. "I know," she said, her voice very low. "I know how grave this is."

"If you don't finish it here, today, then my life is ruined. Rob's, too," Alys loaded her mother's guilt. "Nobody will take him as an apprentice if his mother is a bawd who keeps a bawdy house on the mire. Nobody'll ever marry me with a bastard child and my mother with hers. We'll be ruined whores. My uncle Ned won't even let us on his ferry. We'll never get off the island at high tide. And when they come to drive us out, nobody will save us. Rob will have to watch them throw stones and mud and fish guts at our backs."

Alinor nodded. She could imagine the reflection of torches in the water as the good people of Sealsea Island gathered at dusk to rid themselves of two friendless sluts. "I know."

"Get the herbs ready," Alys ordered. "I'll come home early and we'll do it this evening."

She pulled on her jacket, and she took her distaff, her hank of fleece, and her spindle and she walked out of the door, spinning as she walked up the bank towards the ferry, to go to the mill where she would work as hard as any man, to earn the money for her dowry for the marriage that she was determined to make.

Left alone, Alinor started work on the daily tasks: shooing the hens out of the door, picking up the eggs, sweeping the floor, washing the two wooden gruel bowls, and rinsing the ale mugs. She swept the embers under the earthenware fire guard and made the marks against fire in the ashes of the hearth. She tied her cape around her shoulders, and went outside to gather firewood. And then she stood, looking at the harbor as if she had never seen it before, gazing at the gray horizon, wondering if she would ever again see a ship coming up the deep-water channel and hope that it was bringing the man she loved.

She had been so long in such a daze of missing James, and trusting him to return, that she could not now change the rhythm of her thoughts. She could not understand that she was no longer patiently waiting; now she was in crisis. She could not bring herself to face the problem and solve it. She sank down on the bench and, as the sky overhead darkened with a great flock of wintering geese and she heard their loud complaining cries and heard the beating of their great wings, without knowing it, under her cape her cold hand crept to her flat belly as if she would hold the tiny baby safe inside.

Later that morning Alinor was raking over the barley in the malthouse at Ferry-house. As she leaned on her rake and inhaled the warm scent of the barleycorns, a young lad put his head in the door and said: "Are you the wisewoman?"

Alinor, feeling far from wise, replied: "Yes. Who asks?"

"An oyster fisherwoman," he said. "Down at East Beach."

"Did her husband send for me?" Alinor asked, shoveling the barley grains rapidly into a pile so that they could continue heating.

"He's at sea. His mother sent me for you. She gave me this." The boy handed over a silver sixpence.

"I'll come at once," Alinor said, reassured that there would be money to pay her fee. East Beach fishermen were notorious: on a poor island they did poorly. "I've got to fetch my things."

"I'm to come with you and help carry," the youth said. He was pale with fright at having to serve a wisewoman. Alinor was known on East Beach to be a mistress of unknown arts. The fishermen of East Beach had drunk with Zachary when he had boasted about his wife's strange powers. And then Zachary was gone, and his ship was gone, for no reason, on a clear day, and one or two said that she had sent him down with his ship and her faerie lover had danced like St. Elmo's fire, in the rigging.

"We'll walk across the mire to St. Wilfrid's and then to East Beach," Alinor decided.

He gaped. "Through the waters?"

"It's low tide. I know the paths."

The boy gulped down his fear and followed in her footsteps as she closed the door on the malting floor, shouted an explanation to Ned, who was plaiting a new rope for the ferry on the pier, and headed along the bank to her own cottage to collect the herbs and oils that she would need, putting them in the bag that she always took for childbirth. Alinor walked ahead of the boy along the bank, down to the white shingle shore, and then deep into the harbor, following the hidden paths, hearing him pattering along behind her, sometimes splashing in the puddles left by the receding tide.

They cut the corner by the church, crossing through the churchyard, and went past the big iron gates of the Priory. Alinor, glancing down the drive, saw Rob and Walter riding up the broad sweep. She waved at them but did not check her stride, and was pleased when Rob clicked to his horse and rode up to catch her up.

"Ma!"

"God bless you, my son."

"Are you called out?" he asked, recognizing her sack of goods and her determined march.

"Yes, to East Beach."

"We can take you up," he said at once. He looked at Walter. "Can't we? We can take my mother and this lad to wherever they need to go?"

"Why not?" said Walter easily. "Here, Mrs. Reekie, will you come up with me?"

Alinor was reluctant to ride with Walter, but her son was already pulling up his horse and putting a hand down to the boy.

"I don't know that I can get up there," she said, looking at Walter's hunter.

"I'll come over to this wall here," he said. "And if you will climb up to the top, then you can step on. He's a good horse, he won't shy."

Alinor could not say that she did not want to jolt the child in her belly. "I've got my bag of physic. Is he steady?"

"I promise you he has smooth paces. You can come behind me and hold tight to me."

Alinor clambered up and then balanced on the top of the knapped flint wall as Walter brought his horse alongside. She stepped into the dangling stirrup and swung a leg over, to ride astride behind him.

"All aboard?" Walter asked as Alinor gripped his waist, the precious sack of oils held tightly between them.

"Yes."

"And now we can go onward," he said, and put the horse into a gentle walk.

"Do you want to go faster?" he asked over his shoulder.

"Not too fast," Alinor said nervously.

Walter put the horse into a smooth controlled canter. Alinor clung on as the big-boned hunter plowed up the lane, onto the track to Sealsea, and then turned a sharp left down a sandy stony path to the hamlet of East Beach.

"You can put me down here," she said breathlessly. "The lad'll guide me to the cottage."

Walter pulled up his horse, jumped down, received her into his arms, and set her on her feet.

"Shall I come with you and see if you need me to fetch anything?" Rob offered.

"If Master Walter can spare you," she said.

"Oh, we do nothing but amuse ourselves now," Walter said. "Our tutor, Mr. Summer, has gone away and will come back to take me to Cambridge in the Lent term."

"Gone?" Alinor asked with painful interest. "Is he not coming back before then?"

She realized that she was looking earnestly from one boy to

another, that she was far too eager for the reply. Lent was dangerously late for her. She would be nearly six months pregnant by then.

"No," Walter said lightly. "Not till February."

"Are you all right, Ma?" Rob asked, looking at her pale face. "Are you ill again?"

"Oh, I have a touch of tertian fever," she said carelessly. "But I'm well enough to care for a good woman in her time. Will you wait here, Rob, and I'll send . . ."

"Jem," he volunteered reluctantly as if he did not want this strange woman and these horsemen, who had appeared from nowhere, to know his name.

"I'll send Jem back to you, if I need anything. If he doesn't come within minutes you can go on with your ride."

"Can we come out in your boat again?" Walter asked. "That was a merry day, wasn't it?"

She felt her pale face flush warm at the memory. "It was a good day," she said, keeping her voice level. "But we can't go out now till the spring. The wind is up, and most days the harbor is too rough for me. And it's cold. We'll go again when it is sunny and calm."

The two young men waited on their horses, as Jem guided Alinor through the narrow ways between the fishermen's cottages. Each little home had a net shed attached, some had huts thrown up as sail lofts, some of them had lean-to hovels where a man might smoke his catch, or salt down fish in a barrel. Every now and then a straight track served as a rope walk, filled with cords snaking up and down, tied to a post at each end, being woven into three-strand or five-strand ropes. It was a jumble of dwellings. The houses were walled with driftwood and clay, the roofs a patchwork of old sails and nets thatched with dried bladder wrack. The smell of old rotting fish, the brine of the nets and the occasional foul breeze of a burning midden filled the air. Not even the wind from the sea could clear it. Jem led her to one of the better houses, set sideways to the sea, the waves sucking on the pebble beach below, with a little garden hedged with driftwood. It had a good slate roof and a chimney built of brick, and sturdy white-painted walls made from ship's timbers and mortar.

"Goody Auster," he said. "In there," and pointed to the front door.

Alinor went in. The house had two downstairs rooms at the front, one for eating and all the household work, and the other one, divided from it by a wall of thick decking planks, was the bedroom. A lean-to room at the back was the scullery and a ladder led up to the upper story where other members of the family slept in the storeroom. Coming down the ladder was Mrs. Grace.

"You're here very quick," she said approvingly.

"My son brought me on his horse," Alinor said. "He's waiting to fetch anything extra that I need."

"You'll want to see her," the older woman said, and opened the little door so that Alinor could go into the downstairs bedroom.

The young woman was leaning against the wall, her hands over her face, her big belly straining against her nightgown. She did not turn her head as Alinor came in, but she winced at the creak of the door. "I want Joshua," she whispered.

"Here's Mrs. Reekie come to help you in your time."

"I want Joshua," was all the young woman said. "Ma, I feel sick as a dog."

Alinor felt a reassuring sense of her own competence. Here, she was not a frightened woman who had ruined the lives of her children and herself; here, she was the only one who knew what should be done, who had witnessed and helped at many births. She went quietly up to the young woman and put the back of her cool hand against the girl's flushed forehead, noting how stiffly she held herself.

"Does your head ache?" she asked her. "Your neck?"

The girl's eyes with dark dilated pupils flicked once at her and then she closed her eyes, leaning her head to the plank wall. "I can hardly bear it," she said.

Alinor went quietly from the room and found Jem waiting outside the front door. "Go to my son and tell him to pick me some feverfew," she said. "A big bunch. And then tell him that I can manage the rest, and he can go."

Jem nodded and took to his heels down the dirt track. Alinor went back inside, smiled at Mrs. Grace, and took the girl's icy hands.

"Now," she said reassuringly. "Let's get you comfortable."

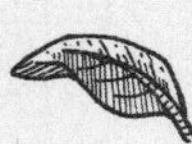

All through the day, other young wives and older women came and went with gifts of ale and bread, apples and cheese, with swaddling bands and birth caps that they had laid away in lavender, staying to gossip at the fireside and send in their best wishes to the birthing chamber, each hoping to be allowed inside. Alinor kept the door shut against them and kept Lisa Auster quiet. She gave her sips of tea made from dried raspberry leaves, and salads of feverfew to eat. Only when her fever had cooled and her headache was soothed did Alinor admit the gossips who had come to see her, and then only two at a time until her pains started to come often, and Alinor judged that her time was coming. Then with her mother and her mother-in-law and two best friends to hold her hands and praise her courage, Lisa walked around the room and finally settled on the bed as they lit the smoking oil lights. The heavy stink of fish oil scented the room. Alinor washed her hands.

"Washing?" Mrs. Grace watched anxiously.

"Yes," Alinor said quietly, and then she came to the girl, who was kneeling against the bed, and persuaded her to squat over the bowl so Alinor could wash her with clean water brewed with lavender and thyme.

"She's not a heifer waiting to calve!" Mrs. Grace objected.

"If I have to help the baby out, it's better," Alinor said quietly.

"She'll catch her death!" the woman warned.

The young woman was growing uneasy, her moans of pain coming more quickly. "Is it now?" she asked Alinor.

"It's soon," Alinor confirmed. "Do you want to kneel up on the bed?"

"Yes. No. I don't know . . ."

"You see where you feel best," Alinor advised her, and watched the girl move around, now leaning over the bed, now lying down. Finally, she settled on the wooden floor, her back against the bed, and the older women gave her a peeled wand of wood to bite and offered her a rope to heave on during the birth. Alinor stood back until they started to speak of the ordeal that was coming and that it might last for hours, even days, and how they had suffered. Then she stepped forward.

"The baby is coming," she told the young woman. "Just let it come. There's no need for pulling on a rope. All the work is in your belly."

Wide-eyed, the girl saw Alinor's face shining with calm conviction. "This is the best day's work we will ever do," Alinor said. "Let the baby come."

The girl squatted, holding to the post of the bed, her belly standing up, every muscle rigid, and she groaned. Alinor knelt before her, watching her frightened face, calming her with a hand on her shoulder. She could see her belly standing up in a spasm, and urged her to push and then rest.

"I can feel! I can feel it . . ."

The women wailed in a wordless chorus with her. "That's right," Alinor said, intently watching the young woman. Then finally she said: "Wait, wait, I can see the head!"

There was a gasp of pleasure and excitement in the room, and everyone crowded closer. "Here you are," said Alinor, her voice filled with joy as she gently took hold of the baby's head and slippery shoulders and, moving with the mother's rhythm, swaying with her, brought the baby into the world. Skillfully she held it by its feet, like a writhing mackerel, and slapped it gently on the back to clear the breath, and then bent her head and sucked the baby's nose and mouth and spat the liquor and blood on the floor. There was a brief silence, a waiting silence, and they all heard the muffled cough and then the wail as the newborn baby breathed air for the first time.

"A girl," Alinor said. "A girl." The cord still pulsed, and the baby opened her mouth and cried. Alinor looked at the perfect hands, the wrinkled skin smeared with white wax and blood, the dark hair plastered on the tiny head, and the small flushed protesting face. She felt the tears rush to her eyes and bit her lip to prevent herself from weeping for pity and joy. "A girl," she said again. "A precious girl, a gift from God Himself."

"Mrs. Reekie, are you all right yourself?" someone asked, and Alinor, recalled to her work, turned to the mother and with her hand still on the pulsing birth cord, delivered the afterbirth. Mrs. Grace held out the shawl that she had kept for her grandchild, and Alinor wrapped the tiny baby closely and handed her to the grandmother, as the young mother climbed onto the bed and Alinor sponged her parts and bound them with moss, her hands moving with their skill while her head was dizzy with the realization that this baby was a precious gift of life, that every baby was precious beyond imagining, that no baby should be lost if they could be saved, if they could have a life where they were loved and cherished.

All the women crowded around, passing the baby from one to another, admiring her and cooing over her. When the baby came back to Alinor, she tied off the cord, snipped it neatly, and handed the baby to the mother. "Here," she said. "Your little girl."

It was as if the baby had come to Alinor's hands to bring her a message, like the robin might sing in her hedge or the seagulls cry over her cottage. "God bless her, and make her well and strong," Alinor said, watching the tiny little head and the way that the dark blue eyes blinked open to see the world for the very first time.

Young Lisa Auster was flushed and proud, leaning back on the heaped bedding, her neighbors crowding round to see the baby and kiss her.

"Let's put her to the breast," Alinor suggested, and waited while the young mother and the baby fumbled towards each other, putting one gentle hand on Mrs. Grace's arm to stop her from interfering.

"Is that right?" the young mother asked. "I don't know if that's right." Then she grimaced as the baby latched on.

"That's right!" Alinor said, beaming with a sense of inexplicable joy. "And it will hurt more, before it hurts less, but you will feel the foremilk come down and you can see the baby is sucking."

She watched the two of them for a moment and then she realized that she was standing, smiling in silence, as if she had realized something of great importance at this poor fishwife's bedside that she had never known before.

"It is a gift," she whispered. "Life. Precious."

"I hoped it would have a caul," Mrs. Grace said. "All of us fishwives would like our babies born with a caul, to protect against drowning."

Alinor nodded. "I know."

"If you have a caul or even a part of one, I would buy it from you?"

"No, I don't trade in such things."

"I thought you were a wisewoman with herbs and secret things?"

"Just herbs," Alinor said levelly. "No secret things."

"Not faerie gold? I heard you had faerie gold."

"I pick up little tokens and pretty shells when I see them. Nothing more than that. Just keepsakes, nothing with any meaning."

"I thought a woman might come to you for all sorts of needs?"

"I've got a need. You could give my old man a potion!" someone interrupted, to bawdy laughter.

Alinor smiled as if she thought it was funny, though she was tired of the question. "I'm sorry, but I only have herbs for illnesses. I sell herbs and attend births, and sometimes I do nursing. I have to take care, Mrs. Grace. You will understand. I have to take care of my good name."

The woman nodded, disbelieving. "But they say you can do all sorts of things. They say you speak to the other world. And they help you."

Alinor shook her head. "I can do nothing better than this," she insisted, looking once again at the girl lying back exhausted in the bed, her face alight with joy, and the baby suckling at her breast. "I think there is nothing finer than this in the whole world. This world—I know nothing about any other."

"Is she well?" Lisa asked. "She's feeding well, isn't she?"

Alinor smiled at her. "She's very well, and when your husband comes home, he will love you both. And now . . ." Alinor started to collect up the bottles of oil and the box of dried moss, and pack them in her sack. "Now I'll go home to my cottage. And if you wish, I'll come back tomorrow to see how you do."

"Jem can go with you with a lantern," Mrs. Grace offered, producing a sixpence. "And I will pay you another shilling when you come tomorrow. I am grateful, Mrs. Reekie. We both are. I hope we have your goodwill? I hope the baby has your good wishes?"

"It is my joy. Praise God," Alinor said, hardly hearing the odd question. She said good night to the other women, hefted her sack, pulled her cape around her and put her hood over her head, and followed Jem's wavering light up the narrow lanes of East Beach.

It was too dark to go across the harbor with the tide coming in, so they went the long way, up the Chichester road, north till they saw the light from the window of Ferry-house. Jem went all the way ahead of her, lantern held high at his side to light her path, as if he was afraid to walk abreast with a wisewoman. He only paused when they got to the brink of the rife and the reflection of the moon, silver on the water, made his lantern seem yellow and weak.

"I'm safe from here," Alinor said. "I know the way, even in the dark. You can go home."

He ducked his head and though she held out half a penny to him, he turned away.

"Here," she said. "This is for you. Thank you for bringing me to Mrs. Auster and home again."

"I don't dare to take it," he said, stepping back, whipping his hands behind his back.

"What d'you mean?" Still, she held out the coin.

"It's faerie gold, I know it!" he burst out. "I'm glad you were pleased with my service, your ladyship. I'll go now, if you will release me." He looked ready to run.

"What did you call me? Boy—Jem—you know that I'm nothing but the widow of the fisherman Zachary Reekie," Alinor said. "You know I work as a midwife. I don't do anything else. I have no faerie gold. There's no call to name me ladyship!"

He was walking backwards, without taking his fearful eyes off her, his face ghastly in the lantern light, hurrying to get away from her. "They told me," he whispered, "that you know things that no mortal woman knows. That your boy lives like a lord at the Priory, and your daughter is to marry the richest farmer in Sussex."

"Well, no—" Alinor started.

"Missis, did you whistle up a storm that blew your husband away?"

Alinor tried to laugh, but his fear was infectious. "This is nonsense," she said, her voice unsteady. "And Mrs. Grace knows it's nonsense, for she sent you for a good honest midwife and I came."

"No," he shook his head. "Not her. They were afraid to send for anyone else in case you ill-wished us. So I fetched you with my fingers crossed, and then you came to her on horseback like a queen, and you sent Sir William's own son to do your bidding. Good night, Mrs. Reekie, your honor. Good night."

Alinor let him go, too shaken to press the coin on him, too frightened by his wide-eyed fear to laugh him into common sense. When Zachary had accused her of being in league with powers beyond this earth, she had taken it as the exaggerated language of courtship when he first saw her, and part of his hatred, as the marriage soured. That he should sow such dangerous slander to his drinking companions and that it should flower into these envious fantasies was something she had never dreamed.

Of course, people would wonder at Rob's good fortune and Alys's betrothal, but she had not thought that people would weave Zachary's superstitious hatred and her survival together into a faerie story of Zachary's doom and her revenge. It was a dark note at the end of a day that had started with thoughts of drowning and dark water. She trudged along the bank, the mud crunching with frost beneath her worn boots, opened the door, and went in.

The cottage was in darkness, the fire under the cover, the candles snuffed out. Alys was asleep on her side of the bed and Alinor felt nothing but relief that she need not speak another word until the morning.

## DOUAI, FRANCE, OCTOBER 1648

James spent a week in penitent silence, sleepless with the conflicting sense of guilt and desire. Every day he met with his confessor and step-by-step they went through his first encounter with Alinor, that she had saved him and without her he would have been lost on the unmapped tidelands. She had been a savior to him.

"But she is not your savior," Father Paul said quietly as they knelt side by side in the chapel and looked up at the altar where the crucified Christ looked down on them, his painted face downcast. "She is no angel. She is an earthly woman and naturally disposed to sin."

James bowed his head. He could not deny that she was disposed to sin. He spoke of the afternoon in the boat, he spoke of her desire. He spoke of the color of her hair and how a curl escaped from her cap and blew against her face. He spoke of her scarred hands and her rough linen.

"She was born into poverty, set in her place by God. It is not for you to defy God and rescue her. Did she ask to be baptized into the true faith?"

"No," James said quietly.

"You have nothing else to offer her."

His voice low and ashamed, James spoke of the feel of her mouth under his, of the strength of her body under the bulky clothes. He spoke of her smile and her little indrawn breath of desire. He said that when he touched her hand, her waist, her breast, he felt that he was, for the first time, a man. That he became himself, in loving her.

"A woman cannot bring insight," Father Paul corrected him. "You do not know yourself by knowing her. All she taught you is carnal knowledge, that is all she knows."

"But that was everything!" James said simply. He did not speak of the loft over the stable, nor of her beauty in the morning light when she had been as naked as Eve and as innocent as Paradise. "I love her, Father. Sin or not."

"It is sin," the priest steadily replied. "Don't call it 'sin or not,' as if you had not received instruction, as if God had not given you reason. It is sin and you must put it from you."

James sat back on his heels, his face pale. "To abandon her would break my word. I have asked her to be my wife."

"You are not free to ask her."

"And she was not free to consent," James conceded. "They speak against her . . ."

"What do they say?"

"Nothing, superstitious nonsense, malice, all malice. Her own husband said she was whore to the faeries," James tried to laugh. "Ignorant nonsense, that foolish countrypeople—"

His confessor did not laugh with him. "My son, you and I, far away from them, don't know what they are speaking of. You can't say that it is nonsense, you don't know what she has done. We would have to inquire. A witchfinder would have to visit and ask questions. This is very serious. Does she have marks upon her?"

"No!" James was horrified.

"Does she fear the word of God in church, or the works of God, like deep water or high cliffs?"

James hesitated, thinking of her horror of water.

"Does she have a familiar, an animal that communes with her?"

He thought of the hens that clucked around her feet and slept in the corner of the little cottage, of Red the dog, of the bees, of the robin in her garden: "But this is her life . . ."

"Is her husband not likely to know better than you, who has been seduced by her? What if she is beautiful because Satan has thrown a glamour on her? What if she makes spells as well as physic? You told me that she expected to speak with the dead? What if this is not a helpless poor woman but an evil one?"

## TIDELANDS, OCTOBER, 1648

Alys woke to the familiar sound of the small ale being poured from the jug and the scrape of the wooden spoon in the bottom of the iron pot of gruel. She got up from the bed and pushed her tumbled hair out of her eyes, pulling on her shirt over her head, and stepping into her skirt, haphazard, without looking.

Alinor pulled up her stool at the table and bowed her head in grace as Alys sat down at the other side and said: "Amen."

They ate in silence and then Alys got to her feet and fetched the comb for her hair. Without speaking she handed it to her mother and sat at her feet as if she were a little girl again. Alinor gently unbraided her daughter's long fair hair and combed it, gently teasing out every tangle and picking out the occasional twig or piece of straw.

"What on earth have you been doing?" she asked as she tossed a leaf into the fire.

"Picking sloes," Alys replied. "Since Mrs. Miller learned that Richard and I are to be married, she sends me out over the fields. As if she can stop us seeing each other! As if she gets any gain by putting me to humble work."

Alinor combed the golden sweep of hair, watching the light fall on the thick waves, and then started to plait, starting from the front, so that it coiled around Alys's pretty head.

"Have you decided?" Alys asked quietly, looking up trustingly into her mother's face. "I came home early to help you, and Uncle told me you'd been called to East Beach. But I've told Mrs. Miller I was ill. She won't expect me today. I can stay home today and help you be rid of this."

"I have decided what to do." Alinor drew a breath and told her. "It came to me yesterday almost like a vision, Alys, when I delivered Lisa Auster's baby. I held her in my arms. She was no bigger than a kitten, and I saw how precious she was, such a miracle. Everything about her was perfect; she was a tiny person, her little eyelashes and her nails as small as the smallest shells on Wittering beach, and her eyes were dark blue, like yours were when you were born. I could see the light of the world in her. I can't destroy such a perfect thing, Alys. It would be like breaking a blackbird's egg. I understood what is sacred, for the first time in my life. This baby has come to me when I thought I would never have another. And I won't kill it."

"But you do know how?" Alys persisted.

"I know how, yes," Alinor said quietly.

"Did your mother ever do it?"

"Yes, she did. When she judged it was best for the mother, or best for the child, poor thing, misconceived, miscarried, miserable. She would do it to spare suffering. I would do it, to spare another's suffering. I believe it is right to do it—to spare pain. If I had my way a woman would be able to choose—whether to conceive, whether to labor, whether or not to bear a child. Men should not rule this, it is a woman's own life and that of her child. But I won't do it to my baby. I would rather have the pain than lose the baby."

"Is it herbs?"

"Herbs first, and if the baby does not come away, then you take a spindle or a tanner's needle, a long thin knife or a bodkin, and you pass it up inside the woman to stab the baby as it lies, curled inside," Alinor said steadily as Alys listened horrified, her hands over her mouth.

"Six times you push the needle up, and you don't know whether you are piercing the baby's head, going through an eye or an ear or a mouth, or stabbing right through into the woman's body. It is as savage as butchering a calf. Worse. You're completely blind: you don't know what you're doing. The woman can bleed to death inside, or the baby can die but not come away and rot inside her. Or she seems to miscarry, but dies in fever. It is death for the baby and sometimes death for the mother. Do you wish that on me?"

Alys leaned against her mother's knee and closed her eyes. "Of course not."

"D'you want to take a tanner's needle and stab your unborn sister in the face as she grows inside me?"

"Of course not," the girl whispered as quiet as her mother.

"Neither do I," Alinor said. "I can't do it. I can't bring myself to do it."

"But what are we to do, Ma? This will ruin me, and you, and Rob."

"I know," Alinor said. "And it's my shame, not yours nor Rob's. I'll think of a way that I can take it, all to myself."

Alys leaned back against her mother's knees. "There's no way. Unless you go away, right away, right now, before anyone knows, and then what will become of Rob and me? We're too young to lose both mother and father. You'll make us orphans. And where would you go? And how can I be married without you? How can I have my baby without you?"

"I'm so sorry," Alinor said, humbled before her daughter. "I really am, Alys. I will pray for guidance, and I'll do anything that I can. Anything but killing this baby."

"Whose baby?" Alinor turned and looked up at her mother. "Whose baby is it? Is it Sir William's? Because he can pay for you to go away. Everyone knows he—"

"It's not Sir William's," Alinor interrupted her. "And I can't say whose it is. It's not my secret, Alys. I've done very wrong, but I won't make it worse by betraying him as well as myself."

"It's he who has betrayed you," the girl said resentfully. "He's ruined all three of us. He's no better than my da."

She stopped as she saw her mother flinch.

"Don't say that, Alys. You don't know—"

"He is worse than my da," she persisted. "We'd have been less hurt if he had beaten you, like my da used to do. You protected Rob and me from our da. I've seen you take a beating that I thought would kill you. You stood between Da and us. But you won't save us from this. What does it mean—if you won't save us from this?"

## DOUAI, FRANCE, NOVEMBER 1648

James felt that he walked everywhere under a glass bell jar, observed but silenced, an echo in his head, breathing a strange air of faithlessness. He prayed that something pure and rare and potent was being exhaled from his constant daily ordeal; but he did not feel he was being purified; he felt he was being distilled into nothing.

One morning Dr. Sean came to him in the little side chapel where James prayed after confession, and said: "I bring you news that will lift a burden from you, Brother James."

"I should be glad of that," James replied, rising from his feet.

"The king is to escape from his keepers. The proposals that the parliament has put before him are too small for his divine greatness and the pardons for his followers are too mean. He has told them that he cannot agree with them, and he has written secretly that he is ready to join the queen and his son Prince Charles in exile."

James felt the familiar sense of dread. "Do you want me to go to him?" he asked. "Am I to go again, and bring him away?" His voice did not falter, but he thought they would be certain to send him to his death this time.

"No, no, a local man is to get him away. A man from Newport. The king is allowed to walk out, to take the air, even to go riding. They suspect nothing. They think he is considering their offer. But riders will meet him and gallop with him to the coast. A ship will be waiting for him. He will get to sea and sail to Cherbourg. With God's grace he may be there already. My letter is days old. God have mercy on us, we might even see him here."

James crossed himself. "Amen," he whispered. "Amen." He was ashamed to find himself dizzy with fear. "But it's not that easy. Are they sure of the ship? With a safe master? And will he take it? How many people has he told about the plan?"

"The local man has made all the arrangements," the professor repeated. "Thank God that the king is ready to leave at last."

"But they have to get a reliable ship and a safe meeting place at sea. It's not easy to—"

"The king has commanded it. He has chosen his ship's master. God will guide him."

"Amen," James said again, silencing his own doubts, knowing that his own fears were born from his own experience. Perhaps someone else would succeed where he had, so miserably, failed. Perhaps this time it would be quite different. "Amen."

# TIDELANDS, NOVEMBER 1648

Alys and Alinor walked together along the bank to Ferry-house, the ground iron hard and icy beneath their feet, and kissed good-bye without speaking at the pier. Ned pulled the ferry over for his niece, his face beaming, his dog standing beside him waving its feathery tail.

"Good day," he said joyfully. "And a good day it is for me and for all the friends of freedom."

"What's happened?" Alinor asked as Alys stepped into the ferry. Alinor shook her head at Ned's outstretched hand. "No, I'm not crossing. I've come to start chitting the barley."

"The army is going to capture the king, I swear it," he said triumphantly.

"Why? How do you know?"

"The wool merchant came through—he left you some more wool for spinning; it's in the store—told me that the news was all over Chichester. The parliament men have got nowhere near agreement with the king. And now it turns out His Majesty was about to break his royal word, break his parole, and run away. The governor of Carisbrooke Castle, Colonel Hammond, is recalled to headquarters to answer for it. The plotters have been arrested. The army has had enough, and now they will take the king for themselves."

"But how ever does a Chichester wool merchant know that the king was planning to escape?" Alys asked skeptically.

"Who's been arrested?" Alinor interrupted, breathless with anxiety for James. "Who was caught—helping the king?"

"His guards at the castle; but the whole island knew of it," Ned said contemptuously. "Half a dozen men were in the plot. He must've written a letter to everyone he knew, telling them that he could not agree with parliament and that he was ready to run away."

Dizzy with fear, Alinor leaned against the mooring post. "It was just his guards arrested?"

"Yes, two of them. Alinor, are you all right?" Ned asked her.

"Uncle, I've got to go to work," Alys said, twitching the guide rope to distract him from her mother's pallor. "Will you take me across? Ma, see you tonight. We're baking at the mill today. I'll bring home a loaf."

"Yes, yes, God bless," Alinor said distractedly, and turned from her brother's scrutiny to the malting house.

The peace of the malthouse steadied her as she took up the barley rake, the handle smooth with decades of use. The low-ceilinged room was warm compared with the wintry chill outside, scented with the sweet smell of barley. The barleycorns were in a steeply shoveled pile, warming through and starting to split. Ned had left a bucket of clean water from the ferry-house dipping pond, out of the way of the overnight frost. She raked the barleycorns flat on the floor and stirred them round, mixing them together. Once they were spread out, she took a brush made from broom twigs and sprinkled them thoroughly with the water, raked them round again, and then took the blunt wide shovel, and piled them back into a heap. There was no way of telling that each seed was bursting with life, but she knew that the miracle of life was here in hundreds and thousands, in millions. Life in secret, a spark so small that it could live in every single barley seed, so powerful that it would split the seed and grow. She leaned on the handle of the shovel and thought that here she was: turning barley, picking herbs, attending a new-born baby, with the miracle of life like a candle flame, hidden inside her; and far away, somewhere, perhaps on the Isle of Wight, perhaps at his college in France, James was thinking of her, coming to her, with the miracle of his passion inside him.

Once she had not known if he was a man to keep his word, if he would come back to her. But now she trusted him; she knew that he would come. And when he came, she would tell him that she was with child, that life was urgently growing inside her. She would not deny him again, she would go with him to his home in the faraway county of Yorkshire, to London, to France, to wherever he wished.

She leaned the malt shovel against the wall, pushed at the door, and swung it open as if she might see the sail of his boat. Before her, the tide was coming in, the seagulls crying over the splashing waves. The water was radiantly blue, the hushing well a familiar distant whisper, the wintry sun hard and bright. Alinor thought that anything in this world was possible: the king might escape, James might regain his home, he would come for her and she would have his child. Why not, in this new world where anything could happen?

"I want to talk," Alinor said to her daughter, ending days of unhappy silence. They were preparing the little cottage for the night, shoveling the red embers of the fire under the earthenware pot guard, shooing the hens into their corner, undressing to their linen shifts and lastly tamping out the rushlights. The foul scent of tallow smoke breathed around the little room like rancid bacon. The cottage was gloomy, lit by bars of moonlight shining through the shutters.

"At last," Alys said irritably. "I wondered how long it'd take before you spoke. D'you have any idea what you're going to do?"

Alinor bowed her head. “Alys, all I can say is that I’m sorry. But I do have hopes.”

The young woman sat heavily on the bed. “Name one.”

“The father of my baby is a good man. He asked me to marry him, and when I can, I will.”

“You can’t, you’re married to my da.”

“I can say he’s dead, and six years from now I’ll be free to marry. It’s in the law. When a man has been missing for seven years.”

“Say he’s dead?” Alys was shocked. “Name our da as a dead man?”

“It’s not ill-wishing!” Alinor exclaimed.

“It is! That’s exactly what it is. You’ll tell everyone he’s dead—what? Drowned?—and name yourself as a widow?”

“Alys, your da’s never coming back,” Alinor said quietly. “He told Rob, he met him at Newport. He’s never coming home.”

“What? Rob saw him?”

“Your da ran from him, and missed the next meeting. He didn’t want to be found. He told the tutor that he wasn’t coming back.”

“And nobody told me?”

“No . . . You remember? You didn’t want to know. You wanted to go to the Stoneys’ farm without a lie in your mouth.”

“My da isn’t coming back? Ever?”

“No. He says not.”

Alys put her hand over her eyes. “Just like that? And nobody told me?”

“I’m sorry, Alys.” Alinor spread her work-worn hands. “There’s been so much—” She broke off when she saw her daughter was fiercely rubbing her eyes with her shawl. “I’m very sorry, Alys. He wasn’t a good father to you or to Rob. He wasn’t a good husband. He’s not a good man. You said you didn’t care. You said you didn’t want to know.” She paused. “Are you crying for him?”

The girl showed her a sulky face rubbed dry of any tears. “Not at all.”

Alinor pressed on. "So, you see, I don't have to wait forever for him to come home."

"Looks like you didn't wait at all," Alys said spitefully.

Alinor bowed her head against the accusation. "But in six years' time I can marry the father of my child."

"Who says you can do this?"

"It's the law."

"Who says so?"

Alinor's eyes dropped from her daughter's demanding glare. "Rob's tutor told me so."

"Does everyone know about this but me? Does Uncle Ned?"

"No! Only the tutor, because he met your da with Rob at Newport."

"And the law says you can marry seven years from my da going?"

"Yes, and I will."

Alys's strained face showed no relief. "That'll be a comfort for your six-year-old bastard. But we've still got to get through the six years."

Alinor gritted her teeth. "That's why I'll say nothing, and nobody will know I'm with child until you're safely married. Then, when you're happy at Stoney Farm, I'll go away."

"Leave me," the girl said flatly. "And Rob."

Alinor's face was as calm as a carved statue of a saint, but her eyes filled with tears. "To spare you both, yes," she said. "Isn't it what you want?"

The girl sighed and lifted her head. "No good can come from this," she predicted. "If this is what comes when a woman is free to make her own choices then I don't think very much of Uncle Ned's new England."

"It's nothing to do with Uncle Ned," Alinor said, startled. "Nothing to do with the new England."

"He says that men and women can choose their destiny, that they shan't be ruled by their betters. But all that's happened is that you've chosen a terrible mistake and we'll suffer worse than when you were a poor widow on the side of the sea with a wasteful landlord ruling you and a wicked king over him. Because nothing's really changed. We might have got rid of the king but not of the rule of men. You're still ruined and this man is free to come and go as he wants. What if he doesn't come back for you, ever?"

Alinor shook her head as if to rid herself of the blank misery of her daughter's face. "The man I love will come back to help me," she promised. "He'll marry me when he can. I'll not be shamed and neither will you. We'll get through your wedding, and when you're safely married I'll go away and have my child, and in six years I shall be safely married too."

"There's a lot of hoping in this," Alys said bitterly. "And we're not a family that's done well on hope. If it were me, telling you this, you would beat me."

For the first time, Alinor smiled at her beloved daughter. "I would never beat you."

"You would be furiously angry with me."

"Aren't you furiously angry with me?"

Alys did not return the smile. She turned her head away.

## DOUAI, FRANCE, NOVEMBER 1648

James tapped on the door of the guest room in Douai College and braced himself when he heard his mother's voice call "*Entrez!*" and then correct herself: "Come! Come in!"

He went in as she was turning from the window that overlooked the market square outside, and she hurried towards him with her arms out. "My son!" she said warmly. "My son!"

James knelt for her blessing and felt her hand on his head, and then rose and kissed her on both cheeks. She smelled of perfume and clean silk. His father got up from his chair at the table, where he had been turning the pages of a beautiful illuminated manuscript, and James knelt to him too. He rose up and the three of them stood looking from one to another, as if they could hardly believe they were reunited.

"Hear you've been home?" his father said shortly, his piercing glance taking in his son's bleak appearance: from his pale face to his sandals.

"Yes," James said. Out of habit he glanced behind him to see that the door was closed. "To England . . . not . . . not to our own home."

"I heard there were problems."

The young man nodded, and his father seated himself at the head of the dark wood refectory table, and gestured that his son should sit. His mother took her place at the foot. James thought that it was three years since they had been seated at the head and foot of their great table in their own home, three years of living on what rents they could collect from their English estate, three years of living off the hand-to-mouth royal courts, three years of exile from home.

"How do you hear?" James asked. "For really, no one should hear anything at all."

"It's this damned country," his mother said wearily. "Everyone knows everything. Nothing is ever private, no one is discreet. Everyone gossips and makes things up."

"It puts me in danger," James pointed out. "And everyone who goes to England to serve the faith, or the king. Don't people realize that? And it puts our cause in danger too. Don't they understand they must serve in secret? Keep silence?"

"Were you in danger, *cheri*?" his mother asked.

"Yes," James said flatly. "Of course. Every day."

His mother blanched. "But you are unhurt?" She put her white hand over his and scanned his face, as if she might see a hidden mortal wound.

"Did you see His Majesty?" his father asked him. "Are you allowed to say?"

"Yes, I saw him. I had organized an escape for him, as I imagine you know, since the queen's court knows, I suppose all of Paris knows. But he didn't come. He wouldn't come."

"He refused rescue?" his father asked incredulously.

"Didn't the gossips tell you that?"

"I only heard that it miscarried. I am sorry, I thought it was—"

"Me that failed?" James interposed bitterly. "No. It's true to say that my rescue failed. But it was because he would not walk out of the open door, to the boat that I had waiting, to the men risking their lives to guard him."

"Was it not safe?"

"Of course it was as safe as it could be! I would never have taken him into danger," James said angrily. "I had arranged it, but he wouldn't come. He believed he could outwit parliament.

Play them off against the army. Threaten them with the Irish, or with an invasion from France."

His father made a quick gesture with his hand. "There will be no invasion from France. There's no money, and God knows . . ."

James looked at his father. "God knows . . . ?" he asked.

Now it was the older man who glanced at the door to see it was tightly closed. "No leadership," he said quietly. "No common sense at the queen's court, no discipline at the court of the prince. No one you would trust with a spaniel, let alone an army. A court of favorites and backbiting and endless gossip, quarrels about nothing, and scandals. Good men throwing what's left of their fortunes away on desperate plans. People dreaming of a future and swearing they will have revenge. Nothing reliable. No one to rely on. Rewards promised, bribes handed out. It's sickening."

James's mother rose from the table and looked out of the window again as if the little market square in the small provincial town had anything to interest her. "Don't speak like that," she said quietly. "Not while James is risking his life."

"Has he escaped?" James asked his father very quietly. "I heard he was to ride away, that there was a ship waiting for him. Is he safe?"

His father shook his head. "It didn't happen. The plot was discovered."

"Hardly surprising," James said sourly.

His mother turned back from the window. "Don't be bitter," she said quietly. "Don't let these times spoil you."

"They have spoiled me," James confessed. "I have lost my faith. Lost my faith in the cause, and lost my faith in God, too. But I suppose you know that? I suppose Dr. Sean sent for you? That is why you are here?"

His father was too honest a man to lie to his only son. "They sent for us the moment you came in," he said. "They said you had been brought very low. Is it your faith in the king and God that is troubling you? Or is there a woman in it too?"

James hesitated, as his mother came to the table and rested her white hand on it, the beautiful lace from her cuff reflected in the polished wood. "You can speak in front of me," she said. "I'm very sure I have heard worse over the last few years. We have been in a ragtag court in exile, with the morals of stable cats for long enough for me to hear everything."

"Are you spoiled?" James asked her with a crooked smile.

"I'm hardened," she admitted. "You can't tell me anything new."

"There is a woman," he confessed. "A workingwoman, not a lady, but she is very beautiful and very brave and very . . ." He tried to think of a description that would do justice to Alinor. "Interesting," he said. "She's interesting. She is a herbalist, but quite uneducated. She is a simple woman but she has her own mind, her own thoughts. She lives—" He broke off, thinking that he could not describe the hovel at the side of Foulmire, and the ferry-house and the army brother. "She lives very simply," he said, avoiding a description of her poverty. "But she saved my life the night that she first met me, and took me into hiding."

"Her family?" his mother prompted.

"She has two children: a boy and a girl."

Her aghast face told him of his mistake.

"I didn't mean that! I meant to ask: is she of a good family?"

"She has children? She's a widow?" his father asked.

James answered his mother first. "She has a little standing in her village, with her neighbors. There's gossip—but there's always gossip in these poor little places, you know that! Her husband has gone. He's probably dead. They are poor people." He hesitated, looking from one to another. "I'm not explaining this well. They don't have land, or a family, or a name."

He looked at his mother, as if willing her to see the mire as he saw it, a place of eerie beauty, and Alinor as a woman of the place, strange and beautiful too. "They are not people like us," he tried to explain.

"But she did at least have a husband? She was married once? She's not a—"

"No! Her parents are dead but she has a brother. He's a good man."

"Did her husband die in the war?" his mother asked. "On our side?"

"Er, no . . ." James said awkwardly. "He's just missing."

"She's a deserted wife?" his mother asked. "Abandoned?"

"Yeoman stock?" his father asked hopefully. "This brother? Has he got his own land? Or is he a tenant farmer?"

James shook his head, forcing himself to be honest. "He keeps the ferry. They have the tenancy to the ferry and the ferry-house, and they grow vegetables and trees and keep hens in an acre behind the house. They sell ale out of the window. They're poor people, sir, on poor land, on the very edge of England as it turns into sea. It's marshland, tidelands, neither one thing nor another. And it's true to say, she owns almost nothing. She was given a few shillings for bringing me to safety and she used it to buy a boat."

He did not know that he was smiling at the thought of the boat and the courage of the woman he loved. "It meant everything to her. She fishes from the boat, and sells her catch. She said—" He broke off as he realized that he could not tell them of her joke that saving him was of the same value as catching a fat salmon. "She grows herbs and makes physic. She's a healer and a midwife in the little village. It's a little fishing village, very poor."

His mother was blanched with horror. "A fisherwoman?" she repeated. "A midwife? Like a cunning woman?"

"Yes," he said steadily. "She's no grander than that." He turned to his father. "But she saved me when I had nowhere to go. And then, later, she nursed me when I was near to death, when anyone else would have locked the doors and abandoned me, for fear of plague. But she chose to stay with me, and be locked up with me. And I have asked her to marry me."

His mother gave a suppressed moan and put her hand over her mouth, closing her eyes.

His father's face was dark. "This is not what we planned for you," he said shortly.

"Sir, I know it. But we did not plan a world like this."

"We are exiles and all but penniless. We're defeated in this world, but we have not sunk so low that you can break your vows to the Church to marry a village midwife with a brace of lowborn children."

"I am sorry, sir. I am sorry, Lady Mother."

She shook her head, her hand shading her eyes, as if she could not bear to look at him.

"We allowed you to go to the Church," his father said begrudgingly. "That was not easy for us. We gave up all hopes of grandchildren and a daughter-in-law then. That was your choice. You said you had a calling and we believed you. That was the hardest thing I ever did—to give up my only son to the Church. And now you tell us that was for nothing? And we are to give you up again? But this time, for something of no value at all? For a woman who—by your own description—is valueless?"

James heard the rising volume of his father's anger. "I know. I know. You were good to let me go to the Church. I longed to be in the Church then. I was certain. But . . . going back to England, and seeing the defeat of everything that we believe and the king so—"

"The king so what?" His mother rounded on him in a cold fury. "Is all this—all this!—because you have discovered that the king is a fool? I could have told you that ten years ago!"

Her husband moved his hand to silence her but she went on. "No! I will speak. The boy should know. He knows already! Yes! The king is a fool and a cat's-paw, and his son is two parts a villain. But still he is the king. That never changes! And you are a priest, and that never changes. Whether he is a good king or a bad one, that never changes. Whether you are a good priest or a bad one, that never changes! Just as your father is and always will be Sir Roger Avery of Northside Manor, Northallerton. It never changes. Whether we live there, in our house, or not, whether it is overrun with rabble or not, whether you live there or not. It is still our name, it is still our house. England never changes and neither will you."

There was silence in the little room. Sir Roger looked from his son to his wife.

"Did the woman accept you?" he asked as if it were a matter of secondary interest.

"Whyever would she not?" Lady Avery demanded angrily. "D'you think she would prefer to stay where she is? In nowhere? Half drowned in the tidelands?"

James raised his head. "No, she did not. She said it was not fitting."

"She's right!"

"Did she really say that?" his father asked, interested.

James nodded. "Yes, I told you she was unusual. But I said that I would be released from my order, that I would ask you if we might pay the fine to parliament and return to Northside, and that I would ask your permission to marry her, and bring her to our home as my wife. She has to wait until she can be declared a widow."

"Pay the fine to parliament and live beneath their rule? Deny our service to the king?"

"Yes," James said steadily. "He does not want my service. I don't want to offer it ever again."

"Betray your oath of loyalty to him?"

"Break it."

Lady Avery took an embroidered handkerchief from her lace-trimmed sleeve and put it to her eyes. Her husband looked steadily at the down-turned face of his son.

"Does she even know your name?" he asked.

The young man looked up and for the first time his father saw his boyish smile. "No," he said. "She knows me as Father James. I pass as a tutor called Mr. Summer. She has risked everything for me and she doesn't even know my name."

# TIDELANDS, NOVEMBER 1648

Alinor knocked on the door of the Mill Farm dairy and entered on Mrs. Miller's irritated shout. Richard Stoney was carrying in extra pails of milk, the maid ahead of him with the yoke on her shoulder.

"I've come for two pails of milk, if you've any for sale," Alinor said.

"We've more than we can use today," Mrs. Miller said. "Bessy's calf fell into the ditch and broke her neck. Bessy's still in milk."

"Oh, poor thing," Alinor said. Mrs. Miller looked at her askance.

"Poor me," she said. "I've lost a good calf. I'll have to have it butchered for veal."

"Yes," Alinor agreed, who had never tasted the luxury meat in her life. "I thought I'd make cheese for Chichester market."

"I'll carry the milk to Ferry-house for you, Mrs. Reekie," Richard said politely.

Mrs. Miller scowled at him. "She's not your mother-in-law yet," she said coldly. "And you work for me."

The young man flushed. "I beg pardon," he said shortly.

"I can manage, if I may borrow the yoke," Alinor said. "Will you take it off Alys's wages?"

"You're asking for credit?" Mrs. Miller said nastily.

"I can pay you now, if you prefer," Alinor said steadily.

"No, no, you can keep your ha'pennies. I'll take it off her wages at the end of the week.

"Thank you." Alinor smiled, and put the well-worn wooden yoke on her shoulders, lifted the two brimming pails, and set her shoulders to find her balance. Richard opened the dairy door for her.

"You get yourself into the mill," Mrs. Miller ordered Richard. "He's milling this morning and the tide won't wait, not even for such as you."

Richard ducked his head and trotted across the yard. As Alinor walked slowly with the yoke across her shoulders, watching the milk slopping in the pails, she heard the miller shout to Richard to open the sluice. She stood for a moment at the yard gate to watch the lad lightly running along the pond wall to turn the great iron key to open the sluice. The water from the pond poured into the millrace, and slowly, the mill wheel started to turn. There was a roar of creaking wood as the rush of waters forced the wheel round and round, and then the tumble of water on the other side of the tide-mill quay as the millrace gushed like a waterfall out into the harbor, bursting like a tide of green foam into the muddy rife. Alinor walked towards the wadeway, her head turned from the raging water of the millrace as the miller engaged the grinding stones inside the mill and there was a deafening rumble of stone against stone. Alinor crossed on the wet cobbles of the wadeway, stepping around the puddles of icy water, to the ferry-house on the other side.

Ned was felling an old apple tree in the garden at the rear of Ferry-house. The trunk was wide and knotted, and Ned had sharpened his axe and stripped to the waist to swing, and then hammer in the wedges so the spreading boughs fell away from the house. He raised his hand to Alinor as she came around the house and into the back door of the dairy.

"The copper's boiling in the laundry room for you," he called to her.

"Thank you!" she shouted back and went into the dairy.

The room was freezing cold, and the floor still damp from washing. Alinor poured one pail of milk and then another into the wooden trough, and then went to and fro from the laundry with earthenware jugs filled with boiling water from the copper. She put the jugs among the milk until it was warmed through, and then poured in a small measure of rennet. Outside, she could hear the regular thud of the blade into the wood and the occasional pause when Ned rested on the handle and drew a breath.

Slowly, the warmed milk was splitting into curds and whey, solidifying. Alinor took down a seashell, one of the cleaned clam shells that her mother had always used to test the thickness of the curds and whey. She spun it on the surface, and when it was steady, she rolled up her sleeves and drew her hands, her fingers outstretched like claws, through the thickening mixture. The curds were growing solid. It was time to drain them.

The stink of the milk and rennet turned Alinor's stomach and she opened the dairy door to take a few breaths of cold air at the doorway. Red, the dog, sat up and looked hopeful that he might get into the dairy and steal cream.

"You sick?" Ned shouted from the yard. "Sick again? You're white as whey!"

"I'm fine," Alinor lied, and went back to her work.

From the front of the house she could hear the clang of the metal bar against the hanging horseshoe as a traveler on the far side of the rife summoned the ferry.

"Alinor, can you do it?" Ned asked her, gesturing at his nakedness, and the tree half felled. "It's low tide. It's dead calm."

Alinor shook her head. "Forgive me, Brother," she said. "You know I can't."

"You're like a cat agauwed of water," he complained, pulling his shirt over his head. "And you should be like a ship's cat that learns to keep itself dry but can go to sea."

"I'm sorry," Alinor repeated. "But I stink of whey."

Ned went round the house to the rife, Red at his heels, and Alinor could not resist trailing after him to see the traveler. She saw a saddle horse on the far side, and a man standing beside it. Alinor's hand went to her belly, her other hand felt her speeding heart. But even as she breathed James's name, she saw it was not him. It was an itinerant preacher in a shabby cloak, with a weary old horse that James would never ride—a godly man come to encourage the puritans of Sealsea Island. Silently, she turned and went back to the dairy. She did not allow herself to feel disappointment. She knew he would come when he could. She trusted him to come to her.

## DOUAI, FRANCE, DECEMBER 1648

James's parents were leaving the guesthouse at Douai. Their horses, waiting outside in the damp cold of early December, stamped their feet and blew out clouds of breath on the freezing air. Lady Avery came out of the house, wrapped in a traveling cloak with a fur-lined hood, and her son helped her up the steps of the mounting block and onto her steady horse. She was riding side-saddle, and she arranged her green wool riding habit so it fell over her leather boots. He climbed up on the block himself, so that they were level, head-to-head and she could hear his penitent whisper.

"I beg you to forgive me, Lady Mother," he said, but she would not even meet his eyes. She turned her head away and stroked her horse's mane. "I cannot withdraw from this woman. She holds my heart. She truly does. I am going back to see her and I will marry her when she is free. I beg that you forgive me, and let me bring her to you as your daughter."

She turned her face to him and he could see from her pale pinched face and red eyelids that she had endured a sleepless night. “I shall pray for you and for me,” was all she said. “But I did not bring you into the world, and give you to the Holy Church for you to bed a fishwife.”

He bowed his head for her blessing and he barely felt the light touch of her hand on his thick hair.

“Forgive me,” he said. “I am promised to her.”

“You are promised to the Church,” she said flatly. “You are promised to be obedient to me and your father, and we forbid this.”

“I shall write to you,” he offered.

“Not if you write of her,” she said steadily.

The door of the abbey guesthouse opened and Sir Roger came out quickly, his thick cloak heavy on his shoulders. Dr. Sean hurried behind him, a sheet of paper in his hand.

“Something’s happened,” Sir Roger said shortly to his son. “Changes everything.” He stepped to his wife’s horse, took hold of her bridle, and said quietly to her: “We can’t leave now. Get down and come in.”

“Is it the king?” she asked, dismounting at once.

He nodded, but his dark look warned her that it was not news of a successful escape from the Isle of Wight that Dr. Sean held in his hand. At once, without another word, she gave her hand to James, stepped down from the mounting block, and they hurried inside.

“What now?” she demanded as Dr. Sean closed the door behind the four of them.

“The army has taken over parliament,” he said. “I have this from one of our spies in London. One of the most radical wicked colonels captured the door of the House of Commons with his regiment, and only admitted those members of parliament who are sworn to Cromwell, bought and sold, wholly his. Such a house will never make an agreement with His Majesty. The true members are thrown out, the army has captured the House of Commons.”

Lady Avery turned to her husband. “Is this to force an agreement on the king?”

"God knows what wickedness they plan!" Dr. Sean exclaimed.

Sir Roger nodded. "My dear, we'd better get back to court. The queen and the Prince of Wales won't allow the king to fall into the hands of the army. This is worse than when he ran away from Hampton Court. Then the army had him, but at least parliament could defend him. Now there is no one to speak for him. Nothing like this has ever happened in the world before. A parliament to rule a king? It's like the end of days."

"It might be worse. They may be thinking of a trial," James warned.

His father turned on him. "A trial? What d'you mean?"

"When I was in Sussex I met a man, a veteran from Cromwell's army, who said that the radicals among them, levelers and men of that sort, believed that the king should answer to them for making war."

"It can't be done!" his father said, frowning. "How would men like that ever bring a charge against a king?"

"Who was this man?" his mother demanded acutely. "One of her friends?"

James flushed with shame.

"Will you return to England and report for us?" Dr. Sean asked bluntly. He gestured to the paper in his hand. "The young man who sent this is already on his way back here. He was in hiding with one of the members of parliament who has been barred from his seat. He's left London already, this came from"—he broke off—"another port. He'll come back to us as soon as he can get a passage."

James felt a deep sense of dread. He looked from his mother and father to his tutor. "You know I have lost my faith," he said. "I can't go."

"This is a matter of the king, not of God," his father said bluntly. "You can do your duty to the king. These are—Lord knows—earthly troubles. We have to know what they plan. If you're right—if there's any possibility of a trial—then we have to get him away."

"I couldn't make him come last time," James reminded them. "I failed. He refused me."

"He'll come now," Dr. Sean predicted. "He knows he must not fall into the power of the army. Besides, all you have to do is to take our young man's place: deliver some money, a letter, and report back."

"Is it safe for him to go back to England?" Lady Avery turned to her son. "What if that woman betrays you?"

"She doesn't come to London. She never leaves Sussex."

"You're only to go to London, deliver the money and the orders, find out what is happening, and report to The Hague," Dr. Sean said.

"Don't go to her," his mother added. "Not when you're on the king's business, not when you're in danger. I don't trust her."

"I'll get you the letters, the address of the safe house in London, and the gold." Dr. Sean hurried to his private room. "I'll have it all ready within the hour."

"You can take my horse," James's father said. He stepped towards his son and hugged him tightly. "Leave him at the inn at Dunkirk. Here, take my cloak as well. It's a cold day, and it will be worse at sea. Go, my son, I am proud of you. Do your duty to the king and then we'll see what is ahead of us. You're a young man, and these are times that change with every tide. Don't promise anything to anyone. We don't know where we will be next year! Come back safely."

James felt his father's heavy cloak swung around his shoulders like an extra burden to carry, saw his mother's anguished face.

"Come back," was all she said. "Don't go to her."

# TIDELANDS, DECEMBER 1648

Alinor and Alys walked in silence to the ferry-house, their shawled heads bowed against the icy wind that blew down the mire. They looked like two hooded beasts, crawling across a wet desert. They were each bent over a large basket filled with little bottles of oils, and twists of waxed paper filled with dried herbs. At the ferry-house Alinor opened the side door, went into the storeroom, and loaded another basket with jars of bottled plums, dried apples, dried black currants, red currants, and blackberries.

Ned appeared in the doorway, Red at his heels. "I'll come with you," he said abruptly. "I'll carry this stuff for you. I'm on my way to London."

"What?" Alinor asked. Her first thought was that he must somehow know that she was with child, and he was leaving them forever. "What? Ned? What d'you mean? You can't leave?"

"Colonel Pride has taken the House of Commons," he said, stammering with excitement. "God bless him, he's one of the commander's best men, so this must be on his orders. It must be. It's war on parliament, as it was war on the king."

"Whose orders?"

"Cromwell's himself! Noll Cromwell himself!"

"What's he done now?" Alys appeared beside her mother, pushing back the scarf from her cold face.

"Taken the houses of parliament, as if they were a royal palace—which they were! They were! The members of parliament will never again throw away an army victory. The army has barred the door to the king's placemen, thrown out the traitor members. They're not going to allow a deal with the king over our heads! They're not going to put him back on the throne with some kind of cobbled oath that he'll break as soon as he can. Us army men saw through his lies from the very beginning, we who were there, we who were there at Marston Moor, we who were there at Naseby."

Alinor put down her basket and took her brother's cold hands in her own, trying to hold him still. "Hush, Ned. I don't understand you. You can't go to London. Who'll keep the ferry?"

"You must," he said bluntly. "Look, I beg you. I'm sorry, but I have to go. I can't miss this. Colonel Pride has taken the houses of parliament, praise God. The army will put in its own men, and they'll vote down all these empty agreements with the king! I've got to be there. If they need an old soldier, I've got to stand with them. I have to see this. I can't be down here, on the edge of the mire, getting news three weeks late, and wondering all the time what's happening. I can't be stuck in Foulmire like a frozen sheep in mud for the last days of my war. Alinor! This is the last battle. These were the greatest days of my life. These are the last days of the kingdom. I've got to be there. I was there at the beginning, I must see the end."

Alinor closed her eyes to block out his flushed face. "I can't keep the ferry," she said. "I can't. You know I can't."

"Nobody will want the ferry in the days before Christmas," he lied. "After the Chichester Christmas market nobody'll go off Sealsea Island. God knows, nobody'll come here. They'll all stay home for the season."

"They will! They will!" Alinor was more and more distressed. "Nobody wants to go through the wadeway in winter. They'll all want to go on the ferry, even at low tide, and at high tide they'll load horses. I can't do it, Brother. Not on cold water. Not on the winter tides. Don't make me! I can't—I swear that I can't."

"But I can," Alys said suddenly from behind her. "I'll keep the ferry for you, Uncle Ned."

"You?"

"Yes, but you have to pay me. You know I don't have all my dowry yet. I'll keep the ferry for you for five shillings. I mean five shillings on top of the money you've promised me as a gift. Five shillings and I keep all the ferry fees."

"You can't," Alinor turned to her daughter. "You can't be on the water. I couldn't bear it. You're not strong enough, when the tide's high . . ."

"Yes, she can," Ned said. "What harm'll come to her? And Rob can come back from the Priory and help."

Alinor closed her eyes at the thought of her children on the dark waters of the winter mire. "Please," she said quietly. "Please don't do this. You know I can't spare them."

"Five shillings for my wedding," Alys bargained. "And I keep all the fees."

Ned held out his hand. "Done." To his sister he said: "I'm sorry; I have to go. I know that the army'll bring the king to London. I pray that they'll charge him with treason against us, the people. He's guilty as sin, and I want to see him answer for his crimes. He's destroyed the peace of England and been the death of thousands of good men—it's all been for nothing unless we gain our freedom from him. And I want to see him punished as I'd want to see a witch drowned. This is the end of tyrants in England, this is the start of our new country. I must be there to see him humbled. Sister, I have to be there."

Alys, her face bright and uncaring, handed over the basket of oils to her uncle. "You can carry those for Ma," she said, "as you go together to Chichester. And I'll stay here. I'll start today."

He grinned like a lad. "Pull us over then," he said.

"A halfpenny for the two of you," she said, putting out her hand and slipping the coin that he gave her into the pocket of her gown. Ned took Alinor's arm and helped her onto the ferry; she clamped her scarred hands on the wooden rail.

"Don't fear," he said to her. "No harm will come to her on the water. How should it? There's nothing to fear except your dreams of drowning. And I'll come back soon."

"When?" she demanded.

"When it's over," he said, his face bright. "When the king has begged pardon of the people of England."

Alinor and Ned parted at the Market Cross in the center of Chichester where the stone cross marked the roads that ran north and south, east and west. Ned was going to walk north to London, confident that someone would offer him a lift on the way, the wagons rolling easily on the frozen roads.

"There'll be many old soldiers going to London for news," he said confidently. "Many of us have waited for this for years."

"But you'll come back when it's all over?" Alinor asked, putting her hand on his sleeve. "You won't enlist again? Not even if the Irish rise against us, or the Scots invade again? You won't go with Cromwell's army?"

"That's finished," he said certainly. "There'll be no more wars, there'll be no more uprisings. The king will have to swear on his life to live in peace, and all the poor men who marched on one side or the other will be able to go home, and the brave women who kept the houses against their enemies will be able to live in peace at last."

"I ask you, because I have troubles that I haven't told you," Alinor said choosing her words with care. "I'm going to need you at home, Brother. I'm going to need your help."

At once, he was alert. "Has Zachary come back? Have you heard from him?"

"No, God be praised, no," she said quickly. "But I have to get Alys married and Rob into his work and I have a difficulty, a difficulty of my own. I'll need your help."

He put his broad rough hand over hers. "Alys is earning her

dowry even now," he reassured her. "No need to fear for her. And Rob has his place promised to him and the Peacheys are paying his entrance fee. I'll come back, but you've nothing to fear. Are you ill? Is that it?"

She made herself smile at him. "I'll tell you when you come back," she said. "It'll keep."

Only his excitement would have made him overlook her pallor. "You'd better stay at Ferry-house while Alys is keeping the ferry."

"Yes, we will."

"Look after the dog. He's getting old now. He feels the cold."

"I'll let him sleep by the fire."

"And when I come home, you can stay on. There's no point going back to your cottage alone when Alys is wed and Rob away. We'll tell everyone that Zachary is never coming home, and you can keep house for me. You can come back to your old home."

Like a vision, Alinor imagined her childhood home as her own home once again, and the man she loved riding down the road to the ferry, just as he had done before. She thought that he would see her, standing at the garden gate of the ferry-house, with the deep water before her, and know that she was a free woman, waiting for him. She thought that when he crossed on the ferry and took her hands she would tell him that she was carrying his child.

Ned was dazzled by her smile, as bright as the winter sun.

"Yes," she said. "Very well."

## LONDON, DECEMBER 1648

James took ship from France on a cold December morning with a westerly wind filling the sails of the Thames barge that took him into the pool of London. He disembarked with papers that showed him to be a wine merchant, coming to trade with the Vintners' Company of London. He was waved ashore by an exciseman whose main concern was to check the hold of the ship, and had no time for anyone who did not have gossip to tell from the extraordinary royal courts in exile in France and the Low Countries.

"No, I heard nothing," James spoke with a slight French accent. "What matter, eh? Can you direct me to the Vintners' Hall?"

"Behind the watergate, and Three Cranes Wharf." The man waved his hand.

"And how may I know Three Cranes Wharf?"

"Because there are three cranes on it," the man said with exaggerated patience.

James, satisfied the exciseman would remember the French wine merchant, hefted his bag over his shoulder and climbed the damp steps set into the quay wall of Queenhithe. The quayside was crowded with vendors of little goods, porters, hawkers, and pedlars. James disappeared among the people trying to sell him things that he did not want, and took Trinity Lane up the hill, and then a roundabout route to his destination: a small counting house off Bread Street. When he reached the door with the curiously wrought door knocker he tapped twice and let himself inside.

In the gloom he could see a middle-aged woman rise up from the table where she was weighing small coins in the dim light from the barred window. “Good day, sir. Can I help you?” she asked.

“Yes,” he replied. “I am Simon de Porte.”

“You are welcome,” she said. “Are you sure that no one followed you from the docks?”

“I am sure,” he said. “I turned several corners and I stopped and doubled back twice. There was no one.”

She hesitated as if she was afraid to trust him. “Have you done this before?” she asked, and then she saw how weary he looked. His handsome young face was grooved with lines of fatigue. Clearly, he had done this before; clearly, he had done it too many times.

“Yes,” he said shortly.

“You can put your bag in the cellar,” she said, gesturing to a hatch in the floor under her chair. Together, they pushed her table to one side and she gave him a candle to light his way down the wooden ladder. At the foot was a small bed, a table, and another candle.

“If there’s a raid, bolt the hatch from the inside. There is a secret way into the cellar next door, behind that rack of wine,” she said. “And from there, in the opposite wall, there is a low delivery door out to the next lane. If someone comes, and you need to escape, then go that way quickly and quietly and you might get away.”

“Thank you,” he said looking up into her worn face framed with gray hair pinned back under her cap. “Is Master Clare at home?”

“I’ll fetch him,” she said. “He’s in his workshop.”

James climbed back up the stairs, she dropped the hatch, and together they pulled back the table. James saw that she was dressed very plainly in a gray gown with a rough apron, not at all like the wealthy cavalier supporters who had hidden him in the past.

"A cup of ale?" she offered him.

"I'd be glad of one."

She poured the ale from a jug on the sideboard and then put her shawl around her head. "I'll fetch the master," she said. "You wait here."

James sat at the table, feeling the odd sensation of the floor moving under his feet, as if he were still riding the horse to the coast, still rising and falling on the waves of the sea. It was only travel sickness, but he thought that it would last forever: never again would the ground be firm beneath his feet. Then the door opened and a slight man came in, dressed in the neat modest clothes of a London tradesman. He shook James's hand with a steady grip.

"You won't be staying long." It was a statement rather than a question.

"I won't," James promised him. "I'm grateful to you for the refuge."

The man nodded.

"You're not of the old faith?" James asked tentatively.

"No," the man said. "I'm a Presbyterian, though I think, as Cromwell does, that a man should be free to worship in his own way. But unlike the radicals, I think the country is best ruled by a king and lords. I can't see that a man can be a plowman by day and a lawmaker by night. We each have our trade, we should stick to it."

"Was the king a good brother in the guild of monarchy?" James asked him, smiling slightly.

"Not the best," the man said frankly. "But if my goldsmith does faulty work I make a complaint and ask him to do it again. I don't put my baker in his place."

"Are there many who think like you in London?"

"A few," the man said. "Not enough for your purposes."

"My purpose is to get information for the queen and prince and a letter to their friends," James said cautiously. "That's all."

"That's only half the job. Your purpose should be to get him back to his throne and you back to your own home, wherever that is. All of us in the place we were born to. All of us doing the trade we were brought up to."

James nodded. "In the end, of course." Briefly he thought of his home and his mother's herb garden, and of his dream of Alinor standing at the gate. "I have hopes," he admitted. "But for now, I have to know what is happening."

"I'll take you to Westminster," his host said. "You can see for yourself. A wonder I never thought I'd see. The army holding the gate of the houses of parliament and the king commanded to answer to them."

## TIDELANDS, DECEMBER 1648

In the cold dark days of December Alys kept the ferry, pulling it over to the north side as soon as she heard the clang of the iron bar against the horseshoe, and answering every knock on the door or holler from the road. She was polite and cheerful with every traveler, and more than one wagoner paid her a penny tip as well as his threepenny fee for her pretty smile. The two women moved into the ferry-house at once. It was the only way that Alys could mind the ferry in the hours of darkness, and they were both glad to be in the bigger warmer house when the east wind brought frost across the harbor and the rain turned to sleet.

Alinor, waking in her childhood bed, seeing once again the familiar painted beams on the limewashed ceiling, felt as if she had never been married and never left home to live with

Zachary in the little cottage. Sometimes she woke and thought that her mother was in the little bedroom next door and her brother, Ned, snoring in the bed beside her own, but then she felt the baby move deep in her belly, and remembered that she was a girl no longer; she had given birth to two children and was now expecting a third.

The two women worked side by side during much of the day, weeding the winter garden, brewing ale and selling it at the kitchen window to people crossing on the ferry, baking bread with the yeast from the ale froth, dipping rushlights in the wax from the bees, and sorting seeds for spring. Their pregnancies were easy to hide. The growing curve of Alinor's belly was disguised under her voluminous winter skirt and aprons, and Alys spent her days wrapped in her uncle Ned's canvas cloak to keep her warm and dry on the water.

There was little hard laboring work to be done on Mill Farm in the winter months. The men did most of the hedging and the ditching. Plowing and harrowing would not start till spring. Alinor took her daughter's place at the mill, working in the kitchen and dairy: breadmaking, ale brewing, and cheese making.

Before sunrise in the morning, and at sunset every winter afternoon, Richard Stoney walked down the track from the mill to sit with Alys in the ferry-house kitchen, or to pull the ferry for her so she could stay indoors and spin. Alinor came upon the two of them, wrapped in each other's arms, when it was time for Richard to go home.

"Soon you won't be parted," she told them.

"And then we'll never be parted again," Richard promised.

Alinor was cooking dinner, a fish stew made from Alys's catch from Broad Rife, when there was a sharp bark from Red, and then a loud knocking on the back door of the ferry-house. Her first thought was of James, but when she threw open the door, it was one of the Sealsea Island famers standing on the stone doorstep.

"It's my mother," he said. "Granny Hebden. She's sinking fast."

"God bless her," Alinor said at once.

"We want you to sit with her, and then . . . all the rest."

"Is she sick?" Alys demanded over her mother's shoulder. "Does she have a fever?"

"I'll come," Alinor said. She said to her daughter: "It's the wrong time of year for plague, but I've got to go and see. She's an old lady; she's likely just slipping away."

"I can't have you bringing sickness back here," Alys said stubbornly. "You know why."

"I wouldn't risk it for myself," Alinor replied with a faint smile. "You know why!"

"I'll get your basket," Alys said, and while her mother put on a shawl and her cape around her shoulders, the younger woman picked up Alinor's basket of herbs and oils. "I'll leave you some of the stew."

"I mightn't get back tonight," Alinor warned. "Shall you go to the Priory and get Rob?"

"Richard will stay with me," Alys said confidently.

Alinor went out into the darkness. The young man had a horn lantern and he held it before them. As she closed the door, Red slipped through, determined to come with her.

"I've got the dog," Alinor called. With the dog at her heels, her path illuminated by the dipping light, Alinor and the farmer hurried down the track running south. The road was frozen, the ruts were white with frost, the winter moon encircled by a yellow haze in the cloudless sky. They could easily see the way. They went at a brisk pace, their breaths coming in misty puffs, until they reached a gateway and the farmer said: "Here we are," and guided Alinor through the orchard to the little house.

He opened the door and they went into the hall of the farmhouse. Alinor said, "Wait here, Red," and the dog lay down on the threshold.

Alinor went towards the fireside where an old lady, bent double with age, shrunk to the size of a child, was seated on a stool beside the fire. The farmer's wife rose up from her stool on the other side of the stone hearth.

"How is she?" the farmer asked his wife.

"Just the same."

"Here's Mrs. Reekie, come to see her."

"I doubt she'll know her."

"I'll talk to her," Alinor said gently. "Let me talk to her."

She knelt on the stone floor before the old woman and waited while the milky eyes turned to her and the old lady smiled. "Oh, Alinor, my dear. Why have they sent for you?"

"Hello, Granny Hebden. They tell me you're not very well?"

The old lady reached out her hands. "Oh, no, my dear, they're all wrong, as usual. I'm quite well: just dying."

"Are you?"

"Yes. But I want to go here, at the fireside, warm. I've lived in this house for more than eighty years, you know."

"Have you?" Alinor asked gently. She could see that the old woman had no fever: her face was pale, her hands cool. But her breathing was labored, with a little catch in every pant.

"Or longer. They have no idea."

"Course they don't," Alinor whispered. "I remember coming here with my mother to see you when I was just a little girl."

"And your grandmother. She brought you when I broke my leg falling from the apple tree. Three generations of wisewomen in your family, and faerie blood, no doubt. Does your daughter have the sight?"

"We don't speak of it now, in these days."

A grimace showed what the old lady thought of the mealy-mouthed generation. "Faerie crafts are a great thing to have in the family. But these days—well, nothing's allowed, is it?"

"The minister must guide us," Alinor said tactfully.

The old lady shrugged irritably. "What does he know?" she asked. "It's not as if he's a proper priest. He doesn't even read the Mass."

"Hush, Grandmother." Alinor gave her the courtesy title for an old woman. "You know, he's the minister appointed to guide us. And the rest of it is against the law now."

"I think I can say what I like with my last breath."

"Does your breath hurt you?" Alinor asked.

"I've had something pressing on my belly for years," the old woman said. "It's been squeezing the life out of me."

"Why didn't you send for me before?"

"What could you have done, my dear?"

Alinor nodded. If the woman had a growth in her belly then nothing could be done. A physician might dare to cut a brave man or woman for a gallstone, a barber surgeon might cut a tongue tie, or slice the gum to pull out a rotting tooth. Alinor herself had once cut a live baby from the belly of a dead woman; but a growth deep in the belly of a living patient was untouchable.

"I could've given you something for the pain."

"I take a little brandy," the old lady said with simple dignity. "And then sometimes I take a little of the Scots usquebaugh. And sometimes—on bad days—I take them both together."

Alinor smiled at her. "Would you like some herbs to ease the pain now?"

"I'll take a little brandy," she agreed. "In hot water. With your herbs. And you can ask the girl—what's her name?—if the minister comes out these days, and if there are prayers for the dying, for I think I'm ready."

"I'll ask Mrs. Hebden, your daughter-in-law," Alinor reminded her.

"Yes, that's her." The old lady nodded. "Ask her what the minister does for the dying, if he does anything these days? Or if that's all changed as well?"

Alinor rose to her feet and found that William Hebden was hovering at the scullery door. "She wants some brandy in hot water," she said.

"We've got a little keg of brandy," he said. "It was a gift. Not bought."

Alinor understood at once that it was contraband: smuggled brandy. “No matter to me,” she reassured him. “And she wants to know if the minister will come to say the prayers for the dying?”

“Not to the likes of us,” he said shortly. “We’re not grand enough for him. We don’t pay enough in tithes for him to come out to us. The chaplain at the Priory, that Mr. Summer, he’d have come for asking. He came out for free, came twice.”

Alinor flushed scarlet at his name. “Did he?” she asked. She thought that anyone would be able to hear the love in her voice. “Did he go to people for free?”

“He came and prayed with her.” William shifted his feet. “Old prayers,” he said. “Those that she likes. Probably not allowed now. But she was that ill . . .”

“Anyway, Mr. Summer has gone away,” Alinor said.

“Aye. But he left his Prayer Book here. He said she could hold it in her hand if there was no one that could read them. He said to keep it hidden, but she could hold it if it comforted her.”

“Did he?” She was swept by a longing to see anything that had belonged to James.

“He said anyone could read the prayers to her. You’re a midwife, you could say them, couldn’t you? It would be as good as a minister?”

“I can say them,” Alinor offered. “I could read them from his book. It wouldn’t be as good as him, but it’s his prayers.”

She went back to the fireside with some brandy in an earthenware cup, added a tincture of fennel, and topped it up with hot water from the pot that stood on a trivet by the fire.

Greedily, the old lady took it into her hands, wrapping her cold fingers around the cup. “Now,” she said. “Now I’m ready.”

Alinor took up James’s missal and started to spell out the beautiful old words in Latin, not knowing what they meant; but hearing the music of the sounds, knowing that he would have known them by heart, knowing that this was his faith and his God, believing that his child in her belly could perhaps hear them and feeling closer to him now, reading the office for the dying to an old lady, than she had been in all the long weeks that he had been away.

## LONDON, DECEMBER 1648

James, not knowing that his prayers were being whispered by the woman he loved, went quietly through the darkened streets of the city of London, keeping to the center of the street, picking his way through the frozen muck and rubbish rather than risk walking close to the dark doorways and shadows. He turned into a grand gateway and nodded to the silent watchman, and then went down the side of the house where a single lantern was hung on a bent nail outside a narrow door.

The door opened easily when he turned the ring of the handle, and he stepped into a stone-flagged corridor, which led to the kitchen one way and to the great hall of the house the other. Before him was a small storeroom with a lighted candle on the table. James went in and seated himself at the scrubbed table.

"You're John Makepeace?" The man came in so quietly that James had not heard his footfall.

"Yes."

"Password?"

"Godspeed."

"God Will Not Fail Us," the man replied. "Have you come from the queen?"

"Yes. I have this." James passed a thick letter.

The man broke the seal. "It's in code," he said irritably. "D'you know what it says?"

"Yes, I was ordered to memorize it in case I had to destroy it. It instructs you to reach the king and get him to Deptford. There's a ship waiting for him, a coastal trader, that will take him to France. She's called the *Dilly*. If you tell me when it will be, I can send a message to His Highness's fleet and see that you are met by them, to give you safe passage on the seas."

"And the two royal children?"

"I have no instructions for them."

Startled, the man looked up from the sealed letter. "What? Do they understand that the army will never let the children out of the country, if he gets away? He will never see them again? Are they to be abandoned among their enemies? Are we to just leave them here?"

"Those are the instructions," James said steadily.

The man dropped into a chair and glared at James. "He was supposed to get away at Newport."

"I know it."

"It failed."

"No one knows that better than me."

"And from Hurst Castle."

"Hurst?"

"Yes, there too. That miscarried as well. And at Bagshot he was supposed to have the fastest horse in England, but it went lame the day he was to go, and nobody had a second horse. Or a second plan."

James forced himself not to reveal his contempt for these half-baked plots. "You speak as if it is hopeless."

"I think it is. My hope has drained away month after month. No one decides what to do and does it. All we can do now is pray that they give him a fair trial and that they listen to what he has to say. That he can put the case for all that he has done."

"And then?"

"God knows. That's the madness of failing to get him away. We don't know what they intend or even if they have any intention beyond shaming him. Will they limit his power as they think best? Or will he agree to hand the throne over to Prince

Charles? Is he to live quietly and let his son rule? Will Prince Charles be bound by them? And will both king and prince swear never to raise an army, outside the kingdom or inside it? Parliament won't stand for anything less."

"It is to unmake royal power. For him—and for his sons. For all kings everywhere?"

"I think he has no choice. This is the army in power now, not parliament, and they are ill-disposed to the man who killed their comrades, surrendered, and then marched out again. They're men of action, not endless words. The army is a different beast again. They speak a different language, they come from different worlds."

"Your orders are to rescue him," James insisted. "Whatever the case. You can decode and read them; but they're as I say. I have to take a reply. What am I to tell them when I report back?"

"Tell them I'll try," the man said miserably. "But I won't send a message to you, to tell you when. I won't fix a date. The fewer men who know, the better."

"You're never going to risk him at sea, without the protection of the fleet?"

"What protection? What fleet? Who's to say the prince's sailors wouldn't kidnap him, and sail right back to London to claim the ransom money? They changed their tune once; they'll do it again, won't they?"

James recoiled from the man's bitter cynicism. "You don't trust the royal fleet? Under the command of the Prince of Wales?"

"D'you think you are the only man in England who has lost faith?"

"I never said I had lost my faith!"

"It's in your face and in every step you take," the man said with contempt. "You look like we all do—whipped."

# TIDELANDS, DECEMBER 1648

Alys and Alinor walked along the harbor bank to church on Christmas Day, a hard frost turning the inland water meadows white as snow on their right hand, the harbor frozen like iron on the other. They were dressed in layer upon layer of winter clothes but they had no special ribbons or favors pinned to their capes. The new parliament had ruled that Christmas was not to be marked with any feasting or merrymaking, but must be a day like any day. Red trotted ahead of them and then circled back, the only joyful one.

Alinor looked at the winter sun, casting shadows that underlined every bank and puddle and reedbed on the wet harbor. She wondered if James was with his family, if he were thinking of her. She hoped he was somewhere warm and merry. She loved him so much, she even wished him happiness without her.

The church was cold and plain and bare, and there was no singing and no Christmas carols. The minister preached a sermon announcing that it was the birth of Jesus Christ and that the day should be filled with quiet reflection, that wassailing and Christmas ales and special puddings and roast dinners were nothing but worldly show and greed. The birth of our Lord should be considered reverently and thoughtfully. Godly work could and should be done; it was not a holiday for visiting and dancing and carousing. How would the birth of God be served by people sinning? How should the Lord be greeted, if not by quiet reflection and steady labor?

The prayers for parishioners who were sick or dying went on for long minutes; the cold weather was always hard on the poor of Sealsea Island. Alinor bowed her head and thanked God that she and Alys were well housed in the ferry-house and Rob lived in luxury at the Priory. The minister prayed for the soul of old Mrs. Hebden, buried in frost-hard ground, and invoked God's aid for other men and women who would not survive the cold season and were going hungry to save their winter stores. The church was freezing, the service dragged on and on, longer than ever, and when the congregation was finally released and spilled out of the porch, it started to snow.

"The dog looks for you," the minister complained to Alinor as she went past him. "He sits in the church porch and looks for you."

"He does not harm, he's a good dog, my brother's dog."

"People remark it," he said.

"It means nothing," Alinor said quickly. "Just a dog missing his master."

"It's ungodly how he attends to you," the man complained.

"I'll leave him at home next Sunday. I apologize. He's pining for my brother."

"Is Edward still in London?" the minister asked.

"Yes, sir," she said, glad to change from the dangerous topic of a loyal animal, a familiar.

"He wanted to be with his old regiment in these important times, I suppose?"

"That was his plan."

"Godly work," he said. "Witness to the end of days."

"Yes," Alinor said. "He's very devout. Praise the Lord."

She curtseyed to him and then went to the squire's household. Alinor curtseyed to Sir William and to Walter and then kissed Rob. "Happy Christmas," she whispered to him.

"You'd better come back to the Priory," Mrs. Wheatley invited her. "We're going to be having a good dinner: Christmas or no Christmas."

"Do come," Rob supplemented.

"I'd better not," Alinor said. "My brother wouldn't like it. And Alys has to keep the ferry."

"Just come for dinner," Rob urged her. "I'll come back with you and work the ferry on the evening tide."

"Do let's," said Alys.

"Oh, very well," Alinor said. "But we have to get back to the ferry for high tide this afternoon. You know that Christmas is not a holiday anymore."

"It is at the Priory," Rob whispered to her. "We keep to the old ways. You should see what Mrs. Wheatley has been cooking!"

Alinor took his arm and they walked side by side after the Peachey household towards the big house, Red trotting behind them, his tail waving like a standard.

"This'll be my one and only Christmas at the Priory," Rob reminded her. "Next year, I'll be at Chichester."

"And I'll be married," Alys chimed in from her mother's other side.

Alinor, happy to be between her two children, hugged Rob's arm, took Alys's hand, and wondered where she would be next year, and if she would be walking to church with James carrying their child.

## THE HAGUE, NETHERLANDS, DECEMBER 1648

James spent his Christmas at The Hague with the advisors to the Prince of Wales, trying to convince them that they should not rely upon the king making an escape to avoid a trial.

"Why not? It is his wish," one of the lords said impatiently to James. There were ten of them seated around a big wooden table. Too many, James thought: ten men who would pass on every word of this conversation to their wives, their servants, their mistresses, and their children. They had once ruled a country—they could not resist demonstrating their importance.

One of them leaned forward. "Once His Majesty believed our enemies might be brought to an agreement. Now we know they are completely false, so he is ready to leave. You have delivered our instructions? Our men are all working together, preparing escape?"

"It's not a question of issuing instructions." James hid his impatience. "I delivered the messages, but the man did not confide in me. He would not trust me, nor anyone. He did not want to work with me or with your other agents. There are not many of them left anymore. In London, all His Majesty's known friends are watched. Many of them have given up. Only six months ago I met with men who will no longer open their doors to me."

"Sir William Peachey?" one of the men queried.

James glanced towards the door. "I won't say names," he said.

"Well, you know who I mean. Won't he help? He's got a neat little port on his lands, hasn't he?"

"Nothing more than a quay at high tide," James said, thinking of the tide mill and Alinor's cottage that faced it across the mire. "Anyway, he's done enough."

"You have money," one of the men pointed out to him bitterly. "We have beggared ourselves in raising money. Can't you hire someone?"

"I have done what you asked me. I've told you where His Majesty is housed and the arrangements for his trial. I gave your gold to the man who said he will attempt a rescue. But I am warning you that he may not succeed. His Majesty is well guarded, and the men who watch him are not for sale. The common soldiers used to respect kingship, but not now. I don't think they can be bribed. So I don't know that you can get him away. I beg you to start bargaining with the Cromwell government. That's the only way we can be sure that His Majesty will be freed."

"Freed? By their agreement?" a man said incredulously. "Are you forgetting that he is the King of England? I won't haggle with criminals!"

"Bargain with Cromwell?" One of the lords raised a well-plucked eyebrow. "With Cromwell? Oliver Cromwell of Ely?"

Another man laughed scoffingly. "Where would they imprison him? In the Tower? It's a royal palace anyway! You're forgetting this is majesty. The moment they meet him face-to-face they will fall to their knees."

James nodded, restraining his temper. "But what if they do not? They could well imprison him. It's been done before. The newspapers and scandal sheets in London are filled with stories of Henry VI and Edward II, and that they were imprisoned and their thrones taken."

"Henry VI!" a man laughed. "Who cares for Henry VI?"

"If they decide to house him in the Tower, it will be very hard to get him away," James persisted.

"For God's sake!" One of the men jumped up from the table.

"Do we need a priest to come and give us a history lesson? You! Summers, or Avery, or whatever is your name, did we ask you to come and disappoint us?"

James rose too. "I am sorry not to be able to give you better news," he said, controlling his rising temper. "I volunteered for this work and it is a thankless task. If you dismiss me I will go without another word. All I ask is that you do not speak of me, my name, or those I have worked with."

"No, don't go, don't go," the first advisor said. "Don't be hasty. Don't take offense. We're all working, as you are, for His Majesty's safety. We are safe to name names here. This is our palace; all the servants are loyal. You don't understand our situation. We're doing all we can. Just as you suggest, the queen is speaking to all her royal relations, the French king among them; and Prince Charles is calling on all the crowned heads of Europe to protect His Majesty. We're demanding the freeing of the royal children as well: Princess Elizabeth and Prince Henry. Especially, we have to get the prince out of England."

"Both children," James said stubbornly. "They should never have been left behind. She's only thirteen and living as a prisoner, trying to care for her little brother. Both children should be restored to their mother."

"Only the prince matters. What if they cram the crown on his head and have a puppet king? He can't be trusted not to take his father's throne. Really, you should go to Prince Henry and tell him, he's to refuse any proposal—"

"He's eight!" James exclaimed. "Do you think you can give orders to an eight-year-old? What do you expect of a child? He should never have been left in their power."

"We're doing all we can here," the senior advisor repeated. "And we're concerned for the children too, of course. First the king's escape, then theirs. We want you to go and watch for us, report back."

"I promised to go, deliver gold, meet with your man, and come back and report to you. I'm bound to do nothing more," James said coldly.

There was a brief silence. "I apologize," the man said who had called him Summers or Avery. "I should not have named you, nor complained of what you have done. Because . . . to tell the truth . . . we've got no one else. No one else who can go. We need you to go back."

"You've not been identified as a spy?" the chief advisor said.

"No," James said unwillingly. "I think not."

"Then we have to ask it of you. This will be the last time."

James looked around the table at the anxious faces, felt the familiar mixture of frustration and despair. "Very well."

"Go back to London, and send us news. We have to know where they are keeping him and what they plan to do with him. We will give your reports to the prince himself and he will take them to the King of France. We will plan a rescue based on what you tell us."

James bowed his head. "Very well. I'll go and I'll report." He got to his feet.

The chief advisor stood up, and came round the table to put a hand on the young man's shoulder, then walked with him to the door. "I'm grateful. You will be rewarded. Prince Charles will know your name and what you are doing for his father."

James glanced sideways, his face tight and closed. "I thank you but I'd rather that nobody named me," he said. "Not while I am in England passing as a Frenchman, or a German, or something else entirely. It's safer for my mother and father and for our lands, too, if my name is kept secret."

"Very well. Report to us. Daily if needs be. And get word to us the moment that you think it is going against him?"

"Oh, that I can do readily," James said bitterly. "It's now. It's going against him now."

# TIDELANDS, JANUARY 1649

In the first cold days of January a fox got into the ferry-house barn and savaged three chickens before the anguished clucking of the flock brought Alinor running barefoot in her shift. As she flung the door open a streak of russet brown dashed out past her. One hen was dead on the floor, one beyond saving—Alinor picked her up and wrung her neck—but the third was bruised and bloodstained, and Alinor put her in a basket and took her into the house, washed the teeth marks on her breast, and kept her by the fireside in a basket. The hens were laying poorly in the cold dark days, so Alinor did not miss the income from the few eggs, but it was still a loss to the smallholding. Even if they could have afforded to lose three hens, Alinor would still have been grieved. She knew each bird by name and took pride in their glossy health.

"I know it's stupid to weep for a hen, but I can't forgive that fox," she said to Alys.

"Tell the Peachey huntsmen where the earth is," Alys said. "They'd be glad of a good run and a kill."

"Oh, I couldn't betray an animal to the hunt."

Alys laughed. "Then until the resurrection and the life eternal you'll always be sorrowing for something that's been killed by something else. I can't wait to eat her. Are you going to make chicken stew?"

"Yes, of course," Alinor said. "I'm not such a fool as to not eat fresh meat in winter when it's come our way. But you're very hard-hearted for poor Mrs. Hoppy."

"I'm hungry," Alys said. "I'm hungry all the time. Aren't you?"

"Yes," Alinor said, noting that her daughter, for the first time in five months, was prepared to share signs of pregnancy. "And I need to piss every moment."

The girl laughed. "I wish it was summer," she said. "I was telling Richard that I wouldn't mind going out to the midden if it wasn't so cold."

"He knows then?" Alinor asked. "You've told him?"

"I told him as soon as I was sure," the young woman said. "He's glad."

"Will he tell his mother and father?" Alinor asked nervously, thinking of the formidable woman who would be Alys's mother-in-law.

"He's told them," Alys said confidently. "And his father is one for the old ways." She made a disdainful little face. "He jokes about it. He likes a fertile bride. She said that it was good to know that I'd continue the line—he said you only buy a cow in calf."

Alinor laughed at Alys's offended expression. "Well, at least they've no objection."

"As long as I've got my dowry. That's all she cares about." She paused. "They said you're to come and stay with me, when I'm near to my time. You'll have to be with me, Ma, when I have my baby."

"I hope so," Alinor said slowly. "I pray for it, Alys. I am hoping and praying for us both, all the time."

"Why don't you send a message to this man? Why doesn't he come and make everything right, if he loves you as you say?"

"He will come," Alinor said steadily. "I don't have to send for him. He will be coming as fast as he can."

In the morning, Red, the ferry-house dog, did not get out of his corner and sit on the pier to watch the ferry, as he usually did.

"And we had a fox," Alinor scolded him. "Are you getting lazy?"

The dog looked at her with his ale-brown eyes and turned away. Alinor put her hand on his head. "Oh, no, Red," she said quietly. "What's wrong?"

He sighed as if he would speak to her. Alinor took his broad head in both hands and looked at him as she would one of her patients.

"Won't you wait till Ned comes home?" she whispered.

He stirred his feathery tail and then turned around three times and lay down. Alinor stroked his soft forehead where his frown wrinkled the fur, and let him stay in his bed.

Alys pulled the icy rope of the ferry as Alinor crossed the mire at low tide to go to work at the mill. It was bitterly cold, the ground slippery with frost. The sandbanks in the mire were white as snow.

"Get back in the warm," Alinor said to her daughter. "And take care on the water."

Alys's face was white with cold, her mittened hands gripping the rope. "I'm fine," she said. "You mind that you don't slip."

Mrs. Miller arranged the work of the farm and house so that she and her little boy, Peter, and daughter, Jane, stayed indoors in bad weather and sent her maid-of-all-work and Alinor into the cold. Alinor started in the barn where the cows were waiting patiently in their stalls. She took a three-legged stool down from the hook and set it beside the first cow, leaning her forehead against the warm flank, talking quietly to her, as she pulled on the udders, alternating her hands, and the milk hissed into the pail. It was so cold in the barn, the milk steamed and Alinor sniffed the rich creamy smell, longing to drink it. She carried the heavy pail to the dairy, and poured it into a bowl to separate for churning into butter later.

"I'll thank you to check the dovecot for eggs." Mrs. Miller poked her head into the icy dairy. "And after that, you can go home. I won't need you for anything this afternoon."

Alinor pulled her shawl over her head again, took the heavy basket, and went back out into the yard.

Richard Stoney, shoveling wheat into the dangling pan of the weighbeam in the barn, caught sight of her through the barn door as she was walking carefully across the frozen yard. "I'll put down some straw so you don't slip." He hurried out to her.

She turned to him, the shawl over her head stiff with frost from her frozen breath. "You can't," she said shortly. "They never straw the yard. Only if the cows are coming out."

"So the cows don't fall, but you can!" he exclaimed. "Let me give you my arm then."

She shook her head. "She'll be watching from the window. Let me do my work, Richard. I won't freeze and I won't fall."

"You're never going up the ladder!"

Before Alinor could answer, the farmhouse kitchen door opened and Mrs. Miller shouted into the yard, "Richard Stoney, are you weighing grain or taking a stroll?"

"Go on," said Alinor. "Back to work."

"Can I come to Ferry-house on my way home? Is Alys well today?" he whispered urgently, as he raised a hand to acknowledge Mrs. Miller.

"She's well. Of course you can come!" Alinor called, as she walked on towards the dovecot. Inside the circular tower she reached under her sheepskin jacket and rolled up the waistband of her skirt so it was hitched above her knees and she would not stumble on the hem as she went up the ladder.

She put her hands on the rung and looked upwards at the dovecot interior wall. It seemed like a long way up, and the ladder was old and rickety, but she could see a dove sitting on a nest. Alinor moved the ladder to the nesting dove, checked that it was firmly placed, hitched her basket on her arm, and started to climb. Each rung was freezing cold to the touch and slippery with frost. Up and up she went, step by step, not looking down, and paying no attention to the ominous creaking of the old wood. In some part of her mind she thought that a fall and a miscarriage would solve all her problems. Then she smiled to herself as she saw that at the thought of losing her baby she at once took a stronger grip on the ladder, and put her feet carefully on the rungs. She was as committed to her own life, and to the life of her child, as she had been that first cold morning when she had sworn that she would not be a victim of sorrows, but would bring this baby into the world and win a place for it.

There was a dove nesting in the pigeonhole; she did not move as Alinor climbed up within reach. Gently, Alinor put her hand under the warm soft breast. "I'm sorry, Goody Dove," she said quietly. "But I am sent to get these. You lay more for yourself."

Ignoring the bird's indignant pecks to her cold hands, she lifted all the eggs but one from the nest, and put them carefully in the basket. They were small white eggs, warm from the mother's breast feathers. Alinor climbed carefully down the ladder and looked upwards to see if another bird was nesting. Four times she moved the ladder and went up and down for eggs, and then she walked carefully back to the house with a dozen eggs in her basket. Mrs. Miller opened the door to her and managed a thin smile.

"I'd have thought you'd have sent Alys to do the work on a cold day like this," she said. "Too grand for dove eggs now, is she? Now that she's planning to marry so well? Playing the lady?"

"Oh, no," Alinor said pleasantly. "But she's still keeping the ferry for Ned."

"Who's going to cross in this cold weather? I hear the river has frozen in London and they're walking from one side to another. You won't get any fees if that happens here!"

"It feels cold enough to freeze," Alinor agreed. "And the freshwater in the rife is frozen hard; but the tide still comes in."

"And Ned still not home? I'm surprised he has the time and the money to go jauntering off to London."

"It matters so much to him."

"None of his business," Mrs. Miller said sourly.

Alinor smiled. "Certainly, none of mine," she said.

Mrs. Miller recovered a little good humor, unpacking the

eggs from the basket and putting them in the crock. "Aye, I suppose so. You don't take an interest in it?"

"I'm interested," Alinor said carefully. "But I don't take sides."

"There's not many that don't think the king should be punished for his sins," Mrs. Miller declared. "Making war on his own people! And the taxes! Would you like two eggs for your dinner?"

"Thank you," Alinor replied, thinking that now there was no handsome stranger and noble party from the Priory, Mrs. Miller had reverted to being an envious roundhead. "Thank you very much for the eggs," she said.

When she got to the rife, walking companionably with a Sealsea Island farmer's wife, the ferry was waiting for her.

"Red's missing," Alys said as Alinor climbed cautiously aboard, the ferry rocking on the ebbing tide. "He didn't come out to the pier this morning and he wasn't in his corner at noon."

"Yes, I know," Alinor spoke unguardedly. "Poor Red. I said good-bye to him this morning."

"You knew the dog would go missing?" the farmer's wife demanded. "How did you know?"

"She didn't know," Alys interrupted rudely. "It's just an old dog and he was lazy getting up this morning. She didn't know."

Alinor looked up, surprised at Alys's harsh tone.

"Nobody could know such a thing," Alys ruled.

The farmer's wife remarked that sometimes she had premonitions herself, and her mother had been a terrible one for dreaming. "And of course your grandma had the sight," she reminded Alys.

"Not us," Alys declared roundly, bringing the ferry to the pier as Alinor got off, and turned to help the woman off the ferry. "We don't believe in stuff like that. Good night!" she called. "See you tomorrow."

"I did know about Red," Alinor remarked mildly as Alys tied the ferry up and came up the steps.

"I know you did; but we can't say things like that," Alys said abruptly. "Not even to Mrs. Bellman. Anyway, I suppose he's under a hedge somewhere," she said.

"We'll look," Alinor promised her. "And I have an egg for your tea. A dove egg."

"Lord, she exceeded herself!" Alys exclaimed. "How lucky are we? Two tiny eggs! She's spoiling us. You go that way, I'll go this. We'll find him."

The dog was not far from the house. He had gone quietly, as wise old dogs do, to die alone. It was Alinor who found him, as she knew she would, curled as if he was asleep; but his coat was cool and his nose was cold and his eyes were shut.

"The ground's too hard for us to bury him," Alys said. "What'll we do? It doesn't seem right to burn him, or put him on the midden."

"I'll dig a hole in the soft mud of the mire," Alinor said. "You go and start dinner. I won't be long."

She took a shovel from the lean-to in the fruit garden and went out on one of the little shingle paths that led out into the deep mire. It would be flooded at high tide, but now, as the moon came up and the cold wind blew across the water, it was dry enough for her to walk along and to dig a deep hole in the soft mud at the side of the track.

When the pit was broad enough and deep enough she took the stiffening body, which now seemed so small and light, and laid it in the bottom of the hole. She knew that Ned would ask her if his dog had been properly buried, and that he would trust her. She filled the grave with shingle from the path to keep the body deep under the moving silt of the harbor floor. "Good-bye, Red," she said gently. "You're a very good dog."

She shoveled a pile of silt and went to tamp it down when a glint of silver caught her eye, bright as a star in the dark night sky. She knelt down and found a tiny coin, shaved and thin but twinkling brightly in the mud. It was faerie gold, a coin from the old people, from the old days, with a crest on one side and a crown on the other, too rubbed and worn to be deciphered, too old to be recognized, too light to be valuable.

"Thank you," Alinor said to Red. She accepted without a second thought that this was his burial fee, which he had sent to her from the other side, a country as far away and as misty as the distant side of the mire. "God bless, good dog. Godspeed."

She put the coin in her pocket and the shovel over her shoulder, and she went heavily up the freezing shingle path to where the lights of the ferry-house gleamed over the cold waters.

## WESTMINSTER PALACE, LONDON, JANUARY 1649

The two men went through the crowded streets, stepping over the dirty gutters in the cobbled ways, picking their way down muddy lanes till the great walls of the palace were before them and they could see the soldiers of the New Model Army on guard before the gates. There was a small crowd outside the gates, looking towards the gray carved stone walls and the snow on the slate roof.

"Where is the king housed now?" James asked, keeping his voice down.

"In St. James's Palace. They've called a hundred and thirty-five judges to London to sit in a high court to try him. But I swear half of them won't dare to come. And even if they do, he won't answer to them. How are they even going to get him into court?"

"But if they come, and if he answers—"

The nameless man interrupted him. "He won't," he insisted. "By what rights can they summon him? You can't summon a king. Nobody's ever summoned a king. Would his father, King James, have come to the parliament whistle? Would Queen Elizabeth have trotted obediently along? No country in the world has ever called their king into a court. No English monarch has ever obeyed parliament."

James nodded; it was incredible that the conflict between king and parliament, which should have been resolved on the first battlefield, or at least at Newport, had come so quickly to this unimaginable state. "But suppose they do," he said. "Have they named a day and a time?"

"Tomorrow."

"What?"

"Yes."

"Can I get the names of the judges?"

"You can get the names of those who were called. But nobody knows who will come. They won't know themselves. More than one will be sleepless tonight, trying to decide what he should do."

"Is it possible that none of them will come, and the trial collapse?"

James's guide spat into the frozen gutter. "The devil knows. It's his idea, surely. But I would think Noll Cromwell will be there, wouldn't you? And men who are faithful to him, and those that go beyond him?"

"The trial is open to the public?"

"Yes, but don't think you can burst out of the crowd and save him. He'll be so closely guarded, no one will get near him. They'll be expecting a rescue attempt. They'll take no risks."

"The best time to get him away would be when he comes

from his rooms at St. James's to here at Westminster." James was thinking aloud. "Probably by barge . . ."

The man ducked his head. "Don't tell me, I don't want to know. And I have no opinion."

"I have none either," James said. "I'm whistling in the dark. Let's get the names of the judges."

## TIDELANDS, JANUARY 1649

At dawn, the late cold dawn of January, Alinor woke to hear the cracking of ice and the sound of horses splashing through the cold waters as a carriage skidded down the wadeway and forded the ebbing tide. She rubbed the frost flowers off the inside of her bedroom window and squinted to her left. In the half-light she could see the lumbering bulk of the Peachey carriage.

"Alys! The Peachey carriage is going over the wadeway," she said to the girl still sleeping in the bed behind her.

"Doesn't matter," Alys replied, unmoving. "He doesn't pay."

"I wonder if Rob is with them. And where they're going."

"To London, I expect, chasing after the king, like everyone else."

"They'll have left Rob at the Priory then," Alinor said. "Surely, they wouldn't take him?"

The rattle of the front door answered her. "That'll be him now!" Alinor said gladly. She called down the ladder stairs: "Is that you, Rob?"

"Aye, Mother," he shouted cheerfully. "I'm to stay with you till Candlemas and then Mr. Tudeley is to take me to Chichester. I'm to go to Mr. Sharpe, the Chichester apothecary. My term starts with him then."

Alinor tied her shawl around her thickening waist, and climbed down the stair. She hugged Rob and stepped back to admire him. "I swear you've grown again."

"In the three weeks since Christmas Day?" he teased her.

"You're becoming a man," she said. "Think of you going as an apprentice!"

He dropped to his knee for her blessing and when he rose up he asked, "Have you breakfasted?"

"Of course not. Alys isn't even up yet. Are you hungry?"

"Starving," he said.

"Sit down then and I'll light the fire." Alinor pressed him into the fireside chair, lifted the cover off the embers, and put the kindling driftwood and twigs on the red glow.

"Is Sir William going to London about the king?" she asked.

"Yes, he's called to be a judge. He's taking Walter on to Cambridge."

"Is there really to be a trial of the king?"

"Everyone says so, but I don't think Sir William'll attend the court. He's going to see if he can be excused."

"How will the king get a fair hearing if the only men who judge him are parliament men?" Alys asked, coming down the stairs.

"That's it," Rob said. "He won't."

"He won't?" repeated Alinor.

"He won't get a fair hearing," Rob predicted. "That's what Sir William says. If they can get him into trial at all, there'll be no justice for him."

"So the royalists won't be there?" Alinor asked, thinking of James.

"They'll stay away."

## LONDON, JANUARY 1649

James, reading the list of the men who had been called as judges, saw Sir William's name, and went, his hat pulled low over his face, to the Golden Cross, at Charing Cross, the inn that the Sussex gentry favored on their trips to London. The landlord, rushed by the arrival of so many country gentlemen, shouted, "Yes! He's upstairs in the private sitting room!" and went by without looking twice at James or asking for a name. James was able to go up the stairs and tap at the door without anyone noticing him.

"God bless," Sir William said shortly as James came in. "I didn't think to see you here." He glanced at the closed door. "You're sure you've not been followed? These are terrible times. Every man is a spy."

"I am certain that I'm not being followed. I pass as a French tutor on this trip, and I'm not visiting any of our old friends. I'm only gathering news on the streets. His wife and her friends—you know who I mean—want to know what's happening."

"Damned if anyone knows, do they?" Sir William asked. "Oh, sit down, sit down, we'll have a glass of something. Walter's out with my steward, seeing the sights. We're alone."

"Did you bring Robert Reekie with you?"

"No, left the lad at Sealsea Island with his mother."

"Did you see her?"

"No," Sir William said, surprised at the question. "No, why?"

"Nothing," James tried to recover. "I just hoped that she didn't take my sickness."

"I don't think so. I'd have heard." Sir William opened the door and shouted down the stairs for a bottle of red wine and two glasses. "Now," he said, closing the door carefully, "d'you know what's going to happen to the king?"

"I think only one man knows, and that's Cromwell," James replied. "He's behind it all. And unless someone does something to stop him, I think it'll all go his way."

"He's a fair man, Cromwell. He wouldn't be unjust."

"He thinks this is justice. And he's got to satisfy the army, as well as the parliament."

"Can he muster enough judges to find the king guilty?"

James nodded. "That must be his intention. He's called in more than a hundred gentlemen. Won't you serve?"

"How can I? As far as anyone knows, I've turned my coat. I'm a parliament man now. I've paid my fine and promised my son that his inheritance is safe. I can't now turn again and join the king's side. I've got too much to lose."

A rap on the door was followed by the taproom boy with a bottle of wine and two glasses. The men were silent as he put the glasses and bottle on the table and went out again.

"But what if they find him guilty?" James asked quietly, checking that the door was shut.

"Of what?" Sir William scoffed. "And then what? Exile him? I doubt the French would want him; the Scots handed him back last time. Lock him up somewhere? Back to Carisbrooke Castle? How does that solve the mire that they're stuck in? They've fought him for six years and had him under arrest for two—they need to change everything, if they want to change anything at all."

"I don't know," James said, taking a glass of wine. "I really don't know."

Sir William held up his glass. "His Majesty the king," he said very quietly, and the two men put their glasses together and then drank. It struck James that the toast was as quiet and as solemn as it would be at a wake.

"Sir, I am sure that nobody knows what will happen but Cromwell. But clearly he is planning a trial and he must be hoping for a finding of guilt. Why else do it?"

"The trial will never happen," Sir William predicted stoutly. "And I shan't be part of it. I won't even witness it. I'm taking Walter to Cambridge to start the Lent term. I won't witness and I won't judge on it. And no good man will witness and judge, so they won't get their trial, for they won't get their commissioners. No Englishman can try his king. You'd do better to come to Cambridge with us and teach Walter there."

"I have to stay," James said quietly. "His wife and her friends sent me to report."

"You'll have nothing to report," Sir William assured him. "It'll not come to that. But come to me when it's all over. Come to the Priory before you go abroad again?"

James hesitated, thinking of his promise to his mother not to go to Alinor. "I am bound to go straight back to my seminary."

"You can leave from the tide-mill quay," Sir William assured him. "You can get a French-bound coaster from there, if you want to come for a visit?"

"Yes," James said. He longed to see Alinor. "I do."

James elbowed his way into Westminster Hall, paid a fee for a place in the stand so he could see over the heads of the halberdiers that lined a cleared square in the center of the hall. The vaulted ceiling echoed the noise as people pushed and argued and thrust themselves into the standing room. Above, in the galleries, people were taking their seats and urging each other to move up to make space on the benches. In the center of the cleared space was a great table draped in a tapestry, with a sword and a mace mounted before the Lord President of the court. Behind him were benches of judges, sixty-eight of them, gravely sitting as an extraordinary court, though more than a hundred had been called and refused to come, or had hidden themselves away. Before the Lord President, standing alone like a little island of self-importance, was a red velvet chair with a side table equipped with paper, pen, and ink, enclosed by a carved wooden partition. James could not believe that the king, who had owned all of England, would be brought into this court of his enemies, like an ordinary man. Although judges had been sworn, witnesses prepared, and the courtroom made ready, half the people had come expecting to see the trial called off.

There was a sudden increase in noise and then an awed silence spread from the judges, who turned their heads all at once, like players in a masque, and looked towards the entrance. At once, the deafening chatter in the stone hall was stilled as everyone leaned forward and craned their necks to look to the entrance door. Charles, the king, stood in the great doorway, like a dancer pausing before making a grand entrance, dressed all in black, with a collar of finest white linen trimmed with rich lace. He came in slowly, as if to make his presence felt, his hat on his head, his cane in his hand, walked towards the chair in the enclosure, and halted before it. He was waiting for someone to open the door for him; he looked around at the hall, the judges, the Lord President, the soldiers, the audience, the gallery, and the stands. There was a long awkward pause and when nobody moved to open the door for him, he swung it open for himself and sat, without invitation, on the velvet chair, as calm and relaxed as if he was in his grand banqueting suite at Whitehall. He did not remove his hat before the court. He would doff it for nobody. He kept it on, as if it were his crown.

James saw at once a difference between the man who sat so calmly before the staring judges and the man he had begged to escape from Newport. The king had aged. His thick dark hair had threads of silver, his face was rounder and weary, deeply grooved with lines. No longer was he lighthearted, like a man certain to outwit his enemies. Now he looked like a saint, priding himself on persecution. The king, who had delighted in double-dealing with his parliament, who had boasted of cheating them, had finished his careless play. Now he was relishing defeat. The comedy was over; he was anticipating a tragedy.

"God help us," James said under his breath, recognizing the signs of a man longing for the morbid importance of martyrdom.

There was a rustle of alarm as the king suddenly got to his feet as if he would leave. James and everyone around him rose to their feet in habitual respect. James thought that if the king walked out as proudly as he had walked in, nobody would dare to stop him. The trial would be over before it had begun.

But the king turned his back on the bench, and looked all around the hall, at the people in the stands, at the judges, at the people who had paid for their seats, some who had risen at his entry and now stood again, looking awkward. He looked at them all, as if he were inspecting a guard of honor. James ducked his head as the mournful dark gaze raked the hall. He did not trust the king not to exclaim in recognition. He did not trust him at all.

The king turned back to the front and seated himself again, and everyone who had risen with him and taken off their hats also subsided again into their places.

A man rose to address the court.

"Who's that?" James asked his neighbor, a well-to-do London merchant.

"John Cook," came the muttered reply. "Prosecutor."

Cook rose to his feet and started reading a list of charges, facing the Lord President and the table with the ornate tapestry, his back half turned to the king.

"Hold a little," the king said. He had never sat behind anyone, since the death of his father, James, the previous king. Court etiquette demanded that everyone face the king to make their bow, and walk backwards, bowing once more at the door. He had not seen the back of a head for twenty-three years. James himself, humiliated and afraid, had awkwardly reversed out of the door at Newport. He flushed at the memory and realized that he must have looked ridiculous. Every time anyone left Charles's presence, the king was reminded of their inferiority, and his own greatness. At this, the lowest point of his life, he was still insisting on deference.

"Hold a little," the king said, raising his voice to Cook's back.

Determinedly deaf to the greatest man in the world, Cook carried on reading the charges, a little breathless as if he were anxious to get through them all. James found he was gritting his teeth as the prosecutor steadfastly ignored his king, continuing to list that the king had traitorously and maliciously . . .

"Hold a little," the king interrupted again, and then shockingly, leaned forwards, lifted his black ebony cane, and poked the prosecutor, hard, in the back.

"God, no," James said to himself.

Cook caught his breath but continued with accusations, the king poked at him again, and again, then, like the slow unfolding of a nightmare, the silver tip at the end of the cane fell to the floor with a heavy thud and rolled loudly to a standstill. Cook paid no attention to the stick against his shoulder, nor to the king's interruption, but as the silver ring rolled to a standstill he froze, as still as the ferrule, as if he were afraid to look round to see what the king would do next. He took a breath as if to continue with the prosecution case. But he did not speak.

Nobody moved. James realized he was gripping his wooden seat, stopping himself getting up and picking up the silver ferrule for the king. Half the audience were holding themselves rigid so that they did not betray themselves by getting to their feet to serve the man who had never had to do anything for himself. Nobody was attending to the prosecutor anymore. Everyone was looking from the shining tip of the cane on the floor, to the king, who had never in his life picked up anything.

The silver ring lay on the floor beside the prosecutor's polished shoes, the prosecutor standing like a statue beside it. The bench of judges was still, the Lord President frozen. Nobody knew what to do, and everyone felt it was strangely important.

Slowly, in the long silence, Charles himself rose from his chair, opened the little door to his enclosure, came out, bent down, and picked up the heavy cane tip, twisting it back into place on the handsome stick. He looked from the Lord President to the prosecutor as if he could not understand that they had not stopped everything to serve him. All his life someone had bent and fetched and carried for him, but here, with more than a thousand subjects in the room, nobody had moved. He smiled slightly, inclining his head a little, as if he had learned something important and disagreeable, and then he went back to his chair in a silence so profound that James thought they could have been passing a sentence of death.

James left the hall at the end of the day's hearing, sick to his belly from lack of food and at what he had heard and seen. He went back to his safe house and, with his head thumping, wrote his report, translated it into the code that they had agreed, and took the letter down to Queenhithe. The master of a ship was waiting for him.

"We sail with the tide," he warned.

"Go now," James said. "This is all I have to send. Someone will be waiting for you when you dock. They'll ask for the paperwork from Monsieur St. Jean."

"I'm guessing it's not good news," the captain said, looking at James's darkened face.

"Just give him the letter," James said wearily, and turned away from the river and the bobbing ships and his own longing to go with them.

Alinor's brother, Ned, was among the crowd that pushed their way into the Westminster Hall on the first day of the trial, but he did not see James. Nor did James, who kept his head down and his hat pulled low over his face, notice the ferryman. The two men, without knowing it, shared a vigil, each of them incredulous that the trial was going ahead, both of them doubtful that there could be a guilty verdict. The roundhead veteran doubted that the judges would hold their nerve for long enough to find their king guilty of treason. And even if they did, Ned was certain they would have no appetite for a death sentence. How could subjects pass a death sentence on their king? All the courts in the land were by royal appointment, bound to keep the king's laws. Who had the power to judge the lawgiver? For the first time in his life, that cold day in January, Ned saw his king in the semidivine flesh, seated on his velvet cushion, with his tall hat like a crown on his head, and thought, confusingly, that a man so arrogant as to bring himself before a court by his refusal to speak to his fellow men, or to keep his word when it was given, deserved that they should act against him. But at the same time, he could not stop himself thinking that a man so long-fingered, so beautifully dressed, with such mournful beauty, must be, as he claimed: half god, and entirely above justice.

*Saturday— It is unlikely that an attempt to rescue him by force could succeed. He is brought by river to a private house before entering Westminster and intensely guarded. I think his only chance of freedom is on the insistence of the princes of Europe, especially if they threaten war on this half-hearted half-attending parliament. Many MPs have been excluded from parliament, less than half the summoned judges are attending, the people are not calling for the king to be sentenced. The decision of the court is by no means certain, the king is refusing to answer to it, and claims that it has no authority. I believe it could be adjourned without a verdict if the king's fellow-monarchs and kinsmen demand it. If the trial continues there is a real danger of a verdict of "guilty," and tho' a verdict is not a sentence, His Royal Highness the Prince of Wales would be well advised to demand an assurance that they will not go from verdict to a sentence of exile or imprisonment.*

*They will call witnesses to give evidence of His Majesty breaking peace treaties, dishonoring his parole, denying his word, and lying to the parliament; and this can only cause more bad feeling. The mood of the hall is growing darker. The king has been fatally ill-advised to say nothing. Since he makes no explanation nor defense, it appears as if he has no defense. Worse, he looks as if he is relishing the accusations. But it does not stop them. We have only one advantage right now: that they have adjourned till Monday. There is time for you to make demands and stop this trial.*

James sent his coded letter of advice into the darkness, into the hands of a ship's captain crossing the stormy seas of the Channel in winter. He had no reply, but he expected none. There was no reason that the lords in exile should reassure him that they were taking steps to save the king. On Sunday, he attended the church for the empty service of protestant communion, and prayed fervently in his own room. He went down three times to Queenhithe in case a ship had come in with a letter for him. Not even his father had written.

On Monday he wrote again to his masters at The Hague that the court had met, and still the king would not answer to them.

*Tomorrow they will meet without the presence of His Majesty to hear witnesses. It is essential that someone contradicts their testimony. Can one of you lords or gentlemen attend to cross-question the witnesses? If they say that the king is a liar it does not matter that the court is unconstitutional—it is something that should never be said. If we do not challenge this, we are teaching the people of England that they can say anything.*

As the days went on, and James sent daily reports and received no reply, not even acknowledgment, he felt more and more that he, like the king, had been forgotten, and that he and the king would go on forever in this strange life in which every word uttered was of life or death importance, every word was on oath, and yet the boredom and banality of day after day in the Painted Chamber at Westminster, as the witnesses listed one dishonorable folly after another, was as painful as a man sucking on a decaying tooth.

Ned, listening as hard as he could, pushed into a corner at the very back of the room, found it incomprehensible that the judges could find the courage to sit in judgment on their king, but not to force him to answer. He feared, as the bitterly cold January drew to an end, that the king would escape all justice by the simple technique of denying that anyone had the right to judge him. He denied their right to speak of him, he denied their right to listen, he denied their right to be.

"It's as if none of us is here," he complained to his landlady in the cramped little inn that evening. "It's as if none of it ever happened at all. He's not even listening to the evidence against him. He's not even attending now. They've let him off his own trial. He's—well, I don't know what he's doing. Playing golf at St. James's?"

"We're nothing to the likes of them," she said.

"I'm not nothing," Ned said doubtfully. "On my ferry, on the mire. I'm not nothing there."

On the evening of Saturday, January 27, James wrote his last letter in code and sent it to the unnamed man who had asked him to report, but not told him what he should do in the case of a disaster. Now the disaster had come and James wrote slowly, feeling that the time for urgency was past, and either they had an escape which they had not troubled to explain to him, or they had heard his warnings and done nothing. Either way his purgatory of misery had been completely wasted.

> *I regret to report that they have found him guilty and, with the verdict, they passed sentence of death. They recorded that they judged him tyrant, traitor, murderer, and public enemy to the good people of the nation, to be put to death by the severing of his head from his body.*
>
> *If you have influence for mercy or pardon or a plan for escape it should be deployed now. They have not set a date for execution, but he is to see his children, Princess Elizabeth and her little brother Prince Henry, on Monday. His execution must follow unless you have prevented it.*

James paused, wanting to believe that his part in this had been so unimportant, that all along a conspirator with a great name, or a man with a great fortune, or the French ambassador or the Prince of Wales himself had been meeting with the judges, or with Oliver Cromwell, and an arrangement had been made for the king's safety. Perhaps even now a secret door in Whitehall Palace was being opened to the stairs down to the river and a ship was raising her sails and taking him away.

> *I truly believe that they intend to execute him within days. Of course, I beg that you save him and prevent this terrible martyrdom. Send me orders as to what I can do. Tell me at least that you have received this?*

# TIDELANDS, FEBRUARY 1649

The iron bar clanged loudly on the horseshoe and Alys rose up from the breakfast table, wiped her mouth with the back of her hand, and went to the door. The cold wintry air swirled in as she banged the door behind her. "Lord, is that you, Uncle Ned?" Alinor heard her call. "I thought you'd never come home!"

Alinor threw open the front door to look out, shading her eyes against the bright wintry sun that burned low, just rising over the harbor. Against the white brightness she could only see the outline of a man, pack on his back, hat on his head, soldier's boots, but she recognized her brother as he stepped down into the ferry, kissed his niece, and let her haul him over, solemnly paying her his fee.

"You're welcome to your home, Brother," Alinor said as Ned stepped ashore. She moved into the warm hug of his cape. He smelled of London, of strange stables, of damp beds, of beer rather than ale, fires of charcoal, not wood. "You've been gone so long. We've had no news. What happened? Did they finish the trial? We only heard that it had begun."

"Aye, they did," he replied, sitting down on his stool and pulling off his boots.

"Never!" Alys exclaimed. "I swore they would not dare."

"They dared do more than that," Ned said wonderingly. "All the way home, I've been puzzling about it. But they did more than charge him with betrayal, they accused him of treason, with a death sentence. And it's done. He's dead and we are a kingdom without a king."

Alinor gasped and put her hand to the base of her throat and felt her pulse thud. "Really? Truly? He's dead? The king is dead?"

"Yes. You're like everyone else that I've told, all the way down the London road. Everyone acts like it was a shock, but he was on trial before a court, in full sight of the people, and he had it coming since Nottingham. Why should anyone be surprised that time ran out for him?"

"Because he's the king," Alinor said simply.

"But not above the law, as it turns out, as he thought."

"How did they do it?" Alys asked curiously.

Alinor went to the foot of the staircase and shouted for Rob to wake and come down, for his uncle was home, poured her brother a cup of ale and sat beside him. She could hardly bear to listen, knowing what this would mean for James. But she had to know: a kingdom without a king was a puzzle that the people of England would have to solve. And how would a people as diverse as the minister, or Mrs. Wheatley, or the Chichester apothecary agree as to how they should be governed? Or would it all be decided by the likes of Sir William and nothing really changed at all?

"They did it lawfully," Ned answered his niece. "In a court of law, though he denied it to the last."

"I mean the execution? We knew that he was on trial. But nobody thought he would be executed. We had sight of a newssheet after the first day, and then nothing."

He sighed. "I was glad to see it done, and it had to be done, and it was just that it was done. But, Lord knows, it's always pitiful to see a man die."

Rob, tying the laces on his breeches, came downstairs, shook hands with his uncle, and sat at the table to listen.

"Where's Red?" Ned suddenly asked, looking under the table, sensing an absence where his dog should be.

Alinor put her hand on his. "I'm sorry, Ned," she said. "He died. He was in no pain. He was just very tired one morning, and by evening, he was asleep."

He shook his head a little. "Ah," he said. "My dog."

They were silent for a moment, and Alinor cut Ned a slice from the breakfast loaf and put it on a wooden platter before him.

"What about the king?" Rob prompted.

"They beheaded him?" Alys pressed.

"They beheaded him. Quickly and well, on a cold morning. He stepped out of a window of glass so tall and so wide that it was like a door to his palace of Whitehall. So he was never in a cell, though they found him guilty. He was never chained, though they named him a criminal. He spoke for a little while, but nobody could hear him—there were thousands of us there, crowded in the street—and then he laid himself down and the executioner took his head off. One blow. It was well done. He did not give the executioner pardon, which was sour. He said he was a 'martyr to the people.' I heard that much: the idiot." Ned coughed and spat into the fire. "He died with a lie in his mouth, as was fitting. It was us who were a martyr to him. He lied to the very end."

"God forgive him," Alinor whispered.

"I never will," Ned said staunchly. "And neither will any man who ever fought against him, over and over, still fighting after he had declared peace and admitted he was beat. Over and over. Never forget it."

"God forgive him," Alinor repeated.

"So what happens now, Uncle?" Rob asked. "Will everything change for us all?"

"That's the question," Ned said. "Everything has changed, everything must change. But will it? And how?"

## LONDON, FEBRUARY 1649

James waited a day and a night in case there were instructions for him, but when he heard nothing from either Paris or The Hague, from his spymaster, his professor, or his father, he concluded that his work was done and there was nothing more for him to do. Sourly, he thought that there had never been anything for him to do, except to bury the king and there were others to do that. Bitterly, he thought that someone might have told him at least that they had received the letters and that they were grateful for his service; but then he remembered his mother telling him that the king was a fool and the prince a rogue and royal service was a thankless task—but one that could not be avoided.

He walked through the silent city, which was like a town in mourning, like a family in shock. He took a ferry to the south side of the river, hired a horse in Lambeth, and headed down the long road to Chichester, and to Sealsea Island.

The horse was old and weary of the road, and James was happy to go at a shambling walk. He was glad to take time away from the terror of these unpredictable days, when words would not save the king, and words could not be spoken, and think in silence what his future might be, what his life might be in this new world into which all Englishmen had stumbled. He would be a man of words no more. He knew that everything had changed for him. Everything had changed from that day at

Newport, when the king had refused to come away though there was a boat waiting for him and his son's fleet at sea.

James pulled himself back from the daydream of a victory, a comforting reverie in days of defeat. He feared that dreaming would keep the royalists trapped in exile, forever hoping for better times, forever hashing over old mistakes. Instead, he tried to think what this new England might mean for him, for his parents, and for Alinor. He doubted that his parents would stay at the court of the queen now that she would never receive a message from her triumphant husband, now that she would never return home in victory. He doubted that they would transfer their loyalty to Prince Charles, who might call himself Charles II—though it was hard to see how he would ever be crowned in Westminster Abbey, so near to Westminster Hall where his father had been sentenced to death. Surely, England must be without a king forever. Would James's parents know they were defeated? Would they come home instead of dreaming and hoping? James thought that they would. People who had sworn loyalty and risked their lives and fortunes for the king would not necessarily transfer their faith to his son, especially a man with nothing but the fading charm of a prince in exile, surrounded by favorites, corrupt advisors, and reckless women, scattering empty promises that he was certain never to repay. Now that he was king in waiting, his court would become even more desperate, even more fatalistic. Only those with hopes of nothing better would support him. Only the homeless would be fellow travelers.

There was little chance, James thought, that his mother, Lady Avery, would join such a court, to serve an uncrowned king. His father would never compete for office or duties with corrupt adventurers, and if they were not appointed by the king in exile, why would they stay in exile? They would come home, James thought. They must come home to Northallerton in Yorkshire and James would be able to return with them to his own fields, to his childhood home, and feel the cold winds blow off the moors again, and hear the cry of the peewit as it tumbled, spade-winged, in the clear sky.

He would present Alinor to his parents as the woman that he loved and intended to marry, and surely they would allow him to live with her, in a new house that he would build, perhaps in the fields below the great house: perhaps a small house, a manor house, set in a walled garden for her herbs, with a fruit orchard. He would present her to the village and the parish as his wife, acknowledging that they could not yet be legally married, but calling her his betrothed, and demanding for her the respect that an Avery commanded in the manor of Northside. And he was certain that, though people would gossip behind their hands, though his mother would disapprove, in a world of such momentous change in which everything was turned upside down, and a middling farmer from Cambridgeshire was running the country, the fact that the future Lady Avery was not yet married to the son and heir would quickly become old news.

All he had to do, James thought as the road wound over the height of the South Downs, so pale and gray and misty in the bitterly cold morning, was convince Alinor to leave her little fisherman's cottage, her beloved daughter and her adored son, and come north with him. Confidently, James thought he could do that. She could bring her daughter and son, if she wanted, if that was the price of her coming. Or they could visit. Or anything, James thought passionately, any condition she wanted to make. If she would only come to him.

## TIDELANDS, FEBRUARY 1649

Ned, Rob, Alinor, and Alys walked along the bank at the side of the harbor, past Alinor's old cottage and net shed, through the quickthorn tunnel, dropping down to the shingle beach, bending their heads beneath the low boughs of the overhanging oak tree, then climbing up the rough steps cut out of the sea wall to the footpath to the church. The rumbling of the millstones across the mire and the rush of the millrace water sounded loud on the cold air, and Alinor glanced back as if she feared that the waters were rising up after them. Ned helped the two women over the stile into the churchyard and they went silently in single file along the path that wound through the gravestones. Ned and Alinor paused before the plain stone that marked their parents' burial site.

"I wish he could have lived to see this day," Ned said of his father. "He would never have believed it possible."

Alinor bowed her head in silence. "I miss her," was all she said.

The four of them turned and went into church, Alys and Alinor going up the stairs to the wooden gallery where the workingwomen of the parish stood in silence, Ned and Rob stood at the left of the nave where the men of the parish waited bare-headed for the Peachey household to enter and Sir William to take his seat. Only when the nobility arrived would the service to God take place. Ned muttered to Rob that nothing would ever change in the tidelands, no matter what took place elsewhere.

There was only one chair: his lordship's, placed before the chancel steps like a throne. Walter was in Cambridge, and there were no guests at the Priory to sit in the Priory pews. The household stood behind the empty seats. Alinor, looking down from the gallery on his lordship's beautiful dark felted hat trimmed with a dark feather and a silver pin, as he processed slowly into church, wondered if he missed his son, or if he had heard anything from his son's former tutor. She knew that she could never ask him, nor anyone of his household. She tightened her thick winter shawl over her round belly, and watched the minister step towards the lectern, bow low to his lordship, and begin.

The service—the new service, as designed by the parliament and delivered by the Church that obeyed them—went through the usual prayers and readings. But when it came to the sermon the minister looked at the men at the back of the church and said, "Edward Ferryman, are you there?"

"Present!" Ned replied with the promptness of an old soldier at roll call.

"Would you tell us what you have witnessed in London, so that we may all know what has befallen the king who betrayed his people?"

The men either side of Ned parted to make him a path to the chancel steps. He came cautiously forward.

"I was not party to any councils or explanations," he said. "I can only tell you what I saw."

"The view of an honest man. The report of an honest man is all we want from you," the minister assured him, and some of the more godly parishioners said: "Amen."

Alinor found she was holding her hands tightly under the shelter of her shawl. She did not know what Sir William would make of Ned's report; she did not know if Ned might, with this encouragement, overstep the line of deference. Rob glanced upwards over his shoulder, to the gallery where his mother stood, and she knew he would be thinking the same thing. His apprenticeship in Chichester did not start till the next day. His chance could be blighted before it had even begun.

Ned walked to the minister and then turned to the people in the church. He bowed slightly to Sir William, who gestured that he should speak.

"King Charles was put on trial for eight days," he said. "I was present from first till last. I was there on the first day in Westminster Hall, when they brought him in."

Alinor saw Sir William shift slightly in his seat.

"There were more than sixty judges sitting to hear how the king answered the accusation of tyranny and betrayal of the people," Ned went on.

The door at the back of the church opened for a latecomer, but no one turned at the gust of cold air. The congregation was completely attentive to Ned's story.

"The king did not speak as they read the charges, and when he did speak he refused to plead guilty or not guilty."

"Why?" someone called out. "Why would he not speak up?"

"He spoke," Ned specified. "He spoke. But he would not plead."

"Why not?"

"I don't know for certain," Ned admitted. "It was a lawyer's argument."

There was a quiet rumble of disapproval. "But why didn't they let the king answer?"

"It was he that would not speak to them. They called witnesses against him, in a smaller room, but he did not even attend. Men who had seen him on the battlefield taking arms against his own people. They had many witnesses for that. I saw it myself."

"May I speak?"

Everyone in the body of the church turned to the doorway to see the latecomer, but he was standing beneath the public gallery and neither Alinor nor Alys could see who it was.

"I, too, was at the trial. I, too, have come directly from London."

Alinor recognized his voice at once, cramming her fist against her mouth so she did not cry out, biting her fingers against the sudden wave of faintness.

"Who is it?" Alys nudged her mother.

"I don't know," Alinor whispered.

He walked up the central nave of the church, the collar of his dark traveling cape set square on his shoulders, the hem of it brushing the tops of his polished riding boots. Alinor, looking down from the gallery, could see only his hat, and when he doffed it, his dark curly head. She could see nothing but his assured stride to the chancel steps and the swirl of his expensive cape.

"Is that you? Mr. Summer?" the minister asked.

James bowed to Sir William and then stood before the minister. "It is I, James Summer, tutor to Sir William's son, Walter. I was in London for business, and I attended the trial of the king. Now I am here for a brief visit to Sir William. I should be happy to tell you what I understood and add my witness to that of Edward Ferryman's."

The preacher made a gesture, inviting James to bear witness. James turned towards the congregation and nodded at Ned. For the first time Alinor saw his face. He was pale. His determined expression made him look older than when she had seen him last, drunk with desire, recklessly in love. She put her hand on her belly and felt the child stir as if he knew his father had come for him.

"It is just as Edward Ferryman says," James confirmed. "The king would not plead for two reasons. He said that the court was not legally created: there has never been a court commissioned by parliament. There have only been courts commissioned by kings. And he said that no court could try a king who was ordained by God." James paused. "Legally, I think his argument was good. But it would mean that no king could ever be tried by his people; and the parliament and the judges were convinced that the king should answer."

"He'd made war on us," Ned interrupted. "And when he promised peace he broke his promise. He brought the Scots down on us, and he was planning to bring the Irish against us. What d'you think his wife, his papist wife, is doing in Paris, if not trying to persuade the French to invade us? What d'you think his son is doing in The Hague but meeting with our enemies? All enemies of Englishmen! Tell me this: if he was at war with Englishmen, allied to our enemies, commanding our enemies, how was he our king?"

There was a murmur in the church supporting Ned. Everyone had suffered during the wars, many had lost fathers, brothers, and sons who followed Sir William to the disaster at Marston Moor.

"I think it is a tragedy," James said frankly. "I think he was ill-advised from the beginning, but I wish, at the end, that he would have pleaded guilty and gone into exile."

"Aye, but would he have stayed in exile?" Ned demanded hotly. "He was in prison for years, and he wouldn't stay in prison."

James bowed his head and then looked up to meet Ned's furious gaze. "Perhaps not," he said calmly. "But I know that he lost good men, when he lost the loyalty of men like you."

"Nothing to do with me!" Ned shrugged off the compliment. "It's nothing to do with what you think of me, or what you think of him. It's wrong for a king to be a tyrant to his people and we have stopped him. From this day on there will never be a tyrant ruling Englishmen. We will be free."

James nodded and said nothing. Sir William shifted in his chair and bowed his head, as if in thought.

"Did he make a godly end?" the minister asked.

Ned glanced at James, but answered for both of them. "Aye, he did. There were thousands watching in the street outside the palace, and they told us that he spent the night in prayer. He stepped out bravely enough, put his head on the block, and signaled that he was ready. The public executioner beheaded him with one blow."

There was a sigh all around the church. Somewhere in the gallery a woman was weeping.

"God will judge him now," James said. "And that is a court to which we all must come."

"Amen," the minister said. "And now I have to call the banns for a marriage for the third and final time."

The two men, Alinor's brother and her lover, turned without looking at each other again and Ned took up his place at the back of the church among the workingmen, and James stood beside Sir William's chair.

"I publish the banns for the marriage of Alys Reekie, spinster of this parish, and Richard Stoney, bachelor of Sidlesham," the minister said.

Alinor felt Alys's hand come into hers, and she squeezed it and found a smile for her daughter.

"This is the third and final time of asking."

There was a little ripple of interest and pleasure from the congregation, and young Richard Stoney, attending St. Wilfrid's to hear his banns called, craned around and looked up into the women's gallery and winked at Alys.

"If any of you know cause or just impediment why these two persons should not be joined together in holy matrimony, ye are to declare it."

"Does anyone ever stand up and declare an impediment?" Alys whispered to her mother.

"No," Alinor replied. "Who would try to make a bigamous marriage on Sealsea Island where everyone knows everyone else's business?"

"The marriage will take place next Sunday," the minister declared.

As they left the church Alinor knew that she must go and pay her respects to Sir William and meet James before the curious gaze of the entire congregation. With Alys and Rob on either side of her, and Ned following reluctantly behind, she walked across the frosty grass and curtseyed to her landlord, keeping her eyes fixed on his expressionless face.

"Mrs. Reekie." He nodded at her and at Ned, but had a smile for Rob. "How now, Robert?"

"I'm well, sir. Going to Chichester tomorrow."

"All arranged, is it?" Sir William looked over his shoulder to Mr. Tudeley.

"Yes, the boy's expected, and I will go myself to pay his fee tomorrow, when his mother signs his articles."

"We're very grateful," Alinor said.

"And here's your patient. D'you think he's looking well?"

Alinor dropped a curtsey to James and finally turned towards him. She felt physically shocked by the warmth of his smile and the intensity of his gaze. She felt frozen as if she could not step towards him and fall into his arms, nor could she run away. She swallowed, but she could not speak. She felt his baby heavy in her belly and could not believe that he did not know that he had fathered the child that she carried. She wrapped her shawl closely about her as if to shield her swelling belly, and said, "I'm glad to see you look so well, Mr. Summer."

"Hello, Mrs. Reekie," he said. "I am glad to see you again. And how is my pupil?"

Rob grinned. "Keeping up my Latin," he said. "Sir William lets me borrow books from his library. Have you seen Walter, sir?"

"He's very grand now that he's at Cambridge," James laughed. "But I hope to visit him after term starts."

"And you're to be married?" His lordship nodded at Alys. "Young man from Sidlesham parish?"

Alys turned and beckoned to Richard, and he came up and made a respectful bow to Sir William. Alinor noticed the carefully graded deference: Richard Stoney was the son of a freeholder, not a Peachey tenant, and he would never forget the difference.

"Wish you happy," Sir William said without much interest. He nodded to Mr. Tudeley to give Alys a shilling, and then turned back to Rob: "You can come for dinner." Pointedly he did not extend the invitation to Alinor or Alys, who were out of favor as the women in the household of a roundhead. Clearly, he was not going to even acknowledge Ned, who stood to one side, hat in hand, stubbornly not bowing.

"Thank you," Rob said easily. "And I will write to you, sir, when I start work at Chichester."

His lordship nodded and turned away, ignoring Ned. James glanced back for one look at Alinor, and then followed his lordship, while the congregation, released from deference, crowded around Ned to ask him more about the trial, about the execution, and about the parliament, and what about London itself, now that it was a royal city without a king anymore?

Alinor and Alys walked back to Ferry-house along the bank of the harbor with Ned following behind them, accompanied by people walking part of the way, to ask for more details of the trial and execution. Ned answered everyone patiently. His own sense of pride in having been a witness to great events made him glad to tell his story over and over again. Nothing had ever been heard like it in the tidelands. Nothing like it had ever been heard in England. It was the end of one sort of world and the start of another.

The sea was coming in, so the people from the mainland, who had earlier walked across the frozen wadeway to church, now wanted the ferry across the rife, and Alys let Ned take the fees and pull the ferry across.

"D'you remember how to do it?" she taunted him. "Haven't your hands gone too soft for the rope?"

"I swear I'd forgotten how cold it is," he replied.

He came into the house blowing on his fingers and stood by

the fire as Alinor raked the embers and put on a big log of driftwood.

"Before I went away," he said quietly so that Alys, upstairs in the bedroom, would not hear, "you said that you would need my help and you would tell me when I returned."

Alinor did not know what she should say. Clearly, she must speak to James. They would decide together what to do, and how the news should be announced.

"It's Alys," she said. "She's with child."

Ned was not shocked. In the country, especially in areas as remote as the tidelands, many couples married in the old way: a promise to marry, and then a long time of courtship and love-making while finding a house or saving for marriage. Many brides carried a big belly on their wedding day. Some had a child or even two walking behind them to the altar.

"Did they promise to each other before God? They hand-fasted and prayed together? It's a godly union? She's not been light or wanton? He didn't force her?"

"Oh, no," Alinor assured him. "They're sure of each other, fully betrothed. And he's given her a ring. It's the dowry that they're waiting on. That's my worry. The parents insist on it. That's why we've been scraping around in such a rush."

"Why the hurry?"

"Alys wants to have the baby in the Stoney farmhouse that he's to inherit. She'd like him to be born into the family, with his father's name."

"I'm sorry I've not come home any richer," Ned said. "It's a place of terrible expense, London. But she's had the fees from the ferry. She can add it up and tell us if she's short. I'll come with you to Stoney Farm tomorrow and talk with them, if you need me. And didn't young Richard promise his inheritance?"

"Yes. I'd rather we didn't take it, but, she says Richard will see us right."

Ned chuckled. "Lord! That girl! She's borrowing her dowry from her betrothed?"

"It's the only way she'd find it. They asked for a fortune.

We've earned all we can. He's making up the difference. She's determined that the wedding goes ahead next Sunday."

He smiled. "Well, it's good that we have a new life coming into the new world that we're making. If it's a boy she could call him 'Oliver' for old Noll!"

"She could," Alinor agreed, thinking that James would never allow it.

"D'you like living in your old home again?"

"Of course," Alinor confirmed. "But if you ever find a wife you want to bring back here, I'll be happy to go back to my cottage. Or somewhere else."

He laughed at her. "Not I. And anyway, where else would you go?"

Alinor smiled. "Oh, I don't know."

James thought that the easiest way to see Alinor would be to walk back with Rob after dinner on the hidden tracks through the harbor, as the sky darkened to the early dusk of winter. He said that he needed herbs against the return of his fever.

"She won't sell herbs on a Sunday," Rob reminded him.

"I can tell her what I need, and she can bring them to the Priory when she is passing," James invented.

Overhead, above the thick gray clouds, he could hear the flocks of winter geese coming in to roost on the shingle beds out in the harbor, and once, the unearthly creaking noise of swans' wings. It was too dark to see anything but the track beneath their feet and the occasional glimpse of a slim moon between the raveled clouds. Rob went sure-footed on the well-known twisting paths but James had to follow him carefully. He could not even see the route that the boy was taking.

"And your mother is well?" he asked, trying to keep up.

"Winter's always hard on the mire," Rob answered. "And Alys had to work on the ferry every day, even on the coldest days, and my mother was afraid every moment that she was out on the rife. When I went over to take a turn it was even worse for her. She's terrified of deep water. But she's well enough. It's more comfortable living in the ferry-house, than in the old cottage."

"They're in the ferry-house? Why did they move from the cottage?"

Rob looked away from his tutor, ashamed of his father's desertion. "We're going to tell everyone that we think my father is dead," he said. "After Alys's wedding. But for my mother to keep her work and her good name, she can't be seen as a woman living alone." He stumbled and stopped and turned to his tutor. "It's better for her to be thought of as a widow, under the protection of her brother, especially when Alys and I leave home. I am sorry to lie, sir. But we really have to."

James dropped his hand on Rob's hunched shoulder. "You're doing the right thing," he said. "It's no shame to you, nor to her, that your father chose not to come home. It's no lie to say that you don't expect him. And I'll tell no one that I saw him in Newport. He's dead to me, too."

Rob visibly brightened. "It's such a little island. She can't live here without a good name."

"And Alys is to be married?" James turned the conversation from the boy's discomfort, as they started to walk again.

"Next Sunday. She's had to save every penny for her dowry."

"Your mother must be happy for her."

"It's taken all of her savings."

James thought he was a fool not to have sent money. But how would she have explained it? And he would have been stealing money that had been given for his work for the king. He had no money of his own. How could he have robbed the cause he was sworn to, for the woman that he was forbidden to love? But the thought of Alinor in hardship made him flush with shame.

"Your uncle Ned should never have left her for so long," he said irritably.

"It was Alys that did the ferry. Ma wouldn't touch it. D'you really believe that my father isn't coming home, sir?"

James was glad to climb the bank that led towards the rife and see the looming darkness of Ferry-house. "It's what he said. And better for your mother if he does not, don't you think?"

"Better for Alys too. The Stoneys would never have her if my da was still here."

"And better for you?"

Rob flushed. "The apothecary wouldn't have me as an apprentice if he met my da."

"Your mother will be a free woman in six years," James said.

"That's such a long time," Rob said, as a young man will say, and James—a young man only twenty-two years old himself—could not disagree.

They reached the ferry-house door. Rob turned the latch and the door yielded. "Mr. Summer came with me," he said as he went in and James stepped in behind him.

After the darkness of the harbor, the room was bright, though it was only lit by firelight and rushlights. Ned was seated at the table, sharpening a pocket knife, Alinor and Alys either side of the fire, spinning, with their distaffs propped beside them and their spindles whirling at their feet. As James came in, Alinor jumped up with a gasp, her spindle skittering away under the settle.

"You're very welcome," she said, recovering.

"I thought I'd walk over with Robert," James said awkwardly. "I thought I'd ask you for some herbs against my fever . . . if it comes back again. I didn't mean to disturb you all."

Ned barely raised his eyes from his work but bobbed his head in a nod.

"Will you take a glass of ale?" Alinor asked. "Please, sit." She gestured to her stool at the fireside.

"Thank you, and then I'll walk back by the road."

"Dark night," Ned observed.

"Yes indeed."

There was a silence as Alinor went to the cool buttery at the back of the house and drew a glass of ale each for James and Rob, and then brought another for Ned. Rob sat beside her on the bench against the wall.

"Is it strange to be home?" James asked Ned.

Ned shrugged. "It's not the life I'd have chosen, but none of us can live the life we'd have chosen." He paused. "Maybe you can," he said. "Maybe his lordship does."

"Not anymore," James said honestly. "I never thought this would happen, and I never thought it would end this way."

Ned put his knife carefully in the worn leather sheath and put the whetstone to one side. "Pity that you didn't," he said gruffly. "Could've been stopped years ago."

"I agree," James said, trying to find some common ground. "I have thought for a long time that we should have found a way ahead without going to war. That we should have made an agreement so that we could find a way to end our differences and live together."

"Well, now we have," Ned said with a little smile. "Though p'raps not the agreement you'd have wished. Can you live in this new England?"

"I hope to," James said. "I hope to regain my home, and I hope to live there, with my family, and help . . ."

"Help what?"

"The ruling and governing of the kingdom . . . of the country."

Ned raised his head and stared at James as if he could not believe the quiet words. "And why should you, and the likes of you, rule and govern us, when you've disturbed our peace for nearly ten years?"

James swallowed. "Because I am an Englishman and I want to live in peace."

"I'm sure we all want peace," Alinor interrupted.

Ned smiled at her. "Aye. I know you do, Sister. And I hope that we'll have it now. What's your opinion on how the country should be run?"

Alinor flushed a little. "Ah, Ned, you know I only know my trade. I think midwives should be licensed, and women should be churched after their confinement. For the rest—how would I know?"

James had a sudden sharp memory of his mother's astute vision, which had guided their family through years of change; she knew the world as well as her husband, and could calculate political advantage quicker than any man.

"Are you in favor of petticoat government?" James asked Ned, trying to smile.

"I'd rather be ruled by good-hearted women than by all the cavaliers who will be turning their collars, and flocking back to their houses, now they've lost."

James flushed with anger. "I can't agree with you," he said shortly. "I think we'll have to differ."

Ned rose from the table. "Have done," he advised James. "It's as I thought. You're what I thought. If you weren't on cavalier business, or papist business, it was secret business and bad business. As for me, I don't care what you did, as long as you cease doing it now."

"Mr. Summer was my tutor," Rob spoke up for him. "I'd not have had a chance at an apprenticeship without his teaching."

Ned nodded, and put his hand on the seated boy's shoulder. "I know. I know he did well by you." He paused. "I'm going to bed," he said. "Some of us have to work early in the morning. And this lad has to start at Chichester tomorrow morning, and that's a great beginning for him. He should be early to bed and early to rise."

"Yes." James got to his feet. "I'm going. I just came for some herbs, for fever. I'm sorry we can't agree."

"I'll see you out," Alinor said, quickly going to the front door. "I'll walk you round to the road."

"Don't let him fall in the rife and drown," Ned remarked with such a bitter smile that his words seemed more of a threat than a joke. "That'd be a loss to the future government. Good night, Mr. Summer. Or will you go by another name when you take up your lands? Was that ever your name at all?"

James turned back towards Ned and stretched out his hand. "I will have another name, and I am sorry to have sailed under false colors with you. I lost my faith some time ago, and we were both a witness to the death of my king. I have been waiting to make my peace with all my countrymen and with you. I hope you will, one day, forgive me for my sins as I forgive those you have done unto me."

Ned was surprised into taking the man's hand and shaking it. "Aye, very well," he said. "And no false dealing in future?"

"None," James said. "The war is over for both of us, and for the king."

"Aye," Ned said with quiet satisfaction. "It's surely over for him."

Alinor was waiting at the front door with a shawl over her head. "I'll shut up the hens," she called back to the firelit room.

As they stepped out into the still cold air James could see the pale outline of her face and her dark eyes in the light of the sickle moon. He thought that he had never seen anything more beautiful in his life than this woman in this bleached and blackened landscape, with the harbor water shining like a sheet of pewter behind her, and the sliver of an ice-white moon in the sky above her.

"Aren't you cold?" he asked, and put his arms around her as if he would straighten her shawl, but found himself holding her, as easily and naturally as if they had never been parted. She came into his arms but at once he felt a difference in her. Through the layers of homespun he could feel her body but it was strange to him. Something about her touch horrified him, as if she was a shape-changer in a frightening story, and he flinched, stepped back, and looked at her. He saw that the pallor of her face was not just moonlight.

"J-James," she said, stumbling over his name.

"My love?"

"You came back for me?"

"As I promised, the minute that I could."

She sighed, and he realized she had been holding her breath from the moment he had stepped over the threshold. Her anxiety only alarmed him more. He glanced back at the darkened doorway, and she took him by the hand and led him around the corner of the house and through a gate into the vegetable garden that ran alongside the deserted road.

"I have to tell you something," she said.

At the sound of her voice, the hens, warm in their house, clucked sleepily to her. She bent, and latched the door of their house, bolting it at the top and at the bottom.

"I have to tell you something first," he said rapidly. "I met with my parents, with my mother and my father. I told them of you. I told them that I will pay my fine to parliament and regain our house. I will take you there, and in six years' time, when you are declared a widow, we will marry."

He saw her blanched lips tremble and he was afraid that she was about to argue. But, to his surprise, she consented at once: "Yes," she said quietly. "Yes, I will marry you and live wherever you wish. Yes. And I have something to tell you."

"You will come with me?" He could hardly believe her words.

"I will. But I have to—"

"My love! My love! You will come with me!"

"I have to tell you something."

"Anything! Anything!"

The hens clucked again at the voices. "Hush," she said, drawing him away from the henhouse. "I have to tell you . . ."

He took her hand. "Of course. What is it, my love?"

She drew a breath again, as if she could not speak. Then her words were so soft he had to lean towards her to catch them. "I am with child," she said.

For a moment he did not understand what she was saying; he could not hear the words. Each single word made sense, but together they made no sense at all and he could not understand it—coming from her, to him.

"What?"

"I am with child."

"How?" he asked stupidly.

She found a ghost of a smile. "The way it usually happens. When we were in the hayloft together."

"But how?" he asked again. "How could it be?"

"What should prevent it?"

"I thought you would prevent it!" he retorted, too loudly for caution.

"Hush," she said again, and led him farther down the path to the bottom gate, so that they could not be heard from the house.

Irrelevantly, he suddenly thought how much he hated a winter vegetable garden, so dark and muddy and nothing growing. He thought how poor it was, and how ugly. He thought how much he disliked it that the hens recognized her voice and clucked back at her. The future Lady Avery should not pull turnips and feed her own hens; and her hand in his was rough. "Are you sure?"

Now she smiled. "Of course I am sure."

Her smile infuriated him, as if she thought him a fool. "I do understand well enough," he snapped. "It's not that I know nothing. It's just that I thought that you—a married woman, a wisewoman—would have made sure that it did not happen."

She shook her head; she was maddeningly serene. "I don't do that sort of work."

"It's not work when it is for yourself!" he argued like a Jesuit. "It would be work, and a sin, if you were preventing the child of another: a sinful woman, or an adulteress. But for yourself there is no sin in a woman choosing to eat some herbs, or drink some drink, as soon as you knew. Or better still, before you did the act!"

"Did the act?" she repeated, as if she could not understand his words.

"Then it would be no sin at all as there would be no intent.

D'you see? If there is no evil intent then there is no sin. Why did you not take the herbs the morning that we parted?"

"I was thinking of nothing but us, nothing but us and the hayloft as if it were a time outside time," she admitted. "I was longing for the evening when I would see you again. Then you were gone, and I was just longing."

She tightened the shawl across her rounded belly. "Of course, once I knew, I thought what I should do. I thought about it all night long. It was a long night, and a cold one . . ." She trailed off. She wanted to tell him how bright the beach of shells had been in the moonlight, the heavy stones that she had chosen, the thought of walking into the mire, the certainty of death by drowning, and her revelation that the life of their baby was a joy to her.

Then she saw his face, closed and angry. "But I would never have done it. I wouldn't use herbs to poison any baby. I certainly wouldn't poison my baby. And I'd rather die than poison a baby of ours."

She saw his shoulders hunch with an instant revulsion. "It's not a baby yet," he said. "Not in law. Not till it quickens. Not in the sight of God. Has it quickened yet? No?"

Wonderingly she looked from his scowling eyes to his hardened mouth. "Yes," she said quietly. "Of course. We conceived him in September. I felt him move at Christmas. I know there is life in him. He sleeps and wakes inside me, I can feel him. Perhaps he dreams."

"It's not a boy child!"

Again, she looked at him with her steady dark gaze. "Of course, no one can say for sure. But it is a child, and I believe it is a boy."

"It's not. It's a nothing. It's not too late . . ."

"Too late for what?"

"For you to take the herb or the drink or whatever it is that you know. Not too late for that."

"Not too late for me to push a bodkin into my belly to kill it in the womb," she remarked.

He gulped. "Of course, I wouldn't want you to do that. But, Alinor . . ."

"Yes?"

"Alinor, I want to take you to my home, I want you to live there as my wife. You will be the next Lady Avery."

At once she was diverted. "Is that your name?"

"Yes, yes, what of it? That's not the point. What I am saying is that I cannot take you to my mother and my father if you are big with a child and you are still another man's wife. If you allow it to be born, it will take Zachary's name. I cannot raise a child named Reekie in my own home! Bad enough that my mother will have Alys and Robert as her grandchildren! I cannot, Alinor. You must understand, I cannot. It would be to shame you, and shame me and my name."

"I didn't know that was your name," she repeated. "Avery! Are you Lord Avery?"

"No. My father is a baronet. Not that it matters."

"But I've thought of you all this time as James Summer. Is your given name not James? How shall I call you anything else?"

She was so ridiculous, so frivolous, that he grabbed her by the shoulders and at once, she jerked back to avoid a blow, following an old lesson that a shaking was followed by a blow, and if she let herself be knocked to the ground she would get a kick to the belly or in the face. At once he released her, horrified, dropping his hands from her shoulders and spreading them wide as if to show that he had no weapon.

"Don't!" he said. "For Christ's sake, don't! I'm not that brute. I wouldn't hurt you. Forgive me, forgive me! But I can't make you hear me! Alinor, you must listen to me."

"I'm listening," she said, recovering herself faster than he could do. "I'm listening. But I can't do what you ask."

"Forgive me . . ." He was trying to calm the furious thudding of his heart. "It has been a terrible month, a terrible year. The very moment that I met with my parents—and they were so angry—we learned of the arrest of the king. So I couldn't leave my seminary, as I was preparing to do, but had to go back into royal service. Since then I've been in London and The Hague, and then to London again, trying desperately—you have no idea—meeting with men who had no hope, asking for money from paupers, asking for them to act when they dared not, sending messages and getting no reply and now—God forgive us—now he is dead, and it is all over, and we have lost worse than we ever lost before, and I have to listen to your brother taunting—"

"Ned didn't taunt you."

"He did. You don't understand. It was between men. It was about our country, our war."

"My war, too," she observed. "My country, too."

He took a swift step away from her to the gate as if he would fling himself out of the gate and down the road, in a rage. "This is not the point! You aren't listening to me!"

She stood as still and silent as a deer when it scents danger but does not know what is coming. She stood as innocent as a deer, as intent as a deer scenting the wind. He stepped back towards her, his fists clenched at his sides, and fought to find the words to explain. "You have given me a terrible shock. I don't know what to say."

A barn owl with a great spread of white wings flew along the hedgerow of the lane towards them, lifted clear of the bushes, and disappeared into the field on the other side of the garden. James saw how she watched it, as if it was warning her of something, and he thought that it was impossible for a man like him—an educated man, a spiritual man—to understand a woman like her, in a place like this.

"What?" he demanded, and she turned her gaze back to him.

"I was just watching the owl," she said quietly, knowing that he was irritated but not knowing why. "I was attending to you. I was just watching her."

"You're cold," he said, but it was he who shivered. "And Ned will be wondering where you are."

"He knows where I am. I told him I was shutting up the hens."

He had to bite his tongue on his irritation. "What I mean is, we can't talk now. We can't talk here. We must talk tomorrow. We must meet tomorrow somewhere and talk. Where will you meet me?"

"I have to take Rob to Chichester tomorrow."

Again, he bit the inside of his mouth and tasted blood. "Can't Edward take him?"

"Oh, no!" She was shocked that he would suggest it. "I want to see Rob's master and his home, and where he will work. Mr. Tudeley will pay over the money. I have to sign Rob's indentures. They will accept a woman's signature. I have a good name in Chichester."

He tried to be calm. "Yes, indeed. Then I will come to Chichester and meet you there."

She nodded without speaking, and opened the garden gate for him to leave. He was astounded by her calmness.

"Alinor, we must be together, we must be lovers again. I will make you my wife. I will give you my name—my real name. You will become accustomed! I love you, I want you. More than anything in the world. You are all that I have left! I have lost everything else. You are all that is left for me."

She nodded, saying nothing.

He thought her unnaturally serene while he was sweating with a mixture of anger and frustrated desire. "Where shall we meet?"

"The Market Cross?" she asked. "Before noon?"

"I'll be there. Nobody knows of this, do they?" He jabbed towards her belly with his hand. "You've not told anyone?"

She lied to him, for the first time, before she had even thought of it. "Nobody," she said.

"Then it will be all right," he tried to reassure her, though it was he who looked panicked. She was as cool as the sickle moon.

"It will be all right," she agreed through pale lips, and she closed the gate on him and turned back to the frozen garden. As he walked away he heard her speak softly to her hens, in the same gentle tones as she had used to soothe him.

Alys wanted to walk to Chichester with her mother and Rob, see Rob's new employer, collect some more wool for spinning, and perhaps even buy a ribbon to trim her wedding dress.

"It's only the Monday market," Alinor said discouragingly. "The ribbon stall is far better on Saturday. And the wool merchant is bringing wool and leaving it here, when he comes next week."

Alys made a face. "Anyway, I suppose I should go to work at the mill," she said.

"You should," Alinor agreed.

"I'd almost rather work the ferry than spend the day with Mrs. Miller."

"You could ask your uncle Ned to take his turn in the dairy?"

Unwillingly, Alys laughed.

"Ah, she's not so bad," Alinor told her daughter. "And it's baking day today. The other women will be there for the firing of the oven and you can bake us a loaf."

Alys wrapped a shawl around her shoulders and tightened her apron at her broad waist. "I'll go to Stoney Farm when I've finished work. I'll have my dinner there, and walk back here later," she said.

"Yes, yes," Alinor said absently. She went to the foot of the stairs and called Rob and heard his answering shout.

"Help me with the copper into the scullery for Rob."

The two women slid the pole through the carry rings and lifted the copper filled with hot water to the center of the room, then Alinor kissed her daughter and saw her out of the front door, turned to the foot of the stairs, and shouted for Rob again.

He came downstairs in his shirt and stripped naked, and washed himself, using the gray soap as Alinor poured jugs of hot water over his shoulders and over his head.

He stepped, long-legged as a calf, out of the water onto a little mat that Alinor put before him, and rubbed himself down with a linen sheet. He sat, wrapped in the sheet on a stool before the fire, as Alinor trimmed his thick brown hair and rubbed it dry with her own mixture of olive oil and apple vinegar and then combed it through with a lice comb. Rob dressed himself in the clean linen that they had given him at the Priory, and a pair of breeches belonging to Walter Peachey.

"Eat some breakfast," Alinor urged him, and put some bread and small ale before him on the kitchen table.

When he had finished, he lifted the copper with her and carried it back to the scullery. "Shall I pour it away?" he asked her. "It's heavy for you."

"I'll wash down the floors with it later," she said. "Leave it there."

Alinor had bought him good secondhand hose in Chichester market and he could still get into the shoes they had given him for Christmas at the Priory, though they were tight across the toes. He had a secondhand jacket which once belonged to Walter.

Alinor stroked the thick wool of the sleeve. "It's very fine," she said.

"It's nothing. It's his old one, his second-best. He wore velvet to go to university."

"I am sorry . . ." she started to say.

Rob grinned at her. "Sorry that I don't have a velvet jacket? Sorry that I can't eat my dinners at Cambridge? Ma, it is me that's sorry that my earnings are stopped from the Priory, and Alys can't get enough for her dowry, and you have to work all the hours of daylight. I know how lucky I am. I know how blessed we've been. And as soon as I earn my first wages you shall have them all."

Alinor reached for him and he bowed his head and allowed her to embrace him, but he no longer clung to her as he used to do, when he was her little boy.

"You're growing up," she said mournfully.

"I'm an apprentice lad!" he said proudly.

"I feel like I'm losing you," she said. "Like you're slipping away."

"It's Chichester," he reminded her. "I'm not going to sea."

"No, and I thank God for that at least," she said. "I'll look in to see you when I come to market, and you'll come home for Alys's wedding on Sunday, and then Lady Day."

Gently he detached himself from her embrace. "Of course. You'll see me within the week."

"Are you ready to go?" she asked him, half hoping he would say no and they would have more time together.

"I'll get my sack," he said.

He ran up the ladder to his loft bedroom and came down again carrying his little sack with some clean linen, his spoon, his cup, his knife, a change of hose and—a gift from Sir William—a notebook with blank pages for him to start his own book of recipes and remedies that he would learn from the apothecary. He had his own pen, a knife to trim it, and a small pot of ink from the Priory schoolroom.

"Everything?" Alinor asked him.

"Yes."

"Well, if you need something, you can always send a message."

They went out of the house, closing the door carefully behind them. Ned was rehanging the horseshoe that served as a chiming bell on the far side of the mire, but when he saw them he pulled the ferry over and held it steady as Alinor got on board.

"All ready?" he asked Rob. "You're the first of us Ferrymans to have an apprenticeship. The first to be headed to clean work. The first to work indoors."

"I'm ready," Rob said.

"Our mother would have died of pride," Ned said to Alinor. "Just shows you what study can do . . . and favor," he added.

"Rob was always bright, even as a baby," Alinor said. "Mother saw that in him, though she would never have dreamed of today. And he's earned the favor of the Peacheys, fair and square. He learned enough at school to be able to study alongside Master Walter. And they made friends, real friends."

"Born to be a lord?" Ned teased her, as he made the ferry fast and took her hand to help her out.

"Of course not," she said. "But it tells you something that he and Master Walter were studying side by side and now Walter is fit to be a lawyer, or at any rate a gentleman."

"It tells you that there are always places for placemen, and nothing changes," Ned said.

"Everything is changing," Rob said surprisingly, leaping from ferry to pier and helping Alinor to dry land. "Everything is changing. We have a parliament instead of a king. We can speak to our masters on our own two feet, we don't have to kneel. I am going to earn a wage, not be paid in pennies. We're never going to go hungry again." He turned to his uncle and the two men embraced. "Thank you, Uncle Ned," Rob said. "I'll be back on Sunday."

"Have this in the meantime," his uncle said, pressing a sixpence into his hand. "Take it, you might need it. They might not feed you well and then you can buy yourself a pie or a loaf of bread. And if they don't treat you well, you must tell us, you know. You're right: we aren't so poor that anyone can do anything to us. And we don't take a beating from anyone."

"I'll be fine," Rob promised.

Alinor took his arm and they started up the road together, turning away from the mire and the road to the mill, and heading towards the Chichester road.

"Godspeed, Nephew," Ned called. "God speed you."

They took a lift with a charcoal burner who worked the Sealsea Island forest, on his way to deliver to the kitchens of Chichester. He let the two of them sit on the wagoner's bench beside him, rather than spoil their clean clothes on the sooty sacks. He let them off at the Market Cross and went to Eastgate for the needlemakers' furnaces.

Alinor and Rob walked up North Street to the apothecary's house. Like many of the tradesmen he used the front room of the house as his shop, with wooden shutters on the windows that were propped up to serve as an awning when the shop was open. At the back of the shop, behind the counter, he had a few little flasks, distillation glasses, and a drying oven for the herbs and spices. His wife, smart in a white coif and apron, served customers, calling her husband forward for consultations, and wrapping pills and pouring drafts herself. She made the cordials and dispensed drams. In a brewhouse in the backyard she made special flavored ales, brewed with herbs and spices to aid digestion, to increase heat, or prevent fatigue.

Alinor tapped on the door and stepped inside. Rob followed her, blinking as the interior of the house was so dark compared with the brightness of the street outside.

"Ah, Mrs. Reekie," said the apothecary.

"Good day, Mrs. Reekie," said his wife. "And this is your boy?"

Alinor stepped back, but she did not have to push Rob forward as she would have done last year. He stepped forward himself with the confidence that he had learned at the Priory and made a little bow to the mistress and to his new master. "I'm Robert Reekie," he said. "Thank you for accepting me as your apprentice."

Alinor saw Mrs. Sharpe smile at Rob's good looks and manners as Mr. Sharpe stretched his hand out for Rob to shake. The shop doorbell tinkled and Mr. Tudeley, the steward from the Priory, stepped into the shop.

"Ah, good day, good day," he said. "Glad you are punctual, Mrs. Reekie, Robert. Good day to you, Mr. and Mrs. Sharpe. Do you have Robert's deeds of apprenticeship?"

"Right here." Mr. Sharpe produced an apprenticeship

deed from his guild, with Robert's name and his own already written in clerkly script. He weighed down the corners of the parchment with the brass weights from the dry goods scale, so they could all see the imposing document, with red seals and ribbons at the foot. Rob stepped up to the desk and took the quill. Alinor watched, loving him as he signed his name without hesitation or a blot of ink, not scratching an "X" on the page like his illiterate father. Then Mr. Tudeley made his signature as Robert's sponsor, and Mr. Sharpe signed his name as his master and the guildsman who would introduce Rob to the Apothecaries' Guild of Chichester, when he had served his time.

Alinor stepped forward and signed her name as Widow Reekie, Rob's parent and guardian, and signed her occupation as a midwife.

"It's done," Mr. Tudeley said. "Robert, I expect you to be a credit to the Priory and to your mother."

"I will, Mr. Tudeley," Rob said. "Please thank his lordship for giving me such a chance in life."

"You'll want to see his room," Mrs. Sharpe said to Alinor.

"I'd be grateful," Alinor said.

The mistress led Alinor and Rob up the staircase to the two rooms over the little shop. From the landing there was a loft ladder, which led upstairs to where the maidservant slept on one side, and the little room that Rob was to have, under the eaves on the other side.

The three of them crowded into the little space and Alinor bent down to look through the window to the street below.

"He'll eat at our table," the mistress said. "And one Sunday a month he has the afternoon off."

"And may I come and see him?" Alinor asked. "When I come to Chichester for the market?"

"You can come in the shop if he's not busy serving. But he can't come out to meet you. We've had apprentice boys before. They've got to settle."

"He's lived away from home," Alinor reassured her. "At the

Priory for the last two quarters. But I'm grateful you're letting him home this Sunday, for his sister's wedding."

"She's to marry the Stoney boy, isn't she?"

"Yes," Alinor said.

"Mr. Tudeley told me, when he came for Rob's apprenticeship. You must be proud of both your children!"

They went down the ladder, then down the stair and back to the little shop. Mr. Tudeley had already left, with a sachet of rose petals as a gift. Alinor curtseyed to Mr. Sharpe and kissed Mrs. Sharpe on both cheeks, and Rob went with her to the shop door and stepped outside to say good-bye.

Alinor faced her young son. His head was up to her shoulder, now. She thought that he was still her little boy, tied to her apron strings, wrapped around her heartstrings, and at the same time he was near to a young man: she could see the broadness of his shoulders and the confidence of his stance. Already he had book learning that she would never know, already he had manners that no one had taught her. He would rise in the world, away from her, and she should be glad to see him go. Her task as a mother now was not to keep him safe and hold him to her heart, but to release him and let him fly, as if she were a falconer, hacking a beautiful hawk into the wild.

"God bless you, Rob." Her voice was choked with emotion. "You know to be a good boy, and let me know how you are. Send a message that everything's all right?"

"Don't you worry about me," he said cheerfully. "I'll be home on Sunday for the wedding!"

Rob was waiting and the Sharpes inside the shop were waiting for her to leave. Alinor knew she could do nothing but walk away. Still, her feet did not move.

Rob kissed her. "Go on," he said, more like a man than her boy. "Go on, Ma. It'll be all right. You'll see."

Alinor smiled shakily and turned and walked away.

The Market Cross was at the center of the town and the streets were crowded with townsmen and women, people delivering goods, and traders setting up stalls or just standing with baskets on their arms or pedlars' packs at their feet and shouting their wares. Alinor, with her hood pulled up over her head, hiding her face, went to the steps of the cross and found James Summer at her side, appearing as if from nowhere.

He took her hand without saying anything and drew her into the front room of the nearby inn. She hesitated at the door.

"I can't come in here," she said, shocked. "What if someone saw me?"

"It's not a tavern," he corrected her. "It's an inn. Lady travelers can dine here and drink. It's perfectly—"

"Nobody would take me for an honest woman, seeing me in here with you."

"Not at all! Look . . ." A family party climbed down from their traveling coach and walked through the hall to their private dining room, without glancing at her. "My own mother dines at inns," he told her. "It's perfectly all right."

"I've never set foot in such a place," she resisted him.

He realized that a poor woman from the country would never have seen the inside of a coaching inn, would not understand the distinction between a grubby village alehouse and the respectable coaching inn of a small town like Chichester. He realized that he must learn to be patient with her—and introduce her slowly to his world. "Alinor, please, we have to go somewhere that we can talk. Come. I promise you that nobody will see you, and it is quite all right if they do. You have to trust me. I will judge for you now, and in the future."

He took her by the hand and led her to where he had reserved a table in the corner of the dining room, with a jug of mulled ale for both of them and a plate of bread and meats.

She sat nervously on the edge of the chair that he drew out for her and peered around her. He repressed his irritation that this Alinor was not the fey stranger that he had met in the churchyard, nor the free countrywoman who had cooked fish on sticks. Here, she was a poor woman afraid of the judgment of others.

"Has Robert started work? Were you happy with his place?" He realized he was speaking loudly as if to someone hard of hearing, or simple.

She took the cup of warm ale and wrapped her cold hands around it. "Yes, yes," she said. "I think he'll do very well there. They've a good trade and the mistress brews her own . . ." She trailed away as she saw the darkness in his face and realized that he had no real interest in Rob's work. "You don't want to know about that."

"We have to decide what we are going to do."

She nodded, put down her cup, and folded her hands in her lap. She had not taken so much as a sip, and he thought his indifference about Rob had hurt her, and now she was putting on serenity as if she were drawing a cape around her shoulders.

"You are determined not to be worried?"

"Of course I'm worried." She found a faint smile. "I've been thinking of you day and night. If I could've sent you a message, I would've done. I've been sleepless wondering what you'd think. I didn't mean to spring this on you, but what else could I do? I've been waiting and hoping that you'd come back."

"My love, beloved . . ." Now that he was faced with her luminous beauty, shining against her poor clothes, as out of place here as in the tidelands, he lost the words that he had assembled overnight, in the sleepless hours when he had prayed for guidance, knowing that his own prayers were a sin. "I can imagine my future with you; but not with a child. It can't be."

He saw her slowly inhale the meaning of his words. For a moment she made no answer. Her dark gray gaze went down to her worn shoes and back to his face. "No child? Then what would you have me do?"

He felt strangely awkward. "Is it not possible for you to take something that would make it disappear?"

"No," she said simply. "There is nothing in the world that can make a baby disappear."

"You know what I mean."

"I know I won't pretend with words."

He took up his cup of ale and took a sip of the hot sweetness to hide his rising temper. "I don't mean to pretend with words. It's just—"

"It's a terrible thing to speak of. Worse to do," she said, as if agreeing with him.

"But it's not too late to do something?"

Gravely, she shook her head. "It's never too late to do something."

"What d'you mean?"

"Some women smother the baby as it's born and say it was a stillbirth. Is that what you want me to do?"

"No!" He had raised his voice, and he looked around, embarrassed. Nobody had noticed them. "But would you do something now? For us? For our life together?"

"If I did it, we would have a life together?"

He could not believe that he had won so quickly. "I swear it. I will go with you now into the cathedral and swear it."

"You want it dead."

He looked at her set face. "Only so that I can be with you."

She drew a shuddering breath, and then slowly she shook her head as if her pale lips could not speak. "That is a terrible bargain. No. No. I could not."

"Because you think it is a sin? I can explain—"

"No," she interrupted him. "Because I could not bear it. Whether it's a sin against God or not. Whatever you could say. It would be . . ." she sought for the word ". . . it would be an offense to me." She shot him a swift glance. "It would be a deep offense to me, against myself."

"It doesn't matter—"

"It matters to me. I matter: in this, I matter."

"We will have other children."

"We would not," she contradicted him. "No child would come to my womb if I had poisoned his brother."

He tried to laugh. "This is superstition and nonsense! This is folly!"

His barking laughter died away when she did not reply, and they sat in silence, waiting for the other to speak.

Then, he used the worst threat against her that he could do: "You know what you're saying? You will not come to me, and be my love and be my wife? You chose this—this nothing—over me? Over the life we would live, and what we could do for Rob and for Alys? You will let them be spoken of as children of a missing father, or worse. When they could be stepchildren to a baronet? You favor this nothing over them? As well as over me?"

He thought she would faint, she had gone so white, but he thought he must be cruel to her, to save them both.

He underestimated her. When she spoke, her voice was steady, she was far from fainting: "Yes, if I have to."

They were both silent at the enormity of what she had said. He thought that not even when the king had died had he felt this disbelieving misery. "Alinor, I cannot take a child that goes by your husband's name into my honorable home. Even if I wanted to do so. I could not own you as my wife."

She nodded. He saw her reach for the cup of ale and realized that she was blinded with tears, but she kept her head down so he could not see. Her grief only made him harder.

"I will regain my home, and go and live there without you, and I will never see you again. You condemn me to being alone, where I had thought we would be happy together. Where you should be my wife."

Her hand found the cup and she held it. Even her scarred fingers were white.

"I have loved you more than anything in the world and I will spend the rest of my life without you," he said.

Speechlessly, she nodded.

"And I will marry someone so that my name continues, so that I have a son. But I will never love her as I have loved you, and I will spend the rest of my life missing you."

Her hand was shaking so hard that the warm ale spilled onto the skirt of her gown.

"Is this your wish?" he asked incredulously. "Is this what you want for me? This misery?"

The maid of the inn came up to them. "Everything all right here?" she asked very loudly, breaking into the spell he was weaving around her. "Want another jug of ale?"

"Nothing, nothing," James said, waving her away.

"Tell me that you will marry me," he whispered. "Tell me that you love me as I love you—more than anything else in the world."

Finally, Alinor looked up at him and he saw that her eyes were darkened with unshed tears. "I wouldn't stoop to marry a man who'd kill his own child," she said simply. "It's not an honor that you offer me. If you're the man who'd destroy his own baby in the womb then you're not the man that I thought you were, and you're not the man for me."

He was as shaken as if she had slapped his handsome face. "Don't you dare to judge me!" he burst out.

She shook her head, quite unafraid. "I don't judge you. I'm just telling you that I agree with you. You won't have me with the baby that I carry; I won't come to you without it. We're both losers, I think."

She rose from her chair, and at once he got to his feet and put his hand on her arm. "You can't go like this!"

"I can't stay," she replied quietly.

"I mean . . ." He meant that he could not believe that she could defy him, that she could turn down his wealth and name and love. He could not believe that she could refuse him, and prefer such a little thing—not even a baby yet—a homunculus that had barely quickened. It was a nothing, it was a nothing, less than a hen's egg that he might eat for his breakfast, and yet she was putting it between them. It was not possible to imagine that she should choose a life of poverty and shame with a fatherless child over the comfort and wealth that he could offer her, and his name, his pride and his name.

"But I love you!" he burst out.

There was a world of sadness in the smile that she turned on him. "Oh, I love you," she replied. "I always will. And I'll take a comfort in that, when you're gone away to your beautiful house and I'm here alone."

Without another word, she turned and walked away from him, just as if he were not a young gentleman, and the son of a great man, just as if he were not the greatest prospect of her life: a husband of unimaginable wealth and position, and her savior from shame. She walked away from him without looking back. She walked away from him as if she were never coming back, and she left him alone at the table laid with breakfast in the best coaching inn of Chichester.

Alinor went home in a dream, setting one foot before the other. She did not hail any passing cart for a lift. There was only one that went by her, and she did not see or hear it. As she walked, it started to snow, little specks of white snow like a dust that whirled around her, and she pulled up the hood of her cloak and let it settle on her head and her shoulders. She could not feel cold; she did not know that it was snowing.

She watched her feet in her worn boots going steadily south down the road, through the village of Hunston, through Street End, and she felt the familiar rub of the ill-fitting left boot against her heel. She held her cape tied tightly around her waist and changed her basket from one frozen grip to another, hardly noticing the weight on one side or the other, nor how her back ached.

She sat on a milestone to catch her breath after an hour's walking, and watched the snow fall on her gown, a speckle of white against the brown wool. When she got to her feet she brushed herself off and shook out her cape, gathered it around herself again, and walked on. She did not notice that her hands were so cold that they were white as the snow and her stubby fingernails were blue.

Ned's ferry was tied up on the far side of the rife, outside the house, so Alinor clanged the dangling horseshoe with the new bar and saw him open the top half of the ferry-house door and then come out, a piece of sacking over his head and shoulders. He went hand over hand till the ferry was at her side and held the raft against the ebbing tide as she stepped in.

"You brought the snow with you," he remarked.

"All the way," she said as she stepped into the gently rocking ferry.

He noticed that she did not grasp his hand or cling to the side as she usually did. He guessed that she was distressed at Rob going away.

"How's our lad? Was it all right there?"

"Fair," she said. "They're good people."

"Did you leave him gladly?"

"Fair," she said again. She gave him a small rueful smile. "He didn't cling to me and beg me not to go."

"Good lad," he said. "He'll do well."

"I don't doubt it."

Hand over hand on the frozen rope, Ned pulled the ferry back to the island side and held it against the pier as she stepped lightly out of the boat. He tied up, and together they went through the half-open door. She took off her cape and shook the snow and the wet out of the door, and then hung it on the peg. She put down her basket and warmed her hands before the little fire. Every action was so familiar that she moved without thinking, as if she had decided not to think.

"Shall I mull you some ale?" he asked, looking at her composed face, and wondering if she would break out in tears, or if she was truly as serene as she seemed.

"That'd be good," she said. "I'm chilled through."

"Could you not get a lift?" he asked, thinking she might be exhausted by walking.

"No. I saw nobody going my way."

"You'll be tired then." He invited her to comment, but still she told him nothing.

The poker hissed as he dipped it into the jug of ale, and he poured her a cup and took one for himself. "This'll put some color in your cheeks," he said uncertainly.

She did not reply, but wrapped her cold hands around the cup and took a sip, her eyes on the leaping flames of the fire.

"Alinor, is anything wrong?" he asked.

She sighed, as if she would tell him everything. But all she said, as she smiled at him through the steam from the ale, was: "I'm well enough."

Richard and Alys walked home late Monday evening from Stoney Farm, and on Tuesday morning Alys was sleepy when Alinor called her. She sat in silence, her head bowed over her bowl of gruel at breakfast time and scowled at her uncle when he said that he hoped she had not missed the early tides when she had been ferryman.

"Are you coming with me to the mill today?" she asked her mother. "She's doing the laundry."

Laundry days at the mill were notorious for Mrs. Miller's bad temper. "Lord," Alinor said smiling, "I'm not surprised you want a companion."

"Also, she'll pay us for eggs. She's not got enough. Not even her hens can bear her."

Ned sat down on his stool at the head of the table. "And do you have your dowry?" he asked.

"Most of it," Alys said.

"I have the five shillings I promised you," he offered. "And I'll add another."

"I'll take it!" she smiled. "And on Saturday we'll have this week's wages."

"You're taking your mother's wages as well as your own?"

"Uncle, I have to," Alys said seriously. "And besides, she'll get it back. When I am Mrs. Stoney of Stoney Farm I'll give her a present every day."

"Oil of roses," Alinor named the one ingredient that she could never afford to buy from the herbalist at Chichester market. "I shall bathe in oil of roses."

"Ah, you're each as mad as the other," Ned said. "Come on, I'll ferry you across."

On Wednesday, the lad who was hedging was taken ill, and the two women clipped and laid the hedge, standing for most of the day in thick mud or in the briny cold ditch, bending and breaking the stubborn stems, their hands bleeding from a hundred scratches.

Alys straightened up, grimacing with pain. "My back aches," she said.

"Have a rest," Alinor urged her. "I can finish the last bit."

"Aren't you tired?"

"No," Alinor lied. "Hardly at all."

"I'll finish," Alys said grimly, and bent again hacking and twisting the stems.

Friday was cheese-making day at the tide mill and Alinor spent the day in the icy dairy, churning the butter, skimming the cream, and pressing the cheese while Alys did the hard work outside. Everything was to be ready for Friday night, and Mrs. Miller would take it herself to Chichester market on Saturday morning.

When Alys had finished the morning chores she came inside and worked alongside her mother in the dairy, their hands red and raw with cold. At noon, when Mrs. Miller rang the bell in the yard, they went into the kitchen and sat at the table to eat: bread from the mill oven and curds from the cheese. They both pressed their hands together and tucked them in the warmth under their arms to bring the feeling back to their numb fingers while Mr. Miller gave thanks for his own good dinner. Richard Stoney and the other mill lad sat opposite them, their faces pinched with cold. Mrs. Miller, seated at the head of the table, had fine white bread to eat and soft cheese, her daughter Jane on one side, little Peter on the other. Mr. Miller sat in silence at the end of the table before a solitary leg of ham. He went out as soon as he had eaten to make sure that the outside workers did not take too long over their break. Richard winked at Alys, nodded his head to Mrs. Miller and Alinor, and followed him with the other lad.

"You'll be brewing wedding ale?" Mrs. Miller asked Alinor.

"I'll strain it and pour it tomorrow," Alinor said. "I think it'll be very good. Mr. Stoney is picking it up when he drives to church on Sunday morning."

"They set a good table at Stoney Farm. You're a lucky girl," Mrs. Miller said to Alys, who forced herself to smile and nod. Mrs. Miller turned to Alinor. "I doubt they'd even have allowed the wedding if she hadn't worked here so long. They know I've taught her well."

"Never even have met if she hadn't worked here," Jane chimed in.

"Yes." Alinor leaned her shoulder gently against Alys to make her keep silence. "We're both grateful."

"The Stoneys wouldn't have trusted anyone else with their Richard," she added. "There's not another mill in Sussex that would be good enough for them."

"I'll always remember your harvest home," Alinor said, turning the conversation. "When the two of them brought in the harvest together? That was a merry day."

Alinor had meant to divert Mrs. Miller to pride in her harvest home but she had accidentally summoned a vivid memory of

James Summer standing before her, and her own flare of temper when he said she must not dance.

She bowed her head as if she were giving thanks for her food; but in reality she was hiding a pain so sharp that she might almost think that her heart was breaking. She took a deep shuddering breath and turned her mind to the dairy and the work they still had to do. She had promised herself that she would not think about losing James, nor about how she would manage without him. She would not think of anything, until after Sunday, Alys's wedding day. Only then, when Alys was married, and safe, would she allow herself to look clear-eyed at the ruin she had made of her life.

"I always give a good harvest home," Mrs. Miller said complacently. "Sir William always says so. Says he would rather be at my harvest home than anywhere in the county. D'you remember, he brought the tutor, didn't he? Mr. Summer?"

"Yes," Alinor said steadily. "Mr. Summer. D'you want to see the butter before I set it into shape?"

Mrs. Miller rose from the table and left Jane and Alys to clear up. "You can wash the plates," she said over her shoulder, and went into the dairy with Alinor. She closed the door behind them to keep the dairy cool, though it was already as cold as the ice house at the Priory.

"That's doing well," she said, looking into the churn where the butter was pale and creamy and starting to separate from the buttermilk. "It always comes so quick for you, Alinor."

Alinor smiled. She knew it was because she worked harder and churned faster than Mrs. Miller, but the woman would never say so.

"I tell my husband, you must whisper a charm into the milk," Mrs. Miller said. "A good charm, of course. I wouldn't suggest other . . ."

"It's rich milk," Alinor said easily. "There's no need for charming. If you're happy with this, I'll make squares for market."

"Don't make them too big," Mrs. Miller said. "One pound each only. No point in giving it away."

"Exactly," Alinor said patiently.

"If it's slightly underweight that's better than over. They don't weigh at the market."

"Certainly. And I'll wrap them."

"And you'll come Saturday morning to pack the cart for me?"

"Yes," Alinor said. "And Alys will come, too. D'you want us all the day?"

"You can mind the farm and the mill while we're at market. Low tide at dinnertime, but I won't ask you to open the sluice and turn the wheel."

Alinor smiled at the weak joke, as the door from the kitchen opened. "Am I to check the hens' eggs?" Alys asked.

"Haven't you done that already?" Mrs. Miller asked crossly. "Go and do it now, lazy girl."

Saturday morning Alinor was up at dawn to do the final strain and pour of the wedding ale. Alys helped her mother and they both sniffed the rich yeasty aroma.

"It's going to be good," Alinor said with satisfaction.

Ned put his head around the brewhouse door. "I hope it's not too strong?"

"It's wedding ale," Alinor replied. "It's as it should be."

"I want no drunkenness, and no bawdy games," Ned specified.

"What sort of woman do you take me for?" Alinor demanded.

"You're one that loves the old ways, and you know it. But this is to be a godly, quiet, and temperate marriage."

"No wedding ale?" asked Alinor. "Shall I pour this in the rife?"

"Well, no wines," he specified. "And no strong waters."

"In that case," Alinor said regretfully, "I shall have to beg Mrs. Stoney, for once, to stay sober."

Ned could not stifle a chuckle. Mrs. Stoney had already impressed him with her grim puritanism. "She's a godly woman," he reproved his sister. "She shouldn't be mocked."

"I know!" Alinor replied, and gave the wedding ale a final stir, before putting on her cape to go to the mill.

When Alinor and Alys walked into the mill yard the cart was at the door and clean straw in the bottom. A sprinkling of snow made it cold enough for the squares of butter to be loaded in their baskets without fear of them going soft. Alinor, Alys, and Jane loaded big round cheeses and eggs in baskets as well, until Mrs. Miller came out of the house, wrapped to her eyes in furs as if she was going to Russia, and took her place on the cart seat. Peter and Jane climbed up beside their mother.

Mr. Miller hurried to take up the reins. He knew that his wife would not tolerate delay. "Good day!" he said to Alinor, with a smile for Alys. "You're in charge, you know! We'll be home by dinnertime!"

Working at the mill without the constant critical commentary of Mrs. Miller and the hangdog eyes of her husband was like working in their own yard. Richard and the miller's lad cleaned out the barn where the plowing oxen were stabled, and Alys and Alinor fed and watered them. The women turned the horses out into the frozen pasture for a few hours while the young men mucked out the stables. Alinor pumped the buckets of water and Alys carried them. They raked out the kennels and the henhouses, the pen for the geese and the cows' stalls. The two women milked the cows and carried the pails to the dairy. They collected hens' eggs from the henhouse and looked in the little warm nooks around the barns where the hens sometimes laid away; but Mrs. Miller had gone around at dawn and taken every one she could find to market. Every time anyone went past a fallen branch they carried it back to the yard and piled it up for the boy to break it into kindling or split it for logs.

They fired up the baking oven for those villagers who would bring their bread or homemade dinners to use the big oven at sunset, and Alys kneaded dough for their own breadmaking. They worked all day until the sun started to sink over the western mire and Alinor said with relief, "Time to go home."

"Not without our wages," Alys said. "I need them for tomorrow."

"Alys, how much of your dowry do you have, exactly? Because we can't be short tomorrow. They won't call it off for the want of a shilling, but we don't want to look like we're robbing them on the church doorstep on the very day of your wedding."

"Richard will give me whatever is missing. But I'd like to do as much as I can. I want my wages for today, since we've worked so hard. And Richard will give me his."

Alinor was about to reply when they heard a shout from the gate and the rumble of wheels. Alys ran to open it and then she called to her mother: "Look who they've brought from Chichester!"

For a moment Alinor's head bobbed up in the certainty that it was James Summer, come to claim her before them all. "Who?"

"It's Rob!"

Alinor hurried out to the gate. "Oh, Rob! Oh, Rob!"

"Now then," said Mr. Miller kindly. "You would think he'd been gone to Afric and back. He's only been away a week."

"But I didn't think he'd come till tomorrow morning for his sister's wedding!" Alinor exclaimed. "How are you, son? How was your first week?"

Rob, smartly dressed and grinning, bounded down from the mill wagon and hugged his mother, ducked down for her blessing, and kissed his sister. "Mrs. Miller came into the shop and bought some ratsbane, asked them if she could give me a lift home, and they were happy to let me go early," he said. "I'm to be back at work Monday morning at eight o'clock, so I can stay for the wedding and overnight."

"How kind of you." Alinor turned to Mrs. Miller, her face glowing with happiness. "Neighborly indeed. I thank you."

"Ah well," the other woman said with unusual generosity. "He's a fine young man and a credit to you. Is all well here?"

"Oh, yes," Alinor said. "And we made a meat pie for your dinner. I didn't know what you would get at market."

"He dined well enough." Mrs. Miller nodded towards her husband, whose red face and merry smile indicated a long stay in the market tavern while his wife and children were selling their cheeses, butter, and eggs. "But we shall be glad of something to eat."

"I shall be glad of one of Mrs. Reekie's pies," Mr. Miller said cheerfully. "Nobody makes a meat pie like Mrs. Reekie."

Alinor shook her head deprecatingly as Mrs. Miller surged past her into the kitchen. Alys and Alinor took the horse from the wagon, led him into the stable, hung up his heavy collar and bridle on the hook while Richard and the lad pushed the wagon into its place and unloaded the goods. Mrs. Miller had bought sacks of wool in the wagon for spinning, a new milking stool, some wooden bowls, and two feather pillows.

"Spent all that she earned," Mr. Miller confided to Alinor.

"Shame on you," Alinor said loyally. "Mrs. Miller is one of the best housewives on the island."

"And what about this girl of yours?" Mr. Miller asked, giving Alys a casual slap on her bottom. "Is she going to make a good housewife to Richard Stoney?"

"I hope so," Alinor said, drawing Alys to her and detaching her from Mr. Miller.

"Have you put the horse away?" Mrs. Miller bawled from the kitchen doorway.

"Aye!" Mr. Miller hollered back. "I've done all my work for one day. And they've done theirs. Are they getting paid today?"

Mrs. Miller disappeared back into the house and came out with their wages, a shilling for the two of them.

"Thank you very much," Alinor said, as Mrs. Miller went back into the house and Alys and Alinor turned towards the yard gate.

"Is that right?" Mr. Miller asked suddenly. "A shilling, for a day's work when you've done everything on the farm today?"

"It's right," Alinor said stiffly. She could have added—but hardly generous for a girl getting married tomorrow—but she would not say a word. Rob beside her stiffened, and she put her hand under his arm and gave it a little squeeze.

"It's not right," Mr. Miller said with the resentful persistence of a slightly drunken man. "Here! Betty Miller! You come out here!"

"Really," Alinor said. "It's right, Mr. Miller. Shilling a day, for the whole day, because we stopped at sunset." She gave Rob a little push towards the yard gate.

Mrs. Miller came bustling out of her kitchen door. "And who's shouting me out like I was a milkmaid?" she demanded.

Rob nodded to Mr. Miller. "Thank you for the lift in the wagon, Mr. Miller," he said. "Good evening to you, Mrs. Miller." Tactfully, he went to the yard gate and waited for his mother out of earshot as Mrs. Miller surged out and stood, hands on hips, glaring at her husband and Alinor.

"What's this?" she demanded.

Alinor shook her head. "Nothing," she said. "Really, nothing."

"You've underpaid the Reekies," Mr. Miller said mulishly. "Mother and the maid."

"Sixpence each, as I always have done."

"Sole charge!" he said, like a man who has discovered a password. "Sole charge. They had sole charge of the farm today, so that makes them like a yard man. Or like a bailiff. Sole charge. Good as a man. Good as two men."

"You want to pay a woman and a maid as much as two yard men?" Mrs. Miller demanded scathingly.

"No," he said, "course not. But they should have . . . and the pretty maid is getting married . . ."

Alinor noted the fatal slip of calling Alys "pretty" to his slate-faced wife.

"Who pays them?" Mrs. Miller suddenly demanded of him, going close and taking him by his linen collar as if she would choke him.

"Why, you do?"

"And who watches them, and keeps them right and clears up after their mistakes, and all the mess they make?"

Alinor let her gaze slip away from Mr. Miller's crestfallen face to the creamy rosy sky over the harbor, glanced towards her son,

Rob, waiting at the gate and wished herself home, with her children at the dinner table.

"You do," Mr. Miller said sulkily.

"So, I think it's best left to me and them, isn't it? Without any man coming in and wanting extra payment for 'pretty'?"

Mr. Miller had been defeated twenty years ago by the iron determination and chronic bad temper of his wife. "I was just saying—"

"Best not to say anything," Mrs. Miller advised him smartly.

"Feeding the horse," he said, as if to himself, and turned towards the stable.

"And we have to go," Alinor said smoothly.

"Old fool that he is," Mrs. Miller said.

"Good night, Mrs. Miller. We'll see you tomorrow at church," Alinor said.

"Good night, Mrs. Reekie," she replied, recovering her temper now that she had won. "And God bless you tomorrow, Alys."

Alinor and her two children walked down the track to the ferry crossing, where Rob ran ahead like a boy to ring the chime.

# TIDELANDS, FEBRUARY 1649

The wedding was to be simple. Alys and Richard would be married before the usual Sunday morning congregation at St. Wilfrid's Church, Alys in her best gown with her new white apron and new white linen cap. Richard would wear his best jacket, and Ned would lead the bride to the altar. The service would follow the new style as ordered by parliament: Richard would make brief promises, and Alys would assent to her own vows. After the wedding in St. Wilfrid's, they would all cross the rife, take a goodwill drink at the tide mill, and then go on to Stoney Farm for the wedding feast. There would be good food, and healths drunk, and finally the young people would go to bed in the big bedroom under the thatched eaves.

Alys did not sleep until the crowing cock from the barn told her that the night was nearly over, and then she turned on her side, sighed with anticipation, and slept deeply.

The morning of her wedding day was freezing cold but clear, the ice on the harbor so white that the seagulls whirling above it were bright against the blue sky and then invisible against the blanched landscape. Alys, waking late and tumbling down the stairs to eat gruel at the kitchen table, swore that she would not wear her cape but would go into church in her gown and new apron and cap.

"You'll freeze," said her mother. "You have to wear your cape, Alys."

"Let her freeze," Ned advised. "It's her wedding day."

Alinor granted the one liberty that Alys had set her heart on. "Oh, very well. But this is what comes of a winter wedding. And no flowers to be had but a posy of dried herbs!"

"As long as I can wear my new pinny," Alys stipulated.

"Oh, wear it!" Alinor said. "But you'll put your cape on when you're going home in the wagon to Stoney Farm."

"I will! I will!"

Rob came down the stair from the loft, wearing his new work jacket and the Christmas shoes.

"And how fine d'you look, lad?" Ned asked, slapping him on the back. "This is a proud day for the Ferrymans."

The children did not mention their father's name, and Alinor, tightening her cape around her broadening waist, thought that if she had not needed a name for her baby she might never have heard the words Zachary Reekie again.

"All right, Ma?" Rob asked gently.

She smiled at him. "I'm fine."

"She's missing Alys before we're rid of her," Ned advised, but Rob's brown eyes were fixed on his mother's pale face.

"Are you really all right?"

Alinor held her breath. From childhood, Rob had been able to see beyond the surface of things, to illness and sorrow. She wondered if he could see her heartbreak, she wondered if he could sense her baby, his half brother.

She shook her head and smiled. "It's as your uncle says," she lied. "I'm seeing you and Alys out the house, both of you, in the same week and I feel like a broody hen with all her eggs stolen."

"I'll be working at the mill with you tomorrow," Alys pointed out. "You'll see me at first light. And Rob'll be home at Lady Day."

"I know, I know," Alinor said. "And I couldn't be happier for both of you. Come along now, Rob, and eat some breakfast. Alys, have you had anything?"

"I can't," she said at once. "I've no appetite."

"Don't you go fainting away at the altar for hunger," Ned warned her.

"Take some small ale and a little bread," Alinor urged her. "And I have eggs as well."

Alys sat at the table as she was ordered, her uncle on one hand and her brother on another, and smiled up at her mother. "My last breakfast here," she said. "My last breakfast as Alys Reekie."

"Stop it," Ned advised swiftly. "Or you'll set your mother off again."

Mr. Stoney, his wife, and son in their wagon rang the chime for the ferry just as the family was finishing breakfast, and Ned went out to bring them across the high water. Once they were on the island side Alinor rolled out the barrels of wedding ale for them, and the two men loaded them into the wagon. Alinor had two big wheels of cheese and two loaves of bread baked in the big oven at the mill.

"And are you ready?" Mr. Stoney asked Alys. "All your little things packed up?"

"I'm ready, I'm ready!" she said breathlessly.

Richard jumped down from the back of the wagon, his face pink with cold and shyness. He took her hands and kissed each one, and then he kissed her on the lips.

Mrs. Stoney climbed down from the seat at the front of the wagon and Alys curtseyed and kissed her mother-in-law, and as the adults greeted each other, she slid her hand in Richard Stoney's warm grip.

"I'll get her things," Ned said to Alinor. "Are they all ready?"

Alinor and Ned went into the house and brought out a small pile of good linen, the best that Ferry-house had, and a knapsack of Alys's personal goods. Mrs. Stoney's eyes flickered over the little bag, but she said nothing. Richard gave Alinor his hand to help her into the back of the cart and lifted Alys in.

"We'll walk over the mire," Ned said for him and Rob. "See you at the church door!"

"Don't delay!" Alys warned him. "Don't get your shoes muddy—go round by the bank!"

"I shan't be stolen by mermaids," Rob teased her. "We'll get there before you do!"

Mr. Stoney clicked to his pair of horses and they headed south as Ned put the cover over the fire, shut the back door, and walked with Rob on the little paths across the flooded harbor to church.

The whole parish turned out to witness the wedding of the pretty Reekie girl to the wealthy farmer's son, many of them glad to see Alinor's daughter doing so well, a few murmuring that it was a shame she was going off the island. Ned was known to everyone in Sealsea Island because of his long service on the ferry, and his father before him, and most of the women had consulted Alinor for their health or for the delivery of a baby. The marriage was an extraordinary upward leap for the family who had worked the ferry on the island for as long as anyone could remember, but everyone conceded that if any girl was likely to marry well for her looks, that would be Alys.

There were a lot of comments about Rob as he took his place in the men's pews at the back. Some people who had seen him in the summer processing to the front of the church with the Peacheys were glad to see him returned to a lowly place. But the young people, especially the young women, remarked on the difference between Rob their former playmate, son of the missing fisherman Zachary Reekie, and this new Rob, with his command of Latin, his apprenticeship in Chichester, and his well-cut jacket.

Nobody remarked aloud that the two Reekie children had been blessed with extraordinary opportunities, given that they had been born in a fisherman's cottage to a ferryman's daughter and a wastrel father who was now missing. Nobody said that their good luck could only be something other than chance, charm, or ability. Nobody repeated the old story that they were faerie born, that their own father had sworn it, and that their good looks and good fortune were the gifts of their mother—a faerie concubine, beloved of the unseen world, and guided by it. But almost everyone thought: how else could the Reekie children be so undeservingly blessed? How else could their mother walk out of a violent marriage with her head high and not a mark on her? How else should Zachary so conveniently disappear? Nobody would say such a thing on Alys's wedding day, but a number of people thought it, and glanced to each other, and saw that others were thinking it too.

Alys was about to go into church and Alinor about to follow her when Mrs. Stoney delayed them at the church porch. "D'you have the dowry?" she asked. "You're supposed to give it to me here."

Alinor halted, and turned to her daughter. Alys flushed a little, and reached into the pocket of her gown under her apron.

"If it's short you'd better tell me now," Mrs. Stoney said harshly. "Before you go a step farther."

"It's not short," Alys said.

Alinor tried to nod as if she were confident that Alys had all the money. They had worked all the hours at the mill, and spun, but even with the ferry money and Rob's wages, she thought that Richard must have donated all his inheritance.

Triumphantly, Alys handed over the purse, and Mrs. Stoney weighed it in her hand and then opened it and peeped inside. Alys's face was like a sculpture in stone as she looked at her mother-in-law. The woman tipped the coins into her hand: gold crowns, silver shillings, no small coins, no coppers at all: a fortune.

"You got it," she said, as if she still could not believe it.

"Of course," Alys said.

"Of course," Alinor repeated.

Mrs. Stoney tucked the purse into the pocket of her cape.

"Then we can go in," she said. "I'll put this in our treasure chest at Stoney Farm tonight."

She turned and went into church, past the standing room for the workingmen at the rear of the church, and took a seat in a pew near the front, while the usual pew owner shifted up sulkily. Alys took her mother's hand and went to stand at the back, waiting to be called up to the altar. Richard was waiting at the front of the church.

"Next Sunday, that's where I'll be," Alys whispered to her mother, nodding at Mrs. Stoney's determined occupation of the prestigious front pew. "And you shall sit beside me. That's worth scraping up for pennies, isn't it? We'll have our own pew."

"That wasn't pennies," Alinor said, still stunned that Alys had a dowry purse with the full amount.

Her daughter smiled up at her. "Richard," she whispered. "I told you he would not risk losing me."

The door of the church behind them opened, and Sir William strolled up the aisle of the church, nodding to his tenants left and right, showing no signs of mourning for the king he had lost and the defeat of his cause. His face was set in its usual lines of calm indifference. His eyes flickered over the men at the back of the church and he ignored Ned and other known roundheads. Behind him, as always, in order of precedence came his household; before them came his guest: James Summer.

Alinor, standing with Alys, unnoticed at the rear of the church, closed her eyes. She felt herself go rigid as an iron bar on an anvil. She had not thought that James would still be at the Priory. It had not occurred to her that he would come to church for Alys's wedding day. Alinor gripped the back of the pew against the falling sense of faintness. She bit her lip. She held herself as if she were a fragile thing that might crack and dissolve, as if she might be exhaled if she did not hold her breath.

The minister announced the first hymn, the parish stumbled through an unfamiliar song with the musicians sawing away on tabor and fiddle. Alinor opened her eyes, came to her senses, and opened and closed her mouth as if she were singing too.

Her heart was thudding with relief that she had not confided in Alys, who glanced without interest at the Priory household. Alinor thought that if her daughter had known that James was the father of the baby that she was carrying, and seen him walk past her without exchanging a glance, her shame and humiliation would have been unbearable. Alinor turned her head a little so her gaze was directed away from the Priory pew. Perhaps this was her punishment for foolishly trusting a young man who spoke of priceless love but lived inside an expensive world, who called himself mad for her but was all too thoughtful when it came to his future. Alinor realized that the hymn had finished and sank obediently to her knees for the prayers. There was nothing she could do to stop the man who had betrayed her from witnessing her daughter's wedding. The best thing she could do was to try to share Alys's joy in this day, and not let her own unhappiness distract her. Alinor closed her eyes and bent her head. She could not find words for a prayer; but she could only wish herself through her daughter's wedding, and for the day to be over without betraying herself.

James, at the front of the church, sensed Alinor's presence behind him, and had to fight the temptation to glance back to see if she was looking for him. He had not thought that he could bear to walk past her; he did not think he could get through the long church service. He had forgotten that it was Alys's wedding day, and it was of no importance to Sir William. The cook, Mrs. Wheatley, could have told him, and that she had baked a great cake to take to Stoney Farm for the wedding feast, but she did not know that he had any interest in Alinor. She would not have dreamed that he was shaking with desire as he knelt and laid his head on his hands, and prayed to God to keep him from sin and from folly.

When the service was finally over, the minister did not walk to the back of the church to greet and reprimand his parishioners as usual. James waited impatiently for the Priory household to lead the way out of church and release him from this vigil—and then he realized that they were not leaving.

"Today we celebrate a wedding," the minister said. "Those of you not wishing to attend may leave. Please do not linger in the churchyard and don't allow children to play around the tombstones."

There was a little murmur from the church wardens, who agreed with the minister, that the parish's traditional use of the church as a gathering point was ungodly. "And those of you witnessing the wedding, please step closer," he said.

James, looking around in surprise, glimpsed Alinor's pale face from the corner of his eye, and remembered, with a jolt, that it was her daughter's wedding day. He longed for Sir William to lead his household out, and a moment later, realized, with dread, that his lordship was keeping his seat in his grand chair, honoring the wedding with his presence.

Richard Stoney walked up to his place at the foot of the chancel steps, just before the altar table, which now stood, plain and unvarnished, blocking the way before the stone carved rood screen and the empty eastern end of the church.

Alinor concentrated on the wedding, erasing all thoughts of James from her mind. She smiled lovingly at Alys. "God bless," she said. "Go on."

Ned came from the men's side of the church and offered his arm to Alys, as formal as a lord. Alys, very pale but smiling, smoothed the front of the new apron over the swell of her belly, and put her hand on his arm. Alinor, carrying Alys's cape, walked behind the two of them as they made their way up the aisle towards the communion table. Ned and Alys halted before the minister so that Alinor, standing behind them, was immediately next to James in the Priory pew. It was almost as if the two of them were at the front of the church on their own wedding day. James stared fixedly ahead, his eyes blind to the wooden lectern that held the Bible in front of him. Alinor looked at the back of her daughter's cap where the little bow trembled.

The minister read the newly approved words of the wedding service and Richard and Alys repeated their vows. Ned passed Alys's little hand to Richard and he slipped the wedding ring on her finger. It was done. Under the shield of Alys's cape, which Alinor held before her belly, she released the grip she had on her fingers. Relief flowed through her. It was done and Alys was now Mrs. Stoney, a married woman. Whatever became of her mother, Alys's good name was secured, her future was guaranteed. Alinor felt hot tears behind her eyelids: Alys was a married woman; she was Mrs. Stoney of Stoney Farm. Alys was safe.

"Amen," said Sir William loudly, and everyone repeated it.

Richard kissed his bride and everyone moved forward to congratulate the young couple. Alys, rosy and smiling, kissed everyone. Richard was slapped on the back and congratulated. They paused before Sir William, who kissed the bride. James smiled his congratulations and shook Richard's hand. Then suddenly the crowd of well-wishers parted, and James was facing Alinor. She felt it was as if they were quite alone, in a silent world.

"I congratulate you on your daughter's happiness, Mrs. Reekie." He found he could hardly speak, as if he had taken a blow to the mouth and his face was numb.

"Thank you."

He could hardly hear her above the chatter of people congratulating the young couple, the creak of the church door, and people going out into the freezing churchyard outside and exclaiming about the cold. He tried to say other words of goodwill, but he could not speak. She glanced at him once, and looked down.

"We'll call in at the wedding dinner," Sir William announced jovially. "We were riding up to Chichester anyway."

"Delighted!" Mrs. Stoney said, stepping forward, blushing with pride. "We should be so pleased."

Alinor did not look at James to prompt him to refuse. It was as if they had nothing between them, no secret, no love, and he would not have understood why she did not want him at her daughter's wedding feast. It was as if everything was forgotten, as if they were strangers, as he had said they would be. She curtseyed to her landlord, and to the man she had adored, turned away without another word, and followed Alys out into the cold winter sunshine.

Ned and Rob had already gone back to man the ferry for the many people who were walking to Stoney Farm. Farmer Stoney was waiting on the box of the wagon outside the lych-gate.

"That was a good day's work, Mrs. Reekie," he said, pleased as Alinor came through the gate.

"Yes indeed," Alinor said, smiling.

"I never thought you'd get the dowry together," he said, a twinkle in his eye. "You must have sold young Rob to Virginia, rather than an apprenticeship."

Alinor tried to laugh. "She's a good girl," she said. "She's been working every day, and spinning all night."

"Even so," he said. "I know that won't have covered it. I hope you haven't put yourselves in debt."

"Alys had her father's gift, and my brother helped," Alinor said, concealing Richard's part.

"Up you get then," he said to her, giving a hand to help her into the wagon. "And here's our little bride."

Alys sat in the seat of honor, beside Mr. Stoney on the box seat. Mrs. Stoney squeezed in beside her, Alinor and Richard sat on the back, and a few of the Stoney neighbors climbed in to save the walk. Mrs. Wheatley came from the Priory with the footman, Stuart, carrying a great fruit cake, and was helped into the wagon and held the cake on her knees.

"All aboard?" Mr. Stoney said, and clicked to the horse to start. Alinor, looking back down the road, saw that James was mounted on horseback already, but someone had delayed Sir William. He was on his horse, speaking to one of his tenants, who was earnestly explaining something, his cap in his hand. The bend in the road hid them from sight. She hoped very much that Sir William and James would be delayed, and then decide against coming at all. She did not know how she would get through Alys's wedding dinner if James were to be there, not looking at her, not speaking to her, not even a stranger to her; but worse than a stranger—a man who had chosen to be rid of her and showed no signs of regret.

The tide was ebbing at the wadeway, low enough for Mr. Stoney to drive the wagon through the water, and the people who were on foot crossed on the ferry, with Ned pulling on the rope. As it was Alys's wedding day, he charged no one and there were many jokes that he would charge them double to get home again. Ned would stay with the ferry till all the guests had crossed the rife, and then he and Rob would follow the bridal party to the tide mill.

"See you later!" Alys called to him. "Don't be late!"

Ned waved and pulled the ferry back to the island as the wagon went towards the mill. Mr. Miller was standing at the five-barred gate to the yard. "Come in! Come in! Toast to the bride!" he exclaimed. "And we have a ham to give you for your wedding feast."

"I'm grateful," Mr. Stoney said, turning the horses into the mill yard.

"We can't stop long," Mrs. Stoney cautioned him, stepping down from the box. "We have to get to Stoney Farm before Sir William. Sir William is coming to our house for the bridal dinner."

"You'll see him riding past," Mr. Miller assured her. "He'll stop for a glass of my ale too, I don't doubt. I've never known him go past my door."

Richard Stoney handed the reins of his father's horses to the stable lad. Mrs. Wheatley carefully put her cake on the wagon floor and climbed down from the tailgate.

"I don't know their ale is that fine," she said quietly to Alinor. "I don't think Sir William needs to leave home to drink good ale."

"Course he doesn't," Alinor replied loyally, hardly knowing what she was saying. "But I'm glad Mrs. Miller is drinking a toast to Alys. She works her so hard!"

"A smoky kitchen," Mrs. Wheatley whispered, using the old description of a shrewish housewife.

Alinor smiled. She could feel the child move in her belly and for a moment she leaned against the doorframe and thought how weary she was, and what a long day stretched before her.

"You all right?" Mrs. Wheatley asked.

"Oh, yes," Alinor said brightly. "I'm happy for Alys; but it's been a strain, you know?"

The two of them went into the kitchen and through to the parlor where previously Alinor had only been before to clean and polish. But today the parlor was open, and the wedding party were invited guests. The round wooden table was set with glasses and biscuits, and Mrs. Miller was wearing her best apron and white cap. Mr. Miller warmed the ale at the fireside and Jane poured a small cup for everyone. "Where is Peter?" Alinor asked Jane.

"Gone to play with the Smith boys," she said.

"Here's to the health of the bride, the new Mrs. Stoney!" Mr. Miller said, holding up his pewter mug. "And to the happiness of the young couple."

"Here's health!" everyone replied, raising their glasses. "Health and happiness!"

Alys, her hand resting on Richard's arm, smiled at everyone. "Thank you," she said.

"God bless us all," Richard added.

Mr. Miller, excited at having the floor to himself, as Mrs. Miller went out to the kitchen, was about to say more. "I well recall my own wedding day . . . ," he started when there was a sudden loud scream from the kitchen.

"Thieves, thieves," Mrs. Miller was shouting. "Thieves in my—"

She burst into the parlor, Jane's red leather dowry purse in her hand, her fingers sooty from the chimney bricks, her face blanched with shock.

"God save us," Mrs. Wheatley said. "Sit down, Mrs. Miller. Sit down. What's wrong?"

Mrs. Miller pushed her aside. "Look!" she said, holding out the purse. "Look!"

"What's this, my dear?" Mr. Miller said. "Surely not . . ."

"My savings purse," Mrs. Miller gabbled. "Jane's dowry money. I got it out just now to give the girl a half crown for her wedding day. Not that I owe her a penny. But I meant to give her a gift, for her wedding day . . . and—"

"Never tell me you've been robbed!" her husband demanded.

In answer she shook the purse at him. There was a reassuring clink of coins, there was a weight to the purse. It was clearly full of coins.

"You're not short," he argued. He took it from her hand and weighed it. "There'll be forty, perhaps fifty, pounds in there," he said. "I can tell from the weight and the chink of the coins. You get to know—"

"I've not been robbed," she said furiously. "Not robbed. I would rather have been robbed than this . . . I've been bewitched."

There was a hiss of superstitious fear from everyone in the little parlor.

"What?" Mr. Miller asked.

"What?" Mrs. Wheatley echoed. "Here, Mrs. Miller, sit down. You don't know what you're saying."

Mrs. Wheatley helped Mrs. Miller into a chair. Alinor came forward and felt her forehead for the flush of fever, and caught a sideways glance from Alys. The bride was as white as if she had seen a ghost. Her lips parted, she turned as if to speak to her mother but she said nothing.

Alinor felt herself grow terribly cold. Her hand dropped from Mrs. Miller's forehead. "What's happened?" she said quietly. "What's happened, Mrs. Miller?"

"Ma . . ." Alys whispered.

Without saying another word, Mrs. Miller snatched the purse from her husband's hand and opened the neck of the purse. "See this? Look what's in here! Look at it. I'll show you!" She gestured towards Alinor, who unthinkingly cupped her hands and Mrs. Miller poured out the contents of the purse. The coins were hot from their hiding place, and strangely light. Alinor held two handfuls of faerie gold, the shaved and chipped coins that she liked to collect, the lost currency of the old ones, the ancient coins of the Saxon shore. Inside the purse they had chinked like coins, weighed like coins, but here, spilled into Alinor's hands, they were clearly counterfeit. With her hands filled with her own collection of coins, Alinor looked across at the blank horror of her daughter's face, and knew at once what she had done.

"Faerie gold," Mrs. Miller said fearfully. "In my house. Changeling treasure. I had a purse here of good gold and silver, Jane's dowry. I rarely touch it. I keep it safe in my chim—in my hiding place. And some witch has exchanged my savings for faerie gold. So that I wouldn't know anything was missing! If I took it out and weighed it in my hands I would think all was well. I've been enchanted, and I didn't even know. Some witch has taken it all. All my money!"

"If I said once, I've said a hundred times: it was a stupid hiding place," Mr. Miller started.

"What about the chest?" She turned on him. "The chest under the bed?"

He blanched and spun on his heel and tore from the room. They could hear his heavy feet pounding up the stair to the bedroom, the creak of the bedroom door, the two swift steps across the wooden floor, and then the noise of the chest being dragged out from under the bed.

Alinor, her hands filled with faerie gold, stood as still as everyone else and listened.

"God save us, God spare us," Mrs. Miller whispered into the silent room. "That's all that we have in the world. We'll be ruined if that's bewitched too."

They could hear him fumbling with the keys and then the creak of the lid. They could hear his sigh of relief and the chink of coins being stirred. Then they heard him slam down the lid, lock up, and come slowly down the stairs, putting the keys in his waistcoat pocket.

"Thank God it's there," he said, gray-faced in the doorway.

"The tide-mill money is safe. It's your savings that have gone. Jane's dowry. How much was there?"

Even in the grip of terrible loss Mrs. Miller was not going to tell her husband how much she had put away over the years. "Pounds, I had," Mrs. Miller said viciously. "More than forty pounds. How am I going to get it back from a witch?"

"Could be a passing thief," Mrs. Wheatley ventured. "Someone from the yard?"

"What thief leaves handfuls of faerie gold? Nobody has come in here; nobody knows where I hide my money. It's a witch. It's got to be a witch. She's magicked away my savings and left me hers in exchange. This is witch money. This is witch work."

The room was silent. The silence thickened, curdled. Slowly, as slowly as a thought dawning, everyone turned to Alinor. Everyone looked at Alinor, who had worked for Mrs. Miller ever since she was a girl, who was known as a cunning woman with skills not of this world. Alinor, who needed gold for her daughter's dowry, her son's apprenticeship, who was said by her own husband to whore for faerie lords. Slowly, everyone looked at Alinor, where she stood, her face very pale, her hands filled with faerie gold.

"You saw me take the purse from the chimney on the day you went to the market for me and bought my lace collar," Mrs. Miller said.

Alinor remembered turning her head away and seeing the reflection of Mrs. Miller fetching her purse in the shiny silver trencher.

She swallowed. "That was months ago," she said. "In the autumn. Last year."

"But you knew of her hiding place?" Mrs. Wheatley asked.

Alinor turned to her friend. "Yes. So did many, I should think."

"But you knew, Alinor?"

"And you needed money," Mrs. Stoney pointed out. "I never thought you would get the dowry together."

"We worked," Alys burst into speech. "Everyone saw us. We

both worked. Like dogs. Here at the mill, everyone saw us working here, and we spun, and I worked the ferry. And my father gave me . . . and my uncle lent us . . ."

"I never thought it'd be enough," Mr. Stoney contributed. "I thought you must've borrowed from someone."

"No!" Alinor said proudly, and then thought she should have said yes.

"I helped Alys," Richard interrupted, and received a savage look from his mother.

"You had no business to," she said sharply.

"And even so," Mr. Stoney said, "you only had your wages."

"His inheritance?" Alinor said. Her hands were shaking, the faerie gold sparkled.

"What inheritance? He's got no inheritance," Mr. Stoney said.

Alys looked at her mother, her eyes huge in her pale face and silently shook her head. There was no inheritance.

"Mrs. Reekie, say it isn't so!" Mr. Miller said to her quietly. "I've known you for years. Say it isn't so."

"Of course it isn't so!" Alinor repeated. Even to her own ears her voice sounded weak, the denial unconvincing. She stretched her hands towards Mr. Miller's reassuring bulk, as if to give him the faerie gold.

"No, I don't want it!" he said, stepping back and whipping his hands behind his back. "I don't want it in my house."

"Let me throw it out the door then!" Alinor turned to the kitchen, and the open door to the yard. But Mrs. Miller suddenly barred the way.

"Not so fast," she said. "You'll have to answer for this. No dashing out. You hold that, till you prove it isn't yours!"

"And where's my dowry?" Jane demanded.

Alinor tried to laugh, her hands sticky with faerie coins. "Mrs. Miller, I've been your neighbor for all my life. My mother delivered you—"

"And everyone said she was a witch."

"No, they didn't."

"She did charming. She was a cunning woman. She could

find things. She could take things," Mrs. Miller reminded her. "She could cast . . ."

"But I don't. You know I don't."

"Your hands are full of faerie gold! Where's it come from?"

"I didn't take your money!" Alinor exclaimed. "I didn't change it into this!"

"Lay ahold of her!" Mrs. Miller said urgently, as if Alinor's raised voice changed everything. "She's cursing us. And you"—she ordered her husband—"you get the other church warden or the minister. She'll have to be charged."

"Back to the church?"

"Are you arguing with me?" Mrs. Miller shouted at him. "A witch in our house with her hands full of faerie gold, and you're standing there arguing with me?"

Mr. Miller cast one incredulous look at Alinor and went out of the parlor into the kitchen, and pulled on his winter cape. He threw open the door to the yard and everyone heard the sound of a horse. "Sir William," Mr. Miller said with evident relief. "His lordship's coming. He's a magistrate. He can decide what's to be done."

Everyone in the parlor crowded around Alinor and led her through the kitchen and out into the mill yard to greet the solitary horseman. But it was not Sir William. It was James Summer.

"His lordship's on his way." He smiled, but then he was silenced as he saw Alinor, her cupped hands filled with coins, surrounded by frightened people. "What is this? What's happening here?"

"It's Mrs. Reekie, taken for a witch," Mrs. Wheatley said, matter-of-fact, going to the horse's head and looking up at James. "Mrs. Miller here has had her savings changed into faerie gold, and she accuses Alinor Reekie, who makes no defense."

"What?" James demanded incredulously.

Alinor could not bring herself to face him, could not speak to him.

"It's not true," Alys said, pushing forwards. "Of course, it's not true."

"Then how are my savings turned into faerie gold, and the true coin gone?" Mrs. Miller demanded. "Who would do that, if not a witch? Who could do such a thing? And doesn't everyone know that Alinor has always loved the faerie gold? Even when she was a girl she would find it and keep it?"

"I didn't steal your money! Of course I knew where you had it hidden. I've known for months—probably everyone does. But I didn't steal it. I wouldn't steal from you, or anyone! I've been in and out of your house and your yard all my life. I go into people's houses all the time. There's not many houses on Sealsea Island that I've not attended, and I've never ever taken anything. I'm a licensed midwife—"

"Not got a license now," a man remarked, making Alinor break off and look at him.

"That's not my fault!" she said. "How can you say that against me?"

"What about Ned's wife and baby?"

Alinor gasped. "She lost her baby. I did everything I knew . . ."

More wedding guests had followed James into the yard. Alinor looked around at a score of her neighbors and saw puzzled and fearful faces.

"You know me. You all know me. I would never . . ." Alinor could barely speak, even in her own defense.

"Well, someone did it," Mr. Miller said heavily, looking up at James, who was still mounted, frozen with indecision, as everyone turned to him to rule on what was to be done. "What do you think, sir?"

"Mrs. Reekie will have to go before a magistrate to clear her name," James said reluctantly.

"Is Sir William following you?" Mr. Stoney asked.

"Yes," James said. "He's on his way."

"He's a magistrate. He'll do. He can hear the case against her now as soon as he comes," said Mr. Miller, a church warden who knew the law. He went a little closer to James and took the reins of his horse. "We don't want her carried off to prison in Chichester," he muttered quickly. "She's a good woman. We don't want her put on trial for a thief. She'll be hanged if more than three pounds are missing, and there was fifty pounds in that purse. Best keep this here, in the village. Best his lordship rules here, where we can keep it among ourselves. Better get started, sir, so no one thinks of Chichester."

James was shocked into action. He dismounted from his horse and the stable lad took it to the barn. "I'll take the evidence here," he said loud enough for everyone to hear. "Sir William and I will confer when he arrives."

He tried to exchange a glance with Alinor, but she was looking away from him, at her daughter. Alys was white. She clung to Richard's arm and her gaze was fixed on her mother's face.

"Where's the defendant's brother?" James asked, thinking Edward would have a strong voice in this frightened community.

"We don't need him," Mrs. Miller interrupted. "He's got no control over her at all. She does whatever she wants. He couldn't even save his own wife. She has no father, and now she says she has no husband, though Zachary Reekie has no grave."

"Just disappeared," someone said from the back of the crowd. "Spoke against her one day, and the next day he was gone."

"Mr. Ferryman is an important witness," James overruled them. "Send for him."

James's calm voice, his tone of authority, was stilling the sense of panic. Mr. Miller, looking around the people crowded into his yard, felt the desire for excitement, for violence, was diminishing.

"Aye, that's for the best. You go and fetch him, lad," he said to the stable boy. He turned back to James. "You'll want a table, and papers, sir," he said, quietly deferential. "Best sit in the kitchen, if you don't mind. It's the biggest room, and we've got the table there and the Carver chair."

James nodded and Mr. Miller led the way into the kitchen, ordered that the big kitchen table be dragged to the back of the room, set the high-backed chair behind it, and indicated that James should sit in justice, with Mr. Miller standing beside him as a makeshift clerk of the court.

"I have no authority," James muttered to him as he took his seat.

"Know Latin?"

"Yes, of course."

"That'll do."

James sat square in his chair and put his hands before him on the table as everyone crowded into the room, sweeping Alinor, with them, still holding the old coins. Mrs. Miller put a sheet of paper before James and Jane set a pot of ink and a pen before him. As if they were watching a mystery play, the wedding guests filled the room, pushing Alinor forwards, to stand isolated before the table. Alys would have gone to her, but Richard took hold of her hand and gently pulled her to his father and mother at the side of the room.

"I want . . ." she whispered to him.

"Better wait here," he whispered back. "See how this goes. Why did she think I had an inheritance?"

"Oh, I don't know," Alys said, silenced.

James dipped the pen in the ink, hoping that Ned would come soon and Sir William swiftly behind him. All he wanted to do now was play for time.

"Name," he said as if to a stranger.

There was a little satisfied sigh. The deep terror of witchcraft was under the control of an authority. They need not scrabble to protect themselves against the unknown powers of the other world: a gentleman who knew Latin was taking responsibility.

"You know my name," Alinor replied sulkily.

There was a murmur against her defiance.

"She's Goodwife Alinor Reekie," Mrs. Miller interrupted. "Sister to Edward Ferryman, of Ferry-house."

James lowered his eyes and wrote his lover's name at the top of the paper.

"Age?" he asked.

"I am twenty-seven," Alinor replied.

"Occupation?"

"I am a licensed midwife and healer."

"No license," someone reminded them all from the back of the room.

Alinor lifted her head. "I am a midwife and healer," she amended. "Of good repute."

"And the accusation?"

Mrs. Miller stepped forward, trembling with anger, her voice low and passionate. "I am Mrs. Miller, of Mill Farm. I keep my savings, my daughter Jane's dowry, in a hiding place in my kitchen." Dramatically she pointed to the fireplace. "There! Right there! Behind a loose brick in the chimney."

Everyone looked to where the brick was missing from the chimney breast, and back to Alinor's white face.

"Months ago, in the autumn, in September it was, she was running an errand for me to Chichester Friday market. I trusted her to buy something for me. I trusted her!"

There was a hushed comment on the notoriously mistrustful nature of Mrs. Miller. She continued: "I made her turn her back as I took my savings purse out of the hiding place. My secret hiding place. But she saw me. She had her back to me, but even so, she saw me!"

There was a ripple of amazement.

"How could this be?" James asked skeptically, his pen poised.

"With her special sight she saw me, though her head was turned away. When she turned round I could see in her face that she had found me out. I just knew. She had seen me, with her witchy eyes."

There was a murmur. Everyone but Mrs. Wheatley and the Stoney family agreed that this must be proof. Mr. Miller shook his head.

"You may not call her a witch until it is proven," James reprimanded her, his level voice cutting through the talk. He turned to Alinor. "Did you see this hiding place?"

"I saw her reflection in the trencher," she said shortly. She gestured to the silver dish ostentatiously displayed on the big wooden dresser. "She told me to face the big platter and I could see her reflection, like in a looking glass. I wasn't looking for her;

but I did see her. But many people know that she kept her savings there. She sometimes paid with hot coins and her fingers were sooty. It was no mystery."

A couple of the Millers' gleaners muttered yes, they had been paid with warm coins.

"Is this the case?" James asked a little too eagerly. "The hiding place was generally known?"

"Only a witch could have seen that reflection," Mrs. Miller said staunchly. "No one else could have made me out."

Mrs. Wheatley pushed her way across the crowded room to the sideboard, looked in the silver platter. "You can see," she reported to James. "You can clearly see."

"Why did you not change your hiding place?" James asked. "If you thought it had been seen?"

Mrs. Miller hesitated. "I didn't," she admitted. "I didn't."

Her words fell a little flat and she struggled to restore her credibility. "Because she enchanted me!" she declared. "I forgot all about it until now. I simply forgot until now, and I trusted her again and again, because I had forgotten that she had seen me. What's that if not spell casting?"

"Do you deny this?" James prompted Alinor, but she was not looking at him. She was looking across the room at Alys's white face, seeing that Richard Stoney was holding her away. Alinor barely heard James; she was gazing at her daughter, her beloved daughter. She was thinking what she might have to do to keep Alys safe.

"You have to answer me," James prompted her.

She turned her head and looked at him indifferently. "Yes, I did see her in the reflection," she confirmed. "But I didn't do anything about it. I'm not a thief. I don't care where she keeps her egg money."

"Egg money! There was more than forty pounds in there!" Mrs. Miller exclaimed.

"My dowry!" Jane reminded everyone.

Alinor shrugged, as contemptuous as a lady of court. "I don't know. I never saw what was inside the purse. I never held the purse. I don't know the weight or how much you had saved. I only ever saw it in your hand as you gave me money to buy your lace. I never even touched it, did I?"

Alinor's disdain was more than Mrs. Miller could bear. "I don't doubt you changed the money into faerie gold without touching it! Without taking the purse from its hiding place!" she shouted. "I don't doubt it for a moment! I don't doubt you never touched it; but did it all at midnight from the mire, where you're always alone, walking in moonlight, on paths that no one else follows, talking to yourself."

Alinor swayed back a little from the venom in the woman's voice.

"She didn't take it!" Alys suddenly spoke up, cutting through the rising noise, stepping forward, pulling away from her new husband. "I know she did not!"

Alinor raised her head and met her daughter's eyes. "Alys, you say nothing," she ordered. She looked past her to Richard's strained face. "Take her away," she said quietly. "It's her wedding day. She shouldn't be here. Take her home. Take her to her new home."

He nodded, his young face shocked, and tried to guide Alys to the door, but she resisted him.

"I won't go," she told him.

"Then stay silent," Richard said. "As your mother tells you."

Alys turned to her mother. "Ma," she said desperately. "You know. . . ."

"Yes, I know." Alinor nodded. "I know. Just go, Alys."

"Plotting!" Mrs. Miller exclaimed. "So there's two of them!"

With relief, James saw Ned enter the kitchen and look around, bewildered. Rob came in behind him. "What's all this?" Ned asked. "What's going on?"

"Mrs. Reekie has been accused of stealing Mrs. Miller's savings by witchcraft and leaving faerie gold in its place," James said.

Ned walked up to the table, brushing through the crowd. "Lord, you people," he said scornfully. "Can't you even go to a wedding feast without stopping for a quarrel?" He went to his sister's side and she turned to him, her hands filled with the coins, and at once he checked, frozen at the sight of them. "What's this?" he said in a quite different voice. "What're you doing with your coins, Alinor?"

"Are these her coins? Her own coins? D'you know them?" Mrs. Miller demanded, her voice sharp with excitement.

"Do you recognize them?" Mr. Miller asked.

"Yes," Ned said simply. "I'd think so. But one looks the same as another to me. I take no interest in them. Alinor—what's happening?"

Rob came to his mother's side and she tried to smile reassuringly, her hands filled with the damning evidence.

Everyone turned to James. Nobody had any doubts about the accusation now. Ned had given absolute confirmation of his sister's guilt.

"Mrs. Reekie, how did your coins get into Mrs. Miller's purse?" James asked quietly.

Mutely, Alinor shook her head. Ned took his hat off his head and she tipped the coins into it. Two of them were such light scraps of silver that they stuck to her sweating palms and she brushed them off. There was a little gasp of horror as if she were peeling faerie gold from her own skin. Ned put his hat down on the table before James as if it were evidence, and he did not want to touch it.

"I don't know," Alinor said steadily. "I have no idea."

"I think we should wait for Sir William's coming," James said.

Alys shot him a desperate look. "You're sitting there, you decide," she said. "This is a mistake, obviously. Let my mother go home. Let's all go on to the wedding."

"Hush, Alys," Alinor whispered to her.

"My mother is innocent of anything, sir," Rob said awkwardly. "Please clear her name."

"Oh, for God's sake," Mrs. Wheatley said under her breath. "These poor children."

"It's her own faerie gold," Mrs. Miller said flatly. "As her brother says. Transformed from my good coin. Like alchemy. Gold to dross. What could this be but enchantment? She must be a witch."

"Prick her," someone said from the back of the room and at once everyone spoke.

"And search her for marks."

"Strip her."

"Get the women to look . . ."

"Devil's teats . . ."

"Test her with a Bible!"

"Moles on her skin . . ."

"The devil leaves his marks."

Alinor was as white as her collar, frozen into stillness.

"Sir," Rob said urgently to his tutor, "they've no right. Don't let them get hold of her. Don't let them . . ."

James tried to assert himself over the rising noise. "I am still taking evidence here," he claimed. "And I will take a decision."

"In writing," Mr. Miller supported him. "Decision in writing."

"Swim her!" someone said, and there was immediate agreement. "Swim her."

"That's the only way!"

"Search her, and then swim her."

For the first time Alinor looked towards James. Her eyes were black with terror. "I can't," she said flatly. "That, I can't."

"She's very afraid of water." Ned spoke rapidly to James. "Very afraid. She's afraid even on my ferry. She can't be swum."

"Stop this!" Alys demanded, her voice high with panic. "Stop this!"

"Sir?" Rob's young face was anguished. "Mr. Summer?"

James rose to his feet. "This is not the time or the place," he ruled. "I am going to order her arrest—"

"She's already arrested!" someone shouted from the back. "We want her tested!"

"Tested now!"

"In water!"

The crowd surged forward and Ned and Rob found they were pushing against grasping hands and a mass of bodies. Ned tried to get his arms around Alinor and pull her towards him, Rob faced out towards the people, who were crowding more and more closely. He slapped their hands away from his mother, trying to get between her and them, but they were coming from every side of the room and he could not block them all. Richard Stoney had hold of Alys, dragging her back from her mother, pulling her away, following his own mother and father, who were leaving, thrusting their way through the crowd, out to the yard to the wedding cart, fearful of what was happening.

"Stop this!" James shouted, but his authority was melting away in the crowd's rising heat. "I order you to stand still!"

Ned got Alinor around the waist and was pulling her away from the crowd in the kitchen, taking her into the house, towards the parlor door. Alinor, with people pulling at her gown, dragging at her apron, snatching off her cap so her hair tumbled down around her frightened white face, was fighting to go with him, pushing as hard as she could to stay in his arms and make their way towards the parlor. James, seeing what they were doing, came out from behind the table and opened the parlor door, got hold of Ned's jacket, and hauled him backwards, the three of them head-to-head when he felt Ned suddenly flinch and recoil: "You've a belly on you!"

Alinor, white as skimmed milk, her jacket ripped from her shoulders, her cap lost, her apron pulled aside so everyone could see the swell of her pregnancy, looked her brother in the face amid all the noise and said: "Yes, God forgive me."

"A belly?"

"Not now," James said quickly, but it was too late: someone in the forefront of the crowd had overheard.

"The witch's whelping," someone exclaimed.

"No!" Mrs. Wheatley exclaimed. She pushed through the crowd to Alinor's side. One glance at her blanched face and her curving body confirmed her guilt. "Oh! Alinor! God forgive you. What've you done?"

"With child?" Mr. Miller asked, disbelievingly. "Alinor Reekie?"

Everyone was stunned into silence and stillness. Alinor turned to face shocked and hostile gazes. Rob was looking at his mother in complete bewilderment. "What? Ma?"

"Whose child?" Mrs. Miller demanded, her voice sharp with renewed fear. "That's what I want to know? Who's the father? What's the father? What has she done now?"

In the frightened silence, they heard Sir William ride into the yard and the clatter as he dismounted and came to the kitchen door.

He took in the scene in one swift glance: Alinor held between her brother and James Summer, her cap off, her hair falling down, her apron torn, and her rounded belly straining against her gown. Nobody said anything.

"Mr. Summer," said his lordship icily. "Come out here, and tell me what the devil is going on."

Everyone spoke at once, but Sir William threw up a hand to silence them. "Mr. Summer, if you please."

James threw one anguished look at Alinor, released her, and went out, the crowd silently parting to let him go. Ned stood between his sister and their neighbors but now there was no need to protect her; nobody wanted to touch her. Nobody moved, or even spoke. They were all straining their ears to hear the low-voiced conversation between the two men on the threshold, and then the snap of Sir William's fingers summoning the miller's lad, and the clip-clop of Sir William's horse being led away to a stable. Alinor fixed her gaze on the floor. Long moments passed, an unseasonal bee buzzed against the parlor window. Alinor, distracted by the noise, turned her head and made a little gesture as if she would release it.

"Leave it," Ned ordered tersely.

Sir William appeared in the doorway. "Good people, don't crush yourselves, now. No need to be all squashed in here. You'd better all come out into the yard," he said generally.

Everyone jostled out into the harsh winter sunshine of the yard. The tide was on the ebb and seagulls were crying over the mire. The millpond gates were bumping closed, pushed together by the deep water in the millpond. There was a trickle of water, overflowing the top of the gates.

"Mrs. Reekie, these good women will have to examine you, you know that," Sir William ruled.

Alinor bowed her head to her landlord.

"Mrs. Wheatley, would you choose three women to take Mrs. Reekie into the house privately, and examine her closely for witch's marks, ask her to name the father of her child, and when she expects to be confined."

Mrs. Wheatley, her lips compressed, looked around the crowd of neighbors, old friends, and some old enemies. Mrs. Stoney flinched back against their wagon. Blandly, Mrs. Wheatley ignored her. "Mrs. Jaden, Mrs. Smith, Mrs. Huntley," she said, naming her cousin, her friend, and a woman who worked as a midwife in the south of the island. Sir William waved them towards the house, and the four women went back inside with Alinor walking slowly between them.

"I won't have her in my house!" Mrs. Miller said furiously. "You should do it in the yard. Strip her naked out here!"

"You will oblige me, Mrs. Miller, I am sure," said his lordship. "We're not complete heathens." He turned aside and spoke quietly with James. Alys tried to edge closer to hear, but Richard Stoney held her tightly. He held to her as if he would save her from drowning, as his mother and his father stood at a little distance, looking at the white face of the daughter-in-law they had never thought good enough.

Mrs. Stoney turned to her husband, put her mouth to his ear. "The dowry," she said quietly. "I have it in my pocket. Should we—"

"Be still," he whispered. "We'll look at it when we get home and this is all over. They're wed, it's the dowry she brought. You saw it, it was good coin. Leave it be for now."

She nodded and waited in silence like all the other neighbors. After a quarter of an hour the searcher women came out of the house again, Alinor walking with them, her cap off, her golden hair tumbled as if they had run their fingers through it, hunting for signs. There was a thin raw scratch on the side of Alinor's neck, and a trickle of blood from her ear to her white collar, which was torn. Rob exclaimed: "Ma!" and she gave him a weary glance. "It's nothing," she tried to reassure him. "Nothing."

Mrs. Wheatley walked up to her employer and stood before him.

"Have you examined Mrs. Reekie?" he asked her.

"We have."

"Is she with child?"

"Yes, sir. She believes that she will be brought to bed in the month of May."

There was a muttered exclamation from the Stoneys. Richard looked at Alys as if he would ask her something, but met such a glare from her blue eyes that he said nothing.

"So the child was conceived . . . ?"

"In August or September, sir."

"Did she name the father of her child?"

James cleared his throat as if to speak; but Mrs. Wheatley continued with her report. "No, sir, she is incorrigible. When we begged her, for the sake of God and for her own good reputation, to give his name she said nothing."

Sir William nodded. "Is it her missing husband's child?" he suggested.

Mrs. Wheatley was quick. "Nobody has seen Zachary the fisherman for over a year, sir. But, of course, he could have come back and visited her secretly."

"Is that what happened?" Sir William asked Alinor, giving her a way out from the accusation of whoring. "Think before you speak, Mrs. Reekie. Think very carefully. Is that what happened?"

"No," she said shortly.

His lordship looked at her for a moment. "Are you sure?"

Alys whispered "Ma!"

Alinor looked towards her. "No," she said again.

Sir William returned his attention to the searcher women. "Did you scratch her for a witch?"

"We did," Mrs. Wheatley said. "With the darning needle that we found in the sewing case in the parlor." She turned politely to Mrs. Miller. "We left it on the table if you want to throw it away."

Mrs. Miller gave an exaggerated shudder. "You take it away. It'll be cursed."

"And did she bleed?" Sir William pursued his inquiry.

"She bled like a mortal woman and she felt the pain. Not very much, but red blood, like any woman." She pointed to the scratch on Alinor's neck. Alinor stood like a statue, her eyes on the ground.

"And did you examine her for witch's marks?"

"We did," Mrs. Smith answered. "She has no extra teats that we could see; but she has a mole in the shape of a moon, very uncommon and very suspicious, on her ribs."

"In the shape of a moon?"

"A new moon. A sickle moon. A witch's moon."

There was a deep satisfied sigh from the listening crowd, and Sir William fell silent at this incriminating evidence. The crowd, staring at Alinor, waited for him to speak, content to wait for his decision, since there could be only one decision from him. It was as if they were enjoying the pause before the final act of a mystery play, the chance to savor the sentence that would come, waiting for the violence that would break out.

"The purse," Sir William said quietly to Alinor. "Did you steal the money? Did you put the old coins in place of Mrs. Miller's savings?"

"I did not," Alinor said.

"These old coins and chips of coins. Are they yours?"

Alinor looked at her brother's hat, which one of the searcher women handed to Mr. Miller, who held it out at arm's length, as if the little silver tokens would burn him.

"They look like my coins."

"You keep them at Ferry-house?"

Alinor glanced at Ned.

"She does," he said miserably.

"Then how did they get from there to here?"

Alinor choked on her answer. She looked at the sky over Sir William's flinty face, she looked at the ground beneath his polished boots. There was a long silence.

"Sir William . . ." Alys began, her voice thin and trembling. "Your lordship . . ." She detached herself from Richard's grip and took one step forwards.

"I did it," Alinor interrupted her daughter.

"Witchcraft!" Mrs. Miller exclaimed. "Just as I said. Witchcraft."

"Oh, Alinor, God forgive you!" Mr. Miller joined in.

"Was she going to pass off her baby as ours?" Richard clamped Alys to his side, his eyes burning. "Are you truly with child? Our baby? Were you going to make me a cuckold twice over—put a faerie child in my cradle, and my wife not the mother?"

"What?" demanded Mr. Stoney.

Sir William and James exchanged shocked glances, but events were moving too fast for them.

"No, no!" said Alys, her hand twisting in his grip, but he held her tightly. "For God's sake, no!"

"But you knew that your mother was with child too? Conceived at the same time? How's that possible?"

Alys looked despairingly towards her white-faced mother. "It's nothing to do with us, Richard. And the money—"

"You hush," Alinor said firmly to her daughter. She was calm now, as if the needle scratch had bled away all shame. She nodded to Richard. "Take her away," she said. "I told you before. Take her to your home. I don't want her here."

"Ma! I have to tell them—"

"Never," Alinor said firmly. "You have nothing to say that can help me. Just go."

"We don't have to do what you say!" Mr. Stoney blustered.

"For pity's sake, take her away," Alinor said simply to him, and Richard nodded and half dragged and half lifted Alys towards the wagon. His father and mother followed, torn between their desire to join their neighbors in the trial of a witch, and the horror that the witch was now related to their family.

They were climbing in the wagon and setting the horses going when someone spoke up from the back of the crowd: "Swim her!"

"I didn't do it with witchcraft, I did it as an exchange," Alinor said rapidly to Sir William. "It was a loan. That's why I left everything that I have, to show that I would pay it back. As a token that it was me and I would repay."

"Faerie gold," someone said. "It'd fade to nothing if anyone but her held it."

"And who's the father of her child?" someone else demanded.

"We should take her to Chichester for the hangman!" someone suggested.

"Satan's child." There was a low hiss from the back of the crowd. "A faerie-born boy."

"Her husband always said Rob was none of his begetting," someone remembered.

Rob turned a horrified look at his mother.

"It's not so!" Alinor cried out. "It's not so! Not so! Rob is a good boy from a bad father!" She turned to Sir William, gabbling in her distress: "Your lordship, don't let them speak ill of Rob! You know what a good boy he is." She turned to Ned. "Take him away," she implored him. "Get him away."

"Enough!" Sir William exclaimed, cutting through the rising shouts that Alinor should be taken to Chichester and hanged. "We'll swim her," he ruled, into the sudden avid silence. "In the millpond. If she comes up alive she's innocent of all charges, and nobody says anything against her again. She repays the money to Mrs. Miller as she says she intended. Agreed? We swim her to see God's will! Agreed? That's my judgment, and my ruling! Agreed?"

"Swim her," half a dozen voices assented.

"Quite right," they said. "Duck her."

Alinor, blank with terror, turned unseeing to her brother, Ned, but he was looking down at the ground, shamed before everyone.

"Ned, take Rob away," she whispered to him. "Ned!"

His head came up at the urgent tone in her voice.

"Take Rob away!"

Her whisper recalled him from his misery at her shame. "Yes," he muttered. "Come on, Rob. Let's get out of here. It'll all be over in a moment."

"They shan't touch her!" Rob exclaimed, pushing between his mother and the crowd, though the searcher women laid hold of her and would not let him take her.

James grabbed his arm. "Better this, than she's accused of theft," he said urgently. "This will be over in a moment. But if they get her to Chichester they'll hang her for theft on the gallows."

"Sir, she can't bear it! The pond is deep water. She can't bear it! You know—"

"Yes, I can," Alinor interrupted him. Her face was white as whey, her eyes huge with fear in her ashen face. "But you go, Rob. I can't stand for you to see this."

Already people were running to the mill to get ropes to truss her up, shuffling their feet and hesitating, not knowing how to lay hold of her, frightened of touching her, but pushed forwards by more people behind them. Sir William watched them, scowling, and nodded to Ned. "Take the lad away," he said. "That's an order. He shouldn't see."

Ned took Rob by the shoulder and forced him through the yard gate, towards the ferry, bobbing on the ebbing tide. "We'll just wait here, beside the ferry," Ned said, his voice gruff. "Then we'll go back and get her when it's over."

"How can she be with child?" Rob whispered to his uncle.

Ned shook his head. "Shamed," was all he said shortly.

"But how can she?"

Ned wrapped the boy in his arms and pushed the young face

against the rough weave of his jacket. "Pray," he advised him. "And don't ask me, I can't bear it. My own sister! Under my roof!"

James watched the two leave. "How can we stop this?" he demanded urgently.

"We can't," said Sir William. "Let them do it. Get it over with."

Alinor did not look at either man as the crowd encircled her, tied her hands behind her back and her legs together with coil after coil of rope around her long skirts. Then they herded her towards the mill, supporting her hobbled walk, half carrying her. She went unresisting, her face so greenish-white that she looked half-drowned already. Mrs. Wheatley was trailing behind, shaking her head, Mrs. Miller angrily leading the way.

They got to the millpond bank and looked in the green weedy depths. The pond was full, the tide gates closed, holding back the water from the mire where the sea was draining away. The gates rubbed against each other with the squeak of damp wood, pressed by the deep mass of water. The pond was limpid, like a deep bowl set beside the muddy harbor. The old walls were slippery and green, the water gates trailing seaweed like hair. But there were no steps to get into the pond and it was too wide for a rope to pull her from one side to another. Nobody wanted to go near the edge: the water was menacing in itself, in its dark depths, deathly cold in winter.

"We need more rope!" someone said.

"Just throw her in from the bank as she is, tied," came the suggestion. "See if she can get out on her own?"

"The mill wheel." Mrs. Miller was inspired by spite. "Strap her on the mill wheel."

Incredulously, her husband looked at her. "On my wheel?" he demanded.

"Two turns!" someone said from the back of the crowd. "Strap her on and turn it twice in the millrace. That's a fair test."

"My wheel?" Mr. Miller said again. He looked at Sir William, horrified.

"It turns fast?" his lordship asked quietly. "You can dunk her and bring her out again?"

"It can turn fast if it's not milling," the man said. "If the stone's not engaged, it will go as fast as the water pours in."

"Two turns," his lordship ruled, raising his voice over the murmurs of excitement. "And if she comes up alive, she's no witch. She repays the money, and she's released. Agreed?"

"Aye. Fair enough, yes. Agreed," the people called out, excited at the prospect of a witch trial, looking from the slight woman to the huge wheel, which stood motionless, the bottom blades deep in the millrace, the upper blades white with frost in the freezing air.

Alinor's knees were buckling beneath her, she swayed on her feet, fainting with fear. She had lost her voice. She barely knew where she was. James could not look at her, as two of the searcher women took her bound arms at the elbows and half led and half dragged her away from the bank of the millpond, to the platform at the side of the wheel. The women tightened her hands behind her back, and twisted the rope around and around her breasts and her swelling belly.

"Better than hanging," Sir William reminded James, as they stepped on the platform beside the wheel.

"She's terrified of water," James whispered.

"Still better than hanging."

The men had to lift her, as limp as a new corpse, up to the mill wheel.

"Put her on the blades of the wheel," Mrs. Miller suggested at the forefront of the crowd. "Tie her on so she don't slip off."

Wordlessly, Mr. Miller gestured to the mill lad to hold the wheel steady by stepping on it with both feet, holding the green blades, and leaning back as a counterweight, as they lifted Alinor by her shoulders and legs and laid her on one of the blades of the wheel. They took another rope and lashed her on.

"Make sure she's tied tight," Sir William ordered. Aside to James he said: "We don't want her falling off and getting trapped under the wheel."

James could see her rounded belly as they laid her on her back on one blade, the second blade just inches above her face, the golden tumble of her hair falling loose against the green of the weedy wooden paddles. She did not cry out, or scream for help; she had not said a word since she had sent Rob away. He realized she was speechless with terror.

"Go on," Sir William said to Mr. Miller. "Get on with it then."

The miller turned abruptly. "I'm opening the head sluice," he said loudly, to warn her of the sudden roar of water, as he turned the great metal key that lifted the gate from the pond to the millrace beneath the wheel.

The cascade of water pouring into the race forced a little sob from Alinor; but no one but James heard her. Now she could smell the icy water rising fast beneath the wheel, the weedy green smell of the mire, the creeping cold breath from the rush of icy water. She could sense it rising higher and higher beneath her. Soon the millrace would be filled, and then the miller would open the drain to the mire, and take the brake off the wheel, the water would pour through the millrace and out into the mire, and the mill wheel would turn, and take her down into the waters.

"Ready!" Mr. Miller shouted from inside the mill.

The miller's lad took his balancing weight off the wheel and it shifted slightly, dropping Alinor towards the water. There was a little gasp of anticipation from everyone.

"Go on," someone said.

"Turn the wheel!" Sir William shouted to Mr. Miller inside the mill.

They heard his shouted reply. "I'm turning now!"

"No!" James said. He stepped towards the blade of the wheel where her bright hair was lifting in the wind. "Alinor!" he shouted at her.

For the first time that day she turned her head and looked directly at him, but he saw from her agonized face that she was beyond hearing him, beyond seeing him. Strapped to the mill wheel, facing the great terror of her life, she was blind to him and heard neither the cascade of water pouring in, nor the creak of the wheel as it started to turn and lift her up.

Stunned, James watched her inexorable rise to the top of the wheel and then her descent on the other side. He took two steps to the back of the wheel and met her terrified gaze as she headed towards the flooding water beneath her. Down she went, into the narrow churning millrace, and he saw her hair swirl around her white face as she went down and down and then, horrifically, the wheel creaked and stopped. It turned no more, it was holding her underwater. There was a silence, there was a long moment.

"God's will," someone whispered in awe. "God has stopped the wheel to drown the witch."

"No! No! It's the weight!" Mr. Miller shouted from inside the mill. "It's her weight on the bottom of the wheel." He came bounding from the mill as everyone crowded round for a glimpse of her golden hair in the pouring water that rushed past the wheel and out to sea.

James understood, and flung himself on the back of the wheel, hands gripping and feet slipping, clinging desperately to the blades hauling it round. He could feel the wheel, yielding, and then slowly he felt it turn again, in the constant pouring swirl of the water, and then lift blade by blade. Slowly, the drowning woman came out of the depths.

He stepped back. Now the wheel was taking up speed. She went over the top of the wheel and past him again and he caught a glimpse of her white face striped with waterweed, water pouring from her clothes, her boots, her open mouth. He heard over the terrible roar of the wheel her retching cough and her gasp for air and then she was plunged under the waters again and she disappeared.

The wheel, turning faster in the churning water, brought her up on the other side, the miller's lad shut off the sluice to hold back the water and Mr. Miller, inside the mill, clamped the grinding stone on its bed to hold the wheel with Alinor at the middle of the turn. There was seaweed in her hair, seawater streaming from her open mouth, her eyes black with terror, her gown plastered to her straining belly. Mr. Miller came from the mill, his face dark with anger, pulled a hefty work knife from his boot, and cut the cords that bound her to the blade of the wheel. Like a sack of flour he pulled her towards him, slung her over his shoulders, stepped back from the wheel. The crowd, awestruck, parted to make way for him as he carried her away from the wheel to the mill yard and dropped her, like a sodden sack, facedown on the cobbles.

Mrs. Wheatley had a stable rug to wrap around her as Alinor heaved and vomited dirty water, and heaved again and again, choking and fighting for her breath.

"So she's not a witch." Sir William climbed down from the mill platform to stand over the retching woman. He addressed his tenants in his most magisterial tones. "She survived the ordeal. As to the theft: I rule that she borrowed Mrs. Miller's savings, planning to return them, leaving her tokens as a promise. This she will do and I will guarantee it. Mrs. Reekie is proven innocent of witchcraft. We have tested her with a fair ordeal and she is no witch."

"Amen," they said, as devout as before they had been frightened.

"What about the baby?" Mrs. Miller demanded. "She's certainly a whore."

"Church court," Sir William ruled swiftly. "Next Sunday."

The sound of a cart distracted everyone. It was the Stoney cart with Alys on the box, her brother, Rob, beside her, Ned in the back. Alys drove the cart into the yard, to where her mother was lying, bundled on the cobbles, wrapped in the horse rug, streaming with water, surrounded by neighbors who would not touch her. Alys passed the reins to Rob, jumped down from the box, and stormed past Sir William as if he was a nobody. She knelt at her mother's side and raised her up. Alinor could not stand, but Mr. Miller took one arm and Alys took the other. Nobody else moved. Together, they dragged her, still choking and retching up green water, across to the waiting cart where Ned reached out for her, and loaded her, like a beached fish, into the back, lying her on her side so she could spew out water.

"Mrs. Reekie is cleared of witchcraft," Sir William declared loudly. "She is innocent."

Alys looked at him and at James with her blue eyes blazing with rage. "Agreed," she said through her teeth, and then she clicked to the horse and they went out of the yard.

As James rode back to the Priory in the early winter dusk he could see a narrow bar of firelight through the closed shutters of Ferry-house, and he stopped his horse, tied the reins to the gate, and tapped on the kitchen door. Alys answered it, a horn lantern in her hand.

"You," she said shortly.

"How is your mother?"

"She has stopped vomiting water but, of course, she could drown later, when it flows into her dreams. She might die of poisoning from the foul water, or she may miscarry her baby and bleed to death."

"Alys, I am so sorry that . . ."

The look of hatred that she shot at him would have silenced any man. He said nothing, then: "Please give her my good wishes for her recovery. I will come tomorrow and—"

"You will not. You will give me a purse of gold for her," she said quietly. "She is going to leave here. I am going with her. We are going to London and we're going to set up a carting business. You are going to buy us a storehouse with a place to live. I've taken the cart and the horse from my husband's family. We'll leave tomorrow at dawn, and we'll set up a business and keep ourselves."

He was astounded by the authority of the young woman. "You're leaving your husband?"

"That's between him and me. I don't have to explain to you. We'll never come back. You'll never see her again."

"You know that the child is mine."

She shook her head. "You lost any rights when you let them strap your child's mother on the mill wheel and put her under the water."

"I have to tell her—"

"Nothing. You have nothing to tell her. You watched your lover accused of whoring and you let them swim her for a witch. You have nothing to do but to give me the money I demand, or I will tell the world that you are the man who forced her. I will name you as a rapist and you will be shamed as she has been shamed. I will name you as a papist spy and I will see you burned to death in front of Chichester Cathedral."

"It was better that she be swum for a witch than hanged for a thief!"

"It was me that should have been hanged for a thief!" she flared at him. "I owe her my life, just as you owe her your honor. She kept my secret and yours, and it has nearly killed her."

He took a breath as he thought of the secrets that she had kept for him.

"For love of us," Alys said through her teeth. "Because she loves you and me so much she faced her worst fear for us, and she nearly died for us. I will repay her with my love. And you will pay too. You will pay for the child that she carries for love of you, you will pay for your betrayal, and you will pay for our silence. That's worth a purse of gold. And you will go now, and bring it here at once."

"I must see her again," he said desperately.

The girl was like a Fury. "I would gouge your eyes out of your head and blind you for life rather than you saw her again," she promised. "Go and get the money. Leave it on the doorstep, and go."

"I don't have that sort of money."

"Steal it," she spat at him. "It's what I did."

It was a cold dawn on the harbor, the tide coming in fast over snowy reeds and icy puddles, the seagulls crying white against the gray light. The barn owl, quartering the hedge line along the harbor, was bright against the dark hedge and then invisible against the frozen bank. A few flakes of snow filtered from the pewter clouds as Alys helped her mother to the seat of the wagon and climbed up beside her.

Alinor was shuddering with cold, and she constantly coughed into the hem of her cloak. Tenderly Alys took up the reins, putting her other arm around Alinor, who rested her head on her daughter's shoulder. Alys clicked to the horse to start up the road to London.

# AUTHOR'S NOTE

A few years ago I realized that, though I still loved my fictionalized biographies of well-known and lesser-known women, I wanted to write a different sort of historical fiction: actually a series of books tracing the rise of a family from obscurity to prosperity. I reread the Forsyte Saga and discovered that my favorite scenes were the few and rather minor moments when the principal character went back to explore his ancestral home. As a reader, I wanted to know more about the story before the saga; as a writer, I understood that I wanted to write a historical fiction series of many generations of an ordinary family.

So many of us are exploring our family histories these days because we want to know who our ancestors were and what they did. Some of us take that very deep, exploring epigenetics. Some of us want to trace our connections with peoples and landscapes that are now strange to us. Some of us find remarkable echoes of our own modern lives in the historical past, as if we have inherited gifts or skills or preferences. Most families are like my family: with the earliest documents showing a family as humble and poor and, by little ordinary acts of courage and years of perseverance, largely unrecorded, rising and prospering—and sometimes, of course, declining.

What is interesting to me as a historian is how the fortunes of every family reflect in their small way the fortunes of the nation. We are all the products of both national and family history. What is interesting to me as a feminist is how these fortunes are so often invisibly guided by women. What is interesting to me as a novelist is whether it is possible to tell a fictional story which tells a historical truth: what the world and the nation were like at the time, what the individuals were thinking, doing, and feeling, and how change comes about for them all.

This is a big ambition, and it's going to be, I hope, a big series, starting with this novel set in an obscure and isolated area of England during the English Civil War, tracing the family through the Restoration, through enlightenment, and empire. I don't know how far my family will travel nor do I know when their story will end. I don't know how many books I will write nor in how many countries they will make a home. But I do know that when I write about ordinary people rather than royals, the story at once becomes more surprising; and when I write about women, I am engaging with a history which is almost always untold.

Between writing the novels for this series I am working on a history of women in England. My interest has moved from the individual women of the court to the millions of women of town and country. I am finding women written off by previous historians as "ordinary," whose experiences are obscured by time and lost to history—widely regarded as not worth recording in the first place. But these are our foremothers—interesting to us for that reason alone. These are women making the nation, just as much as their more visible better-recorded fathers, brothers, and sons. Thinking like this about women's history has led me inevitably to want to write a different sort of historical fiction—the fiction of an unwritten history.

Many fine writers have taken the leap into the unknown to fictionalize little-known history. Ann Baer's *Down the Common* is a particularly interesting example: a fictional account of a working woman who would usually not make the archive, and so not enter history, and so leave no trace for the novelist to animate. Very helpful for the Isle of Wight section of this story was Jan Toms's *To Serve Two Masters: Colonel Robert Hammond, the King's Gaoler,* which is a splendid example of local detailed history that adds so much to the national story. I drew my account of Charles and his trial mostly from two great biographies: D. R. Watson's *The Life and Times of Charles I* and Charles Carlton's *Charles I: The Personal Monarch*, as well as his poignant *Going to the Wars: The Experience of the British Civil Wars, 1638–1651*. For general history I consulted, among many others, Robert Ashton's *The English Civil War: Conservatism and Revolution, 1603–1649*. Lucy Moore's *Lady Fanshawe's Receipt Book: The Life and Times of a Civil War Heroine* was inspiring both for the recipes and for the history of a woman, like James's mother, who went into exile with the royal family. Of course, I read many more books than these titles; and I am grateful to the very many fine historians, and to the staff of West Sussex Records office for their welcome and for the care they take of their local maps and documents. Among these was some fine research from local history groups, a reminder of the importance of libraries and local adult education.

The novel is set in Selsey Island, near Chichester, a place which was my home for several years in the 1980s. I revisited it for research for this book and once again found a small place of extraordinary richness and beauty. The main character, Alinor, is entirely fictional but representative of the working women of her time: excluded from power, from wealth and education, but nonetheless making lives for themselves as best as they can. Women had no formal political power when the whole country was deciding for or against a monarchy, but we see from the debates, from the public demonstrations, from civil disobedience, and from the massive women-only petitions presented to the parliament that they were opinionated, active, and vocal. When we honor women who demanded the vote, sought rights over their own money and their own bodies, we should remember that even before them millions of ordinary women simply assumed the rights they wanted and lived their lives in quiet defiance of the law and of convention. Their successes are rarely recorded (except in specialist studies) because they chose discreet personal victory to acknowledgment. These were not exemplary feminist victories: by one woman for the benefit of all women. They were personal triumphs: one woman for herself and perhaps her daughters. But we see in these individual stories the pattern of female perseverance and success which, in practical day-to-day experience, defies and defeats the oppression of their times. For much of English history women have been legal nonentities. But they always lived as if they mattered.

Alinor is a woman like this. To outside appearances—which at the end, are all that James can see—she is in a hopeless state. The best she can wish for is survival without falling into poverty in a period where poor people died of hunger and want. But, even poor and shamed, Alinor is of interest to herself: she has hopes, she has ambition, she is not fatalistic, she plans a better future. Her terrible trial was not unusual for women of her time—there were uncounted witch trials up and down the country in the seventeenth century; more than three thousand people were named as witches and executed in Britain; many more were questioned and tested, mostly women.

But the rumors about Alinor do not define her, neither does the hardship she endures. She continues to insist on an independent moral judgment and on her own independent thinking and feeling. Dependent upon her neighbors for a living, dependent on a man for her status, she nonetheless thinks, feels, and lives for herself. At a time when women counted for nothing, she values herself. She is—if only to herself—a heroine. Certainly she and all the other women of history who have found their way through unmarked, treacherous times are heroines to me, and *Tidelands* is their story.

# ABOUT THE AUTHOR

PHILIPPA GREGORY is the author of many *New York Times* bestselling novels, including *The Other Boleyn Girl*, and is a recognized authority on women's history. Many of her works have been adapted for the screen, including her recent novel *The Last Tudor,* which is now in production for a television series. She graduated from the University of Sussex and received a Ph.D. from the University of Edinburgh, where she is a Regent. She holds honorary degrees from Teesside University and the University of Sussex, is a fellow of the universities of Sussex and Cardiff, and was awarded the 2016 Harrogate Festival Award for Contribution to Historical Fiction. She is an honorary research fellow at Birkbeck, University of London. She founded Gardens for The Gambia, a charity to dig wells in poor rural schools in The Gambia, and has provided nearly two hundred wells. She welcomes visitors to her website, PhilippaGregory.com.

# GARDENS FOR THE GAMBIA

Philippa Gregory visited The Gambia, one of the driest and poorest countries of sub-Saharan Africa, in 1993 and paid for a well to be hand dug in a village primary school at Sika. Now—more than two hundred wells later—she continues to raise money and commission wells in village schools, in community gardens, and in The Gambia's only agricultural college. She works with her representative in The Gambia, headmaster Ismaila Sisay, and their charity now funds pottery and batik classes, beekeeping, and adult literacy programs.

GARDENS FOR THE GAMBIA is a registered charity in the UK and a registered NGO in The Gambia. Every donation, however small, goes to The Gambia without any deductions. If you would like to learn more about the work that Philippa calls "the best thing that I do," visit her website, PhilippaGregory.com, and click on GARDENS FOR THE GAMBIA, where you can make a donation and join with Philippa in this project.

*"Every well we dig provides drinking water for a school of about 600 children, and waters the gardens where they grow vegetables for the school dinners. I don't know of a more direct way to feed hungry children and teach them to farm for their future."*

Philippa Gregory

# TIDELANDS

## PHILIPPA GREGORY

*This reader's guide for* Tidelands *includes an introduction, discussion questions, ideas for enhancing your book club, and a Q&A wi[…] Philippa Gregory. The suggested questions are intended […] reading group find new and interesting angles and […] discussion. We hope that these ideas will enrich y[…] increase your enjoyment of the book.*

# INTRODUCTION

On Midsummer Eve, Alinor waits in the church graveyard, hoping to encounter her missing husband's ghost and thus confirm his death. Instead, she meets a stranger, a man named James, who is a Catholic priest and a spy in secret service to the exiled King Charles. The political tides are also unpredictable; England is in a civil war, and it is dangerous to take any stand when power shifts daily. Alinor lives in a dangerous no-man's-land—neither maiden, wife, nor widow—a place that mirrors the treacherous, watery landscape that surrounds her tiny village. The suspicious, close-minded villagers watch as her fortunes rise due to her industriousness and her ambitions for her son and daughter. They don't know that Alinor is also walking on a knife-edge of political intrigue as well as having an affair in which she and James are breaking their most sacred vows. Her choices will determine her family's fate for generations to come.

# TOPICS & QUESTIONS FOR DISCUSSION

1. From the opening page, the reader is immediately pulled into the unique setting of the book. Alinor lives in an ever-changing physical landscape known to outsiders as Foulmire. How much does this in-between geography shape the people who live there? How much is it a reflection of the personalities that can manage the ever-changing conditions of the tidelands? Why do you think the author used this setting for a book that takes place during England's Civil War?
2. At their first parting, James tells Alinor, "'I did not know that there could be a woman like you, in a place like this.'" That sentence is repeated throughout the book but with changing meanings. Alinor even rephrases it at the moment she is considering suicide. Ultimately, what kind of woman does James see Alinor as? How does she come to see herself?
3. The story is told in the third person, but alternates between Alinor's perspective and James's. When King Charles refuses to be rescued, the reader feels how deeply James is shaken, losing his faith and his sense of purpose in life. But with the third-person perspective, can the reader see anything James has gained? What else can we see that he has lost by the end of the novel?
4. Ned is a foil for James, in both his political convictions and social status. But neither man is able to help Alinor in her hour of greatest need. Can you defend either of their actions during Alinor's trial for witchcraft? Do you think either of them loves Alinor as much as they claim?

5. When we first meet Alys, she appears to be a good child and an obedient daughter. How does she change throughout the novel? When she argues for Alinor to try to abort her baby, do you think Alys makes a fair case?

6. Alys steals money for her dowry and lets her mother pay for the crime. How do you think Alys justifies this to herself? As a reader, do you find this forgivable? Do you think contemporary readers can fairly judge a woman of the seventeenth century?

7. Mrs. Miller is never portrayed as a kind or generous woman. But when she finds Jane's dowry purse filled with old and valueless coins, is her reaction fair? Given all the events leading to Alinor's witch trial, is Mrs. Miller more to blame than anyone else?

8. In seventeenth-century England, infant mortality was estimated at about 18 percent, and childbirth was often fatal for the mother. But Alinor enjoys her job as a midwife. How do we see childbirth through her eyes? How do we see the women of the tidelands as she interacts with them?

9. Through Rob's placement as a companion for Master Walter, we get to see the inner workings of the wealthiest house on the island. How do Mr. Tudeley and Mrs. Wheatley compare to Mr. and Mrs. Miller? Mr. and Mrs. Stoney? In a world of such rigid class distinctions, do you think Cromwell can really bring about the changes men like Ned want?

10. Characters like Sir William show how the upper class of England had to handle the rise of Cromwell and his New Model Army. Men like Ned believe this adherence to the Protestant faith and new political beliefs will benefit everyone. But as we see more common citizens of the area, is there anything to be said for the old faith? Is the "old faith" Catholicism or something even older?

11. The oldest superstitions on the island help lead to Alinor's trial. The causes of these trials are hard for modern readers to imagine. But given that they were described as an "epidemic" in

mid-sixteenth- through mid-seventeenth-century Europe, does this novel help twenty-first-century readers understand why?

12. The novel ends with King Charles executed and parliament in power. But the political tides are still turning in England. How do you imagine women like Alinor and Alys will fare in this world where so much is changing?

# ENHANCE YOUR BOOK CLUB

1. Alinor is a very compelling main character. She is driven by her desire to secure a better future for her children. Ask your book club to discuss if there are any figures in history like Alinor or any contemporary heroines, in real life or fiction.

2. Have your book club discuss what factors in our current times might have motivated Philippa Gregory to write the story of a woman whose life was severely constrained by her social and financial status.

3. Has anyone in your group read other Philippa Gregory novels? Some of her most famous books are about royalty or those in the royal circle. How does Alinor compare to other Gregory heroines, like Elizabeth of York in *The White Princess* or Mary Boleyn in *The Other Boleyn Girl*?

4. When Alinor and Alys visit the market in Chichester, the lace maker says, "'It's a crime to be poor in this country; it's a sin to be old. It's never good to be a woman.'" How would your group describe conditions for those three categories (poor, old, female) now?

# A CONVERSATION WITH PHILIPPA GREGORY

**You are best known for your series about royal families. But Cromwellian England is a time when the monarchy is out of power. What drew you to start your newest series during this time period?**

It's true that I have set many previous books in the royal courts, but what interested me about them was not the royalty but the concentration of power and therefore jeopardy—which is the heart of any dramatic story. Also, in the royal courts we have records of women that are completely absent further down the social scale, and it was the stories of historical women that I wanted to tell. Further ahead in time there are more records of what ordinary women and men were doing, which I could draw on to root the fiction in a historical reality. By making Alinor a wholly fictional character, I was able to write a historical novel which was true to the time. I don't know that there is any record of the life of an ordinary working woman in this period. The diarists and letter writers simply were not interested in them, so any account is going to have to be mostly fictional.

I wanted to leave the world of the royals—I have tried to write about them without "rose-tinted" vision; but inevitably these are elite people and their difficulties and dangers, though sometimes extreme, are not the difficulties and dangers of people on the edge of poverty. This first book is where my family starts, in poverty. They're going to rise in the world, but they come (as most English families do, however grand they are now) from agricultural laborers on the edge of survival. It's a very leveling thought!

**You have a great ability to flesh out characters only briefly mentioned in the historical record. But at the time Alinor lived, there would be almost no original source material for a poor woman with no social status. Were you still able to use the same research process to build her character?**

There is a wealth of material about working people and working women from historians who are interested in the supporters of Cromwell and parliament—so ordinary people. Though there is nothing (that I could find) about people living in this particular area, there are surveys and reports of poor parts of England as the armies went through. For unruly women there are criminal court records, and a lot of complaints from ministers and vicars and magistrates. There are records of midwives, and herbalists, and of course there is a wealth of documentary evidence when literate men (almost always men) supervised witchcraft hunts and trials and so reported (probably the first time they had ever considered) the private lives of poor women.

**History is said to be written by the winners. But your novels tend to show what it is like to be both in the favor of the powerful and out of favor with the powerful. What inspired you to make James a spy for the losing side?**

James is a spy for the elite—the upper classes—so he starts his life as one of the "winners." His family adhered to the Roman Catholic faith when the rest of the country turned Protestant, but there were many elite Catholics who survive to this day. He would have thought he was on the winning side for most of the war, and I don't think he genuinely imagines defeat until he is responsible for one of the many failed escape attempts by the captured king. Of course, ultimately, he is on the winning side, as the monarchy is restored in the king's son Charles II.

In fiction terms, I wanted a character who would be able to show the weakness of the monarchy case and a character who would expose Alinor to more danger. This was a civil war; it divided families and I wanted to show that, too. Also—this was a book that was very fictional in process as well as outcome—as I was writing, James ran into the book, as he does into Alinor's life, and he turned out to be a royalist spy. I didn't know that was what he would be when he first arrived. I thought he would be a recusant priest, but all the rest unfolded.

**When you wrote the scene between James and King Charles, was there anything in your research that particularly helped you portray the king?**

There's a lot of biographical material about the king and especially about his deterioration during his imprisonment. There are quite a lot of accounts of failed rescue attempts at this stage of his imprisonment, too, so there was a lot of history and historians' opinions to draw on to write this completely fictional scene.

I was especially interested in Charles's change of attitude during his captivity. From his own letters we know that he started confident that he could outwit and outnegotiate the parliamentary representatives, and he was certain that he would negotiate a return to his throne. This was partly because he was convinced that kingship was a state of being, a divinely appointed state, which nothing could alter. He thought everyone would come to realize that they could arrest him but that being a king was intrinsic to him—he would always be king. Ultimately, I think he came to think that to be a martyred king was the best way to demonstrate this.

It's hard for us in the modern world to imagine that someone should think that they are a genuinely superior being to another person—we're so inculcated with democracy now! But Charles believed that he had been chosen by God to be king of England and that meant that he was father to his people, and that they could not reject this relationship.

**Your novels about royalty are told from the first-person perspective. *Tidelands* is written in the third person. Why did you decide to make this change? Was it a challenge or a thrill?**

The first-person characters are women at the royal courts and include commoners (like Mary Boleyn) and indeed imposters (like Hannah in *The Queen's Fool*), so the point of moving from first to third person was not about status but about the story I wanted to tell.

In *Tidelands* I wanted to be able to describe the inner world of more than one person; I wanted to be free to describe events that happened far from the primary character. I wanted Alinor to live like an uneducated woman in a highly complex world—it was important that she was not present at great events. So if I wanted the reader to see James's life at his college in Douai, I had to write in third person (or have a series of first-person narrators). Contradictorily, when it came to the execution of King Charles, I did not use third person! Instead I found it really useful to imbue the account with emotion by letting James and Ned be reporters.

How to tell the story is a huge decision when starting a novel, but since this is book one of a series, I knew that it would be less of a wrench if I did not change the narrator with each book.

**Alinor and Alys are both very compelling women. The reader is able to see their problems from both their points of view. Was it difficult to write the scenes where they are at odds with how to fix the situation in which they find themselves?**

No! Delightfully the mother/daughter conflicts were very fluent to write. I could see each one's point of view. The development of Alys in the story came from her growing up so that she was more than her mother's daughter but was someone with her own ambitions and opinions.

**You have announced that *Tidelands* is part of the Fairmile series, spanning 250 years and three continents. How long did it take you to write this first novel? How much of the series did you have plotted out before you started writing?**

The joy of writing historical fiction which is not fictional biography is that I am so much more free to develop the characters and develop their lives as I wish. I knew at the outset that I wanted to tell the story of an English family which rises in prosperity, as so many English families did through the revolutions in agriculture, industry, and then especially empire. Beyond that, I didn't really have a plan. This first novel developed as I wrote it, sometimes surprising me, and took two years to write—longer than usual. The next one is going to start in London but probably move to Venice and from there probably east. But I think that Ned is the sort of man who would follow his conscience to America.

**You graduated from the University of Sussex. Had you always wanted to write a novel set in that area? Or was there something about this story that drew you back there?**

The novel is set in an area that I lived in for several years, and was where I spent most of my childhood holidays. I love this undeveloped, unspoiled stretch of coastline. It's very peaceful, very rich in wildlife, and incredibly evocative. It's not very large, and it's not very famous, so it's very lovely to visit and write there. It's not far from where I set my first novel, *Wideacre*, so it is now both a fictional landscape and a real place for me.

**Did the #MeToo movement affect how you wanted to write the character of Alinor? Has the persistence of this current women's movement affected your plans for the series as a whole?**

My commitment to feminism as a way of understanding the world and as a hope for the future goes back a long way, and the #MeToo movement has been an inspiration to me in seeing courageous women stand together. I have been guided in this fictional series by my simultaneous work on a new nonfiction book of history which is going to trace the lives of ordinary women (and the obstacles they faced) over a long study from 1066 to 1966 in England. I hope to publish this within five years. As a historian I am particularly interested in the roots of women's oppression and ill treatment, and I think I can make the greatest contribution to the movement by showing how the past contributes to our lives now. It's really shocking to understand how little improvement there has been in terms of assaults on women while we have made great strides in political representation.

**You are very involved with the charity Gardens for The Gambia. Can you share how that came about?**

I founded the charity Gardens for The Gambia with a headmaster of a rural Gambian primary school in 1993 to provide water for wells in the gardens of rural schools in The Gambia. The vegetables they grow provide school dinners for the poorest children in school, who would otherwise have nothing to eat all day; the surplus produce is sold and stationery and educational equipment is bought with the profit; and the children learn the basics of sustainable agriculture. The gardens are planted rather like an English allotment. They grow all sorts of vegetables and salad vegetables. Usually the school also plants an orchard of citrus trees and walnut trees. Often pupils from the senior class of these primary schools will be made responsible for the health of their particular tree. They fence it to protect it from straying animals and they water it every day from the well. We dig the wells with local labor and we go down about sixteen meters to tap clean water. We provide a rope and a bucket and—job done! It's a beautiful little scheme that makes a difference to about two hundred children in every school and we've completed nearly two hundred wells. I pay for it from my own money and from donations—it's only £300 per well [almost $400], so it's extraordinarily good value for money in transforming the lives of the poorest people in Africa. I'm very grateful to people who donate to share this project with me.

Read more at: https://www.philippagregory.com/gardens-for-the-gambia.

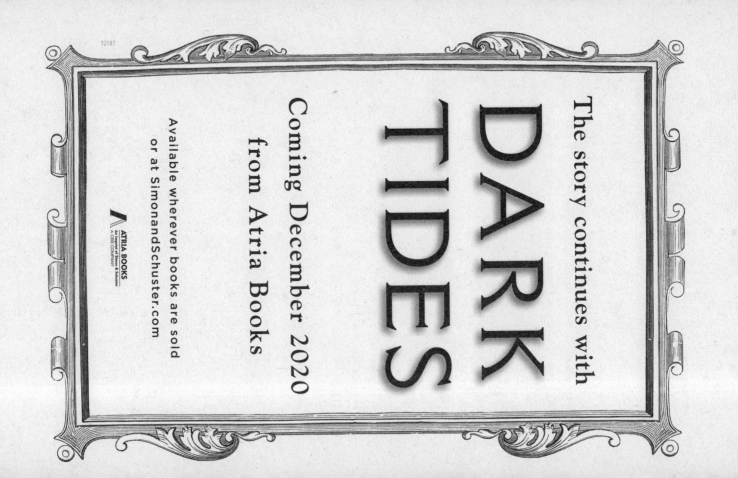

The story continues with
DARK
TIDES
Coming December 2020
from Atria Books
Available wherever books are sold
or at SimonandSchuster.com
ATRIA BOOKS
An Imprint of Simon & Schuster
A CBS COMPANY